The round face of the stranger split into a wide grin, creasing the short beard into the rolls of skin. A plump hand, festooned with rings, reached into the pouch, but then the fellow turned back to the queen, obviously enjoying the suspense.

"This is more than a gift, royal lady. In fact, I return to you something which you have lost. Indeed, I presume it is something you have missed very much."

The hand came forth from the pouch, holding a limp, sickly pale object. Alicia couldn't see what it was, but then the man tossed it contemptuously toward the queen. It landed on the table before her, and the princess couldn't suppress a scream of horror.

The thing was a human hand, bled pallid and shriveled from long immersion in brine. On a finger of the hand, Alicia saw a ring, a jeweled signet that she well knew, for it bore the seal of a king, the head of a great bear. And with that recognition came the understanding that fueled her emotions.

For she knew that this was her father's hand. . . .

FANTASY ADVENTURE

The Coral Kingdom

Douglas Niles

The Druidhome Trilogy: Book Two

THE CORAL KINGDOM

Random House and its affiliate companies have worldwide distribution rights in the book trade for English language products of TSR, Inc.

Distributed to the book and hobby trade in the United Kingdom by TSR, Ltd.

Cover art by Clyde Caldwell.

FORGOTTEN REALMS and DRAGONLANCE are registered trademarks owned by TSR, Inc. The TSR logo is a trademark owned by TSR, Inc.

First Printing: September, 1992
Printed in the United States of America
Library of Congress Catalog Card Number: 91-66493

9 8 7 6 5 4 3 2 1

ISBN: 1-56076-332-9

TSR, Inc.
P.O. Box 756
Lake Geneva, WI 53147
U.S.A.

TSR Ltd.
120 Church End, Cherry Hinton
Cambridge CB1 3LB
United Kingdom

To Bill Larson and Pat McGilligan,
who helped me bring the Moonshaes to life

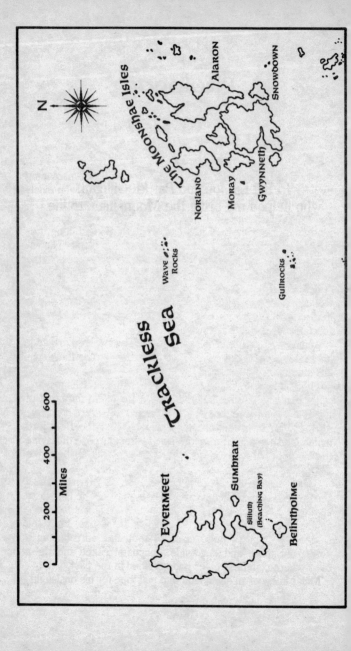

Prologue

An evil god was Malar, the Beastlord—master of marauding monsters and misshapen creatures, deity of those who existed to kill, who relished slaying innocent, helpless victims. The grotesque shape of his immortal body resembled that of a monstrous black beast, like a malformed bear, with long, ripping claws and a coarse coat that dripped fresh blood. The essence of his evil soul formed a staunch pillar of darkness in the pantheon of the gods of the Forgotten Realms.

Restless, Malar seethed within the seat of his immortal throne. Fury fueled his foul nature, boiling, churning within him, compelling as release a savage depredation across the mortal lands beneath his sway.

And as was so often the case when Malar's hatred erupted, his target became the mortal race toward whom he felt a special enmity: the elves.

This is not to say that many dwarves, humans, halflings, and other benign creatures had not perished beneath the brunt of this foul god's wrath, but unquestionably elves were his favorite prey. So favored were they, in fact, that the Beastlord maintained a pet creature expressly for the purpose of slaying the members of that sylvan race. This was Ityak-Ortheel, the Elf-Eater.

In his vindictive hatred, Malar decided that Ityak-Ortheel should once again walk the paths of the Realms. The Beastlord summoned the monster from its mire-choked lair far down among the Lower Planes. The Elf-Eater arose from the sludge, revealing a huge mass of tentacles surrounding a domed carapace and one wide, mucus-streaked mouth—a maw where countless elves had perished in the past.

Malar knew of an elven land that was ripe for his onslaught, for it lay in a valley on a continent in flux, a place where new human cultures invaded, clashing with the old. As was always the case, such conflicts among humans created great dangers for the elves caught in the violence. Regardless of which human force prevailed, it would act vigorously to secure its borders. Any elven communities in the area faced automatic jeopardy.

For his target, this time, the Lord of Bones selected an elven tribe known as the Thy-Tach. The community had existed in peace for more than two millennia among the stately oaks of its pastoral vale. Far from the intrigues of Toril and Kara-Tur, the Thy-Tach elves had prospered without bloodshed or violent conflict for a very long time. They carved tall totems of wood and stone, placing these in honored sites throughout the forest, nourishing and tending the woodlands and wild creatures of the valley for many harmonious centuries.

Ityak-Ortheel changed that status very quickly. Transported through gates of arcane passage, the beast arrived in the midst of the peaceful village as evening approached, appearing with the quickness of a blinking eye. Tentacles flailing, the Elf-Eater lumbered through a pair of wooden houses, smashing them to splinters and quickly gobbling up the female and young elves cowering there. The Elf-Eater's huge bulk balanced upon a trio of legs—each club-footed, of huge girth—and this physical structure gave the monster a rolling appearance as it rumbled forward.

Screams of sheer terror rent the pastoral valley. Wooden walls splintered into a thousand pieces, while horrible tentacles probed, as if they had intelligence of their own, through the wreckage for survivors. When a tendril seized upon an elf—young or old, male or female—the terrified victim faced the consummate horror of the monster's mouth. The blood-red aperture gaped, and the last sights withessed by the doomed elves were the churning plates of cartilage that thrashed, like giant tongues, within that horrid maw.

With a grotesque bellow, the monster roared through the village, crushing buildings, smashing the priceless totems, seizing elves with its snakelike tentacles. Cookfires sizzled and died, squashed by the beast's clublike feet. Great works of art, created from patterns of leaf and crystal, shattered beneath uncaring blows.

Some of the elves tried to fight. The bravest of them, males and females alike, took up bows or spears tipped with enchanted iron heads. The Thy-Tach fired these in courageous futility, watching as the sharp metal bounced harmlessly from the monster's rough carapace. Most of the attackers quickly felt the lashing of a tentacle around the ankle, precursor to a sudden and gruesome death.

Elven clerics, spiritual leaders of the tribe, struggled to gather the surviving Thy-Tach, fleeing into the darkness that settled over the forest. Stragglers fled the ruin of their town, gaining a precious few moments of time while Ityak-Ortheel searched the rubble for survivors—a few of which it found and quickly devoured. But within minutes, the monster knew that the village was empty and turned toward the forest in pursuit of the fleeing survivors.

The chief cleric, a matriarch nearly a thousand years old, led her people up the steep slopes of the valley toward a notched hilltop that had long been a place of honor and meditation among the Thy-Tach. Now, she knew, that place provided their only hope of escape. The cleric held before her a gleaming shape, like a platinum triangle balanced on its point, crossed by a spiderweb of silver threads. Now these threads glowed, and the cleric followed the direction indicated by their emanations.

The horrendous roars of the monster followed them, growing closer by the moment, as the stronger elves helped the weakest, both very young and very old, to make the difficult ascent. Trees splintered behind them, clearly marking the path of the pursuing beast. Seizing vegetation with its tentacles, the bulky monster barged up the slope, uprooting huge trees with the force of its enraged pursuit.

Reaching the hilltop, the priestess raised a powerful prayer to the elven gods, protectors of her race even as elven numbers dwindled across the Realms. The platinum talisman flared into light, and the deities of elvendom heard and granted their favor.

The hilltop surged into brilliant illumination, casting golden light across the darkened hills, opening as a shining passageway before the desperate elves. A broad path appeared, leading upward into the night sky, framed by a silvery arch of gleaming, translucent brilliance. In a single column, the Thy-Tach passed through this gate as the roars of the Elf-Eater grew louder. Infuriated, the creature watched in frustration as its prey slipped from its grasp.

The venerable priestess stood at the rear of the file as the monster loomed out of the darkness, and as the last of her people fled, she passed the gleaming triangle to a younger priest, the last elf to pass through the gate.

Finally the priestess stood alone before the mountainous presence of the Ityak-Ortheel. Serenely she turned to face the hideous form. As bloody tentacles enwrapped her, dragging her to inevitable doom within the monster's cavernous maw, the cleric's face relaxed into an expression of quiet bliss. Then the gate behind her faded, slowly replaced by the star-speckled vista of the night sky.

The monster flailed madly, thrusting its tentacles into the closing aperture. The young priest recoiled as he disappeared from view, but one grasping tendril actually touched the platinum icon before the male cleric stumbled away. Then, as the priestess perished, the light paled and the magical gate shrank into nothing.

The rage of the Elf-Eater was a thing that shook the world to its roots. The monster flailed about the mountaintop, knowing from past experience that its quarry was gone, for this was not the first time the monster had witnessed that hated triangle, had watched a tribe of elves escape through such a magical aperture.

Finally Malar called his pet back to the Lower Planes, where it could wallow in its filth and digest the victims who had failed to reach the glowing gate.

And while the Elf-Eater seethed in hatred, Malar pondered the elven escape. Too often had he been thwarted thus, and frustration was not a pleasurable sensation to a chaotic and vengeful god. He roiled and festered in his rage, trying to focus his fury into a grim determination.

But through his anger burned the memory of the gleaming triangle, the tool that allowed the elven escape. Never had the Ityak-Ortheel come so *close*—it had actually *touched* the thing! The god sensed the essence of the talisman through the touch of Ityak-Ortheel. Now its image burned in his immortal mind, compelling him to find it, for he knew that if he could follow the path of the talisman, he would be able to pursue the elves who dared to frustrate him by their escape.

One day, he vowed, he would learn the path of those who escaped him, and then vengeance would be his.

PART I: SYNNORIA

❦ 1 ❦

A Royal Funeral

Robyn Kendrick, High Queen of the Ffolk, stood at the highest window of her castle, watching the sun-speckled waters of Whitefish Bay, the bustling commerce of Callidyrr, and the thriving fields and pastures that spilled across the moors to the highlands beyond. She looked upon this scene of prosperity and beauty, and she felt as though she would perish from the force of her own despair.

"He *lives!*" she whispered softly. "He is not dead!"

Too often in the past days she had spoken the words aloud, and this had caused the eyes of her daughters or her servants to look at her pityingly. They thought she was losing her mind, she knew, and the queen sensed that now, of all times, she could not let her subjects begin to wonder about her fitness to rule.

"It's *true!*" she told herself, yet even Robyn had begun to wonder how she could continue to cling to such a hollow hope.

True, there had been no body—but when was there ever a body when a ship went down at sea with the loss of all hands? The High King's vessel had sailed on the return leg to the Moonshaes, following an important trading mission to the Sword Coast kingdoms of Callidyrr and Amn. Somewhere in the vast reaches of the Trackless Sea, south of the Moonshae Islands, the ship had encountered a surging tempest of storms typical of the gales that swept across that wide stretch of ocean. The ship had entered the maelstrom and it had failed to emerge.

The news had come to Callidyrr, the great city where the High King had made his capital and his home, more than three weeks before, and in all that time, there had been no information to indicate any chance of his survival. Even the stubborn

Ffolk, grief-stricken and frightened as they were, had begun to accept the reality of the loss of their king.

Robyn's own daughters had faced the grim truth, though each in her own unique way. The elder, High Princess Alicia, had embarked on a vigorous regimen of weapons training, as if her skill with sword and bow might help to avert a future tragedy. In this, Alicia was aided by good friends—most notably Brandon Olafsson, Crown Prince of Gnarhelm and a proud northman sailor. Brandon professed his love for the princess in every expression of his face, every jealous glower in his blue eyes as he looked at the two other men who also stood high in the princess's friendship and affection.

One of these was Hanrald Blackstone, newly appointed as Earl of Fairheight following the death of his father. Hanrald had been trained as a knight, and the honor and chivalry of that calling marked him as clearly as did his plate mail breastplate or his proud, crested helm. Yet that stiffness displayed itself in a reserve that held Hanrald aloof while his more hot-blooded rival pressed his suit vigorously.

The third man, Robyn realized, might not be recognized as a rival by Brandon or Hanrald. Indeed, a cold part of the queen's mind told her that he made a less desirable match for her daughter politically than did either the earl or the prince. Keane of Callidyrr had been Alicia's tutor for more than ten years and still treated the princess with protectiveness as much as affection. Yet of the three, the magic-using teacher came closest to understanding Alicia Kendrick.

Now, however, Robyn knew that the choice of a husband was not Alicia's concern. Instead, she needed the comfort of her friends as she struggled to grasp the reality of her father's loss. Currently, as Robyn looked upon her realm, Brandon captained a longship that carried the princess and her companions to Corwell, where the queen would join them shortly. Because of these friends, thought the queen, the High Princess had adapted better than either her mother or her sister in accepting the loss of the High King.

For a moment, Robyn's thoughts turned to her younger

daughter, Deirdre. As always, her mind raised far more questions than it answered.

Dark-haired Deirdre had a personality that matched the color of her long hair. Distant and cool toward her family—toward everyone—the younger princess had fostered a life in studies, scrolls, and books. She was a young woman of great intelligence and barely concealed ambition. Often, during their childhood, Robyn had worried about the younger girl's jealousy of her older sibling, wondering whether that emotion would grow into the kind of hatred that could rend asunder a kingdom and a people.

Then, during the girls' adolescence, the queen's worries had lessened. Deirdre ceased to display the overt hostility that had characterized her childhood. Though she had never become close to her sister, she had tended to treat her with indifference rather than rage. Alicia, on the other hand, had never lacked for trusted friends, so her sister's coldness hadn't seemed to create a void in her life.

But now, in a matter of months, Robyn's concerns had flared into full-blown fear. Something had happened to Deirdre, something mysterious and darkly menacing. Through her studies, the young woman had touched powers that were not meant for the casual scholar, powers that required from their wielder a price as great as they granted.

True, Deirdre's visible use of that power had been fortuitous. She had employed it to aid Alicia in breaking a thrall of storms and natural violence that had wracked the Moonshaes for several years. Yet in that accomplishment her daughter's arrogance and envy had reasserted itself, so that the queen once more feared that the spite felt by a sister could fan itself into a blaze that might drive a nation to destruction.

Robyn knew that the Moonshae Islands stood at a critical time in their long history. Only once before, under the reign of the hero Cymrych Hugh, had the four kingdoms of the Ffolk stood united under a single throne. Yet Cymrych Hugh had died with no clear heir to the throne, and within a generation, the isles had again broken into political fragments, easy prey for the northmen invaders who had gradually claimed much of the land.

Now Tristan Kendrick, the second High King to unite the Ffolk, had perished. He left a queen—a *strong* queen, Robyn reminded herself—and two daughters. Though the Ffolk, unlike the northmen, had never disparaged the rulership of a queen simply on the basis of her sex, Robyn knew that she would have to prove her fitness to continue the Kendrick line, and in that process, she must ensure that Alicia would inherit the kingdom upon her own death.

Her goal seemed clear, but there were so many obstacles, and as she thought of those obstacles, she came back to the plans that had caused her to pause, musing, at the window in the first place.

A harsh knock at the door, though not unexpected, broke Robyn's reverie. "Come in," she said.

The door opened to reveal Deirdre Kendrick. The princess's black hair floated behind her, unbound and silky long, as she moved softly into her mother's chamber. The two women looked remarkably similar, though the maturity and sorrow of age had unmistakably marked the mother with lines around her mouth and eyes and a fringe of gray that had begun to lighten her long black hair. "You wished to see me?" Deirdre said.

Robyn knew what she needed to say to her daughter, and she knew that Deirdre wouldn't like it. She found it difficult to begin.

"Yes, my daughter. Please come here. I was enjoying the view."

Silently the princess joined her mother.

"Summer," observed the queen. "Such a vital, vibrant season. Doesn't it make you feel *alive?*"

Deirdre smiled, but her eyes remained hooded. "*Books* make me feel alive, Mother—and they do so even in the dark of winter."

Robyn suppressed a sigh, turning to face her daughter squarely. "I wish to speak with you about those books, about the forces you read about and touch. You bring a shadow around yourself. There is a darkness that surrounds you—a darkness you wear about your shoulders like a cloak. It disturbs me. You've opened the doors to places that can't help but change you. The powers you touch are very dangerous things!"

"Of course they're dangerous! But I *know* how to use them, and every day I learn more!" Deirdre's reaction was anger, and her green eyes flashed with the heat of her emotion. "I follow a pathway to power without limit, without restriction—a road I've chosen for myself!"

"Without the limits, for example, imposed by a god—or goddess?" Robyn asked pointedly.

Deirdre shrugged. "You have your own life, Mother, and the goddess has chosen to favor that life. Once again you wear the mantle of the Great Druid, but that's not the way for me!"

"Your sister shows a growing awareness of the Earthmother," the queen said. "She wears the bracers of a druid, and soon she will bear the staff that I'm making for her. I should like to grant you an equal gift, my daughter—but I don't know what it should be."

"There is something that I desire very much," Deirdre replied, her tone level, her eyes serious.

"If it falls within my power—"

"It is *freedom*, Mother—freedom from you, from the goddess! I have to be free to follow my own course, through the spellbooks and scrolls of wizardry. I need to see the hallowed places of magic in the Realms, visit the great sages, have the freedom to learn!"

Her impassioned voice rose as she spoke, and when she stopped suddenly, an almost unnatural silence settled over the room and the world outside, as if the birds and insects, even the wind, paused to see what happened next.

"No," the queen said, quietly and firmly. "You're one of two royal children. You must be prepared to rule should it be required of you. Your place is here, in Callidyrr—in the Moonshaes."

"But there is so much *more* in the world!"

"Your father is dead!" snapped Robyn, and the bluntness of the painful admission was enough to quiet Deirdre for the moment. "The three of us—you, your sister, and I—hold the destiny of the Moonshaes in our hands. The great peace begun by King Tristan can flourish or fail. Do you believe for one moment that the Council of Lords will agree to the continuance of the Kendrick reign for old times' sake?"

"Surely they won't try to wrest the crown from you!" exclaimed the princess.

"Who knows what they'll try?" Robyn sighed. "In three days, in Corwell, we shall see. I know we have allies—the good Earls of Fairheight and Corwell, to name two. And the Grand Mayor of the Halflings, Lord Pawldo, will certainly side with us. As to the others, who can say what schemes they've set in motion."

"They wouldn't *dare!*" There was no fear, just an icy fury, in the younger woman's tone. The queen looked at her daughter sharply, never doubting the threat in her voice.

"If the three of us are united," Robyn said quietly, "then I'm certain there is little that the lords can—or will—do. But if we go into the council squabbling and bickering, I don't doubt that some challenge is inevitable."

"I hear you, Mother," said Deirdre softly.

"But do you *understand* me?" Robyn persisted. "Will you do as I ask?"

The princess stared at her mother, and Robyn saw anger flashing in those dark eyes. She barely heard the reply.

"I will."

Neither woman averted her gaze for a moment, but finally Deirde looked away. "May I go now?" she asked angrily.

With a sigh that was more tired than angry, Robyn nodded, turning back to the window as her daughter left without another word. Once again she saw the sunlit landscape and the dazzling sea, and it was a scene that seemed to mock her. With conscious discipline, she forced her mind to turn back to her plans.

The funeral could not be a simple ceremony. It must be a festival worthy of the passing of a great High King. Yet neither would the normal rites suffice, for they had no body to bury.

Traditionally the great men and women of the Ffolk were put to rest in large barrows, mounds of earth raised over timber enclosures, where the corpse was laid together with an assortment of weapons, treasures, food, and drink—all that the deceased would need on his long journey into the afterlife.

For Tristan Kendrick, there would be no place in the barrows mound, no gifts for him to bear into the realms he now explored. Yet his queen would ensure that his passing was marked with proper ritual and ceremony. This goal had given her strength during the past weeks, and now that the event drew near, it provided a focus for her mind when it would have been so easy to collapse into grief.

Corwell! She knew instinctively that she had made the right choice in the location for the ritual of the king's passage. That pastoral kingdom, childhood home to both Tristan and Robyn, was a place where she could get away from the chaos of the high court, returning like a wounded animal to the den from which she had emerged as a cub.

Corwell was the ancestral home of the Kendricks, and both the queen and her daughters bore that name. The ancient castle—protected still by a palisade of wooden timbers, though the king had ordered a stone wall started some years back—would reinforce in the minds of the lords and kings of the Ffolk that Robyn came by her rank honestly. And that her daughters, too, bore the blood of the island's royal line.

And there was more than political truth to her choice, just as Robyn was more than a queen to the Ffolk. The kingdom of Corwell was on the isle of Gwynneth, and there Robyn would find Myrloch Vale, the heart of the reawakening power of the goddess Earthmother.

Robyn Kendrick had once been the great druid of the isles. With the passing of her goddess, the order of druids had drifted into the wilds of the Moonshaes, their numbers shrinking, their powers gone. But now, thanks primarily to the actions of the two Kendrick daughters, the goddess had surged back to life, her druids reborn.

Robyn herself was no longer a young woman. A return to the isolation of a druid's grove seemed like a strange form of exile now, something she did not desire, nor would have accepted. Yet she had seen the awakening of similar powers within Alicia—powers that Alicia denied, preferring to believe that she would become a warrior queen. Yet now the older princess wore silver bracers on her wrists, the coiled bracelets in the shape of dragons that identified her as a chosen daughter of the goddess.

"Carry me a little longer, Mother. . . please."

Robyn whispered the words like a prayer and felt a lightening of her oppression. She did not feel joy—there were times she believed that happiness was a thing from her distant past—but she could steel herself to her work.

Finally Robyn stepped to the window. The city and the harbor seemed to pause, frozen in tableau. The queen leaned outward, spreading her arms wide, and they became her wings. The human woman fell from the window, but an eagle of purest white flew away from the the castle, away from the town—away from all of Callidyrr.

In two days, that eagle would reach Corwell.

* * * * *

Brigit Cu'Lyrran hauled back on the reins of her white mare. Talloth reared silently, raising her rider so that the elfwoman could see over the screen of quivering aspen branches before her. Her keen eyes had detected a flash of movement up the valley several minutes before, in the direction of the Fey-Alamtine.

She had been right—the Synnorian Gate would open today! Quickly she nudged Talloth with her knees, and the fleet mare exploded into a gallop, carrying her mistress swiftly up the trail. Passing a steep upward branch to the left, a rarely used trail that led to the human kingdom of Corwell, she continued up the main path.

In a few minutes, Talloth slowed to a lope, and then a trot as the trail opened into a clearing. The mare instinctively paused before the Fey-Alamtine, the Synnorian Gate.

A wall of obsidian-black cliff shimmered before Brigit, as if an invisible sheen of water flowed across the surface, but Brigit knew that the rock was dry. The visual effect had a magical cause.

Three or four times in her life the gate had been used, and once before she had been here to witness. Those memories, from a hundred years ago, remained with her as vividly as this morning's. But today she was the only one here, and as the shimmering grew more pronounced, she knew that the gate would open soon.

As captain of the Sisters of Synnoria, Brigit spent much of her time riding the swales and valleys of this tiny elven realm in the Moonshae Islands. Synnoria, and its beautiful capital Chrysalis, bordered the Ffolk kingdom of Corwell, yet the Llewyrr had existed without human intrusion for more than ten centuries. Magical wards and rugged mountains surrounded Synnoria on all sides; indeed, many of the Ffolk believed that the Llewyrr were creatures of history or legend.

Brigit was one of the few Llewyrr to have journeyed beyond the borders of Synnoria. Twenty years earlier, she and a small company of her knights had aided the human king, Tristan Kendrick, in the Darkwalker War. Now she would happily spend the rest of her days riding these valleys and woodlands.

A burst of light washed over her like a cool dawn, and her attention riveted to the Fey-Alamtine. The glossy black wall slowly grew opaque, taking on a rosy hue and an appearance of great depth, as if she looked through a foggy window at a scene many miles away. The shimmering stopped suddenly, replaced by a fixed glow.

Brigit saw a male elf, clad in a dirty, torn cotton tunic, step through the wall, as if he emerged from the heart of the mountain, though she knew that he must have come from far beyond. He blinked in the bright daylight of Synnoria and then gasped when he saw Brigit. He was unarmed, but he clutched a triangle of silvery metal in both of his hands.

"Get out of the way," Brigit suggested gently. "The gate will not remain open indefinitely."

Blinking in surprise, the male quickly nodded and took several steps forward. A female elf, equally dirty and ragged, followed him, clutching a youngster by the hand. The elven child ran forward to clasp the leg of the male who had been the first to emerge.

They came through the shimmering wall in single file, and the elven horsewoman got a good look at them as they emerged into Synnoria: all of them ragged, unkempt, and dirty. Their blond hair was disheveled, trailing back in the wind and plainly revealing the pointed ears of Brigit's elven kindred. She felt no alarm now, only sympathy and a kind of general sadness at the course of advancing history.

The sister knight dismounted, leaving Talloth to wait patiently for her mistress. Brigit advanced slowly toward the leader, whom she marked as a cleric by the golden oak leaf—symbol of Corellon, god of all the elves—embroidered on his sleeves.

The young priest stared at her in mute suspicion—or hope. Brigit held up a hand and advanced at a walk. "Welcome to Synnoria," she said in the language of the elves. "I see that you have traveled the ways of the Fey-Alamtine."

"Yes—in desperate haste," replied the priest, stepping forward. He held his hand on the shoulder of the elven boy who had run to him moments before. The youngster looked up at Brigit with palpable hostility, his hand rested on the hilt of a tiny dagger—a kitchen tool, probably—that he wore in his belt. More and more ragged elves came through, until well over a hundred had assembled in the clearing before the dark cliff.

"We are the Thy-Tach," continued the cleric. Brigit saw that he held the Alamtine Triangle in his hand. She had seen one example of the rare artifact before, the last time a tribe had come through the gate. "Our village was attacked by some monstrous horror, a three-legged creature as big as a hill. We had no recourse but flight!"

"Easy—you're safe now," the knight said, reaching out a hand to clasp the priest on the shoulder. Her touch seemed to steady him.

"My name is Pallarynd," said the priest quietly. "I thank you for your kind welcome."

"I've seen tribes come through the gate of the Fey-Alamtine before in my lifetime, and the shock of the transition is always upsetting. That's why you'll need to rest here for some time before you continue on," Brigit explained.

"It really worked, didn't it?" asked Pallarynd, his tone amazed, looking back at the Fey-Alamtine. The magical gate again looked like a shimmering wall of wet obsidian. "Torcelly had kept this ancient triangle for centuries. She'd never tell me what it was for, but she said that we might need it sometime. Now it has brought the village here, most of us alive."

"It's the way we ensure the survival of our race," Brigit replied. "Only on Evermeet can the elves reign over all the land. Everywhere else the humans press, or, even worse, other creatures. It is the Fey-Alamtine that gives hope to those elves such as yourselves, too isolated or too threatened to flee on foot."

"We're halfway there now, aren't we?" mused Pallarynd, to himself as much as the knight.

"Yes," Brigit said, with a soft smile at the young elf beside the priest. The little fellow squinted, still suspicious, but at least his hand fell away from the knife. The cleric squeezed his shoulder and the boy took the older elf's hand.

Pallarynd turned to his people. The Thy-Tach pressed close to hear his words. "To think we have come safely to Synnoria, the outpost of our people on the Moonshae Islands! The Fey-Alamtine has led us here, and when it is time, it shall lead us on the final leg of our migration as we travel to the eternal elvenhome, Evermeet!"

The Thy-Tach elves, in their ragged leggings and woods-brown tunics, whispered quietly among themselves. Their losses were too recent, and too horrifying, for the elves to feel any joy. Yet as the sister knight turned back down the valley, their relief was palpable to Brigit. She urged Talloth into a fleet canter. The Thy-Tach would find shelters, beds, and food awaiting them when they reached Chrysalis.

* * * * *

The keen bow of the *Coho* sliced the smooth waters of Corwell Firth. Under the steady eye of her captain, Brandon of Gnarhelm, the small longship glided toward the narrow harbor mouth a mile or two away. Soon they passed the breakwater, gliding toward the dock at the conclusion of a smooth five-day journey from Callidyrr.

Two women stood in the bow of the ship. One of them was heavyset, with a smile as broad as the sun and a merry twinkle in her eyes, seemingly amused by everything they saw. The woman's hair was gray, tied in a bun behind her neck, and the wrinkles lining her face gave a grandmotherly cast to her age, but she stood at the gunwale with one foot balanced on the rail, as light on her feet as any young sailor. Around her shoulders was strapped a dark-grained harp, silver strings winking in the sunlight, and a smooth, well-polished body shimmering from the reflections of the waves.

The second woman was much younger, and strikingly beautiful. Her fair hair, like straw tinted with copper, trailed behind her in the wind, but though her lips creased into a smile at the sight of her family home, her good humor did not extend to her eyes. She looked up at the castle, rising above the town and the firth on its rocky knoll, and she missed her father more than ever.

"Look—there's Lord Pawldo!" announced Tavish, the bard.

The diminutive figure of the halfling, clad in an elegant blue waistcoat and shiny, high-topped black boots, waved enthusiastically from the wharf. As the skilled northmen crew, with a few strokes of the oars, brought the vessel bumping gently against the dock, the Lord Mayor Pawldo of Lowhill, longtime friend of the Kendrick family, rushed up to the princess and embraced her. Alicia bravely tried not to cry, but this was the first time she had seen her old friend since her father's death. She couldn't bear the embrace of the halfling, such a great companion of her father's, without shedding tears of grief.

"There, there, child," whispered Pawldo, and for a brief moment, Alicia felt like a little girl. The strength of his shoulder to cry on was a great relief.

But in another moment, she stepped back and wiped her eyes. Pawldo gave her a hand as she stepped up from the hull onto the dock, and again she was a High Princess, returned to the town of her family's clan.

The Ffolk were not a great people to observe formality and ceremony, so there was no turnout of the castle guard or any such display at the wharf. Earl Randolph was present, however, and he quickly joined Pawldo in greeting Alicia and her party.

The earl had been a young captain who fought for King Kendrick twenty years earlier, in the Darkwalker War. When Tristan went to rule in Callidyrr, he appointed the loyal warrior as seneschal in Corwell, and later made him an earl. Now Randolph's eyes, too, were moist as he bowed to the princess. She introduced her companions as they climbed from the *Coho*'s shallow hull.

"Do you recall young Hanrald Blackstone?" she asked Randolph. "Now the Earl of Fairheight?" Hanrald bowed formally, then extended a hand to his fellow earl.

"Indeed—your service to our lady princess has been well told by the bards!" proclaimed Randolph. "It is an honor to have you as my guest."

"And Brandon Olafsson, Prince of Gnarhelm," continued Alicia. "He provides us with the fast transport—and more, for without his aid, we would not have broken the thrall of the Stormbringer."

"King Kendrick has done our people a lasting service when he made peace with the northmen," said Randolph, bowing with easy grace to the prince. "My honor is doubled to have such an esteemed ally as another guest!"

Brandon flushed in embarassment. Such niceties of diplomacy always discomfitted him. "Well, thank you," he finally remembered to say. "And the transportation might have been faster," he reminded Alicia, "if we'd had the use of my own *Gullwing*."

The prince's eyes swept the horizon wistfully, as if he expected that proud longship, sunk by the tempest of Talos the Stormbringer, to come sailing toward them. Alicia knew that one of Brandon's countrymen had willingly given him use of the *Coho*, but the love he had felt for his own vessel was clearly lacking with the new longship.

"Your mother will arrive soon?" inquired Earl Randolph, drawing Alicia's attention.

"Yes. She rides the wind now, as she did when she was younger. The love of the Earthmother, I think, is the only thing that lifts her spirits."

"And your sister?" inquired Randolph, with a meaningful look along the hull of the longship. The rest of the crew, long-haired northmen sailors to the last unshaven face, stared back. It was quite obvious that Princess Deirdre was not present.

"She, too, arrives under powers other than sail," Alicia said, mildly irritated at the thought of Deirdre's icy arrogance when she had declined Brandon's invitation to sail on the *Coho*. Her younger sister's dalliance with magic seemed to Alicia to be a vexing pastime. It annoyed her that Deirdre planned to teleport from Alaron to Gwynneth. Still, Alicia had trouble understanding the stark concern that others, notably Keane and Robyn, had expressed about Deirdre's mysterious powers.

"Many of the lords have gathered," noted the earl, pointing to the field full of colorful tents that lay between the town and the castle. Different banners flew from many, and at first glance, Alicia saw the boar of Lord Koart and the unicorn of Dynnatt, two of the local cantrevs. Farther away streamed the white banner of King Truac of Snowdown. Soon all the lords and kings of the Ffolk would be gathered for the High Queen's court.

And above the field rose Caer Corwell, with its partially

completed stone wall joining the wooden palisade. The towers of the keep rose beyond the wall, and the whole structure crowded the steep-sided knoll that placed it in command of all the ground for miles in every direction.

Suddenly the little castle seemed like home to her—a home she missed very much. Though she had spent most of her life living in Caer Callidyrr, her time in Corwell had included many idyllic summers. Now, as that season came once again to the Moonshaes, she wanted nothing quite so much as to pass through those great doors and enter the cooling shelter of the family hall.

* * * * *

Talos the Stormbringer, god of maelstrom and cyclone, deity of destruction and chaos, brooded malevolently as he pondered his lust for revenge. A monstrously powerful god, Talos was not used to frustration, yet a short while ago, when he had thought that he stood at the brink of his mightiest accomplishment, he had instead suffered the greatest defeat in a long and combative existence.

The crux of his hatred, and his defeat, was the island group called the Moonshaes and the people known as the Ffolk. These enchanted isles were places of sublime and ancient power, but power that had of late drifted in a vacuum. A yawning space had beckoned the Destructor like a bottomless pit, urging his own claim to the lands and seas.

And so Talos had sent Coss-Axell-Sinioth, his most trusted servant, a vile being of corrupt origins and deepest evil, to plant the seeds of war in the land. Talos also enlisted the aid of undersea minions, the sahuagin—ravenous predators, ever eager to serve his cause. The most faithful of these was the king of the fishmen, Sythissal.

Aided by the fierce and bloodthirsty sahuagin, the forces of evil had assailed the Moonshaes. Talos quickly neared complete mastery of the isles. Only the tattered remnants of a dying faith and a dead goddess had stood in his path.

But then those remnants had flared to life. The goddess Earthmother, hallowed mistress of the Moonshaes, surged into the world from an absence that had been perilously near, but not quite, permanent. The goddess reborn infused the land with vitality, and Sinioth, the agent of Talos, had been banished to a nether plane.

There, in the few short weeks that had passed, the avatar of evil had suffered what seemed to be an infinity of torture and suffering, punishment for his failure, meted out to him by his dark master. Now, however, Talos summoned Sinioth to face him. The avatar appeared immediately, assuming the body of a withered old man as he stood trembling beneath the wrath of his awful god.

"Coss-Axell-Sinioth! You failed me once. Do you dare attempt my works again?"

"Please, Master, I beg for a chance to redeem myself!" wheezed the frail form, his voice tremulous.

"Dare I trust you?"

"I beseech you, O Mighty One, allow the chance to prove my worth! It is true that I failed to succeed in your name and deserve nothing more than your immortal scorn, your disgust and loathing! But remember, O Master!"—here the voice became more courageous, wheedling persuasively—"I planted the tool, the mirror of scrying, that still allows you to witness the world, to spy on your enemies!"

"Bah!" snorted Talos haughtily. "I have seen naught of that glass!"

"Time, O Great One . . . it will take only a short time, I am certain, before the Kendrick princess discovers it. She will cherish the mirror, Master, and through it, you will see all that she beholds! She will give you a window into the lives of your greatest enemies!"

"You may speak the truth," mused the god, considering the possibility that this time Sinioth's plan would succeed. Talos also had another source of good fortune—a piece of luck that encouraged him to quickly reenter the fray.

"There is a tool—a bargaining chip—that has come into my

hands," he informed his avatar, "that will prove an even greater asset than the mirror! It is for this purpose I have summoned you!"

Talos sent Coss-Axell-Sinioth back to the Realms, for he needed the avatar to carry word of that asset back to the Ffolk. Talos wanted them to suffer—very much indeed.

♣ 2 ♣

Council In Corwell

The fields and moors around Corwell teemed with tents, makeshift pastures, and practice yards. Riders galloped here and there, and dozens of banners, denoting all the major lords of the Ffolk, streamed from the peaks of the grandest of the tents.

Many of the nobles themselves had been given lodgings in Caer Corwell, or located accommodations in the many inns of the town, all of which charged top price for the several weeks of this unprecedented midsummer court. But teeming Ffolk quickly overran the relatively small community, and thus the sprawling tent city had soon claimed Corwell's environs.

The Ffolk came from all across Gwynneth, and many ships had arrived from the islands of Snowdown, Moray, and of course Alaron. Several tall galleons and a number of tublike curraghs bobbed in the harbor, although the *Coho* was the only longship present.

Jousts and tourneys occurred daily throughout the gathering. Even now, in the morning, both male and female warriors trained vigorously in dozens of impromptu practice yards. Minstrels plied the crowds, while bakers and brewers did a season's worth of business daily. An occasional thief slipped his way among the populace, slicing a purse string here or picking a pocket there, but the Ffolk were an alert and frugal people, not prone to carelessness with their precious coins. Those dishonest rogues unfortunate or careless enough to be apprehended were divested of their belongings and locked up until they could be placed aboard a ship departing for the Sword Coast. Repeat offenders were hanged.

All the festivity had been building for a week as more and more of the Ffolk reached this small town. Not in the lifetime of any human present had Corwell hosted such a gathering. It brought a warmth and pride to thousands of hearts, for the relatively isolated kingdom had always held an important place in the heritage of the Moonshae people. This had been the home of Cymrych Hugh in centuries past, and now, in their own lifetimes, it had given them Tristan Kendrick and unity.

The High Queen arrived dramatically in late morning. She soared in the guise of a great eagle, a huge bird of the purest white. Circling the high tower of the castle three times in an ever-tightening spiral, she drew the eyes of everyone on the fields and in the town or castle. Then, as her talons touched the rim of the parapet, her form quickly shifted back to the human woman who was so adored by her Ffolk. Robyn's black hair, unbound this time, trailed in the breeze as she waved to her people.

Their cheers erupted spontaneously and continued for many minutes, long after the queen had disappeared into the humble castle that had been her home for the first eighteen years of her life.

The grand court would not open until the morrow. On this, the day preceding the formal council, the heralds announced that the queen would host a feast for all of her subjects, to be served on the great commons below the castle.

Word of the impending celebration spread rapidly, and when the queen and her elder daughter emerged from the castle in late afternoon, a cheering crowd shouted their devotion along the raised roadway that led down to the field.

"It *is* like coming home again," Robyn said to Alicia wistfully. "But then, at the same time, it isn't."

"There are memories of Father everywhere around here," Alicia agreed. "It always seemed that, when the family stayed at Corwell, he had more time for us—he *took* the time for us."

Robyn smiled, though the tears began to veil her eyes. "He must have remembered his own father when we were here. He always vowed that he would show his children more affection than King Bryan showed to him."

Alicia looked at the sea of faces spread across the fields below them. She had always enjoyed the attention awarded her rank, and never before had she beheld such a throng. Yet today the sensation was pale, even insignificant. "How can we feel lonely when so many shout their affection for us?"

"Because we've lost the one we really desire to hear it from," Robyn replied. Alicia saw, with surprise, that her mother's face had hardened. The queen smiled at her subjects, a frozen, formal expression, and the crowd fell in behind them as they approached the commons, already covered with cloths, tables, and benches for the feast.

"The Earl of Corwell has done a commendable job," observed the princess, beholding an array of canopied tables and great firepits where several massive oxen rotated on huge spits.

"Lord Randolph has ever been an able administrator," Robyn replied, fondly remembering the young captain to whom Tristan had entrusted his home realm when the High King and Queen first embarked for Callidyrr.

Now all the young Ffolk of the town, it seemed, had turned out to serve the meal, and swiftly the nobles and esteemed citizens were seated. The rest of the Ffolk would eat where they could. Keane, Tavish, Prince Brandon, Pawldo of Lowhill, and the Earl of Fairheight all joined Lord Randolph and the two noblewomen at the head table.

Crusty loaves of bread, hot from the oven, appeared on the tables before them. Wheels of cheese, mild and sharp and all ranges between, complemented the bread, and pitchers of wine and ale overflowed onto the tables. Cooks bustled about, trimming and slicing from the steers and pigs that now entered the final stage of the daylong cooking process.

"Does the lady bard have a song for the occasion?" inquired Robyn, smiling at Tavish.

"There's a tune I've been trying out," the harpist allowed, her eyes twinkling with pleasure. She slung her lute from her shoulder with a casual flip. "It's in the early stages, mind you. I've been planning to put some work into it when I can find the time."

The others watched as she tuned a few recalcitrant strings and then strummed a bright chord. "This is a song about Corwell—in the distant past," Tavish explained as her fingers deftly walked across the strings. "A time when there were as many elves as humans in the isles—more, perhaps. The first verses tell of the birth of the kingdom of Corwell.

"This part of Gwynneth was ruled by King Deric, a good man, brave and heroic. His people lived in peace with the Llewyrr, the elves of Moonshae. Still, the two didn't mix much."

She started to sing the verse then, and her listeners saw the proud King Deric of the Ffolk, astride his white charger. The steed pranced on the beach as his piratical enemies fled from the scene of a disastrous battle. The warriors of Gwynneth had just defeated the greatest invasion ever to menace their shores. King Deric was victorious and triumphant, and he used his prestige to forge all the cantrevs of southern Gwynneth into the fledgling kingdom of Corwell.

The strains of the song floated across the field, compelling the attention of all who could hear. Time passed swiftly as the bard wove her tale.

Deric was a good king, and Corwell flourished beyond any other kingdom in the isles. He was a leader just and wise, decisive and merciful. Even the elves made peace with Deric of Corwell. This was in the age when the numbers of elves and humans on Gwynneth were roughly equal, thus the forging of the peace was no small accomplishment.

Many times Deric journeyed to the elven capital of Chrysalis, there to meet with Kaminas, monarch of the elves.

Yet as the years of Deric's adulthood began to pass, his people worried that he took no wife, left no heir. All the maidens—and a good many of the dames—in his kingdom sought his attention, but he paid them no heed. Unsavory rumors circulated, and the king's loyal companions slew many a gossiper in late-night tavern duels.

In fact, the king was in love, and his beloved would have granted a splendid heir to the kingdom, for her blood was royal, too, of a strain that had ruled for far longer than the clan of Corwell. Yet the match was unacceptable to both the Ffolk and her own people.

Deric's beloved was Herene, princess of Synnoria and daughter of Kaminas, the High Elven Lord.

The Synnorian ruler was appalled by his daughter's attraction to the human king. At first, he tried to coax her toward other beaus, but she showed no interest in even the most handsome elves among all the Llewyrr. Later King Kaminas resorted to sending Herene away from the valley when King Deric's visits were anticipated.

But the lovers found ways to circumvent these precautions as well. The man would arrive unannounced, or the princess would cut short her departure. Finally Kaminas faced a drastic action, but one he felt necessary to the survival of his kingdom: He closed Synnoria to humans, barring their presence there for any reason. The wizards and clerics among the Llewyrr, with the help of mighty Corellon Larethian, god of all elves, weaved a pattern of spells around Synnoria, blocking all its borders against human intrusion.

Though he tried many times throughout the remainder of his life, King Deric was never able to find a path into Synnoria. He never saw the elven princess again. Decades later, he died, childless, and a bitter civil war resulted in a series of brutal tyrants holding the throne and wresting it away from each other.

Herene lived for many centuries, and eventually her father compelled her to marriage, yet she, too, perished without an heir. And from that era to this, the bard concluded, the borders of Synnoria remained closed.

On that note, Tavish let the notes of her final chord fade.

The harpist lowered her instrument and caught her breath. Noticing her own hunger, Alicia finally realized that Tavish had been singing for a long time, though the minutes had seemed to pass with a trancelike beauty.

Now the meat was served, and quickly the guests' attention turned to the food. Pitchers were refilled, but the conversation faded away as men and women alike went to work on their plates.

"Where is the young Princess Deirdre?" Randolph inquired after a while, as they dined on beef and pork, with bowls of thick soup and still more loaves of bread before them. "Will she attend the council?"

"She promised me that she would arrive by tomorrow," the High Queen replied in clipped tones, "though I encouraged her to attend the feast today."

"I see." The Earl of Corwell wisely refrained from further conversation on the topic.

"It's a delight to have the queen's presence at our meager Corwellian table," said the rotund Pawldo, reaching for another rib of pork with both of his ring-bejeweled hands. Though he was a mere three feet tall, his appetite was the match of any of the humans'. The halfling had made his fortune as a merchant but was famed more as the courageous adventurer who had accompanied King Kendrick on his rise to the throne. Now the comforts of his wealth and station generally held him to the confines of Corwell Town or the neighboring halfling community of Lowhill.

"Your table is always sumptuous, and never more than now," Robyn disagreed with a laugh.

"Will my lady princess be attending the dance?" inquired Hanrald, blushing furiously as he spoke to Alicia. Keane and Brandon leaned forward.

"I imagine so," Alicia allowed, enjoying the attention as the three of them sought her pledges to dance. For a moment, she felt the light happiness she had known throughout her life, but then the memory of their purpose here came back with renewed poignancy, as if her father had perished only yesterday.

Festive Ffolk sat at tables all around them, gathered in knots of conversation. Harps and lutes, flutes and horns, rang across the broad field, while jugglers and magicians worked through the crowd, entertaining to exclamations of delight and disbelief. It was altogether a scene of considerable commotion.

Thus the party of strangers approached quite close to the head table before anyone there even took note of their arrival. A band of men and women, dressed as elegantly as any group of noble lords and ladies, advanced through the crowd behind a herald bearing a banner of black, white, and red. They numbered more than a dozen, though none of them were armed, and the few pieces of armor worn by the men appeared purely ceremonial in nature, as evidenced by detailed engraving and graceful but impractical shoulder epaulets.

"Who are those people?" Robyn said, abruptly realizing that she didn't recognize the lords or their banner.

"I recall that tricolor symbol," offered Randolph. "A curragh entered the harbor this morning under a sail of the same colors. I assumed they were a clan from one of the outlying islands."

The High Queen shook her head emphatically. "I would know if they were," she stated. Robyn scrutinized the leading lord, an enormously fat individual with multiple chins concealed under a thin beard. He wore a blue velvet cap that flowed like a pancake out to either side of his head.

It was a style that was new to the Moonshaes, Robyn reflected. It should have looked ridiculous, but the huge man somehow gained from it a sense of noble dignity.

The herald dipped the tricolor banner in deference to the great bear of the Ffolk, the pennant that floated above Robyn's table.

"Greetings, stranger," offered the queen, accepting the lord's deep bow with easy grace. "Will you join our feast? There is plenty for all of your party, but first you must introduce yourselves."

"The High Queen's kindness is, as legend claims, ever flowing!" the lord proclaimed with a grand sweep of his arm. "We had but hoped to find meager lodgings in your town, but this invitation overwhelms my humble self!"

Alicia noticed that Keane, seated beside her, had stopped eating. The wizard's eyes were fixed on the visiting lord's face. Keane was not smiling.

"It is the way of the Ffolk to be hospitable," said Robyn, an edge of curtness to her voice. "Especially when they know who their guests are and from whence they come."

"Allow me to present my entourage. We journey here from a place that is far away, but we bear a most important message for my noble queen!"

"And the land, sir? What place is that? And how are you called?" pressed Robyn. The edge of iron in her voice could not be ignored.

"My name? If you insist that I have one, it shall be what you give me," proclaimed the obese figure, his own voice growing more firm.

"Cease your riddles, sir. If you have a message, produce it. I grow tired of your rudeness and prattling." Robyn gestured subtly with her hand, and Keane mumbled a soft word, performing the delicate motions of a spell with his hands concealed beneath the table.

Alicia noticed several files of men-at-arms, bearing cocked and loaded crossbows, working into position on either side of the visitors. For the first time, the princess noticed that Lord Randolph had left the table. The earl must have sensed danger earlier and summoned the company of guardsmen.

"My message, then," said the stranger, with another overly flourishing bow.

One of his attending lords, a foppish fellow in a large yellow hat—this one *did* look ridiculous, Robyn decided—scampered to the huge man's side, bearing a pouch of smooth leather. The courtier lifted the enclosing flap and held the opened pouch out for his master's inspection.

The round face split into a wide grin, creasing the short beard into the rolls of chin. A plump hand, festooned with rings, reached into the pouch, but then the fellow turned back to the queen, obviously enjoying the suspense.

"This is more than a gift, royal lady. In fact, I return to you something which you have lost. Indeed, I presume it is something you have missed very much."

The hand came forth from the pouch, holding a limp, sickly

pale object. Alicia couldn't see what it was, but then the man tossed it contemptuously toward the queen. It landed on the table before her, and the princess couldn't suppress a scream of horror.

The thing was a human hand, bled pallid and shriveled from long immersion in brine. The ragged stump of the wrist showed the mark of a brutal wound, inflicted by tooth or jagged-bladed sword. For a moment, Alicia's stomach heaved, but she resisted the urge to turn away. Instead, she looked at the appendage more closely, and as she did, her shock turned to horror, and then to a cold, brutal rage.

On a finger of the hand she saw a ring, a jeweled signet that she well knew, for it bore the seal of a king, the head of a great bear. And with that recognition came the understanding that fueled her emotions.

For she knew that this was her father's hand.

*　*　*　*　*

Deirdre poked through the darkest shelves of the great library of Caer Callidyrr. The great white castle was nearly empty, with most of the court gone to Corwell for the council. She would go there, too, but her journey, on the wings of sorcery, would last mere seconds. She had no intention of arriving any earlier than necessary.

As she did so often when her time belonged to herself, Deirdre came to this library. Driven by memories or desires— she didn't know which—she explored the vast, dark shelves and must-covered tomes and scrolls.

It was here, after all, that so much of her awakening knowledge had kindled itself into the flame of her current power, here where the mysterious one had come to her, infusing her with the mastery of great magic, allowing her potential to grow wildly. She hadn't known his name, but she had called him Malawar.

For a time, she had trusted him, learned from him—even given herself to him in in faith and affection—until in the end he had cruelly betrayed her. Now she knew the reason he had kept his identity secret. His power was centered in his name, and if she had learned it, she could have mastered him. As it was, she had barely been able to evade his own attempt to control her.

She had only discovered his true face at the end, but ultimately she had banished the thing, driving it away from her world. Yet in her contest with this potent being, something had happened to her—some reserve within her had broken open, allowing her to draw power from him, to tap resources normally barred to human spell-casters. She had gained astounding abilities in a short period of time, but even so she felt as though she had only begun to scrape the surface of her potential.

Every once in a while she had to wonder, with a little tremor of apprehension, whether this all had come to her free. Sooner or later, would she be called upon to pay? Angrily, as always, she brushed aside those apprehensions.

Worries faded as she pressed through new tomes, dusty volumes that hadn't felt the touch of human hand in decades, perhaps longer. Some compulsion drove her to seek in these shadowy niches where she had never looked before. Carrying a long taper, she poked through stiff curtains and examined heavy, dust-laden shelves.

Finally, in one of the back alcoves, she felt a sudden thrill of discovery, though she didn't know what she had found. Setting the candle down on a shelf, she reached forward to grasp a long, flat object, wrapped in brittle leather as protection against dust and disturbance. Slowly, breathlessly, she tore the stiff and moldy skin away, revealing a glimmering surface of pure reflection.

She studied herself in the mirror, astounded by the clarity of the image staring back at her. Even here, in an alcove virtually devoid of light, she saw each detail of her white skin and her dark black hair that swept across her forehead and framed each side of her coldly beautiful face. "I *am* beautiful," she observed softly. This was no mere expression of vanity, however. Instead, it represented the confirmation of still another weapon in her inventory of powers.

The mirror seemed to beckon her like a bottomless well of crystal water. For a brief moment, she felt herself falling, a dizzying sensation that swirled around her even as she felt her feet firmly planted on the floor. Then she looked into the glass again, and her reflection slowly faded from view. She felt a sense of wonder, a trembling excitement that numbed her fingers as she gripped the frame tightly.

Deirdre allowed her mind to wander beyond the walls of the castle, beyond the island of Alaron. In moments, her attention soared, and the image in the mirror shifted to match. She saw a great expanse of water, steel gray even under a pale blue sky—the Sea of Moonshae. Trees lined the horizon, then great highlands sprouted from the land, and she knew that she beheld the island of Gwynneth.

Next pastoral Corwell appeared, and she sought the small castle where her parents had been raised. Caer Corwell looked the same as always, jutting peremptorily atop its little knoll. The mirror zoomed in, and the princess saw the field dotted with tents and tables, in the midst of some incomprehensibly boring feast.

How amusing, Deirdre thought, quickly grasping the potential of this rare device. She could be the perfect spy. She could eavesdrop on anything, anywhere she wanted. Cautiously, as if she feared detection, she urged the picture closer, and soon she found the heavy table where her mother, her sister, and a number of their sycophants sat. They were not eating, but insead stared at an object lying on the table. Deirdre felt a secret contempt as she watched. How pitiful were their interests and concerns! Simple and small, as befitted their powers.

But then her vision encountered the being who stood before the great table, the obese ambassador from the unknown region. Robyn spoke sharply to this fellow, but already Deirdre stared in shock, and then in growing rage. She cared not what her mother said or did, for in the clarity of the mirror, she saw who this was. He was no human ambassador from the Sword

Coast or anywhere else. She recognized him with a sensation of cold terror, but it was terror mixed with fascination, even attraction, such as the moth finds in the flame.

For this grotesque being who now stood before the queen was none other than the avatar of evil, the one Deirdre had known as Malawar.

* * * * *

"Foul bastard!" shouted Lord Hanrald, springing to his feet so quickly that his chair tumbled over backward. "You'll pay for your insolence with your life!"

Keane cursed beneath his breath. The shock of the hand's appearance had disrupted the concentration of his spell.

Only Robyn remained fixed in place, displaying no reaction. "Why do you bring me my husband's hand? Tell me quickly—before you die! Did you kill him?"

"No, esteemed matriarch!" exclaimed the plump visitor, his features contorting into a mask of indignation. "I am no murderer, nor do I come to torment you! Indeed, you should greet me with joy, for I bring you glad tidings!"

Alicia saw the ranks of crossbowmen raise their weapons. Her mother's hands were clenched into fists on the table before her, but Robyn's gaze never left the hatefully pleasant face of the stranger.

"Do you claim that my husband is alive?" she asked with deadly calm.

"Very much so, albeit a trifle sore. After all, we needed to carry positive proof to you of his existence. He is our guest, and we shall keep him safe until such time as he can return to his home."

"And what is the ransom?" Robyn asked. Only her daughter heard the slight tremor in her mother's voice. Alicia's own heart had soared for a brief moment, until the grim reality of the situation became clear. The fat man's visage shimmered, and slowly his human appearance melted away, as if his features were wax, heated by an intense flame. They distorted, a grotesque mask of slimy meat, to a chorus of gasps and screams from all sides. People scrambled away in horror, toppling tables and benches to the ground, while the creatures eyes dripped streaks of ichor as they blazed with infernal hatred.

"You, the humans of the Moonshaes, must abandon the seas to us," hissed the now featureless horror. The mouth was a mucus-streaked gap in the flowing ooze that had replaced its face. "And you must furnish slaves, five hundred in number—humans that we will take to the Coral Kingdom and put to work in our mines! Only when your ships—all of them—have been drawn onto the shores and the slaves have been delivered to our warriors will the king of Moonshae be returned to his people."

"This is *madness!*" shouted Alicia, fury overcoming self-discipline. Quickly she sprang to her feet, wishing she wore a weapon.

"Wait." Robyn's hand, on her daughter's arm, had the effect of a calming spell upon the princess. Alicia stood still, breathing deeply but slowly, as the High Queen confronted the messenger from the depths. Robyn's demeanor accented the sudden pallor of her face with an expression that might have been etched into the surface of an icy cliff.

"Your ghastly missive cannot be met with other than loathing," Robyn declared, pure force running like bedrock in her voice. "Presuming for the moment that I were willing to deliver my people into certain death, the High King himself would never consent to such an exchange. But even more contemptibly, you seek to inflame with a bit of a corpse the hopes of a widow and a kingdom. You tell us that he who is dead lives, and for this you deserve worse than scorn!"

Alicia noticed that her mother's left hand had remained still for some time. Now the queen abruptly made a chopping motion with that hand. Immediately the crossbows of the guardsmen came up. Ladies screamed, and Ffolk dove for cover all around the commons. The princess seized a long carving knife and sprang over the table, Hanrald and Brandon diving forward to stand at her sides.

The princess heard dual intonations and sensed that both Keane and her mother were casting spells. Alicia paused in a fighting crouch, ready to defend the pair with her blade should the hateful ambassador or his party attack.

All of this happened in a scant few seconds, but the next split moment became a frozen image in Alicia Kendrick's mind. She saw a wall of fire spring from the ground, sputtering upward among the visitors—her mother's druid magic, she knew. Crossbow quarrels whistled through the air, a deadly crossfire of steel-headed death. And then Keane's spell thundered, followed by a deluge of rocks from the sky, pounding like meteors into the pulpy earth.

But amid the chaos of the lethal attacks, the princess saw one other thing in that split second before the murderous barrage impacted its target. The visitors, the ambassador and his entire party, had *disappeared!*

"Stop! They're gone," announced the queen, raising a hand to the reloading crossbowmen. The flames sank back into the earth, and the meteor barrage ceased.

"To where?" asked Prince Brandon, bashing his fist into the palm of his other hand. "We'll be after them with the first tide!"

"To the Coral Kingdom," Alicia remembered. "At least, that's where he said. . . ." Her voice choked in helpless fury as she remembered the words that the horrible visitor had uttered.

"A legendary place, the Coral Kingdom—at least, so I had always thought," announced Tavish, the most well traveled of them all.

"Where is it?" demanded Alicia.

"Hundreds of miles to the south of here, somewhere across the Trackless Sea," explained Keane when no one else answered.

"There's nothing for a thousand miles," objected Alicia. "Barely a few tiny islands!"

"You heard it was a legend. That's because no human has

been there to prove its existence. The Coral Kingdom lies a hundred fathoms beneath the sea," concluded Keane, grimly quiet.

* * * * *

Talos chortled in unholy pleasure. The stroke of good fortune that had brought Tristan Kendrick into the hands of his undersea minions was too sweet, too ironic. Also, there was the fact of the mirror. The princess had discovered it and used it. Her power and ambition burned like a fire in the glass, with an allure that drew the evil god's interest and desire.

Now he was nearly ready to move for mastery of the isles, but first, he would take one more precaution. In the wake of his earlier defeat, he had determined to seek an immortal partner. A pair of divine beings, coupled in the same destructive goal, would certainly allow the cause of evil to gain justly deserved vengeance. He cast about for the name of a likely ally, and he decided to approach Malar, the Beastlord. That vengeful god was known for the force of his wrath. Indeed, he had recently demolished an entire community of elves for no purpose other than his own gruesome pleasure.

Thus he was interested when Talos proposed to him that they unite to attack the Moonshaes. But one question was paramount to the Beastlord.

"Are there elves? I must smite the elves!"

"Aye," rumbled Talos. "Called the Llewyrr, they are—but they are elves."

As proof, Talos summoned the image of the mirror, unknown to Princess Deirdre, who slumbered nearby. The Stormbringer showed Malar an image of Synnoria, with its pristine lake and crystal city.

"That can only be a place of elves," grunted Malar, pleased with his discovery. As he studied the scene more intently, his pleasure turned to keen excitement. He looked closely, drawn by powerful emanations that pulled his attention stronger than any visual cue.

"There!" he spat, focusing on one of the elves in this sylvan vale, on one particular elf who walked at the head of a group. That one bore a platinum triangle at his waist, and Malar knew he had found the answer: For centuries, elven populations had escaped him through the use of that hateful talisman. They had disappeared, untraceable and immune to his vengeance, because he didn't know where they had gone.

Now he did.

♣ 3 ♣

Urgent Endeavor

"You've heard of the Coral Kingdom?" By habit, Alicia asked the question of Keane. The wreckage left by the brief battle with the unnatural ambassador still smoldered around them, and they all struggled to grasp the truth—or falsehood—of the visitor's extravagant claims.

It was Tavish who replied, however. "Those legends, that's all—so foreign to humankind that it remains completely unknown, if in fact it exists at all."

"An undersea domain," added Robyn. "As immense in its own way as all the isles of the Moonshaes combined, and even more inviolate in its territory. It is ruled by the sea trolls, the scrags. They are even more horrible than the sahuagin—the fishmen, whom we've had to fight before."

"Then Father . . . then the king *must be* dead," Alicia argued, to herself more than anyone. "How could any human survive in such a place?"

"It *is* possible," the mage, Keane, observed tentatively. "There are many spells that will grant one the ability to survive without breathing for a matter of hours, long enough for the sahuagin or scrags to drag a victim to an undersea lair, there to imprison the unfortunate soul in an air-filled cave. No cell can be more impervious to escape."

Alicia's heart leaped again, wanting to believe beyond all reason that her father still lived. The loss of a hand didn't matter. In fact, a powerful priest could repair such damage. What was important was that Tristan lived!

"A few hours," muttered Brandon in frustration. "That would hardly be enough time to mount a rescue even if we could swim to the bottom of the ocean."

"I have heard in the past of other ways," Tavish noted. This time no one interrupted. "It is said that the elves once waged war under the sea, using ships enchanted with powerful magic that not only journeyed below the surface but also kept their crews alive, breathing air."

"Even so, they must have been helpless beyond the hull of their vessel!" objected the prince.

"Ah, but there a wizard's spell magic can come to the aid of his crew. Enchanted by water-breathing spells, elves could sally forth from their galleys, driving the creatures of the sea before them. In this way, it is said, the elves eventually gained mastery of the surface of the sea for all air-breathing creatures."

"Look out!" Brandon cried, springing to Alicia's side before anyone else reacted. A sudden movement nearby drew their attention, and the companions whirled to face one who had not been there a second before.

"Greetings," said Princess Deirdre wryly. She gestured at the craters left by Keane's meteor shower, the singed grass where the wall of fire had roared. "Did the celebration get a little too wild?"

"Great timing," Alicia snapped. "We could have used your help a few minutes ago."

The dark-haired princess said nothing. She wore a plain woolen traveling cloak, with a large bundle strapped to her back. The outline of the flat mirror, through which she had watched the entire fight, was lost in the shapeless bulk of the mass.

Robyn's eyes flashed, and for a moment, she fixed Deirdre with a harsh stare, an expression her daughter ignored. After a moment, the queen's face softened, shadowed once more by grief.

No one stopped to explain what had transpired to the newcomer, however, and Deirdre didn't bother to ask. Instead, they turned their attention back to the discussion that had been interrupted.

"Now?" persisted Alicia. "Is such a voyage under the sea possible today?"

"There you'll have to ask the elves," Tavish said with a sigh. "And it's most unlikely that they'll tell you much!"

"But we can try, can't we?" asked the princess, suddenly excited by the possibilities. "There are elves right here on Gwynneth! The Llewyrr, in Synnoria."

"Indeed," her mother noted with a wry smile. "Have you ever been to Synnoria? Has anyone here—anyone within the borders of Corwell—been to Synnoria?"

"Yes, my queen," came the unexpected reply, from Lord Pawldo. "You have—and so have I."

Robyn laughed, and the sound broke some of the tension. "Yes, beneath blindfolds, our ears masked by the sound of a harp!" Her face grew wistful at the memory. "Yet even then our presence was not desired by the Llewyrr. And the passes into the valley, remember, cannot be seen by humans—not even with aid of a sorcerer."

"That doesn't matter!" Alicia declared forcefully. She regretted her tone immediately, but surprisingly, her mother merely nodded and waited for her to continue.

"I'll start out first thing in the morning! I'll circle every side of that mountain range if I have to until I find a way in or they come out to get me!"

"I'm with you, my princess!" declared Lord Hanrald, grinding his fist into his palm, wishing he held a sword that he could brandish.

"And I!" Brandon was quick to pledge his axe.

Unconsciously the princess found herself looking at Keane. She saw an expression of unabashed dismay cross the mage's face.

Indeed, to the wizard, the difficulties of the task loomed paramount. Keane had no faith in their ability to find a path into Synnoria. It was known to be impervious to most forms of detection and orientation spells. And even if they did manage to find their way to the hidden land, he very much doubted that the elves would willingly aid them. Not that they *could* be of much help, he noted in his silent tally of insurmountable obstacles. He didn't believe for a moment that the secret to sailing a ship under the sea could be discovered in a landlocked mountain kingdom. But finally Keane spoke.

"What time do we leave?" the magic-user asked with a sigh of resignation.

* * * * *

Brigit removed the supple steel gauntlets from her hands and then stopped to doff her helmet and loosen the straps of her armor. Several young Llewyrr led her mare to the watering pool, and she knew that they would brush and feed the animal with care.

Flowing golden hair spilled across Brigit's shoulders, concealing the pointed tips of her elven ears. Barely an inch over five feet tall and quite slender even in her armor, she concealed a great amount of fighting prowess in that tiny form.

"Captain?" Another sister knight stepped through the stable door.

"Oh, hello, Myra. What is it?"

"That priest who came through the Fey-Alamtine goes to see Erashanoor today. The elder wondered if you could join them."

"Of course," Brigit replied without hesitation. Normally the elven knight preferred the pastoral quiet and chaotic splendor of the forest to the well-manicured beauty of Chrysalis, but an invitation from the elder sage of Synnoria was always an intriguing prospect.

Erashanoor was, in many ways, Brigit's mentor—at least in scholarship, if not in knighthood. She saw him only rarely, however, for the old elf could spare little time from his work. He was reputedly writing a detailed history of Synnoria. Nevertheless, on those rare occasions when the Fey-Alamtine was used, Erashanoor always spent considerable time with the refugees.

The sage's offices were located on the highest level in the Argen-Tellirynd, the Palace of the Ages in the heart of Chrysalis. The city itself occupied an island in the Crystaloch, while the stables and barracks of the knights—along with the farms, forests, and parks of all Synnoria—sprawled across the broad valley floor surrounding the lake. Three wide roadways, each smoothly paved with tight-fitting blocks of white marble, crossed the lake at different points, connecting the island city to the shore.

Brigit crossed the causeway on foot, passing through the narrow silver gates—standing open, as always. Soon the gleaming towers of Chrysalis loomed around her, and the winding roads of smoothly polished alabaster stone swerved with artistic perfection among flower bushes and delicately shaped evergreens.

But she must attend to business, she reminded herself. She strolled down the quiet avenues, passing other Llewyrr who walked with casual grace about the city. There was no sense of urgency here, though all of these elves undoubtedly had business to tend to. Such is the way of members of a race whose lifespans commonly pass five centuries.

Brigit moved with the same unconscious ease, at last arriving at a clear, multifaceted wall that cast dazzling patterns of sunlight on the ground at her feet. She stood before the crowning glory of Chrysalis, the structure that had served as the ceremonial capital of the Llewyrr for as long as their city had stood.

The Argen-Tellirynd was surrounded by a crystal wall in the shape of a perfect triangle, enclosing pools, gardens, and walkways within its bright confines. The palace itself rose in a steeply sloping pyramid in the center of the courtyard. The structure had three sides, but Brigit could only see one from her current vantage. Gates as clear as glass swung wide at Brigit's approach, and two elven footmen nodded politely to the knight as she passed.

"The elder is expecting you, Lady Brigit," offered one.

The sister knight meandered through the maze of reflective pools and graceful hedges that filled the courtyard of the Argen-Tellirynd. Finally, unconsciously quickening her steps, she reached the gates of the palace structure itself.

A triangular door in the side of the palace structure slid sideways, revealing a wide, silver-floored corridor. Walls of crystal sloped upward to meet in a point, twenty feet over her head.

A few twists and turns brought her to a wide staircase, and at the top, she reached the elder sage's library. She knew even before she entered that he was within; the telltale scent of his pipe smoke lingered in the air. With a wry smile, Brigit knocked on the door and entered.

"Ah, welcome, my child, welcome!" Erashanoor waved absently. The sage sat in his high-backed leather chair, holding a long-stemmed pipe in his hand and leaning forward, his posture intent upon Pallarynd. The Thy-Tach priest, his face streaked by tears, looked down as Brigit joined them in a third chair.

"The Thy-Tach have undergone an incredible ordeal," explained the sage, puffing absently and sending clouds of smoke into the air over his head. Smoking was a virtually unknown practice among the Llewyrr and would not have been tolerated in closed quarters from anyone less influential than the elder sage. Unlike many of her people, however, Brigit had always enjoyed the burnt-almond smell of Erashanoor's blended herbs.

"Until we encountered you yesterday," Pallarynd said to Brigit, his composure recovered, "we weren't even sure we would survive. Not just from the threat of the beast, but from the flight through the paths of ether."

"I believe they were attacked by Ityak-Ortheel," explained Erashanoor. "The one called 'Elf-Eater.' The monster has plagued our race throughout known history. Barely a century passes wherein a village or community does not feel its wrathful attack, and this attack always drives the survivors to the Fey-Alamtine. No means of defeating the Elf-Eater has ever been discovered."

"Is that creature the reason the gate was constructed?" asked Pallarynd.

"No—at least, not the only reason." Erashanoor took several pensive puffs on his pipe, leaning back in his chair and collecting his thoughts like scribbled notes scattered across a messy desk.

"You see, the destiny of our race is one of epic greatness, but also finite dimension," he began. "We live longer than the humans, or any other populous and—allegedly—civilized race. Our artists create the most glorious sculptures, our musicians script the most beautiful songs—even our weaponsmiths make the finest sword steel!"

Brigit knew of a dwarf or two who would disagree with the last statement, but she kept the notion private as the sage continued with a sigh.

"The price of our longevity, our greatness, is that our numbers shall ever remain small. If we wage war against a human realm, their numbers are replenished after a few generations. We elves, however, never recover from such conflicts.

"And this limitation is coupled with another certainty: Despite our best efforts, humans and other lesser creatures who border elven lands will eventually covet those lands. It is the way of the short-lived ones to employ hasty means, such as violence, to accomplish their goals. Too, many of them are propelled by gods of evil, or the simple pressures of growing population. They breed like rabbits, these humans," Erashanoor noted with a disgusted shake of his head. He paused to puff a few smoke rings, his narrow face creased into a scowl. He nodded to himself before he resumed.

"This is why Evermeet is so well protected. That island, the eternal elvenhome, will provide a land for our peoples that will last as long as the Realms themselves. It is guarded by wards and barriers both magical and mundane, protection against approach by the legions of creatures who threaten us. For that reason, the passages by which even we elves can approach the great island are strictly limited."

"Limited to one route only—the Fey-Alamtine," Brigit interjected.

"The reason Synnoria must remain inviolate," Erashanoor quickly explained, "is that we are the only gate to Evermeet. This is why you must bring the Alamtine triangle with you when you enter the gate, and why someone must always remain behind, to see that nothing follows when the Fey-Alamtine closes."

"That was a near thing," noted Pallarynd. "This 'Elf-Eater,' I believe you called it, reached after me as we departed. It seemed to seek the triangle. The tentacle touched it and tried to pull it from my grasp."

"It is a very good thing for all of us that it did not," Erashanoor replied sternly. "Else it could have followed you here. If the secret of Synnoria becomes known to the enemies of the elves, our existence becomes tenuous at best. Even the touch of the Alamtine Triangle can give our enemies knowledge that endangers us."

"Do you suppose that the Elf-Eater . . . ?" Brigit felt an icy stab of fear. The picture of a creature such as the Ityak-Ortheel entering Synnoria brought bleak images of death and devastation to her mind.

"The creature didn't take the triangle. Therefore I suspect the risk is minimal. It may know the shape of the key, but it still does not know where the gate leads. As long as that knowledge remains concealed, we are safe."

* * * * *

"Walk with me for a moment, my daughter." The warmth of Robyn's tone touched Alicia, and she quickly rose and joined the queen at the fringe of the firelight cast by the hearty blaze.

The time approached midnight, Alicia knew without needing to look at the brilliant stars.

Several dozen Ffolk—Alicia's companions, and other lords, knights, and even druids—had gathered around the fire some hours before to discuss the import of the day's events. The queen had naturally canceled the upcoming Council of Lords. They could not proceed with a memorial for a king who might still be alive. They all realized that the prospects of a rescue seemed slim to nonexistent, but they also knew that the attempt must be made.

Alicia and her companions would embark for Synnoria on the morrow, seeking a secret that would allow them to take a ship under the sea. Robyn had returned to the castle after the disastrous banquet, and this was her first reappearance on the commons.

"Are you all right?" inquired the princess, laying a hand on her mother's arm. Robyn replied by placing her own hand over her daughter's and pressing gently.

For a time, they did not speak, and Alicia realized with surprise that her mother led her toward Corwell's small druids' grove and its sacred Moonwell. Soon they passed under the flat-topped stone arch, the entrance to the grove, and approached the small, milk-white pool of water. Even beneath the starlight and a half-full waxing moon, the illumination of the water cast a pale wash of light throughout the sacred clearing in the heart of the grove.

"I had a talk with your sister before I departed from Callidyrr," Robyn opened the conversation.

"Deirdre has changed—a great deal," Alicia remarked thoughtfully.

"You've seen it, too." For a moment, Robyn was silent. "This spring she mastered a great deal of sorcery in a very short period of time. Keane swears that he doesn't know how she did this, though he, too, has observed her power. Do you know anything more?"

Alicia shook her head regretfully. "We were apart for most of that month, and when we met again, at the Fairheight Moonwell, she had the powers of an accomplished sorceress. But she'll tell me nothing about what happened to her in that space of time."

"A mystery—and a disturbing one," Robyn noted. "There is danger here, for Deirdre and for all of us, that I don't believe she fully understands."

Alicia remained silent. She had sensed the same threat as her mother, and it comforted her somewhat to know that she was not alone in her apprehensions. Nevertheless, she didn't know what she could do to open a door of communication with her aloof sibling.

Robyn strolled along the shore of the shallow pond, as if looking for something on the ground. "Here," said the High Queen finally. "I placed this here this morning to let the blessings of the goddess surround it."

The High Queen knelt at the edge of the pool and lifted up a long shaft that had lain in the shadows. Rising and turning, she offered it to Alicia.

"Your staff?" questioned the younger woman. "But surely you'll need it now!"

Robyn raised a hand. "Not my staff. Yours."

"But—"

"This is a changestaff. I made it for you in honor of your accomplishments. It may aid you in your service to the goddess."

Alicia touched the wood, which was smooth and vaguely warm beneath her fingertips. A sense of wonder overwhelmed her. The surface was carved intricately in the design of a leafy tendril that coiled about the staff over its entire length.

"It's beautiful," she breathed. "I'll cherish it more than anything I know."

"When you need an ally, plant the base of the staff in the ground. Use the command word '*Phyrosyne.*' "

"What will it do?" Alicia wondered.

"You'll see. It's not what the *staff* does, but what the goddess does through the agent of the wood." The queen's smile was wistful, and Alicia waited for her to continue. "I fear you'll need it, and much more, in the days and weeks to come."

"But Father lives! Doesn't he?" The disturbing fear that the ambassador might have been lying pushed its way to the forefront of Alicia's mind, but angrily she forced it back. "He *must* be alive! Can't you tell somehow?"

"Aye, Daughter. I believe that I can." Robyn sighed, sinking to a stone bench beside the pool. Alicia sat beside her. "I didn't realize it at first. When the news came that the ship was lost and everyone had drowned, I tried to accept the fact that Tristan was dead. There could be no other explanation, no other real hope.

"Yet as the days and weeks went by, I couldn't bring myself to believe it. I dreamed about him almost every night, and there was something so *real* about those dreams that I came to believe that he must be alive somewhere.

"Now this messenger comes, with these claims that they hold the High King prisoner, and I find it all too easy to believe."

"Then you must have faith, Mother!" Alicia insisted. "He's lived this long, and when I get to Synnoria I promise that I'll find a way to go after him!"

Robyn smiled, forcing her expression to brighten. "I believe you, my daughter—and more than that, I will help."

"What do you mean?"

"Tomorrow, when you begin your journey along the Corwell Road in search of the Llewyrr, I intend to ride with you."

* * * * *

During the long afternoon and evening, Deirdre watched the preparations of her sister's party in the mirror of scrying. She viewed the scene with the same wry amusement with which she had greeted the images of the disrupted festival. She kept the fact of her spying crystal a secret, spending long hours secluded in her room while she observed the activities around the castle in the glass.

Then, when Alicia, the queen, and their companions rode through the gate in the morning, she amused herself by watching their progress, trying to imagine the substance of their undoubtedly trivial conversations. The mirror provided no sound for the scene being observed.

Eventually she tired of this eavesdropping and turned back to her books. She went about her own business, relieved that the burden of court and council could be delayed to some nebulous future hour. Deirdre had brought several tomes with her, carried in a large sack over her shoulder, and she spread these on the desk near the room's window. Bright sunshine flooded the land of Corwell, and in its light, she would be able to read easily.

She returned to a book she had started the day before, a treatise on travel—both voluntary and involuntary—through the ethereal stuff that connected the planes of existence. Her nimble mind absorbed each detail, recognizing where the writer overextended his arguments and where he had touched upon a real germ of truth.

As she progressed through the book, the sun sank into the west and the household servants brought her some food and lit several candles for her reading. The former remained untouched and the latter burned low as the princess learned more, and more, and more.

* * * * *

The supple bay raced along Corwell Road, and Alicia gave the horse her head. Her companions trailed along the smooth surface of the highway, riding at the easy lope that for two days had carried them across central Corwell. Hanrald led the way, alternately lumbering forward on his huge war-horse or probing possible places of concealment along the road to either side, while Alicia and Robyn alternately raced, trotted, or walked. Keane, Brandon, Pawldo, and Tavish followed at a more sedate pace, trailing some distance behind the others for hours at a time.

The journey to the borders of Synnoria would take three or four days. The first part of the trip followed good roads, but for the last day or two they must branch off the highway and enter the rougher country of the highlands. Once there, they intended to seek some entry into the elven realm. Alicia was determined not to worry about that problem until it confronted them.

The companion who had most surprised Alicia rode at the side of the princess: the High Queen herself. The younger woman had not expected that her mother would want to accompany the party, yet now, as they rode together, Alicia couldn't imagine traveling without her.

Her mother had seemed like a new woman since the start of the journey. Years of age seemed to melt away from her, and she rode with a spirit almost equal to Alicia's, who was quite skilled as a horsewoman. Robyn carried her own staff lashed to the saddle behind her and wore a plain silver torque around her neck, the symbol of her status as Great Druid.

Both of them rode with renewed hopes, however tenuous. For the first time since Tristan's disappearance, they had a course of action to follow; they could *do* something besides sit around and grieve. The challenges of their quest remained daunting, to be sure, but both mother and daughter felt confident that they would be able to deal with any obstacles that might arise.

Rather than tiring, the horses had seemed to gain in strength and excitement as each day passed. Now, in the late morning of the third day, Alicia knew they must soon turn off the wide road, following the winding vale that the High Queen had described.

Soon they found the turn, marked by a hill called Freeman's Down. That night they made camp in a high valley, where an unseasonably chill wind scoured the ground and whistled through the trees. They built a great fire and huddled around its warmth, each of them wrapped within private thoughts, weighing their chances for success or failure.

"Somewhere along here, off to our right, will be the valley that Tristan, Pawldo, and I came down when we left Synnoria," Robyn told them, describing as best she could her experiences of twenty summers before. "I'm not sure that I'll recognize it, though. We might have to try a few different routes."

"One of them will take us there—I'm sure of it!" Alicia proclaimed, and the others found her confidence heartwarming, but not necessarily contagious.

"It can't be that hard to find," suggested Hanrald. "After all, Gwynneth itself isn't very big, and we're talking about a good-sized, populous valley located in a specific range of highlands!"

"It's not the size of Synnoria that gives it concealment," argued Tavish heatedly. "It has more to do with the nature of the place. Legends say that a person can walk straight toward it, and then turn aside without even taking notice of the fact that he is near it. You'll walk past and never know that you've missed it."

"But surely farmers and herdsmen around here must have some kind of idea!" objected Alicia.

"You've seen the state of the country," Keane pointed out, pleased with the verbal opening that would allow him to join the conversation. "We didn't pass a single farm once we moved beyond the Corwell Road. And the grass was long—I don't think the land is used by herdsmen either."

"The Ffolk sense that this land is not for mundane employment," Robyn said. "Synnoria is a place of enchantment, of power that is drawn from the earth itself, not from the skills of mortal wizards. It's the same power that gives life to the goddess and makes the Moonshae Islands a place of special beauty."

The queen paused, her face relaxing into a reflective smile. After a moment, she looked up, aware that the others waited for her to continue. "King—then he was 'Prince'—Tristan and I came through here near the start of the Darkwalker War. It was the detour through Synnoria that allowed us to reach Corwell Road before an invading army of northmen, and also to gain the aid of dwarves from Myrloch Vale, and even a company of the Sisters of Synnoria."

The history of that war was well known to them all. The aid of the elven riders and their resolute captain, Brigit Cu'Lyrran, had proven decisive in stopping the original attacks against Corwell.

"But the passage through Synnoria lingers in my mind," continued the queen. "Perhaps because I didn't *see* it. They blindfolded us, remember, Pawldo?"

The halfling nodded, suppressing a shudder as he looked into the darkness beyond the camp.

"They told us that the fabulous beauty of the place would surely drive us humans mad, and perhaps it would have, judging by the sounds we heard. Even those—the trilling of waterfalls, the mingling of birdsong and breeze—would have captivated us all. . . ."

"Except for the bard!" finished Tavish with a smile.

"Indeed. The harpist Keren banged against his harp and made the most awful sounds you could imagine. For a full day, he kept it up while the sisters led us along their trails. Those jarring notes, I'm sure, were all that kept us alive. Finally we came out on a broad and rounded ridge. Synnoria was behind us. . . ."

Robyn's face grew sad as she remembered the darker moments in the path of her life since then. Suddenly she missed Tristan terribly, and it was all she could do to hold back her tears.

"So you see, there's a lot of magic to contend with," warned Pawldo, wiggling a finger at Alicia. "I wouldn't be surprised if half of us are turned into bugs before this is over!" His face was jocular, but his tone indicated more than a little apprehension on this point.

Alicia slumped backward but didn't concede defeat. "You can argue reality all you want," she said, "but I've never doubted, from the moment we started out, that we'd find our way into that valley somehow!"

"Hold that faith, child," said Tavish with a soft laugh. "It may be all we need."

* * * * *

"Arise, Ityak-Ortheel, and answer your master's summons!"

The command of Malar rang through the ether, past the vortices of the gods and down—far, far down—into the Abyssal depths of the lower planes. Here the one known as Elf-Eater raised its muck-streaked maw from the primordial sludge that was its home and, upon hearing the call, uttered a rumbling belch of assent.

Talos observed the activities of his ally with cruel pleasure. The discovery of the platinum triangle on the Moonshae Islands had infused Malar with vengeful hatred. The Beastlord would waste no time in setting his pet creature against those insolent elves—and this vengeance suited the Stormbringer's plans as well.

The image of Malar's muzzled skull, bristling with fangs and resting upon huge, many-taloned paws, appeared before the Elf-Eater. Slowly, with gruesome majesty, Ityak-Ortheel rose from the sheltering sludge until it crouched before the figure of its god. Only the illusionary presence of the deity allowed Malar to loom over his pet, for Ityak-Ortheel was itself the size of a massive dragon.

But size was the thing's only resemblance to those comparatively noble serpents. The Elf-Eater had a mouth but no teeth. Instead, the aperture was a moist, sucking hole in the side of the thing's domelike body. The maw was capable of expanding to a gaping width or compressing into a long, probing snout, and it was surrounded by many long tentacles, each equipped with multiple, weblike pods used to trap a victim and drag it toward that obscene orifice.

And also unlike a dragon, Ityak-Ortheel had no tail nor wings—and only three legs, each as broad as a gnarled oak stump. Upon those limbs, however, it could lumber as fast as a galloping horse. It had no eyes nor ears, but it could sense the presence of warm-blooded beings on all sides, and could easily distinguish which were elves.

With the summons of Malar, all the Elf-Eater's dim intellect focused on the gnawing emptiness within the great body. Quivering in eagerness, the elephantine shape awaited the further words of its god.

The words it wanted to hear were not forthcoming. Instead, Malar seized the spiritual essence of Iytak Ortheel and hauled it upward into the ether. Malar focused his attention on the target, and Talos used his still-awesome power to enact a powerful spell.

Iytak-Ortheel, the Elf-Eater, shook its great body, exploding through a dark wall of stone to plant its three feet firmly on grassy soil. No longer did it fester in the pits of sludge, it knew. Instead, it had come to a place surrounded by a world of mortals. . . a place called Synnoria.

A place of elves.

❧ 4 ❧

The Elf-Eater

Robyn awakened suddenly amid the stillness of the sleeping camp. For a brief moment, her mind flashed back to younger days. How long had it been since she had slept beneath a canopy of stars? Too long, she decided.

But then, in the clarity of her growing awareness, she wondered what it was that had interrupted her slumber. Sitting up and pulling her woolen cloak about her shoulders, she looked around the silent camp.

The outline of a large, broad-shouldered man was visible some distance above the rest of them. She recognized Hanrald and remembered that the Earl of Fairheight had taken the midnight watch. A swift glance at the stars confirmed her estimate of the time.

The unseasonal chill remained in the air, but to the High Queen, the brisk weather was a bracing welcome, an embrace of nature, ushering her back to her favorite domain.

No longer questioning, Robyn followed an instinctive sense, slowly approaching the glowing mound of coals that marked the place where their fire had blazed hours earlier. She stopped several feet away from the firepit but close enough to feel the radiant warmth on her face, and then she spread the blanket apart with her arms, allowing the heat to caress her entire body.

Slowly the dull red of the coals began to brighten, though the steady radiance of heat remained comfortably constant. Robyn stared at the embers, watching spots of light grow from orange pinpricks to blazing yellow circles in her eyes, as if she stared at the sun near noon of a high summer day.

Yet instead of feeling pain, she felt a powerful sense of exultation, a kind of energy she hadn't known for two decades.

This was the power of the Earthmother, she knew, and it flowed into the willing woman who again was the Great Druid of that goddess.

Finally the power became too great, and Robyn fell to her knees. Still she did not lower her eyes, and slowly the lights that dazzled her shifted into cooler spectrums—red, blue, and finally a pale violet that seemed to linger for hours, soothing the druid's taut nerves and acting as a balm for the grave troubles that worried her.

Then, when next Robyn raised her eyes, she saw a misty form begin to gather in the air above the fire. A whirling vapor coalesced in the night, growing more substantial as it slowed the rate of its rotation. Finally the mist solidified, just for a moment, into the image of a proud wolf's-head. Yellow eyes gleamed at Robyn, seeming to blink against the darkness.

"There is evil . . ." The wolf spoke to her, in a voice like the hunting cry of a distant pack. It pierced her heart with a plaintive, savagely beautiful song. At the same time, Robyn heard a firm undertone of danger, of a deep and imminent menace that intruded into this place like a cancerous tumor.

The long, narrow jaws seemed to grin, revealing ivory fangs that gleamed in the darkness. The yellow eyes stared with unblinking intensity, bright and powerful. Robyn Kendrick opened her heart and her mind, letting the sign wash over her. She listened, for the first time since she had been a very young woman, to the pure voice of her goddess.

"Seek . . . seek the evil. . . ." Again the soft cry floated through the night. *"For there you will find good . . ."*

The sound and image faded for many wondrous minutes, as if the pack ranged over distant hills, each rise carrying the sound farther and farther, until nothing remained but the wind whispering among the full summer leaves.

"I understand, my Mother," Robyn said softly.

The coals had sunk to mere shadowy remnants of their previous warmth. But as the queen returned to her bedrolls and wrapped her blanket against the chill, the warmth of the fire glowed with the warmth of her spirit and her mind.

* * * * *

Talloth cantered easily up the gentle forest trail, and Brigit felt the full joy of a Synnorian sunrise fill her body and her spirit. The morning had dawned clear, and the sun was no more than two handspans over the eastern horizon.

These hours, when the mist still lingered among the trees and the flowers glistened with fresh dew, were the captain's favorite time to ride. Llewyrr gardeners who had begun to work their fields waved as the silver knight on her white mare rode past.

She came to the trout farm and turned Talloth from the trail, riding among the clear pools that dotted this large glade in the forest. Several Llewyrr, breeders and netmen, looked up from their tasks. They were opening a sluicegate to fill a newly excavated pool.

Brigit observed the brilliant fish darting back and forth in their clear pools. One pond held trout of purest golden color, each more than a foot long; another contained even larger fish, striped with the full spectrum of a rainbow. The fish would be introduced into the streams and lakes, ensuring that they remained a viable food source and a beautiful part of the natural scenery of Synnoria.

After a few minutes, Brigit rode on, passing other Llewyrr who were hauling buckets full of fingerlings to the stream. Then, in a few moments, the full peace of the forest surrounded her again. She continued up the valley, intending to ride all the way to the Fey-Alamtine gate.

Then she stiffened. A sound came to her, and Talloth halted instinctively. Hoofbeats approached down this same trail. In moments, she saw a flash of white in the woods, and then Brigit identified the form of one of her knights.

The sister shouted at the sight of her captain.

"Humans! They approach from the west, up the Vale of Clouds!" The knight's shout of alarm sounded a jarring note in the pastoral sunrise. Brigit recognized the rider as Colleen, one of the border patrol. The pounding gallop of the white horse drowned out most of Colleen's voice, but the urgency in the young scout's demeanor was apparent to Brigit even from a half mile away.

The captain spurred Talloth, and the mare leaped forward. In a few moments, they met and Brigit reined in, taking the bridle of the scout's horse. The young Llewyrr rider, her blonde hair tossed raggedly by the wind in her ride, gasped for breath while Brigit gestured to her to collect herself.

"I saw them myself," Colleen reported after a moment. "Humans, about six of them. They ride horses—two of the steeds are as white as Synnorian mares!"

"They climb the western valley?"

"The Vale of Clouds." The young sister nodded. She wore the mottled greenish tunic of a scout over her silver breastplate. Her helmet was lashed to the saddle of her horse, while a deep hood attached to her cloak could quickly be pulled up to cover her white-blonde hair.

"They'll pass the boundary and turn aside," Brigit announced, more calm in her voice than she actually felt.

It disturbed her, this sudden appearance of humans at the borders of Synnoria so soon after she had resolved to be especially vigilant against intrusion. "Still, it's best if I have a look at them. Lead on!"

Colleen reversed her gelding and galloped back up the trail, Brigit close behind. The two sister knights rode without taking notice of the wonders around them. Even though the bright flowers and verdant woods were familiar sights, they rarely failed to attract the attention and delight of the Llewyrr who passed among them. But now the elfwomen remained still, intent upon the potential for intrusion.

But those surrounding wonders were splendorous indeed. Waterfalls trilled from the slopes to either side, while a clear brook collected their spumes and carried them with laughing enthusiasm toward the blue waters of Crystaloch. Columbines, daisies, and fleabane all blinked among lush, windblown grasses, each type of flower blooming in a dozen different shades of brilliant color. Tall pines, their long-needled sprouts blanketing the forest in a soft, blue-green hue, waved from the slopes above them.

The Llewyrr on their white horses followed a narrow track that generally traced the streambed up the valley bottom. Much of the ride took them through sun-speckled meadow, or among the few pines growing on the valley floor. After several miles, however, Colleen veered to the left, her gelding plunging between two tall pine trunks onto an almost invisible track in the woods.

The winding path climbed steeply, and the two riders ducked their heads beneath many overhanging limbs. The strong horses bounded over the tangled ground, laboring hard, carrying the two elves steadily upward. After a few minutes, they paused for rest on a shoulder of the valley that gave them a splendid view behind them. The black cliff of the Fey-Alamtine gleamed in the sunlight at the head of the valley.

Then, for many more minutes, they pressed higher through the enclosing forest. Finally the trees gave way abruptly to a rolling, rock-studded ridge. Below them, the wonders of Synnoria sprawled, pristine and heartbreakingly beautiful beneath the dome of blue.

"A little farther," Colleen said. The horses broke into a gallop, approaching the top of the rounded ridge bordering Synnoria on the west.

As they approached the crest, the jagged tors and rocky promontories of the Myrloch highlands came into view over the ridge and then, as the sisters reached the summit, the forested slopes and flat-bottomed valleys, many dotted with lake or fen. Still they cantered, past the crest of the ridge and down the gradual slope that soon grew steeper.

Colleen halted, and the two dismounted behind a large rock. Leaving the horses behind, they slipped forward on hands and knees onto an outcrop of granite that jutted into the air over the twisting valley below.

"I see them," Brigit announced immediately. The figures were still miles away, but she could clearly count seven of them, on five dark and two white horses.

As the two observed from their lofty perch, the party of humans reached a small side valley that flowed into the wider vale they had been following. Without visible hesitation, the intruders turned into the narrow valley. Brigit watched them dismount, taking their horses by the bridles to lead them up the steep, treacherous-looking trail.

"The magic still works," observed the captain with a wry smile.

"They believe that they follow the only route available to them?" asked Colleen. Though the illusionary barrier of Synnoria was understood by all adult Llewyrr, the young scout had never seen it in action.

"Yes. The walls of the main valley appear to merge before them into a tight, cliff-sided draw. The apparent amount of water in the two streams is reversed. A mere trickle comes down the draw, while the humans will think for several miles that they follow a major channel. Imagine their confusion as they move away from Synnoria and it dwindles to its true dimensions!"

"Then they are gone for now?" The scout studied the diminishing figures until they had disappeared behind the first twist in the narrow passage.

"They'll follow that draw until it comes to a little valley with a marsh and a lake. That's the divide. From there, they descend and expect to find Synnoria. Instead, it puts them in the fenland of Myrloch Vale!"

The two knights made their way carefully back to their horses, where they relaxed, safely out of sight of the valley. For a long time, they rested beside the sun-swept boulder, drifting toward a midday nap in the soothing warmth.

Finally Brigit stirred, stretching easily as she stood. "Let's follow the ridgeline for a while," she suggested.

For more than an hour, the two Llewyrr rode the heights, following the border between Synnoria and Corwell until they reached a craggy stretch too rough for the horses. Enjoying the scenery and the silence, they turned back.

"Let's go look for those humans again, to make sure they

haven't come back this way," Brigit said.

Before Colleen could reply, both sisters stiffened. A long, ululating call reached their ears, carried clearly from the valley of Synnoria. Then the sound stopped abruptly, chopped away in midcry.

"The Fey-Alamtine!" cried Colleen.

"Let's go!" barked Brigit. The sound had been a Llewyrr distress cry reserved for the most dire of emergencies. The two white horses pounded forward, streaking over the crest of the ridge, racing back toward the pastoral Synnorian valley the two riders had left scant hours before. They galloped headlong down the steep trail, back toward the valley bottom.

As the valley floor came into sight, the two sisters, even from nearly a thousand feet above, could see that something was horribly changed. A great swath marked the middle of the vale where tall trees had been crushed to either side like blades of grass. The setting was no longer pastoral; indeed, so profound was the transformation that Brigit tried to convince herself that she must be dreaming. Trees of great girth lay sprawled about like matchsticks, pushed outward as if some horrifying, destructive force had forged a path between them.

Colleen gasped in horror. "What happened?" she shouted, clinging to her racing gelding.

Brigit didn't reply. She felt sick to her stomach, grimly determined to discover the source of this abomination.

"Look—the way the trees lie. Whatever did this moved on down the valley," observed Colleen crisply.

"Toward Chrysalis!"

The captain had reached the same conclusion, but to her, it held different significance—not so much where the path was leading, as to where it came from. It originated higher up the valley to their left . . .

From the Fey-Alamtine.

They reached the vantage where they had rested on the climb, and Brigit gazed to the west in uncomprehending shock. The once-shiny cliff no longer gleamed in the morning sunlight. In fact, there was no cliff there to gleam! Instead, a wreckage of splintered obsidian lay at the foot of the slope, as if a horrendous landslide or explosion had ripped open the mountain.

Brigit spurred her horse, and the fleet mare seemed to sprout wings, so gracefully did she sweep along the forest trail. Colleen held as close as possible, but the gelding couldn't match the pace of her captain's mare.

They reached a shelf in the descending valley, and the horses pounded down the winding trail with abandon. Near the bottom, Brigit's mare reared back and the sister knight looked down, appalled, at the trail before her.

A white horse lay there, dead for only moments judging by the steam rising from its freshly exposed bowels. Something had scored a gory wound across the horse's midsection, nearly tearing the hapless beast in two. The tattered remnants of the saddle remained, but there was no sign of the rider.

"Inger's horse," said the white-faced Colleen. She held her longbow across her saddle, her fear-widened eyes darting back and forth among the surrounding trees.

A loud splintering sound reached them, and the Llewyrr felt the massive pain of trees, rended by some awful force. Shrieks of horror, undeniably elven, rang from somewhere down the trail.

Immediately the two sister knights spurred their mounts into a gallop, frantic now to intercept the threat that seemed to move like a landslide toward the heart of Synnoria. They ducked under branches, then lay flat along the pitching backs of the racing steeds, thundering several miles in a blur of speed.

Finally they came through a grove of tall pines into the wide meadow of the trout farm, and here the horses reared back, instinctively terrified.

The first thing that came into Brigit's mind was that a gigantic turtle had somehow appeared among the Llewyrr. At a glance, the domed back, covered by a hard carapace, might have belonged to one of that amphibious race.

But as it moved, the resemblance immediately vanished.

Three legs flexed beneath the beast, carrying it with bounding speed toward several fleeing elves. It loomed over them, the size of a small barn, then scampered with shocking speed this way and that after the terrified Llewyrr. Tentacles lashed outward, seizing the slight forms and dragging them to an unseen fate beneath the monster's overhanging shell.

"The trout farm!" cried Colleen, but Brigit had already seen the damage. The beast stalked among the buildings and sheds, smashing troughs of flowing water, reducing wooden buildings to splinters with a single kick of a tree-sized leg. Panic-stricken Llewyrr fled in all directions. The knights saw several of them seized by the monster's tentacles and dragged screaming to their doom.

"Let's go!" urged Brigit, spurring the frightened Talloth toward the rampaging beast. She wished for her lance, though in her heart, she knew that even that steel-tipped shaft could do little more than prick the monster's skin. Despite the hopelessness of their courageous gesture, Colleen raced at her side. Both of the sister knights drew their swords, raising the blades in a wild attempt to distract the monster from its helpless prey.

The beast must have sensed their approach, for it turned from the wreckage of a shed, where it had been burrowing after survivors with its tentacles, and lumbered toward the froth-flecked horses and their determined riders.

"Break!" shouted Brigit, veering to the right. Colleen, anticipating the command, split to the left. The horses swept around the looming beast, out of range of the awful tendrils, and the monster seemed content to let them pass.

As they came around to the other side, Brigit looked back and, for the first time, saw the distended gap that was the thing's mouth. Blood flowed copiously among a grinding nest of tongue protuberances, hard-edged digits that crunched and scraped against each other or against anything else unfortunate enough to be caught between them. The knight gagged at the thought of the elves—her fellow Llewyrr!—who had perished there, ground to pieces by the churning cartilage.

"Turn back!" she shouted to Colleen, veering sharply toward the creature. A tentacle lashed toward her and she chopped, feeling a grim satisfaction when her steel blade bit into the gruesome flesh. Immediately the limb whipped backward, away from the keen sword.

Colleen darted in on the other side, slashing at a different tentacle, and then the two riders galloped away, pausing across the field to see if the thing would pursue them.

Instead, it stood like a small hillock, as if it would never move anywhere again. "Attack again—but be careful!" Brigit commanded.

Again the two Llewyrr thundered forward, blades at the ready, guiding the sleek horses with the pressure of their knees. Still the three-legged monstrosity remained unmoving, awaiting the charge.

"Break!" cried Brigit again, and once more the two riders swept past the monster. The captain looked for the lashing tentacles again, ready to parry, but no attack came. She darted closer, stabbing with her blade toward the immense body.

But the beast sprang away before she could close. For a fierce, triumphant moment, she thought that it feared her, but then she saw the awful truth.

The monster's leap carried it full into the side of Colleen's gelding. One of the huge legs kicked outward, shockingly nimble, crushing the horse's shoulder with the force of a single blow. With an exclamation of fear, or maybe anger, the scout flew from the saddle, tumbling heavily to the ground. Immediately a lashing tendril whipped over her tumbling body to constrict about her legs. The knight finally stopped rolling, knocked senseless, and the monster tightened its grip.

Slowly the tentacle grew taut, dragging Colleen feetfirst through the grass toward the gigantic beast. The gaping maw narrowed, becoming an extending proboscis with a small, circular opening in its blunt tip. The aperture resembled a giant sucker as it pulsed open and closed, as if tantalized by the approaching morsel.

Brigit had rushed in closer when the monster attacked Colleen, but her blade—of the sharpest, hardest elven steel, and enchanted more than a thousand years earlier by a great Llewyrr wizard—merely bounced from the thing's bony carapace. Talloth fairly flew around the thing, and then Brigit saw the awful doom her comrade faced.

Colleen regained her senses, but the monster ignored her desperate kicks. She grasped despairingly at the grass, but it tore loose in her hands. The moist sucker that was the beast's mouth reached closer, almost touching her leather boot.

The captain of the sister knights sprang from her saddle, landed on her feet between the scout and the creature's mouth, and drove her longsword downward with killing force. The razor-sharp edge bit into the tentacle, scoring a deep groove but failing to sever the tough limb.

Still, the wound distracted the monster enough for Colleen to kick against the tendril and squirm free. Brigit jumped backward, grasping her companion's shoulder and jerking the trembling scout roughly to her feet.

"Onto my mare! Quickly!" she barked as the faithful Talloth circled back to the two Llewyrr. The elves stumbled away from the looming horror, not daring to look backward. Colleen steadied herself and reached for the mare's bridle as the steed galloped closer. Suddenly the animal's eyes widened in fright and it reared back.

Without thinking, Brigit pushed Colleen to the side, diving behind her companion as the ground behind them—the place where they had just stood—shook to the impact of a monstrous body. Looking upward in horror, the captain of the knights saw two tentacles reach toward the panicked mare. They seized Talloth's forelegs and pulled, dragging the steed to the ground. One of the tentacles, heavier than the rest, bashed against the mare's neck.

Brigit saw blood spurt and heard the gurgling death of her loyal war-horse, but she forced the pain and grief from her mind. They had to *move!*

"Run—for all you're worth!" she ordered, bouncing to her feet with the fleet scout at her side. The two elves dashed across the field toward the dark line of the stream, which here flowed between steep banks that were slightly higher than an elf.

They heard a thudding noise behind them again, and then they reached the streambed, flinging themselves from the bank to land in the shallow, gravel-bedded stream.

"This way!" Brigit darted to the left, hearing Colleen behind her. The water barely rose to their ankles, and they sprinted nearly as quickly as they had before.

But not quickly enough. A shadow loomed over them, blocking out the bright sun, the fiery orb that was so yellow, so cheerful that it certainly must be mocking them, Brigit thought in despair. The huge, rounded beast towered above them, reaching forward with tentacles too numerous to count.

Colleen collapsed with a groan of despair, sobbing. Brigit shook her head angrily, ignoring the thunderous voice of hopelessness. Instead, she raised her sword in both hands and prepared to meet the monster squarely.

* * * * *

The High Queen told none of her companions of the goddess's omen, the proud wolf who had spoken to her in the darkest hours of the night. Hanrald mentioned, in the morning, that he had seen the queen sitting beside the dying fire, but that was all. The vision had been for her alone.

Now she pondered the meaning privately as they progressed farther up the valley that, to the best of her memory, would lead them somewhere near Synnoria.

"Are you sure the terrain was this rough?" asked Alicia as, afoot, the companions led their horses higher up the steep, twisting draw. The formerly wide vale had compressed into this ravine in a remarkably short period of time.

"To tell you the truth, it seemed that we rode our horses the whole way," Robyn admitted. "I can't imagine we could have come out this way."

"And look how quickly this stream has dwindled away," observed Hanrald, who had been leading the party up the narrow gully. "There was a lot more water in it a mile back, and yet I haven't seen any tributaries entering the stream since then. How do you explain it being a mere trickle here without the addition of more water?"

"This whole range responds to a detect magic spell," said Keane disgustedly, after examining their surroundings with yet another magical inspection. "I can't tell where any specific effect exists."

The mage disliked walking even more than he loathed riding, and the rugged terrain of this morning's march had done little for his morale. Now he slumped to sit on a boulder, holding the reins of his swaybacked gelding.

"And look." Brandon pointed at the sky, where the sun lay off their right shoulders. "We no longer go east. We've curved to the north somewhere along the way."

"That's funny. The valley seemed pretty straight to me, even though it was a little steep," Alicia noted with surprise. The hair at the back of her neck prickled upward as she realized that they had been deceived by sorcery.

"No doubt we'll be turned into frogs or something equally hideous if we take a few more steps," grumbled Pawldo, looking around nervously. He paused, as if waiting for someone to urge him forward.

"It seems pointless to continue up this gully," agreed Robyn, with an appraising look at the steep climb before them. "We must have passed the trail somewhere below."

"That's the smartest suggestion I've heard in days!" agreed the halfling heartily.

"Nothing like a bit of climbing to get the blood flowing, though. Don't you agree?" said Hanrald, with a hearty clap on the back for Keane.

The mage scowled but climbed stiffly to his feet. "This means we go *down* for a while, right?" he checked.

"Due south," Brandon noted. "Until we figure out where the valley curved from east and west."

The descent passed quickly, though they moved with careful

attention to their surroundings. Keane constantly checked the magical emanations from the surrounding ridge, particularly the steep faces toward the east and north, reporting that the intensity of the enchantment remained steady. Robyn studied her surroundings each step of the way, seeking some feature that would trigger a memory. Brandon kept an eye on the sun, carefully watching their direction of travel.

All of them noticed the gradual change in the terrain as the narrow draw slowly widened, and the cliff walls rolled back to rounded ridges on either side. The ground leveled, and the stream beside them grew placid, losing the urgency that had formerly carried it frothing from the heights. Now it meandered, deep and murky, between earthen banks and grassy meadows.

"Look! We're going west now!" Brandon's voice carried the excitement of discovery, and the significance of the news could not be underplayed.

"The valley appears to run straight—but here it goes east and west, and a mile back it flows north to south!" Alicia realized.

"*That's* the illusion—to make a curved valley appear to be straight!" Keane pointed out.

Robyn held up a hand, silencing the others instantly. They waited as the woman removed her staff from its lashings to her saddle and gently placed the butt of the shaft on the ground. She closed her eyes and murmured a brief phrase of a simple spell. It was an enchantment of detection, but unlike Keane's spell, it didn't search for the presence of magic. Instead, she sought a far different thing—a thing she normally would never have associated with Synnoria, except for words that the vision of the wolf had said to her on the previous night.

Now she performed a spell to detect evil.

For a long while, the queen felt no triggering response, no indication of any presence that was other than natural or benign. But then, just as she began to despair of success, a tiny flicker of darkness and dread tugged at the fringes of her awareness.

Whatever it was, the malignancy remained distant. Yet even through the filter of several miles, she felt the power of this evil, the terrible menace it represented.

Quickly she opened her eyes. The detection spell was a glowing spot in her subconscious, the sense of direction compelling and accurate. She knew which way to go now.

"The route to Synnoria must lie—there!" Robyn pointed, surprising even herself with her certainty.

They followed the direction she indicated to look skeptically at a tiny rivulet of water trilling over a series of precipitous waterfalls, spilling from a lofty height to join the stream before them from the opposite bank.

"Just crossing the river to get over there looks impossible!" Alicia objected. "How could you have come that way—on horses?"

"I know I was never under water," Pawldo inserted. "That's the kind of thing I tend to remember!"

"The crossing is not quite impossible," Hanrald announced. The earl had wandered over to the streambed, and now he gestured to the ground at his feet. "There's a ford here—not very obvious or well used. In fact, it looks as though someone doesn't want it to be found!"

The others joined him, and they all saw that several flat rocks had been placed to form steps leading down into the stream. A ridge of gravel, several feet wide, barely visible under the water, led to a similar avenue on the opposite bank. The ford itself looked to be no more than three feet deep, though much deeper water approached, and flowed away from, the spot.

"That's *it!*" Robyn cried. "We crossed here—or at a ford just like this! I remember the steps leading up out of the water."

"You might be onto something," admitted Lord Pawldo.

They quickly mounted, and the horses needed little urging to enter the cold, slow-moving, water. They crossed in single file and soon emerged onto the far bank.

"It doesn't look nearly so steep from here!" the princess

noted. The slope still climbed away from them, but at a much more gentle angle than before. It looked as if they would have no difficulty walking, though she still doubted that they could ride. Still, she urged her horse forward, and the animal climbed smoothly up a gradual incline. The waterfalls that had trickled downward had disappeared, though the river remained deep and regal beside her. Then, in a flash, the princess understood.

"The river! It comes from here. It looks like a trickle from over there, but this is the real valley! That ravine we followed before is just a little side stream!"

In moments, the excitement of the truth propelling them, they moved forward at a trot, climbing the slowly ascending valley on a much better trail than the illusionary diversion they had followed earlier. It turned out to be an even more gentle grade that Alicia had perceived from this side of the stream. The farther they progressed, the more normal the valley around them became.

As they rode, however, Robyn dampened their joy somewhat with an explanation of the spell she had used to find the path. "It was a *very* strong emanation of evil," she told them. "We have to proceed with caution."

They rode with unsuppressed urgency, fearing what they would find, yet eager to make the discovery. They crossed the highland ridge, and finally the shimmering vista of Synnoria opened before them. In the distance, they saw the blue lake in the center of the main valley, the city of glass gleaming in the sunlight on a verdant island. A wooded side valley passed before them, and the trail dropped steeply toward its floor. They urged the horses down the path at a dangerous pace.

As they plunged lower, Robyn remained alert for any of the seductive effects of Synnoria she had encountered before. But the wind that blew past her ears seemed mundane, and nothing like magic twinkled in the shaking branches of the trees. If anything, it seemed as if they rode into a place of oppression and fear.

When they came to the trail of splintered trees, many of

them more than an armspan in girth, the damage seemed like a monstrous effrontery to this place of beauty. They rode at a gallop now, unspeaking, following the spoor left by something of tremendous proportion and horribly destructive in its passage.

Finally they broke from the enclosing trees, and several of their horses reared in sudden fright. Pools of water, churned to mud, dotted the field. Thousands of colorful fish flopped helplessly in the mud, suffocating. Across the meadow rose a thing that, at first, Alicia mistook for a small domed building.

Then the building moved.

* * * * *

Talos and Malar relished the rampage of the Elf-Eater, vicariously feeding their evil natures on the killing and destruction wrought by their pet. The two gods were well pleased, but for different reasons—Talos, for the blow struck to the Moonshaes; and Malar, for the destruction in the great elven escape path.

Yet the Destructor had other plans to make, and to this end he summoned his avatar, bidding Sinioth to appear in a guise of master in his new domain. Thus, beneath the waters of the Trackless Sea, Coss-Axell-Sinioth assumed the shape of a proper creature. Long tentacles trailed from his head, and a beaklike mouth clamped shut with crushing power. As large as a good-sized ship, the giant squid waited to hear his master's words.

At the same time, Talos summoned Sythissal, king of the sahuagin, into his immortal presence. The scaly creature, his humanoid body layered with supple sinew, a column of bristling spines extending down his back, soon floated before the squid.

"This is your master," came the voice of Talos, like a distant landslide rumbling under the sea. "You will obey him in all his commands!

"The two of you must journey to Kyrasti, to the great city of

the sea trolls in the Coral Kingdom. There, you, Sythissal, are
to assume personal command of the prisoner.

"And you, my favorite pet"—the voice of Talos lowered to
an affectionate growl—"are to prepare my minions for mastery of the Moonshaes!"

❦ 5 ❦

Pawldo of Lowhill

Keane was the first to attack, spurring his horse into a charge across the meadow with reckless abandon. The others raced behind him as the magic-user raised his hand and started barking the commands to a spell.

The awful appearance of the monster before them belied any kind of rational explanation—from its three legs, to its monstrous size, to the lack of any apparent face, except for the fluid opening and closing of its grotesque mouth. Two humanlike figures, barely visible below the banks of a nearby stream, took advantage of the momentary distraction to scramble away from the horror.

The beast turned slowly through a full circle, waving long, whiplike tentacles in the air, as if seeking some clue to the approaching party.

Alicia's first thoughts about the monster told her that the thing was impossibly huge—too big to fight, much less hope to kill. Her second thoughts followed closely as she understood that this was not a beast of this world. But even as these apprehensions whirled through her brain, she spurred her horse to join the thundering charge of her companions trailing after Keane.

The lanky wizard, his robes flapping from the speed of his horse's gait, extended his right hand, pointing a finger toward the monstrosity looming over the riverbank. He shouted hoarsely, his words blurring with the pounding thunder of his suddenly animated steed. In fact, the gelding seemed to have abruptly come to life, throwing every ounce of its strength into a desperate and surprisingly fast gallop.

A crackling bolt of energy exploded from Keane's hand, slashing through the air like a flaming spear to impact against the monster's bony carapace, hissing for a split second as sparks flew from the wound. The domed monster bellowed in a droning, almost metallic sound and reared backward. Tentacles lashed the air before it as it sought the source of the painful attack.

But Keane reined in, well back from the monster's clutching tendrils. The muddy figures in the streambed dropped out of sight, but Alicia caught a glimpse of their wide eyes staring at the fight in the field. One of them wore a steel helmet, its silvery sheen streaked brown with mud.

Robyn joined Keane, leaping down from her saddle to stamp the end of her staff on the ground before her.

"*Caorralis—Etrai!*" she shouted, summoning the power of the goddess from the earth itself.

Immediately a mound of dirt began to rise from the ground, ripping itself free from the surrounding soil, tearing away a great patch of sod and rising into a giant, vaguely human form. Clumps of grass clung to its back and shoulders, for the creature had been formed from the earth itself. Growing steadily, it soon towered like a giant over the heads of the mounted Ffolk. It was an earth elemental, a creature summoned by the power of a druid and sent by the goddess to aid a cause in the world of men.

The elemental tore its great feet free from the ground and clumped toward the monster. A tentacle lashed across the elemental's face, and the creature of earth seized the tendril in hands the size of boulders, planting its feet and tugging. The strand grew taut, and for a moment, the two creatures held in equilibrium, each struggling to dislodge the other.

Warlike chords of music rang through the air as Tavish took up her harp. The music infused the humans with courage. Suddenly Alicia found her fears vanquished, replaced by a grim determination to smite this horrific creature. Hanrald and Brandon urged their horses toward the monster, shouting challenges and raising their weapons—Brandon, his great, double-bladed axe and Hanrald his immensely long sword wielded in both his metal-gauntleted hands.

Even Pawldo darted forward, spurring his pony into a gallop while he drew a shortsword from a sheath on his saddle. Whooping savagely, he dashed up to one of the monster's legs and chopped with all the strength in his small, tough body. The pony skipped nimbly away as the beast swiveled toward the annoying attack.

The earth elemental, its feet still firmly planted, pulled on the monster's tentacle, and the force of the creature was enough to jerk the monster around, allowing Pawldo and his pony to barely escape the beast's clutching grasp.

Alicia spurred her horse and drew her longsword. Her instincts as a warrior ran deep, and loyalty to her companions told her that she belonged beside them. Thus she reacted with outrage when her mother seized the mare's bridle and hauled back as the princess rode past.

"Let go!" demanded Alicia.

"Use the *staff!*" Robyn cried, ignoring her daughter's command.

For a moment, the princess simply stared at her mother as if the queen had lost her mind. Alicia held a perfectly good—indeed, an *exceptionally* good—sword in her hand, and she had trained for much of her life in that weapon's use.

Yet now her mother urged her to set that aside in favor of a shaft made from a piece of wood.

But then Alicia remembered the reborn power of the goddess, and she wasn't so sure. "How?" Alicia asked, one eye on the heroic charge of the fighters. Brandon's axe bounced off the monster's shell, while a tremendous blow from Hanrald's sword inflicted a tiny nick in its bony plate.

Pawldo circled back, darting in with his shortsword raised when he saw an opening. The beast seemed to sense his approach, however, turning back toward the halfling and ignoring the two human warriors. The pony squealed as a tendril seized its foreleg. Another limb with sharp, bony edges slashed at the small horse, ripping a great wound in its flank as Pawldo flew from the saddle.

The halfling bounded to his feet, his face twisted in fury, and was about to charge with his shortsword when Hanrald rode up behind him. Seizing Pawldo by the collar, the earl yanked the little fellow off the ground and carried him, screaming and cursing, away from immediate danger.

"Plant the staff in the ground, then use the *word!*" Alicia's mother said urgently.

In a flash, Alicia remembered Robyn's instructions at the Moonwell. Her mother had been mysterious about the shaft's use, yet there was no time for questions. She pulled the staff from her saddlebags and leaned over to plant its base on the ground.

"*Phyrosyne!*" she shouted, mimicking the word her mother had given her with the staff.

Immediately the wood expanded upward and grew thicker—like a tree undergoing thirty years' growth in mere seconds, the princess thought in amazement. Branches shot out to the sides, armlike appendages with stout, grasping twigs as fingers. The trunk split into two, forming a pair of solid pillars that held the creature upright. Then the mighty legs flexed, to carry the tree thing forward in steady, ponderous strides. It marched as rigidly as a soldier trying to impress a strict sergeant-major. Higher it grew, reaching twice the height of the earth elemental. Alicia gaped at the tree creature in awe.

"Now—*command* it!" her mother urged.

The princess blinked. "Attack!" she shouted, willing the thing to stride forward and strike at the monster. The tree lurched forward, its gait stiff, the two trunklike legs plodding steadily.

The arm limbs came up as tentacles from the monster lashed toward this new combatant. Like the elemental, the walking tree anchored its feet and seized the tendrils and pulled. Indeed it seemed to Alicia that the tree's base sank into the ground like roots, until the thing was as firmly planted as any stately oak. Now the earth elemental held two of the tentacles and pulled one way, while the tree creature entangled more of the monster's tendrils and anchored it on the opposite side.

Keane unleashed a barrage of spells against the beast. Meteors thundered down from the sky, shuddering the ground with the force of their impact; a great fireball blossomed around the monster, searing the faces of the watching humans with the force of its fiery blast. No sooner had the flames died than Keane unleashed a blast of killing frost, a chilling wash of pale light that coated the monster with ice and even froze several of the exposed tentacles so that the brittle limbs broke into pieces when the rampaging creature moved.

The elemental and the tree thing continued to tug in opposite directions, holding the monster immobile against the onslaught of magic.

Two silver-plated fighters scrambled from the stream to join them, and Alicia wasn't surprised to see that they were female. More stunning, to her, was the reality of their blond hair and their small, pointed ears that peeked through their light tresses. These were elves!

Any delight at the sight of them was quashed thoroughly by the menace that had brought them together. The two sister knights charged bravely on foot, trying to strike at the soft, vulnerable-looking mouth. Alicia found that her staff continued its assault without her concentration, so she drew her sword and rode forward, joining the others who battled against the lashing tentacles and probing, sucking aperture.

Despite the damage caused by Keane's spells, the monster met them with a tangled mass of tentacles, reaching forward with whiplike strikes at first one, then another of the attackers. Alicia's horse skipped back from one such thrust, but then she saw the ropelike limb snare one of the elven women around the waist. The Llewyrr warrior screamed in stark panic as her companion, the one who wore the steel helm, darted in to help, only to be knocked aside by another blow.

The Lord of Lowhill tucked his short body into a roll and tumbled forward, springing to his feet directly in front of the monster's maw.

"Pawldo!" Robyn screamed, terrified for her friend.

Before the druid could react, the halfling whirled and

chopped his shortsword into the tentacle that imprisoned the knight. His small body concealed a surprising strength of sinew, and the keen edge bit deep. With a palpable grunt, the monster relaxed its hold, and the elfwoman and halfling tumbled away together.

The fighters rode in again, Hanrald and Brandon close enough to chop at the thing's trunklike legs while Alicia and the helmeted elfwoman chopped at the strands of the monster's limbs that still lashed through the air. The sister knight darted backward, tripping and sprawling to the ground from the intensity of the beast's attack. The monster seemed to seek her over all the rest of the combatants.

Alicia dashed toward the elf, hacking with her sword against the seething nest of tendrils that reached toward the prostrate knight. Hanrald, too, leaped forward to strike. The force of his two-handed blow severed the tentacle closest to the trapped Llewyrr. Then, before the princess could spring away, she felt a cold grasp around her ankle. She tried to jump, but the powerful grip of a tentacle tugged hard, and she sprawled headlong to the ground.

The force of the fall knocked the breath from her lungs, and as Alicia gasped for air, the tendril tightened around her ankle, pulling her toward the monster with shockingly brutal force. She twisted and kicked in desperation, but still she slid along the ground, scrambling for some hold. There was nothing to grab, nothing that could stop her slide!

The Earl of Fairheight leaped from his saddle and landed at her side, bringing his two-handed sword down in a savage chop that completely severed the ropelike tendril. Pawldo grabbed Alicia's hand and pulled her from the lashing limbs. Quickly the princess scrambled away as the unarmored halfling lunged between her and the horrible, devouring monster. Pawldo raised his blade and swung again at the lashing tentacles that reached out in an attempt to encircle the knight.

"Get back!" shouted Alicia, watching in horror as two of the clutching limbs wrapped around the courageous halfling's shoulders. Pawldo stumbled backward, but the grip that held him was too firm.

"Help!" shouted the stocky halfling, desperately struggling against the grasping tentacles.

A fresh surge of explosions rocked the beast backward as Keane saw the danger and blasted every spell that he knew into the looming horror. Brandon raged forward in a berserker frenzy, hacking at the tentacles with his axe, then stumbling away before they could enwrap him. Hanrald, too, attacked without regard for his own safety. The monster kicked brutally, pounding both of the brave warriors back before they could break the grip that imprisoned their comrade.

"Pull!" screamed Alicia, calling to her tree staff, desperate for any hope that could break Pawldo free. The halfling squirmed in grim silence now, dragged closer and closer to doom.

A wall of fire burst from the ground beneath the beast, smoldering into a column of oily black smoke around it. The monster shifted uncomfortably but continued to drag the halfling closer to the mouth that now gaped wetly a few feet from Pawldo's boots.

With a lurching spin, the huge beast shifted its position, exerting enough force to pull the earth elemental and the tree creature loose from their once-firm positions. The two enchanted servants stumbled, and then the monster pulled its tentacles free from their grasps. The earth elemental tumbled to the ground, while the tall tree stood, flailing about with its branchlike limbs.

The two elves dashed forward, chopping with their silver swords, and Alicia, Brandon, and Hanrald joined in the onslaught. The princess reached out desperately, grasping one of Pawldo's small hands just as the extended muzzle of the monster reached the halfling's foot.

Then, with one great gulping sound of air, the Lord of Lowhill was gone.

"No!" shrieked Alicia, disbelieving, appalled. She lunged toward the mouth as if she would drag him out again, and only the strong hands of the two elves and Brandon pulled her back from the same fate that had met the courageous halfling.

"Get back!" Robyn commanded her, and, sobbing, the princess stumbled away from the beast.

"Stop it!" Alicia cried, reeling with shock and horror. She would not accept the brave halfling's demise. "We can't let Pawldo go!" She surged forward once more, ready to attack the monster alone, but Keane's surprisingly strong grip held her back.

"Don't!" he barked, his voice a hiss. The princess whirled, ready to take out her horror and frustration on the loyal tutor, but she could not. Instead, she collapsed against her mother while the others kept a wary eye upon the looming, three-legged beast.

For a moment, they wondered if it would attack them again. The wall of fire still crackled beneath it, and the elemental and the tree creature clung to several tentacles. The monster loomed closer, and the companions raised their weapons as a group, too tired—and too dispirited—to flee. But then the great beast settled back. Somehow it seemed to regard them, though it had no eyes nor any other sensing organs that any of them could see.

And then, as if disparaging them as foes worthy of battle, the monster spun about on its three legs. With a great, earth-shaking leap, it bounded away, and in another moment, it raced into the distance, thundering down the valley like a gigantic, maddened elephant. As it fled away from the companions and their horses, their despair precluded even a momentary relief. Numbly they watched it go, each of them remembering the cheerful and courageous halfling.

Robyn stood stiff, her face a cold mask that belied the torment seething inside of her. Brandon, Keane, and Hanrald exchanged grim glances, and Alicia shook her head, determined to hold back the tears that surged against her will. Later! she vowed. Later they would grieve for Pawldo, but first they would have to avenge him.

* * * * *

Deirdre had watched the progress of her sister's party for several hours, using the mirror of scrying she had brought from the library of Caer Callidyrr. She had found, much to her delight, that the images in the mirror seemed almost more real than life itself. She found herself constantly drawn to the picture there, always fascinated by what she saw.

Eventually the game had grown tiring—not boring, but draining in a way that Deirdre could not ignore. Her neck was stiff and her head hurt when, late at night, she finally laid the mirror aside. She spent several hours, into the gray birth of dawn, studying her teleportation spell. Like all magic-users, she expended the knowledge of a spell when she cast it, and she required a period of study before she could relearn the incantation. The more powerful the spell, the more complicated the routine required to rememorize it. Teleportation was a mighty spell, and thus its reabsorption took a significant amount of time. Despite her fatigue, she found that she grasped the spell easily, its symbols and commands flaring vividly in her mind.

Finally she was finished, but she still wasn't ready for sleep. Instead, she turned to the tome she had been perusing earlier, the volume detailing a host of tactics and procedures for traveling throughout the known planes of existence. It was heady stuff, but Deirdre absorbed it easily, as she did all her reading. She learned much about the dangers, and potentials, of working one's way through the ether, communicating with distant realms for good or ill.

Particularly entrancing was the discussion of a small village that existed some thousand years ago. It had been menaced by a creature from the Lower Planes, and the beast had only been vanquished when the village cleric identified the two symbols holding most power over the monster's plane of origin—in this case, a circle encased within a square. Then the townsfolk had plowed the requisite symbols into the dirt of a lush field and goaded the creature into the trap. At that point, a simple teleportation spell had sufficed to banish the creature back to its unholy lair.

Finally, that lesson completed, Deirdre slept, uncaring of anything for several hours. When she finally awakened in the late morning, it was with the languorous ease of a well-fed feline. She allowed the sunshine to wash over her, basking in the warmth.

When she eventually rose, she didn't partake of the bread and cheese that had been delivered to her anteroom. Instead, she turned to the mirror.

Quickly an image came into focus. It was a picture of Synnoria, the valley that was no longer pastoral. Stark lines of black earth, splintered trees, and muddy wreckage marred the green fields, and Deirdre quickly observed the image of Ityak-Ortheel, the Elf-Eater. The beast, rolling smoothly, rapidly forward on its three legs, moved resolutely down the valley.

For the moment, Deirdre could see no sign of her mother or sister, nor of their companions. But then a small group of riders thundered into sight, and when Keane's lightning bolt exploded against the monster, she knew beyond a doubt that she had found the party of Ffolk.

Deirdre leaned closer to get a better look at the tiny figures in the mirror. A tiny smile creased her mouth. She didn't know why, but she found the spectacle in the looking glass strangely amusing.

* * * * *

"Who's hurt?" asked the queen, her voice a harsh note of reality amid the dreamlike silence that followed the battle.

No one replied, but the companions all held their weapons ready, staring after the diminishing form of the monster as it moved down the valley.

"Pawldo . . ." Alicia spoke her friend's name as if in a daze. "We have to avenge him!"

Robyn laid a hand upon her daughter's shoulder, but her look followed the creature that had slain their friend. The princess gazed after the beast as well, but her mind recalled only the smiling halfling who had brought her treats since she was a little girl. He *can't* be dead! She tried to lie to herself, but her recent memories stubbornly reminded her of the truth.

Then, as if for the first time, the High Queen turned to look at the two disheveled Llewyrr, the pair whose plight had drawn them into the attack in the first place.

"Brigit?" she asked tentatively.

"Robyn—or is it 'Your Majesty'?" replied the elf, shock written across her features.

"Yes," said the human woman, adding a wry laugh. "Though not so unchanged by time as yourself."

"You saved our lives . . ." the elfwoman realized with dawning amazement, quickly turning to suspicion. "And yet by all rights you should not even be here! How did you pass our border? What brings you here at all?"

"Those reasons can wait until later," said the High Queen in a tone as firm as Brigit's. She indicated the tracks of the monster, scoured in the black dirt. "We have a more pressing problem now!"

"The *Llewyrr* have a problem. This is an invasion of Synnoria, not Corwell," the sister knight replied stiffly. "Your aid is appreciated. As I indicated, your presence saved our lives."

"Our *actions* saved your lives!" Alicia snapped, indignant at the elfwoman's arrogance. She would have spoken further except that her mother raised a hand.

"This monster is a horror that menaces all Gwynneth," Robyn declared. "And therefore, it is *my* problem. I am the monarch of the lands beyond your valley! Whether it ravages all Synnoria while we stand here in discussion, or whether we work together to stop it is up to you."

The humans in the party stood silent. Even the elves seemed taken aback. Brigit's eyes flashed, but she worked visibly to hold her tongue. Clearly the situation called for urgency . . . and cooperation.

"You are right . . . Your Majesty. It has been too long since I have seen a human. I had come once more to think of you as the group that is the danger, instead of remembering the individuals who were my friends. Forgive my lack of grace."

"I understand," Robyn answered. "Now—what was that thing? And where is it going?"

They gathered the horses while they talked, mounting an elf behind Alicia and Hanrald, who were the best riders.

Pawldo! He's lost—gone forever, Alicia realized with a tearing pain in her heart. Her eyes blurred, and she went through the motions of riding without thinking. It took a great effort to clear her head enough to listen to the conversation between Robyn and Brigit.

". . . not from this world, nor any place I have ever heard described," the elfwoman was saying. "There are legends, more than a millennia old, of a three-legged giant who preyed upon the elves. I cannot help but wonder if this is an incarnation of the Elf-Eater." She said nothing about the Fey-Alamtine or the recent flight of the Thy-Tach.

"It is most assuredly a being from one of the Lower Planes," Keane observed, riding beside the pair, "requiring a very powerful force to call it hence—not an easy gate to open nor to control."

"Gate?" Brigit's face had gone pale, though she said nothing further. She looked furtively away from Alicia as the princess stared, puzzled, at the elven horsewoman.

"Can we send it back . . . to its own plane?" asked the queen.

"Not a chance that I know of," said Keane, before turning to Brigit. "Unless you have some wizardry in this valley of yours that goes beyond anything I've ever seen!"

"I fear not," replied Brigit. "From what I've seen of your powers, no elven sorcerer could hope to offer something beyond your ken."

"If we can't send it away, we'll have to kill it," observed Brandon, who had been brooding in silence since the battle. His face focused into a grimace of determination as he spoke. It was obvious that his anger had focused into this clear and warlike purpose.

"Yes," agreed Brigit simply.

But none of them had any idea how.

* * * * *

Deirdre reclined on her bed, enjoying the spectacle in the mirror. She had been thrilled by the battle with the Elf-Eater, shocked—and horribly fascinated—by Pawldo's gruesome death, and now intrigued by the challenge presented by the extraplanar beast.

She wondered, for a moment, why she felt no sorrow, no grief, over the death of the halfling she had known all her life. True, she had always thought the Lord of Lowhill a somewhat pompous stuffed shirt, but she had seen him several times a year throughout her life, and he had been a good friend of her parents. Nevertheless, his death triggered no particular emotion in the youngest Kendrick.

The specter of the Elf-Eater, on the other hand, drew her attention with a secret, forbidden excitement. The memory of her recent readings thrilled in her blood, for she now understood how the gates and the planes worked.

She doubted whether the Elf-Eater could be slain. Such was the root of its might that its true life-force existed in some nether place far removed from the world of the Realms. Without access to that soul, those who attacked the beast could at most hope to vanquish the incarnation appearing in the present time and place. If that were accomplished, the thing would be forced back to its lair.

Yet even that relatively straightforward task, she thought, may well prove beyond the abilities of the elves and their human allies. In her readings, the task of controlling a beast such as this required careful research and diligent preparation.

Research? Her lips curled in a tight smile. She rose, padding across the floor in her bare feet to the table where stood her great stack of books. Without hesitation, she lifted several tomes out of the way, found the one that she wanted, and returned to her bed.

There she started to read.

* * * * *

A vast ridge, emerald green in color, loomed beside Sinioth. Soon the towers of great manors, lairs to the noble scrags of the Coral Kingdom, dotted the rolling sea bottom. Great fields of kelp, tended by sahuagin overseers and mermen and dolphin slaves, drifted through the warm currents overhead, while a rolling horizon of coral edifices and dark, green-shaded valleys sprawled in all directions.

Sinioth, in the body of the giant squid, swam with the king of the sahuagin, Sythissal. In these depths, the body of evil's avatar showed as a murky shadow on the coral seabed—the huge, blunt trunk, the long tentacles trailing behind, the powerful flukes driving the creature through the water. The humanoid fishman swam with powerful kicks of his legs, eager to obey the commands of his great master. Together the two would make known the wishes of Talos.

The approach of the giant squid drew scrags and sahuagin, the inhabitants of the submarine city of Kyrasti, from their towers and domes. Great legions of the finned, fanged humanoids swam behind Sinioth as he approached the highest reef, climbing again to where the dark water gave way to soft shades of green and blue.

Before him loomed a place of towering spires. Curved domes of clear shell arched over many enclosed dwellings, while other places spiraled upward, open to the sea on all sides.

A great thrumming sound boomed through the sea, summoning the warriors and the nobles of the Coral Kingdom. A huge scrag swam forth from the palace gates, trailing delicate chains of gold and silver.

This mighty sea troll stood more than ten feet tall when he settled his webbed feet on the coral stair. His scaled skin rippled over folds of taut sinew, and his mouth gaped, sharklike, to reveal rows of needle-sharp teeth. Unlike his smaller cousins, the sahuagin, the scrag had no row of sharp spines down his back, but his head was covered with a kelplike growth of hair that waved about his face in the current, concealing his mouth one moment and then drifting aside at the next.

"Greetings, Master," gurgled this mighty one, floating forward to prostrate himself before the giant squid. "Welcome to Kyrasti, to the palace of Krell-Bane, King of the Sea. Our master, Talos, has brought us together for a great cause!"

Yet even as he groveled, the huge sea troll looked sideways at his new masters, his eyes reflecting jealousy, resentment . . . and hatred.

♣ 6 ♣

Shattered Glass

"Flee! The vengeance of the gods comes upon us!" A dozen panic-stricken elves stumbled toward the causeway leading to Chrysalis. Some of them bled from horrible wounds, and all of them shambled with the half-dead gait of complete exhaustion.

"The trout farm!" gasped one of the Llewyrr, collapsing before a pair of guards at the start of the causeway. "We're the only ones to survive!"

"What?" demanded the guard. "What was it?"

"Horror!" groaned the elf. "I don't know what it was . . . it was huge! And it killed—it killed *everyone!*"

As soon as they got this much of an answer, garbled as it was by fear, one of the watchmen raced toward the city gates, crying a general alarm.

Myra, ranking sister knight in the city, heard the commotion at her post near those silver portals. She raced up the winding stairs into one of the needlelike spires that lined the city's walls. In moments, she heard the shouted explanations from the causeway and ordered the city's permanent garrison of warriors to muster outside the gates.

Where was Brigit? The question loomed paramount in her mind. She knew that today the captain had intended to patrol the same valley of the Fey-Alamtine and the trout farm. Cold fear began to tighten her heart as she looked across the peaceful lake toward the fields and forest beyond. She saw nothing out of the ordinary. Indeed, the idea that some horrific beast was out there seemed unthinkable.

Nevertheless, minutes later the small company of permanent-duty guards, silver speartips gleaming in the sun, followed Myra's orders and filed out the gates and over one of the long causeways connecting the island city to the shore.

Here the elven warriors deployed in a three-rank line of pikes, blocking the most direct route into Chrysalis.

Myra watched them go, telling herself that they were just a precaution. Nothing seemed unusual about the forest as she looked to the west, but the hysteria of the trout farm workers dispelled any sense of security she might have felt. And still she wondered: Where was Brigit? The captain of the sister knights held overall command of Synnoria's troops; Myra was a mere substitute, and she longed for the older elf's guidance.

Meanwhile, the citizens of Synnoria mobilized for their own defense. The young and the old, the pregnant and the infirm Llewyrr, all fled from the far side of the city in an orderly column. Myra would have liked to send them toward the Fey-Alamtine and, if necessary, the ultimate sanctuary of Evermeet. However, the monster's approach precluded that course. Indeed, it was perhaps fortunate that she had no way of knowing that the Synnorian Gate lay in a heap of crumbled rock, shattered by the beast's violent arrival.

Now these refugees would take shelter in the wooded valleys opposite the monster's reported avenue of approach. The adults, meanwhile, gathered any weapons that they could find and began to assemble in the city's parklike grand plaza.

The warriors of the Thy-Tach tribe made haste to join in the defense force, offering nearly four dozen powerfully muscled spearmen. These trotted swiftly along the causeway behind the pikes, ready to form a backup of that formation.

Then, as Myra stared at the bright woods, she sensed that something was horribly wrong. Treetops shivered and fell away one after the other in a clearly defined path—a path that led straight toward the elven city! Myra thought of a field of tall grass where a small dog bounds through, unseen, except these were great trees, many of them centuries old. Whatever crushed them aside possessed unspeakable strength.

Finally the Elf-Eater came into sight on the wooded shore, a looming form pressing the lush pines to either side in a waste of splinters and great, muddy footprints. It rumbled forward in its awkward gait, appearing to roll along like a top reaching the end of its spin. Yet in the case of the Elf-Eater, this clumsiness was completely misleading. Clear of the trees, it leaped forward to race across the grassy field on the shore.

Silver pike tips gleamed in the sun, the same sun that had witnessed the arrival of this beast barely three hours before. The Llewyrr of the guard company stood firm, those in the fore kneeling, the second rank standing with pikes held at the waist, and the third rank with their long weapons held at shoulder height. The effect, to the front, was an array of razor-sharp steel tips, bristling like the spines of a cactus in tightly packed array.

Quickly the Elf-Eater broke from the confines of the forest, advancing across the grassy meadow in broad strides. Mutters of apprehension shook the elves as they got their first good look at the monster. Its broad snout was drawn in, gaping wide below the rim of the domed carapace, revealing its nest of churning appendages, surrounded by the web of flailing tentacles. The creature ran with one leg in front, the two others side by side to the rear.

The massive form rumbled forward, breaking into a rolling gallop on the broad field. The ground shook with each pounding step, and the monster's charge took it straight toward the wall of pikes. The elves in the path of the charge stood firm. Few of them had ever faced a real opponent before, but all of them had trained and prepared for decades—or centuries, in many cases. Now they met the test of that training and passed with fortitude.

Myra held her breath as she watched from the tower. Many more Llewyrr gathered in the streets below. The city's heavy silver gates stood closed, firmly barred. She could do nothing more except pray that the courageous pikemen and the spearthrowers of the Thy-Tach would turn the monster away.

The longest of the beast's tentacles stretched outward as it reached the Llewyrr, grasping pikes below the heads. Some sharp edges met the tendrils with their blades, but even the keen elven steel rarely pierced a leathery limb. The monster tugged against the pikes it still held firmly, jerking them to the sides and disrupting the precision of the steady line.

Not that precision mattered. The elves held their weapons braced with every muscle in their bodies, often with the butts of the weapons planted into the ground. The razor-edged pike heads, crafted of the hardest elven alloys, bore enchantments powerful enough to penetrate the hardest armor, the toughest scaly skin. But the Elf-Eater tucked its body as it rolled into the pikes, so that the bulk of the weapons met the hard carapace. The poles of a dozen pikes snapped simultaneously, the preciously crafted steel falling useless to the ground.

A few of the elves, their pikes held very low, angled the weapons below the carapace and met the skin around the creature's mouth. The weapons plunged in, and the Elf-Eater recoiled for a moment. Then a nest of tentacles converged, plucking the weapons from the wounds and casting them aside. The tentacles descended, and elf after struggling elf was plucked up and cast into the gaping maw.

On her tower-top vantage, Myra felt sick to her stomach. She saw that soon the monster would reach the city gates, and she knew that she would have to be there as well.

"Summon the clerics!" shouted the sister knight. "All the priests and priestesses of the city! Gather here at the wall!"

She cast a last despairing glance for Brigit, but she could see no sign of any white horse or rider in the splintered path of the Elf-Eater's trail. Finally she raced down the spiraling stair, quickly reaching the street, where hundreds of armed but undirected Llweyrr mingled around in growing confusion. Through apertures in the white marble wall they could see the progress of the battle.

Within a few moments of the first impact, the beast's irresistible momentum carried it through all three ranks of the pikemen, scattering the hopelessly courageous Llewyrr in all directions. A dozen vanished into the dripping mouth, and as many more lay on the ground, crushed and broken by the monster's trampling feet.

The line of pikes recoiled, fatally ruptured by the breach through its center. Individual weapons prodded and stabbed the monster, but most of these it ignored. Those pikes that attracted the Elf-Eater's attention were pulled from their wielders' hands and snapped, with the Llewyrr warriors as likely as not to immediately follow their weapons to ruin.

"Flee! Run for your lives!" Panic—an uncommon characteristic among elven warriors—spread rapidly through the rank. Some of the Llewyrr threw down their pikes and raced for the causeway into the city, only to be blocked by the company of Thy-Tach spearmen, still standing firm. Others fled across the field while a small band, perhaps a third of the original company, retained their pikes and formed a bristling square. They moved away from the Elf-Eater toward the trees, and the monster seemed content to let them go.

The Thy-Tach spearmen, standing at the very end of the causeway at the lakeshore, cast their weapons as the Elf-Eater rose above them. Several of the missiles found targets in the gaping mouth, but this did little more than inflame the monster.

The terrifying creature swept tentacles low along the ground, sweeping a half-dozen Thy-Tach from their feet. In the next moment, the monstrous beast rolled over them, muffling their screams with its huge size. When it moved past, these elves had vanished.

Next Ityak-Ortheel turned its attentions to the lake itself, moving toward the white stone causeway that led to the gleaming gates of Chrysalis. As a result of Myra's orders, many Synnorian clerics stood along the wall above the silver-steel gates. Now these clerics called upon Corellon Larethian, Solonar Thelandira, and the other multitudinous gods of the elves, praying in their hour of need for powerful spells.

As the Elf-Eater started across the causeway, leaving crushing footprints in the white stone surface, the waters of the lake responded to the clerical spell-casting and began to rise. First they washed against the banks of the causeway, and then in several places wavelets crossed the road itself. Swiftly the footprints behind the monster filled with water, and in another few moments, the entire causeway vanished under several inches of the steadily rising lake.

Waves tossed and surged over the road, rising into an unnatural mound. The monster continued its advance as water surged upward, several feet higher than the causeway. The effect of the spell was local. The lake didn't flood beyond its banks onto the field or into the streets of the city, but it continued to grow, frothing like a rushing stream, climbing into a higher and higher barrier along the length of the stone roadway, forming a long ridge of turbulence.

Tentacles lashed like eels through the water before and around the Elf-Eater, groping to hold the beast on the raised platform of stone. Waves splashed against it like breakers crashing onto a rock-strewn shore.

Then the clerics raised a great shout, and the spell culminated in an immense wave, washing upward into a peak over the causeway. The dome of the monster's carapace showed like a wet rock in the surf, but all of its body had vanished below the churning water.

No cheer rocked the city wall yet. Even had the thing been slain and dismembered before these Llewyrr, it's doubtful that they would have celebrated. So profound was the shock of the Elf-Eater's intrusion, so obscene and horrifying was its apparent purpose, that even its defeat would merely leave the elves of Synnoria in a state of numbness.

And then even that frail hope vanished, for the rounded back of the Elf-Eater continued to press through the water. White turbulence swirled around it, trailing away behind as the thing continued to move forward. The violent watery onslaught slowed it only momentarily. As long as the monster could feel the causeway, the great legs and feet continued to carry the huge body forward.

The elven clerics tried mightily, with resounding cries for power and for the blessings of their gods. The water rose still higher. Surging whitecaps rolled down the sides of the mound, but tremendous pressure continued to lift it higher. The force of the Elf-Eater's passage raised a white wave, like a frothing bone in the teeth of a fast ship.

Then finally the rising pressure surged beyond its limits. Several of the clerics groaned and staggered, falling to the ground. The dam of magic burst, and the ridge of water plunged away from the road, drawn by gravity across the surface of the lake. Dripping but undaunted, the Elf-Eater advanced toward the gates of Chrysalis.

"Quickly! Make a stand at the gates! Bring those pikes up. You archers—to the walls! Hurry if you want to live!"

Myra barked commands, trying to imagine how Brigit would have faced this challenge. Her captain must be dead, Myra knew. She would certainly have tried to fight this monster if she encountered it in the forest, and there was no way she could have survived such a battle.

"It's up to me then," she told herself quietly, trying to banish her fear. How could she—how could *anyone*—hope to stop this thing?

Archers lined the walls, and now a shower of arrows clacked like hail against the carapace, with no visible effect. The monster reached the gate, and great caldrons were tipped on the wall above, pouring a deluge of hot oil across the Elf-Eater's shell. Torches followed, and in seconds, a crackling inferno, belching black smoke, hissed and roared around the monstrosity.

The monster settled slowly to the ground, drawing its tentacles close, and the fire blazed away. The domed shell covered the legs and mouth; even the ropelike limbs had been drawn inside. For several minutes, the fire blazed, helped along by repeated douses of oil, and once again the Llewyrr dared to hope for deliverance. Flames sputtered and raged, spewing a column of black smoke like a dark beacon into the sky, and still the creature showed no inclination to move.

The silver gates grew dark with soot, as did the white walls of the city and the formerly gleaming towers of its gatehouse. The elven citizenry had by now made their escape from the other side of the city, and all that remained were those Llewyrr and Thy-Tach who carried weapons and were prepared to give their lives for Synnoria.

Finally the elves ceased fueling the blaze, watching carefully and waiting to observe the effect of their fiery attack. Another block of pikemen assembled inside the gate, though they had witnessed the failure of the same weapons in the field. The Llewyrr had no other tactic with which to try and stand against the beast. The flames died further, and only the blackened outline of the Elf-Eater's shell was visible to the watchers on the wall.

Then, in a shocking blur of activity, the great form raised itself from the ground to stand firmly on its three legs. The foreleg knelt low, and the dome tilted until its apex was angled toward the top of the steel gates. In the next moment, the Elf-Eater hurled itself into the portals with a thunderous charge, sending echoes reverberating up and down the valley of Synnoria.

Splinters of steel exploded through the air, knifing into many of the pikemen who stood in their steady formation. The great slabs of silvered metal broke from their hinges to fall among the warriors, crushing dozens. Even the white stone walls of the gate towers splintered and cracked, and the tall pillars swayed for a moment as if they, too, would join the gates in ruin on the ground.

The crushing blow knocked Myra to the side and she lay inside the gate, half-stunned, as the monster loomed above her, then rolled past. She tried to force her muscles to move, but they wouldn't respond to the commands of her mind. Instead, she lay motionless, expecting at any moment to feel the grasp of a clutching tendril, the quick snap of movement that would send her into that dolorous maw. She saw the crystal spire of a guard tower swaying over her head, and for a despairing moment, she prayed that the structure would fall, crushing out her awareness and sparing her the knowledge of her gruesome fate.

But the towers held. Myra saw the monster move through the wreckage of the gates, gobbling up those elves who lay in its path, but then the beast paid the city entrance no more mind, for the path into Chrysalis lay open. The Elf-Eater barged forward, barreling into the scattered pikemen and sending them tumbling like tenpins. Here the thing paused for a few minutes to gruesomely feed, snatching up the slain and wounded elves from the crowded street, snaring by the ankles many who tried to flee. These it dragged slowly, inexorably toward its gaping mouth, almost as if tantalized by the hysterical terror of the doomed elves.

Though the white stone wall surrounded the elven city, Chrysalis was not a place designed for defense. For millennia, the elven valley had stood inviolate, and this bred a long tradition of peace and an almost dazed confidence that the future would remain as untroubled as had the past.

Thus the city's avenues were wide and smoothly paved with the same white granite that had formed the causeways and so much of Chrysalis. Sweeping, open gardens beckoned an attacker, with no enclosing walls or narrow streets to restrict access.

Trees, especially birch and aspen, whose pale trunks complemented the stone so well, had been bred so that they remained green all year around, though Synnoria was subjected to the same snowy winters that affected the rest of Gwynneth. Now these trees waved gently in the breeze, their branches quaking like silver in mockery of the horror that stalked among them.

The Argen-Tellirynd, the Palace of the Ages, gleamed at the end of the wide street. That triangular edifice towered over its own transparent wall, inlaid with panels of glass and silver and diamond and even more exotic gems, sparkling like a gleaming work of jewelry. Even amid the splendor of the white, gold, and green houses and inns, the palace was a thing from another world, an enchanted place.

The Elf-Eater started down the avenue in long, rolling strides. A few elves tried to fight, with pikes and spears and even swords. None of the attacks managed to slow the beast, and few of these courageous attackers escaped with their lives. The creature moved easily between the rows of white tree trunks, coming inexorably closer to the Argen-Tellirynd.

Myra struggled with the numbness that claimed her, and slowly she forced herself to a sitting position. Her head throbbed, and every muscle in her body ached, but she ignored these minor complaints. As long as she lived, she would fight!

Staggering to her feet, she tried to ignore the wreckage of the gates, the carnage among the defenders that surrounded her. Several elves were caught beneath the heavy gates, and their groans tore at her heart. Yet the knight forced their pain from her mind, and instead, stumbled down the avenue after the lumbering Elf-Eater.

Her mind stopped spinning, and Myra forced herself into a trot. She jogged into a side street and quickly reached the small barracks and stable that the sisters maintained within the city proper. Here she found five of her comrades, armed and ready to mount. Myra quickly seized a lance and a sixth horse.

They formed a pathetically small line as they lowered their silver-tipped lances and urged their mounts into a gallop. The white horses leaped forward at the command to charge, and in moments, the riders thundered down the street, straight toward the looming Elf-Eater, their lances angled upward. The monstrous mouth gaped before them, though even that cavernous maw couldn't swallow a horse and rider, let alone a band of them.

Then, at the last instant, the Elf-Eater tucked its shell all the way to the ground. The heavy weapons slammed into the bony surface, and the long shafts splintered. The galloping horses crashed into the monster with stunning force. All of the horses and riders went down as assuredly as if they had ridden full tilt into a brick wall.

Myra flew from her saddle as her lance broke in her hands. She crashed into the monster's shell, hearing bones snap in her shoulder and arm. Involuntarily she cried out in pain as she dropped to the paved street, groaning and helpless in the very shadow of the beast.

One of the sister knights died instantly from a broken neck, but the fate of the others was just as certain—and infinitely more horrible. Haze filled Myra's mind with fiery agony. She remembered the gate, when the monster had left her on the ground in search of other prey. This time, she knew, she would not be so lucky.

Stunned and immobile, the surviving knights watched helplessly or struggled feebly as the beast picked them up, one by one, and gulped them into the drooling pit of its mouth. Myra cried out in rage as she watched her comrades perish—but then a sturdy tentacle grasped her waist. She punched at it, trying in vain to draw her sword—but in the next moment, she followed the other brave sisters into the mindlessly devouring mouth.

That task completed, the Elf-Eater raised itself above the scene of its gory repast, ignoring the injured horses that kicked and whinnied at its feet. Before the monster, glittering in the sunlight like a magnet of beauty, stood the Argen-Tellirynd, the Palace of the Ages.

*   *   *   *   *

Deirdre read for what seemed like a long time. Gradually, however, she found that her mind couldn't concentrate on the words. Instead, she found herself looking at the table, at the silvered glass propped there.

At first, she had purposely turned the mirror to the side, so that she couldn't see her face when she looked up from her reading. But after two hours, she grew restless. Rising to pace, she looked into the glass as she passed. Finally she turned it to face the chair and returned to her tome. She found it strangely comforting to look up and see the image of herself, the great leather-bound volume covering her lap.

She wanted to see the monster again, but the mere thought of projecting the image in the mirror caused her temples to throb and her eyes to burn. The princess knew that she needed rest before she again used the device for scrying, but she felt no desire to sleep.

In fact, her memory had served her well: She found the passage, in Khelben Arunsun's *Walking the Dark Places*, that she had recalled earlier. It bore a striking resemblance, in some respects, to the situation in Synnoria.

Deirdre read about a creature from the Lower Planes, a six-legged menace called Gorathil. That horror had menaced an entire nation of halflings. The monster was the size of an ox, and it scuttled about with a speedy, crablike gait. Arunsun spent much time describing in detail the horrid claws of the monster, which were used to rend the halfling prey alive so that Gorathil's tooth-studded maw could devour the pieces.

Skipping over these details quickly, Deirdre pressed ahead to the end of the section, the equally involved account of the means by which the creature was vanquished. She wondered if perhaps the description in the book was relevant to the conflict now raging in Synnoria.

To Princess Deirdre, the problem was an interesting tactical study on the use of power. The fact that her sister and mother personally fought the monster in Synnoria meant little to her, save that she would earn their respect, perhaps even their fear, if she were able to best this thing.

Carefully, deliberately, she turned away from the mirror and continued to read.

* * * * *

Alicia scrambled through splintered wreckage, all that remained of a once-magnificent row of proud aspens that had lined the avenue beside the Palace of Ages. The Elf-Eater was somewhere ahead of her, invisible in the smoke that drifted across the parklike expanse that had once been the great plaza of Chrysalis. Now it looked like the ground where an epic battle had been lost.

The tree creature of her staff strided along beside her. The great being had used its strength to hold and delay the Elf-Eater but, like the earth elemental, had been unable to inflict serious injury to the beast. Now the changestaff stepped stiffly forward, pausing occasionally to bend forward until its upper half extended nearly parallel to the ground. Alicia wondered what it was doing, but finally she realized that it peered thus to inspect the blind spots around buildings and hedges. She found the uncanny alertness of the beast somewhat reassuring.

Mostly Alicia's mind tried to remain numb, inured by battle to a multitude of disasters. But too often she found herself looking through the smoke and wreckage for Pawldo, and then remembering, with a burning stab of pain, that she would never see him again. Then her thoughts would turn to her father, growing into a tornado of despair and fright.

Another crackling inferno flamed before her, driving her thoughts back to the present. The monster had smashed many houses, and often a cookfire or lantern inside ignited the wreckage. The fine timber blazed like a great bonfire, and the princess crossed to the far side of the street as she passed the ruined dwelling.

For hours, she and her companions and a handful of Llewyrr who had rallied to their city's defense had harassed the Elf-Eater in a great circle. The only thing they had been able to accomplish, at the cost of several elven lives, had been the distraction of the monster, for it had not yet moved in to ravage the palace.

Yet how long could they maintain this ultimately defeatist strategy? Alicia wondered. They had to find some way to damage the beast, to somehow slay it, or at the very least force it away from the otherwise defenseless city.

Keane had expended every spell in his repertoire, and though several had seemed to anger the monster, none had inflicted any noticeable damage. Her mother's wall of fire spell had sent the Elf-Eater plunging away in apparent panic, the first, and only, real setback that any of them had delivered to the dreaded slayer.

But none of it held even the faint hope of eventual victory—and so immense was the monster's apparent power that Alicia had begun to despair of ever finding the hope, let alone the reality, of the Elf-Eater's defeat.

Brigit's voice came to Alicia from somewhere ahead along the dust-shrouded boulevard. "The Elf-Eater moves on the Argen-Tellirynd!"

Desperately weary, Alicia raised her sword and stumbled forward. A shape emerged from the murk to her left, and she smiled weakly at Hanrald as the knight fell in at her side.

"This thing is tougher than I thought," admitted the armored warrior grimly. Nevertheless the Earl of Fairheight tightened his grip on the pommel of his great two-handed sword and marched steadily up the street.

Brigit joined them next. Her smooth face was bruised, her lips puffed and swollen. Her silver breastplate remained smooth, but concealed beneath soot, mud—and blood. She brushed a hand across her eyes, and Alicia noticed that she had lost a gauntlet somewhere.

Colleen, the scout who had fought beside Brigit all day, approached out of the smoke, her expression stricken.

"I found Myra's horse," she said numbly. "Others, too—but the riders were . . ."

"That's enough," replied the captain, closing her eyes in momentary pain. She shook her head. How many lives would end on this day?

"Wait—we go together!" Brandon lurched from another smoky ruin, the northman's axe clutched firmly in his two hands. Others joined them from the places where they had scattered when the Elf-Eater had rumbled through. Robyn emerged from a clump of trees. The High Queen's face was smudged with smoke, but her eyes smoldered with the flame of anger. There was Keane, limping slightly. He pushed himself erect as the others came into view, joining their advance with scarcely a falter in his step.

"Argen-Tellirynd. . . . the palace," Brigit said, her tone dull. "It has stood inviolate for more than three thousand years." She shook her head, as if trying to dispel an enchantment of disbelief. Ahead of them, they saw the Elf-Eater, crouching motionless between a pair of blazing houses, greedily devouring the numerous limp shapes scattered on the ground around it.

Abruptly the thing rose. If it noticed the approach of the companions, it gave no sign. Instead, it rolled forward in its deceptively awkward gait until it once again stood in the middle of the street, less than a hundred paces from Alicia.

Then it started to move, rumbling away from them toward the gleaming facets of Argen-Tellirynd.

"Can you distract it somehow?" Brigit cried to Keane, her tone desperate. "Get it to come this way—anywhere but the palace!"

"When will it have enough?" groaned Keane, weariness making his voice strident. He raised a hand and barked a magical command.

Sparks hissed and crackled in the air, along with the pungent scent of a nearby lightning strike. Three balls of force, hissing and sputtering, trailing flashes and sparks in the air, hurtled into the Elf-Eater's carapace. Each exploded with a violent convulsion, searing into the creature's unnatural flesh, burning and sizzling with released force. The monster picked up speed but continued to lumber away from them.

Keane groaned and staggered. For a moment, Alicia feared that he might collapse, but then he shook his head and stumbled forward with the others. His hand closed around the steel dagger he always carried at his waist.

"For Synnoria—for the Llewyrr, and the Palace of the Ages!" cried Brigit, raising her sword and charging forward on foot. Other sisters joined her, and then Alicia, Hanrald, and Brandon shouted through hoarse throats and added their weight to the ragged charge. The tree of Alicia's changestaff lumbered beside them. Robyn trotted beside Keane, but then the druid queen cried another command. Once more the earth elemental rose from the land. This time, it emerged from among the paving stones in the street, bearing several marble slabs like plate armor, and lumbered toward the Elf-Eater.

But the marauding monster only flicked its tentacles at the pesky mortals attacking its rear. Most of the Ityak-Ortheel's attention focused on the magnificent structure before it.

The high wall, as clear as glass, surrounded the three-sided courtyard of Argen-Tellirynd. In the center of this plaza rose the pyramidical shape of the palace itself, three triangular walls that came together in a sharp peak at the top.

Rumbling faster now, too fast for the companions to keep up, the monster charged straight toward the clear wall—almost as if the thing didn't know the barrier existed. Closer it lumbered, and then it lowered its shell as it had done at the city gates.

The ground shook from the force of the impact, and a sound like thunder crashed through the air. The beast bounced back from the wall and pounded to the earth, but again, with deceptive quickness, it bounced back to its three feet.

"The wall! It didn't break!" shouted the princess, fiercely delighted.

"Look," said Keane grimly, pointing to the glasslike barrier.

Alicia's heart sank as she saw a thin spiderweb of cracks spread along the crystalline wall. The monster backed up several steps and charged forward again, crashing into the wall and stopping in its tracks. This time the sound of splintering rang through Chrysalis.

The wall still held, but obviously not for long. Pieces of the crystalline substance fell away in a glittering shower, and several gaping holes yawned in the barrier. Cracks spread farther to the left and right, casting dazzling prisms on the ground when the sun washed over them.

When the Elf-Eater bashed the wall a third time, the barrier came apart in a shower of sharp crystals. Passing through the gap, the monster entered the huge, triangular courtyard of the Argen-Tellirynd.

*　*　*　*　*

Deirdre returned to her mirror, fiercely determined to prove her strength in such a way that none could ever again deny it. Quickly the image found Synnoria and the city of the Llewyrr. The path of the Elf-Eater gaped like a bleeding wound across the scene, and Deirdre easily followed the trail to the edge of the crystal palace.

Her heart pounded as she saw, again, the broad triangle of the palace courtyard—and the similarly shaped structure within. Perfect!

For once, Deirdre's iron-hard confidence rested on her shoulders with less than total conviction. The task was an awesome one, the enemy a being of unthinkable power.

Yet, if she was right, that enemy had a fatal weakness, and the princess of Callidyrr was the only person who knew where that vulnerability lay.

Finally the image faded from the mirror, and she was ready to put her plans into action. Deirdre wrapped her cloak around her lithe body and closed her eyes, picturing clearly the scene that had last appeared before her eyes.

She spoke three words sharply, and then she was gone.

* * * * *

Sinioth ordered his two lieutenants, each a monarch in his own right, to attend him in the Great Grotto of the Coral Kingdom. This was a huge, domed cavern erected at the height of the coral ridge occupied by Krell-Bane's scrags. The giant squid coiled around a dais in the center of the grotto and waited for the others to speak.

Sythissal floated before his master, while Krell-Bane rested on the coral floor of the grotto. The latter's eyes still flashed hatred. He greatly resented the orders of Talos requiring him to accept a new master in his own realm, but he kept his wrath hidden, observing the conference with rapt attention.

"How do we catch these humans if they take to the sea?" he wondered aloud.

"There I have been making preparations," explained Sythissal, eagerly settling to the floor. His clawed hands flexed as he gestured. "My warriors have built two great ships—ships that will carry us on the surface as fast as the humans can sail! No longer will our enemies outrun us with a favorable wind!"

"These are ships of the surface?" asked the scrag king in genuine surprise.

"They wait for us under the water, but only atop the sea will they gain their highest speed. They are secreted in the Moonshaes now, ready for our master's command!"

Krell-Bane grimaced at his ally's fawning, but he couldn't contain his curiosity. "What are these vessels? Where have they come from?"

"My warriors have created them from the shells of wrecked human ships—hulls and decks we have joined, capable of carrying many hundreds of us. As to what they are," replied Sythissal, his barbed teeth flashing in a self-satisfied grin, "I have decided to call them 'Mantas.'"

❧ 7 ❧

Twin Triangles

Brigit stumbled through the wreckage of the crystal wall, desperate to distract the Elf-Eater from its attack against the Palace of the Ages. Alicia watched, awestruck, admiring the elfwoman's courage even as she recognized her futility. Two other sisters, their armor battered and their faces dirty, accompanied their captain in this headlong advance.

The tall triangle of the palace proper soared skyward before them, blocked only by the pastoral hedges, the curved marble walls and sweeping reflective pools that had once created such harmony in the courtyard. Centered in the midst of this grace, the crystalline walls of the three-sided pyramid once reflected beauty and balance.

The elephantine monster shattered any such pristine memories, lumbering closer to the palace, paying no attention to the insignificant elven warriors to its rear. Instead, Ityak-Ortheel bore straight toward the looming structure, crushing to gravel a marble arch that stood in its path, smashing lush and ancient cedars underfoot so that the sweet scent of green needles permeated the air. Stomping through the wreckage, the monster continued without pause.

Alicia waited with her companions outside the breach in the wall. A sense of wonder bedazzled her, for the shining silver and diamond structure before her, towering to its lofty point in the sky, evoked a strong sense of awe. The Argen-Tellirynd was the grandest building she had ever seen, more elegant and beautiful even than Caer Callidyrr, yet now its grandeur could evoke only a profound sadness, for saving the palace didn't seem like an attainable goal.

Keane groaned wearily, slumping against a crumbling wall. Robyn, too, leaned weakly against the supporting surface.

With a grimace, she pushed herself upward.

"Attack—go!" the queen commanded, and the hulking earthen form of her stone-plated elemental lumbered after the Elf-Eater. The gangly, leaf-covered form of Alicia's change-staff followed in a gait that seemed as awkward as a man on stilts, yet carried the tree being forward with sweeping strides.

Finally Hanrald and Brandon stepped through the broken wall of crystal, followed by Alicia, Robyn, and Keane.

"A diversion!" Brigit cried, turning to cast about for some kind of idea. She looked at them in despair. "We've got to draw that thing away!"

"I don't think we can," the High Queen said quietly, in a voice that still carried clearly to Brigit's ears.

The elfwoman whirled back toward the monster, as if she would run forward and try to drag it back by herself. Then her shoulders slumped, and she staggered in complete dejection. "We can't," she agreed, choking with grief. "Three thousand years . . ."

She didn't finish, but there was nothing anyone could do to change the beast's inexorable advance toward the Palace of the Ages. The Ityak-Ortheel was clearly drawn to the triangular pyramid by some compulsion not understood by the human and elven onlookers.

The monster rumbled through the wide courtyard, trudging through several pristine fishponds. The crystal waters shimmered in a fine spray as they were splashed by the grotesque feet, and then flowed into the muddy depressions left by the Elf-Eater's passage.

Two blue-coated elven warriors, each carrying a silver-bladed halberd, rushed forward from a palace guardpost. They raised their weapons and shouted a fierce cry as they attacked, but before the blades dropped, the Ityak-Ortheel reached out with leathery tentacles and swiped the weapons away.

The hapless fighters struggled vainly in the grip of those same limbs, their screams silenced with shocking speed.

Again Alicia remembered how swiftly Pawldo had disappeared. Anger boiled within her, coupled with furious frustration. There seemed to be *nothing* they could do to slow the monster's onslaught.

More trees splintered—three ancient aspens this time, each thicker in girth than a man could reach around—as the Elf-Eater continued in its direct path toward the palace. The high, shining wall leaned away from it, soaring upward in a perfect triangle to the sharp point in the bright Synnorian sky.

"*Stop!*" shouted Brigit as the first tentacle reached forward to touch the gleaming surface.

"No! Let it go forward!"

The words rang through the air like a peal of thunder, spoken from behind the companions. Shocked, Alicia and her companions wheeled, weapons ready for attack or defense. Even Brigit and Colleen halted their headlong advance to stare in astonishment.

"Deirdre!" gasped Alicia, the first to recover her voice.

"Don't stop it!" The black-haired princess ignored her sister, instead repeating her direction to Brigit as she stalked toward them. She passed through the breach in the wall and marched into the courtyard of the Argen-Tellirynd like some commanding warlord. Wind gusted against Deirdre's black dress, outlining her strong legs and streaming her long hair behind her.

Advancing past her mother and sister silently, the princess finally stopped to confront Brigit with her hands firmly on her hips.

"Who are you?" demanded the white-faced captain of the sister knights.

"My daughter," Robyn replied, her tone icy as she joined the pair. "This is an emergency!" she snapped to Deirdre. "Explain yourself—quickly!"

"The two triangles—the courtyard and the building—give us our only chance to defeat this creature!" the younger woman explained, her voice level, as if the chaos around them was some sort of remote picture. "If we can lure the beast there, I can send it away—at least, I think I can," she said, no trace of doubt in her voice.

Alicia looked for Keane's reaction to her sister's astounding claim. Surprisingly the mage's brows were knitted in concentration. He appeared to be giving serious weight to Deirdre's claim.

"You don't *believe* her, do you?" demanded the older princess.

"I don't know what else to hope for," Keane informed her, and Alicia had no good reply to that.

"Do you know what you countenance?" spat Brigit, still pale with fury. "This is the *Argen-Tellirynd!* It has stood for millennia, and now you ask that we allow this horror within its sacred walls?"

"Only if you want to get rid of it."

Brigit's eyes flashed in anger, but abruptly she turned and confronted Robyn. "What kind of madness is this?" she demanded.

"I . . . don't know," replied the High Queen of the Ffolk, studying her daughter—so much the image of herself—with narrowed eyes.

A crash of crystal, mingled with the incongruously musical ringing of broken silver piping, signaled further destruction as the Ityak-Ortheel bashed through the palace wall, probing with its tendrils, smashing a wider opening for its domed body. Quickly it forced itself through the gap, disappearing within the palace to the sounds of continued destruction.

"Come on," commanded Deirdre. She stepped along the rubble-strewn path of the monster, ignoring the shattered work of age-old sculptors and crushed remains of enchanted gardens. Reaching the gaping hole in the palace wall, she entered the Argen-Tellirynd.

Brigit looked after the young woman with fury etched upon her elven face, but finally she forced herself to clutch at the straw—the desperate, costly hope—extended by Deirdre. If the Elf-Eater could be vanquished, that was the only thing that mattered! She and her sisters, as well as their human companions, fell in behind Deirdre.

"In the center of the building," announced the dark-haired sorceress, watching carefully as the Elf-Eater rumbled ahead. "It must go all the way in."

She picked up the pace of her advance, keeping within a few dozen paces of the monster. They passed toppled pillars of marble, quartz, and silver, saw a hall of tall mirrors, every one of them smashed. High, arching holes marked each wall the Elf-Eater had crashed through, and even when it disappeared from sight around a corner for a moment or two, they had no difficulty remaining close behind.

Finally the beast smashed an opening in a wall of white stone, kicking the rubble out of the way to advance into the great atrium, the triangular heart of the palace. Three walls soared upward, meeting in a narrow peak a hundred feet overhead. Long, narrow windows showered the room with incongruously bright sunlight. A black floor gleamed like a mirror, except where chunks of stone lay scattered from the force of the Elf-Eater's entrance.

Deirdre sprinted ahead, following the beast into the room for several steps before she suddenly stopped. The monster reached the center of the triangle, and Deirdre raised her hands.

The words of her teleportation spell flamed in her mind. The triangles were centered, the three-legged beast vulnerable to her magic. The timing was perfect—now!

"*Bluth-tar—!*" Rigidly concentrating, Deirdre began to chant the spell.

The Elf-Eater whirled with astounding speed, springing toward Princess Deirdre. She screamed and stumbled backward.

"My spell!" she shrieked as the wasted power hissed in the air around her. She reached out, as if to retrieve the useless casting, but her concentration had been broken, leaving her helpless before the full brunt of the leaping Ityak-Ortheel.

But another had carefully watched her—and in a flash, Keane understood what the princess attempted. And she was not the only one who knew the words to a teleportation spell.

"*Bluth-tarith-Erallanor!*"

The chant was completed by the magic-user, his voice as free of tremor and as taut as a fully drawn bowstring. The Elf-Eater, leaping from the center of the triangular atrium, suddenly froze in the air, as if suspended by some kind of restraining rope. It hung there for a moment as a bellow of consumate rage shook the very foundations of Synnoria.

Then it began to grow faint, its image shimmering, the Ityak-Ortheel soon fading into nothing more than foggy illusion.

In a few seconds, it was gone.

* * * * *

Brigit found Erashanoor wandering among the ruined walls of the Argen-Tellirynd. The ancient sage's feet crunched across twisted facets of crystal, tearing his boots and finally cutting into his feet.

"Come, grandfather," she said, helping the old elf to a less littered stretch of the corridor. He blinked at her vaguely, but then his pale eyes focused, reflecting great wells of grief and pain.

"It came through the gate, did it not?" he asked numbly. "Through the Fey-Alamtine?"

"Yes, it did." She could give him nothing less than the truth. "The Synnorian Gate is destroyed—ruined by the creature when it came through."

Erashanoor groaned, his voice tremulous. "This—the palace, these walls and gardens—they can all be rebuilt. But the Fey-Alamtine!"

The elderly elf's thin hands grasped Brigit's shoulders with surprising strength. "The eternal route to Evermeet is closed!"

Brigit's mind refused to consider the long-term problem to which her mentor referred. Instead, she tried to grapple with more immediate concerns—the loss of her friends, the destruction of her city, and the astounding and timely arrival of humans within Synnoria.

"Can you come to the atrium?" she asked. "The Serene Matriarch will be meeting the humans there. She—we—would like your presence."

Erashanoor blinked again, looking around as if he couldn't bear to leave the wreckage without cleaning up. "Humans? Yes—yes, of course!"

His voice grew firm, and he looked at Brigit sternly. "We cannot bear *every* outrage of this grievous day!"

She felt a measure of relief as he fished out his great pipe and tamped down a bowl of his herb. Finally he turned his back on the chaos and followed Brigit toward the atrium, the only part of the Palace of the Ages where the floor was clear enough for a gathering.

* * * * *

Alicia and her companions stood as spectators to a confrontation between two factions of the Llewyrr.

On the one side, albeit reluctantly, stood Brigit Cu'Lyrran and the surviving Sisters of Synnoria. They formed a pathetically small group, though Alicia was heartened to see that the brave Colleen had survived the fight. These Llewyrr had fought the Ityak-Ortheel and knew that without the intervention of the humans, the battle would have ended in unmitigated disaster.

On the other side stood the venerable Erashanoor and the Elders of the Llewyrr, each of whom had lived a minimum of six centuries, representing nearly three thousand years of tradition coupled with implacable prejudice. Yet these elves, like the fighters, still reeled emotionally from the shock of the Elf-Eater's rampage.

The Serene Matriarch of Synnoria, Ate'Niah, sat in an ornately carved wooden chair in the center of the sunlight-filled chamber. Her face was unlined, but still reflected the wisdom of many centuries of life. Silver hair coiled around her head, rising into a peak that bore a small tiara of diamond-studded platinum. Despite the perfection of her coiffure, however, the haste of the meeting was reflected in her muddy boots and the traces of soot that stained her pearl-colored gown.

"I must repeat, Matriarch," announced Erashanoor determinedly, "I protest most strongly the presence of humans here, in the heart of our most sacred chambers!" The elderly Llewyrr, keeper of the Elven Gate for all these long centuries, avoided looking at the visitors, as if their very sight was an affront to his sensibilities. Instead, his gaze came to rest on Brigit, and he glowered with unconcealed anger.

"It has been agreed that their presence will be tolerated," replied the Serene Matriarch Ate'Niah.

"*Tolerated!*" Alicia, who had been struggling to contain her anger and resentment at the elven arrogance, could no longer bear it. "If we hadn't arrived when we did, there'd be no chambers here at all, sacred or otherwise! A brave halfling *died* in that cause!" She glared at the withered form of the gatemaster, daring him to meet her gaze, but he did not.

A touch on Alicia's arm brought her attention around to Robyn. The queen stood beside her daughter, though the princess didn't know how long she had been there. Yet, with the touch on her arm, Alicia felt her tension and anger fade from burning flame to dull coal, like a well-banked fire that nestled a great deal of heat while showing little brightness.

"Serene Matriarch of Synnoria, I thank you for the opportunity to speak in these exalted chambers," Robyn began, bowing politely without seeming abject.

"I know who you are, High Queen Kendrick of Callidyrr," said the thin-faced elven matriarch known as Ate'Niah. Her voice was cool, carefully formal. "The mistress captain has informed me of your acquaintance in the recent past, and your contributions today are known to even the blindest of the Llewyrr."

Recent past! The words brought rueful smiles to Robyn's and Alicia's lips. Her adventures with Brigit had occurred twenty years ago, half of the queen's lifetime, yet the elf could refer to it as the 'recent past'!

"I am pleased that my friend Brigit recalls our alliance in a positive light. The courage of her and her comrades was instrumental in the triumph of King Kendrick and myself." Robyn's tone remained formal, but she smiled at the captain of the sister knights.

"Ah, yes. . . High King Kendrick. The extent of his rule was known to us, even isolated in Synnoria. His reign did not pass without merit."

Again Alicia flushed. Tristan had merely united the four kingdoms of the Ffolk, the first ruler to do so since Cymrych Hugh! "Not without merit" indeed! But she held her tongue, realizing that anger could only jeopardize their hopes.

"I extend our regret regarding his death," continued the matriarch. "The passing of even a short-lived human must be a thing of sorrow."

Robyn stiffened, and for a moment, Alicia wondered if the sublime arrogance of the Llewyrr would overcome even her mother's discipline. It did not.

"He . . . King Tristan . . . may be alive," replied the queen, her words ringing with hope in the vast chamber.

For a time, none of the elves made any reply. At first, Alicia wondered if they'd heard. Then she noticed a raised eyebrow on Erashanoor's creased forehead, a twist of the Matriarch's lips. Brigit alone gasped, and she did that silently.

"How do you know this? Is he a madman, to disappear from the world? Or is he a prisoner?" inquired Matriarch Ate'Niah.

"A prisoner," replied Robyn. "That is why we have come to you—to ask for help in his rescue."

"No!" declared Erashanoor, forcing himself to look at the companions for a moment before turning to the matriarch to plead his case. "It's a snare to trap us in human intrigues!"

"I was about to explain that we have no intention of 'ensnaring' you or even of asking Llewyrr to place themselves in danger," Robyn said, her tone low but icy-hard. The rebuke against the venerable Erashanoor was plain to all the Llewyrr. The matriarch's lips tightened in an expression that might have been grim amusement.

"Who holds King Kendrick, and where?" asked Brigit.

"The scrags—the sea trolls—have imprisoned him in the Coral Kingdom. Their ransom demands are impossible, leaving us no recourse but to abandon him or attempt his rescue."

"It would seem, then, that they have him beyond your reach," observed the sister knight grimly. "How did you hope that we could help?"

"There are tales . . . perhaps little more than legends, though our bards and mages believe them to be grounded in the truth . . . tales of elven ships that, at one time, could sail beneath the sea. If this is true and such magic can be employed to modify our vessels, we intend to mount an expedition to rescue him."

Robyn stated the plan bluntly, and then she waited. If the matriarch or Erashanoor had expected her to plead for help, they were surprised. The queen of Moonshae would make no further attempt to persuade.

It was the ancient gatekeeper who broke the silence, and his tone was the softest it had been during this council. Erashanoor almost looked sad; certainly his attitude was regretful. "Such knowledge was once the province of the elven seafarers, and perhaps two thousand years ago you would have found crafters among the Llewyrr who could help you. But such skills are long since lost to the elves of the Outer Lands."

"Outer Lands? You mean places like Synnoria?" inquired Alicia, her impatience forcing her into the conversation.

"All the elvenlands beyond Evermeet are the Outer Lands," explained the matriarch. "And I'm afraid that the gatemaster is correct. The only repository of such knowledge is in the vast libraries and troves of the eternal elvenhome."

Evermeet! To Alicia—to all the humans—the knowledge might as well have resided on the moon. That mystical isle was hidden somewhere in the mists of the Trackless Sea, reputedly death to any sailors who dared approach. The greatest navigators of humanity disagreed vehemently on its location or even its very existence.

Keane spoke softly, but his voice and his presence—he was the tallest person, man or elf, in the room—commanded the attention of the Synnorian Elders. "It is said—also in legends, of course, though I have heard it from those who call it fact— that there are ways known to the elves, paths that lead to Evermeet from across the Realms. Is there such a way you could employ to aid us?"

There was no mistaking the pain that flashed across Erashanoor's face, and Alicia felt a surge of suspicion. Had the wizard guessed at the secret of the Llewyrr? As quickly as that, her suspicions were replaced by hope. Did that mean that there *was* a route to Evermeet? Could her father be saved?

"That route is closed," Brigit said, unable to conceal her grief. She turned and spoke to the Serene Matriarch, who gasped in shock at Brigit's words. "The Ityak-Ortheel corrupted the Fey-Alamtine—smashed the passage beyond recognition. Evermeet can no longer be reached through the Synnorian Gate."

"So much corruption, such evil . . . and our islands are so small," observed Ate'Niah after a somber pause.

"And shared by our peoples together," observed the queen of the Ffolk. "It is not unreasonable to believe that the forces sending the Elf-Eater against Synnoria are the same dark ones who hold my husband hostage."

"Quite possible, Noble Queen," replied the matriarch of Synnoria. "But alas, it does not change the fact that, so long as our path to Evermeet is closed, we cannot aid you in the rescue of your husband."

The hope that had blossomed in Alicia's mind wilted with this revelation, and despair threatened to claim her. Her father was lost, in truth. There would be, could be, no rescue.

"Evermeet is an island, correct?" asked Brandon, speaking for the first time. His voice was gruff, as if the words came forth only with difficulty. He, too, had been forced to unusual lengths of self-control to maintain his silence.

Erashanoor and the matriarch both nodded somberly, watching the Prince of Gnarhelm carefully. If the Llewyrr regarded the Ffolk with cautious hostility, the northmen they had considered blood enemies for many centuries.

"An island not impossibly far from here, from the Moonshaes." Brand turned to face his companions, his words warming to the topic. "Well, we could *sail* there! It can be no longer a journey than a dozen of my ancestors have made at some time or another!"

"Impossible!" snapped Erashanoor, appalled.

"It cannot be done. You would not survive to reach the island's shores!" confirmed Matriarch Ate'Niah.

"Begging your pardon, Your Royal Matronship, but I can take a ship a good many places others have said a ship was never meant to go!" Brandon pursued.

"You don't know what stands in your path," exclaimed Brigit, her eyes wide and her tone serious. She looked at Brandon with sympathy, but shook her head. "There are magical cyclones that rise from the sea, crushing ships into kindling. There are the Warders, great sea beasts who spend their lives ensuring that no vessel can approach the elvenhome."

"Sea beasts and cyclones!" Brandon laughed, although admittedly the sound was somewhat forced. "Nothing I haven't faced a dozen times before!" Alicia had to admire his bravado. As he spoke, she found herself believing him, wanting to sail with him against these foes.

"And even if you survive the barriers—an unlikely occurrence, assuredly," offered the matriarch, "you would be slain as soon as you stepped ashore. Humans are not welcome on Evermeet."

"Perhaps . . . but perhaps not," noted Robyn thoughtfully.

"What do you mean?" inquired Brigit, intrigued in spite of herself.

"Perhaps we could land safely if we had an escort . . . an *elven* escort!"

"Impossible!" shouted Erashanoor, his wrinkled visage flushing indignantly. "It is as I suspected. You seek to seduce us away from our valley! It won't be—"

"I'll go." Brigit's voice cut like a blade through the gatekeeper's ranting. Erashanoor stopped speaking but forgot to close his mouth in astonishment. "I will sail with you to Evermeet. Once there—*if* we get there—I will act as your agent, presenting your request for aid."

"If you don't believe we can get there, why do you volunteer to come along?" asked Alicia, unable to banish the challenge from her voice.

"Friendship," said Brigit bluntly. "And perhaps a measure of gratitude . . . and respect."

Alicia regretted her tone, her face flushing with embarrassment at the sister knight's generous words. But her mother smoothly moved past the moment.

"I thank you, my old friend," Robyn said, stepping forward to clasp both of Brigit's outstretched hands.

And as quickly as that, the matter was settled.

*   *   *   *   *

"Enough of these distractions!" The voice of Talos, backed by thunder in his rage, echoed and resounded through the halls of his smoking realm.

Even Malar, mortal enemy of elvenkind, would have quailed before that anger, except for the fact that any such display of weakness in the face of a fellow god could have potentially disastrous consequences. So instead, the Beastlord pretended haughty indifference and turned a bored, deathlike eye toward his unholy ally.

"Very well," he agreed, his own voice a basso rumble that could be felt to the core of the plane around them. "Ityak-Ortheel was an amusing diversion, but the Synnorian Gate is still closed—and no doubt the Llewyrr have been driven deeper into their shell than ever. I am satisfied."

"Good—very good!" Talos grumbled, mollified.

"Have the humans replied to Sinioth's demands?" inquired Malar, none too eager to dwell on the previous topic of conversation. Talos shook his head, and the ground rumbled beneath him.

"The king of the Ffolk . . . ?" Malar mused. "Should he be put to death?"

"Not yet!" Talos commanded without hesitation. "We hold a vital trump, my ally. We should not be hasty to discard it!"

"Very well," agreed the Beastlord, phrasing the central question. "What do we do now?"

"We have the glass . . . in the hands of our young tool," Talos noted.

"Proven doubly useful," Malar agreed.

"So we wait," said Talos, his voice low, almost bored. "Then later, after the humans have had time to grasp their impotence, we will send them his other hand."

The other god smiled. The plan had an appealing ring.

PART II: EVERMEET

❧ 8 ❧

The Third Princess of Moonshae

Brandon's eyes swept the horizon with obvious eagerness as the party drew near Corwell on the return from Synnoria. Alicia attributed the northman's eagerness to his love for the sea, assuming that the week-long trek into the highlands had been a hard separation for the sailor.

Of course, the princess herself looked ahead with growing eagerness as their horses alternately cantered, trotted, and walked along the King's Road of Corwell. The solid bulk of Caer Corwell, atop its rocky knoll, would be a clear sign of their homecoming, looming before them for the last six hours of the ride. At the same time, Alicia reminded herself, pastoral Lowhill would come into sight, a clear reminder of their mission's grim cost.

Brigit accompanied the human riders. Her lieutenant, Colleen, had pleaded with her to come as well, but Brigit had agreed that she would be the only elf to accompany the party. This much she was willing to compromise with her mentor, Erashanoor. Despite the fact that a departure from Synnoria—not to mention a sea voyage!—loomed as a major trauma to the Llewyrr, the elf had completed her preparations in the hour following the council in ruined Argen-Tellirynd.

The matriarch had prevailed on the battle-weary companions to spend one night in the elven vale, which they had done gratefully. The hypnotic splendor of the place Robyn recalled from twenty years before remained absent—a fact that was hardly surprising, considering the chaos that had just wracked the valley.

By the following dawn, propelled by unspoken urgency, they were saddled and ready to ride. Deirdre, they discovered as they prepared to depart, was nowhere to be found. She had apparently teleported back to Caer Corwell without any farewells.

The morning of the last day had broken a few hours ago with the promise of Corwellian hearths before nightfall. The absence of Pawldo was a persistent cloud, hovering over members of the party at different times but affecting them all deeply.

Brandon rode beside Alicia. He had been silent for much of this day. Now, however, the other companions had trailed out before them, and they could talk privately. It was the moment he had awaited.

"We're well along the path to your father," he declared. "I *know* that—you have to trust me, Princess!"

"We're not even started yet, really," she replied. "It seems like an impossible dream—that somewhere at the end of this, we'll sail under the ocean and rescue him."

"But I know that this is a dream you'll not abandon, and because of that, neither will I!"

She felt a deep sense of relief to have his help in this quest. At the same time, his presence caused a real ambivalence in her feelings. What would be the cost—in his own mind, and to her own sense of debt and honor—of his courage and sacrifice? Certainly she knew that he didn't help her out of any such selfish motives, but could she separate those issues in her own mind, her own heart?

"When we find your father, will you allow me to ask him for your hand?" pressed Brandon.

"I . . . I don't know!" Alicia replied, suddenly afraid. "I can't decide that—I can't even think about it—now! You have to understand that!"

Unconsciously Alicia picked up the pace so that she and Brandon drew closer to Hanrald and Brigit, who rode in tandem before them. Their nearness, more than Alicia's reluctance, brought Brandon's conversation to a halt.

The two knights, human man and elven woman, were engaged in serious discussion. Though Hanrald loomed over Brigit on foot, the difference was somewhat lessened on horseback. The earl's war-horse was a heavy steed, capable of charging with the knight in plate armor and the horse fully barded in chain. Yet Brigit had selected for her mount an exceptionally long-legged young mare—naturally of purest white. The horse scampered with such a bounce in her gait that she seemed to float above the road.

"The chain armor has its place for scouting and speed," Brigit was saying as Alicia and Brandon drew even with them.

"But there's nothing like solid plate for making a charge or mixing it up in a melee," Hanrald replied.

"True—to a point," Brigit allowed. "But then a good shirt of chain can provide nearly the same protection and also give you the speed to cover your back with your weapon, instead of your armor."

"You'd be talking about better chain than *I've* seen," Hanrald said with a rueful laugh. "Even the best armorsmiths in Callidyrr can't link together anything that'll hold the bite of a northman's axe."

"And what kind of northman would be striking at your back?" demanded Brandon, in mock offense.

"I'll welcome them at my side now," replied Hanrald seriously. "It's no small thing you've done, offering to take a company of foreigners on a quest for their king!"

Alicia flinched. The words were too close to the turmoil she wrestled with so frequently. She turned to Brigit, trying to ignore the men.

"What do you know about the barriers around Evermeet?" the princess asked.

"Very little," admitted Brigit. "And neither Erashanoor nor the sages could tell me much, though I spoke with them about it on the evening before our departure.

"There are the things called cyclones," continued the sister knight. "But whether they're funnel clouds of intense pressure or great masses of storm I can't tell you. As to the Warders, it seems that their nature has been kept—intentionally—a secret."

"We'll need spare rigging and sails, extra oars," Brandon mused. "All things we can gather in Corwell Town."

Alicia nodded. "We'll have no dearth of volunteers, I'm sure—enough to crew your vessel."

Brandon shook his head. "My own men will go, to the last hand. Best we sail with an experienced company."

"There is *some* hope I can offer," Brigit added slowly. She didn't sound terribly enthusiastic. "Erashanoor told me before we left that it's supposed to be possible to reach Evermeet by sea. There were paths laid through the storm belt, and the Warders are not invincible."

"That *is* encouraging news," the princess agreed, her hopes fanned into flame.

"Of course, we don't have any map of those paths, and if the Warders have a weakness, I'm sure *I* don't know what it is!" Brigit reminded her, but Alicia didn't bother to listen because it wasn't what she wanted to hear.

"My ancestors have long avoided a wide stretch of sea a thousand miles to the west of here," Brandon said. "They tell legends of an elven island, dangerous to approach. That's the place you call Evermeet?"

"Yes," Brigit replied. "A large realm, hundreds of miles from north to south."

"With a favoring wind, we might make the voyage in a week or ten days."

"And without a favoring wind?" inquired the sister knight.

This time it was the northman who shook away the question. "We can tack around any wind, and we've got oars if it comes to that!"

"It shouldn't take us too long to get everything collected once we get to town. And Brand's crew is there already, plus his longship."

At her last word, Alicia frowned, realizing that their vessel was one matter in which they must settle for less than ideal preparations. Brandon's own ship, the *Gullwing*, had been lost in a wreck barely two months earlier. As crown prince, he had commandeered the *Coho*, the longship of one of his countrymen, but the craft was smaller and, even to Alicia's unpracticed eye, appeared less seaworthy than had Brand's personal ship. The prince had long before commissioned a new long-ship, but Alicia had seen the vessel under construction little more than a month before. There would still be, she felt certain, much work to do on the new longship.

"The towers of Corwell," announced the High Queen abruptly, and they all cantered ahead to get a look.

None of the others could make out the shape of the hilltop fortress, but within five minutes, a squat outline began to show through the haze of distance.

"How did you see that from back there?" asked Brandon, who had always believed his own eyesight to be perfect.

"Human senses are not always the most acute. Perhaps I borrowed the eyes of something different—a hawk, say. Or perhaps your young eyes are not as keen as you think they are!"

The towers of Corwell Keep soon stood out in individual relief, and then the stone wall that had begun to replace the castle's wooden palisade came into view. Soon the waters of the firth glittered on the far horizon, stretching like a blue highway into the haze of the far west.

The companions unconsciously picked up their pace, allowing the horses to gobble the miles with long, loping strides. The steeds ran as if they could sense the snug stable and fresh oats in their near future.

As they rode, more and more details became apparent—the buildings dotting the snug town, many puffing small wafts of cooksmoke from their chimneys. . . fishing ships, a trading galleon, and a pair of longer vessels as well, dotting the placid waters of Corwell Harbor.

And then Brandon gave a shout of triumph that took them all by surprise. The northman's face was locked in an expression of fierce joy. Alicia stared at the Prince of Gnarhelm and then followed his eyes to the firth.

Two longships in the harbor? She squinted, recognizing first the *Coho* by her battered hull and limp, swaybacked look. The other vessel was anchored just beyond, and though she was the same type of ship, she was as different from the *Coho* as a galleon was from a canoe.

The second longship was more than half again as long as the *Coho*, and her hull planks were so clean that they gleamed. Her gunwales were long and straight, and a proud figurehead rose high above the prow. The ship was quite simply the grandest vessel Alicia had ever seen.

"She's here!" shouted the prince of the north, raising his fist triumphantly.

"*Who's* here?" inquired Keane, peevish from the long ride.

Brandon took them all in with his smile, the wide grin of a man who has just sworn his love for life or has beheld his newborn son for the first time.

And then Alicia knew. She remembered the partially completed hull she had seen in Gnarhelm that spring, the sleek vessel that Brandon had told her would be his own. Even among the builders' stays she had been a grand vessel, and the princess had no doubt that the same ship now awaited them in the harbor of Corwell.

"This is a ship I would take to the edge of the world and sail her along the brink!" declared the northman, his voice thick with pride. "The work was finished in record time, and I left word in Gnarhelm, weeks ago, to bring her here as soon as she was ready to sail."

Now Alicia saw that he eyed her seriously, his expression unusually tentative.

"We shall sail to Evermeet on the grandest vessel of Gnarhelm," Brandon said, his voice thick with pride. "And that vessel required a name befitting her grandness. I hope you can forgive my presumption."

Alicia started at the uncharacteristic humility in his tone. Then her blood thrilled and her throat choked as she understood what he meant.

"She is called the *Princess of Moonshae*," Brandon finished quietly. Deeply touched, Alicia could only nod her thanks, but even through her tear-streaked eyes she could see the warmth and affection shining from the northman's face.

* * * * *

For a long time, Deirdre tried to avoid her mirror, even going to the extent of covering it with the leather wrap and stacking books and scrolls on top of it. In truth, she was terribly tired. She had spent the night in Synnoria relearning her teleportation spell and then, before dawn, she used it to return to Corwell.

Then she had fallen into a slumber that had lasted for two full days—and even now, on the third day, her mind was reluctant to focus. Instead, she found her thoughts drifting to the mirror.

Finally she gave up her resistance, slowly lifting the top books from the stack. She quickly pushed the other volumes out of the way and tore away the cover. Palpable relief swept over her when she saw the comforting reflection in the glass.

Then the picture shimmered, and she settled down to observe her sister and her companions making their plans.

* * * * *

The companions' return to Caer Corwell was marked by an enthusiastic crowd of Ffolk who poured out of the town to line the roadway as soon as the party was sighted. The appearance of the elf among them was greeted by wild cheers.

Immediately upon reaching the courtyard, Robyn ordered a grand feast for those lords and Ffolk still in Corwell. The occasion was a farewell banquet for those who would embark to Evermeet—and also, a memorial and tribute to the queen's lifelong friend, Lord Pawldo of Lowhill.

Tavish sang songs about love and triumphant heroes while the guests mingled about the great hall, beginning the carousing that would go on far into the night. Dozens of kegs were tapped, and ales from palest amber to darkest mahogany overfilled deep and oft-inverted mugs, while the smells of succulent roasts drifted through the hall. Nevertheless, this was not nearly such a grand gathering as the festival of ten days earlier.

The entire affair was held within the keep of the palace.

Keane sensed the preparations for the feast as a vague background confusion against his concentration on the mission before them. The voyage to Evermeet, he guessed, offered the companions a less than fifty percent chance of survival. He had tried to dissuade the queen and the princesses together, and each separately, from participating in the quest. He hadn't expected to succeed with even one of the accursedly stubborn females, but in the case of Deirdre, he found an ally in the queen.

Robyn would not allow the entire family to embark on the quest, and she had decreed that it would be Deirdre who remained behind. The younger daughter had agreed with this suggestion too willingly for Keane's peace of mind. He let his mind consider the younger princess with an undeniable shiver of concern.

How had she known about the Elf-Eater—its rampage, or the means to vanquish it? And what unerring sense had brought her right to the scene of the fight, just when her presence could make a difference? How much did she know—and how did she learn it? A cautionary part of him wanted to remain in Corwell to observe the frightening development of Deirdre's power.

Yet Keane never questioned the importance of his own presence on the mission to rescue the king. Without his spells, the expedition's slim survival chances would be drastically decreased, in the mage's well-considered and unemotional opinion.

He spent many hours in study, and in the transcribing of spells from his great, leather-bound spellbook to a smaller volume that he would take with him aboard the *Princess of Moonshae*. Abruptly the lean magic-user straightened up and sighed, reminded by a pang of jealousy that they would be placing themselves in Brandon Olafsson's hands for the duration of their voyage.

Not that he had any doubts as to the young northman's proficiency as a sailor. In fact, the root of his jealousy was quite the opposite—Brand was such a fine sailor that he was bound to gain stature in the eyes of the Princess Alicia. Keane, on the other hand, would go on being . . . well, Keane.

Still, there was no question of him remaining behind. He thought of Alicia, touching the private part of his heart, the only place where he dared admit the truth. Keane had finally allowed himself to admit that he loved the princess, had loved her since she was little more than a girl. Always he had remained aloof, keeping this part of himself locked away, but he could no longer deny it. He would follow Alicia Kendrick to the farthest corner of the Realms if she set out in that direction.

Of course, Brandon Olafsson would probably be there waiting for them, Keane reflected ruefully. He came to the same woeful conclusion when he considered his other competitor. Hanrald, Earl of Fairheight, seemed like such a confident and capable suitor, and if he didn't press his case with as much vigor as Brandon, he remained a strong and manly presence. Gloomily the magic-user pondered his rivals—if he himself could even be called a participant in that contest.

There were times when he felt that such was not the case. He thought of Alicia's undiluted vitality. In the Palace of the Ages, she had been the one to voice the humans' resentment of Llewyrr arrogance. He had admired her when she had challenged the Serene Matriarch, even as he realized that he could not have uttered such statements himself.

Both the other men were closer to Alicia's age at twenty, and while Keane had a mere eight years on them, there were times when he felt three decades older. Alicia, Brand, and Hanrald were also all people of action. The two Ffolk were splendid riders, the northman a magnificent sea captain. Keane, on the contrary, felt equally uncomfortable bouncing on horseback or pitching deck.

Stop this! Angrily he rebuked himself, realizing that he might precipitate a dive into a dangerous depression. Fifteen minutes had passed since last he had dipped his quill into the inkwell! With a shake of his head, he forced himself to look at his work. Eventually the discipline that had enabled him, at a relatively young age, to master many spells that most magic-users never learned in all their lives allowed him to focus on his preparations.

Three hours later, he was done. He took another fifteen minutes to shave and don a clean tunic and trousers, arriving in the great hall just as the main course—roasts of venison and boar—was served.

As luck would have it, Hanrald had saved him a place at the head table, placing the tutor between the earl himself and Deirdre. Brigit and Alicia sat across the table from them.

"Nice you could join us," said Alicia, her tone cool. Obviously she had expected him earlier.

"I had a little work to do . . . if I'm going to be ready to sail tomorrow."

"At least we have an afternoon tide," Brandon noted, from down the table. He leaned forward and grinned at Keane. He obviously enjoyed the mage's exchange with Alicia.

"I'll be ready," Keane promised, his tone more grim than he intended. He saw Alicia looking at him curiously. Was that concern on her face or annoyance?

Servingmaids brought more pitchers of ale and a few bottles of Calishite rum. They drank toasts with the latter and washed down the rum with the former.

As they talked and ate, Keane found his eyes drawn to Brigit. The elfwoman was mostly silent, speaking only in answer to questions, and then in a soft tone that precluded further discussion in the crowded hall.

She really *is* beautiful, he realized. For once, the sister knight did not wear her silvered plate mail. Her petite form, clad in a gauzy dress, seemed almost frail by comparison to the robust, though hardly large, Alicia. Both of them had light-colored hair, but Alicia's was tinged with red and long, carelessly bound with a scarf that left many rogue strands free to tickle her cheeks and sweep across her shoulders. Brigit's, on the other hand, curled softly in a much shorter cut. When she wore her helm, none of the thin strands, as yellow as spun gold, were visible. Though the elfwoman didn't bind it in any visible way, her hair lay soft and lightly curling against her scalp, hiding the tips of her pointed ears and accentuating the delicate shape of her features.

Brigit joined Alicia for each toast, and as the evening wore on, the two females grew louder and more boisterous. Gradually the sister knight's elven reserve dropped away, and when she and Alicia joined Tavish for a ribald chorus of "The Murderous Maid," the whole hall resounded with cheers.

"Humans!" cried Brigit, slowly stifling her laughter as she settled back into her chair. "I wouldn't have believed it, but your festive spirit is catching!"

"Obviously," murmured Deirdre, too quietly for anyone but Keane to hear. The mage cast a quick look at the princess, who had been silent during the course of the dinner.

"You should try it," Keane couldn't resist pointing out.

Deirdre looked at him frankly, her lip curling into a faint sneer. "Some of us have more important things to do."

Keane looked at his former student with concern. The chaos of the banquet was not the place to talk with her. Tomorrow, he told himself—before we sail—I will speak with her. She hasn't listened before, but perhaps . . .

". . .when the firbolgs saw the Sisters of Synnoria ride over the hill, their faces dropped into every expression of astonishment you could imagine." Keane looked up, realizing that Queen Robyn was relating the story of the battle of Freeman's Down, the first time she and Tristan had fought with the aid of Brigit and the sister knights.

"It was a costly day," continued the queen, her voice dropping sadly. "Many brave Ffolk perished at the ditch, and one of the knights, fell, too. But we held them."

"Just as we'll hold them now," concluded Alicia softly. "May the goddess protect our efforts!"

* * * * *

Through the mirror of scrying, Talos watched the development of the humans' plans. Many options existed for thwarting those plans. Naturally the one he selected called for the use of his favorite avatar. Coss-Axell-Sinioth, now dwelling as master of the Coral Kingdom, would again serve his god in Corwell.

The command of Talos penetrated the depths of the sea, tickling the evil brain of his avatar as Sinioth lolled among the coral pillars of his submarine grotto. The giant squid oozed upward from the bottom, into the pale green of the shallows, as if here it could better absorb the message of its evil god.

"Arise, Coss-Axell-Sinioth, and hear the words of your master!"

"Speak, O Awesome One, and I obey!"

"You will again don the guise of a man," ordered Talos. "And quickly. You must go ashore in Corwell. There is a task you must do for me there. . . ."

When Sinioth heard the wishes of Talos, he could only gurgle in appreciative glee.

❦ 9 ❦

Corwell Town

The streets of Corwell were dark and generally abandoned at this late hour. A few guardsmen marched about, spending most of their time lingering beneath the occasional oil street-lamps, while late-night revelers stumbled from this inn to that tavern, seeking a little more entertainment before giving themselves up to the night.

Of course, every decent Ffolk was home in bed—at least, that would have been the opinion expressed by any city guard one bothered to ask. And for the most part, the man-at-arms would have been right.

This was especially so in the case of one dark side street, and a particularly ill-lighted tavern at the blackest end of that dingy lane, a place frequented by the lowest class of sailors and anyone else lacking the few copper pieces necessary to find better accommodations or entertainment.

In short, The Black Salmon was the seediest dive in Corwell Town, and so it attracted the kind of customer one might expect. Now, in the predawn hours, most of these derelicts had fallen asleep in pools of spilled beer, or staggered off to the common sleeping room or their lodgings elsewhere in town.

The exceptions were few: a painted harlot, alone for the night; a pair of young Ffolkmen spending their last night ashore before embarking, as crewmen, on the trading galleon in the harbor; and two northmen sailors, one profoundly drunk and the other only halfway so.

The fire grew dull, but the grease-stained innkeeper did nothing about it. A few candles guttered and dripped on some of the tables, casting wavering shadows around the room. The barely coherent northman broke the silence abruptly by calling out for two more mugs. The innkeeper poured stale beer from a leaking keg and examined the copper piece he received as if he were a master jeweler assessing the value of a princely ransom.

But even that dullard's eyes widened as a shadowy form moved through the door. One of the sleeping men snored loudly and then started awake. All conversation ceased, and the two pairs of men watched, the drunken northman rubbing his eyes in an attempt to see more clearly.

But nothing could form that shape in the doorway into other than a murk. It was no natural fog that rolled in from the street, sapping the feeble light from the room and bringing with it a chill from the sea . . . or beyond.

Then the haze dissipated, and a man entered the Black Salmon. The stranger was a tall fellow, dressed in black trousers and tunic, with hair and beard to match, and gleaming boots of midnight-dark leather reaching to his knees. He smiled around the inn, flashing white teeth, though his eyes remained hooded by carefully lowered lids.

Then he stalked across the common room to the table where the two northmen sat, pulling up a chair and seating himself without waiting for an invitation.

"Barkeep!" he shouted, a sound that jerked all of the others upward like marionettes seized by frantic puppeteers. "Bring us a pitcher of that . . . ale?" He regarded the contents of a half-filled mug with distaste, but then shrugged and tapped his fingers impatiently while the innkeeper filled a tall jug from his keg and hurried over with it.

The stranger flipped a coin to the server, and silver flashed briefly in the candlelight. The greasy little man seized the coin from the air and scampered back to the shelter of his grimy bar.

"On me, friends," said the newcomer, smiling with his mouth only. The two northmen still gaped at him as if he had two heads or three arms.

"Who *are* you?" demanded the less drunken of the two, finally recovering his voice.

The stranger blinked. "Call me . . . Malawar," he said after a moment. "Malawar of Alaron. And you, if I'm not mistaken, are men of the north."

The two sailors, with their long blond hair tied into twin braids, drooping mustaches, and fur-lined tunics, could hardly have been anything else. Nevertheless, they both nodded and assented seriously, as if a question of great import had been asked.

"That's a sleek ship in the harbor," the stranger continued. "Sailing on her?"

"Soon now," said the one who was still coherent. "With the afternoon tide, tomorrow. We just wanted to sample a little more of the local treasures before we go!" The sailor concluded with a chuckle that grew into a long, ale-flavored belch.

The stranger grimaced at the sight of the amber liquid in the pitcher, with its slight film of white foam. Nevertheless, he reached over and refilled the mugs of each northman. His own glass stood before him, barely touched.

"Did you sail here on that pig scow?" asked the northman, gesturing to the door. The indication of the great galleon was not lost on the one called Malawar.

"No—I've been on Gwynneth for some time now. I came to Corwell across the road from Kingsbay."

The northman shook his head. Why would someone travel from one side of an island to the other on *land?* "D'you know ships?" he demanded belligerently, then slumped back into his chair, not waiting for an answer. "That ship out there—the *Princess!* She's the finest boat ever to put to sea from Gnarhelm. That means she be the finest from anywhere in the Moonshaes, y' unnerstan'?"

The black-haired man nodded easily, and the sailor talked while his companion slumped deeper into coma. The trio passed an hour thus. The conscious northman was named Roloff and proved quite loquacious, telling ribald tales of life in Gnarhelm and revealing that the destination of their morrow's voyage was being kept a mystery by their captain, who was none other than the Crown Prince of Gnarhelm!

Eventually the harlot and the two young seamen left, and

the innkeeper coughed and tapped his foot, then started to clean up. The black-garbed man took note and squinted at his companions.

"Are you men staying here?" asked Malawar, rising to his feet. When the coherent one nodded, the dark figure's lips creased into another pale smile. "I have a splendid suite of rooms up the street at the King's Copper. Why don't you join me? There's plenty of room for the two of you."

The northman blinked suspiciously, but another silver piece flashed as Malawar paid off the innkeeper. The sailor had walked past the King's Copper and knew that it was a splendid place. Also, the rash he had acquired from the straw mat in The Black Salmon's sleeping room was still with him. The thought of real accommodations was too good to ignore.

"Aye," he grunted. "Give me a hand with Luge, here, and we'll take you up on that!"

Without appearing to strain, Malawar took the drunken Luge's shoulder and bore a great portion of the man's weight. They moved out the door and along the darkened street. It was many hours past midnight. Their route took them along the waterfront, beside the black waters of Corwell Harbor, water that extended still and placid toward the firth and the Trackless Sea beyond.

When they reached the King's Copper, Malawar alone carried Luge, bearing him full across his shoulders, hauling him like a sack of potatoes through the deserted common room and along the darkened hallway to his room.

The northman called Roloff was nowhere to be seen.

* * * * *

Alicia stood amid a bustle of controlled chaos on the Corwell waterfront while northmen sailors rowed the *Princess of Moonshae* toward the quay for loading. Brandon stood beside her, his hands on his hips, his eyes scrutinizing every move of the graceful vessel's slow progress.

"Easy there!" he shouted, unable to control himself. "Take

her slow! Now—come about! Watch it!"

The Prince of Gnarhelm paced in agitation, though the vessel was clearly in no danger. At the rudder stood the fiercely scowling figure of Knaff the Elder, as experienced a helmsman as ever sailed the Sea of Moonshae, and the longship, propelled by a half-dozen oars, barely crept through the water.

"Easy!" cried Brandon as a tublike fishing vessel raised sail a hundred paces away from the *Princess*.

"Can't hear myself think out here!" grumbled Knaff, loud enough for his voice to carry to shore.

"He can bring it in safely, don't you think?" suggested Alicia with a laugh. "You're like a proud papa getting his first look at his little boy!"

The captain grinned sheepishly. "You're right," he admitted. Brandon forced himself to keep his mouth shut, but his eyes studied every move of the sleek vessel, and he couldn't help but flinch at each change of course or speed.

At last the longship touched the wharf, very gently. Ropes made fast her stern and prow, and the crew quickly began loading aboard the crates of food and barrels of drinking water to provision a possibly long voyage.

Hanrald and Brigit carefully crossed the gangplank, each carrying a bundle containing polished armor. The two knights stowed their packages beside the mast.

Some distance down the dock, Alicia saw another northman she recognized—gigantic Wultha, a hulking, well-muscled specimen of a warrior. He stood with several of his crewmates, and for a moment the princess thought, oddly, that they were fishing. Then the big man waved to his prince and Brandon walked over to them. Alicia saw them talking seriously, saw Brandon's brows suddenly tighten into a scowl.

Concerned, Alicia started toward them, joined by Robyn and Keane. The Prince of Gnarhelm met them halfway, Alicia's disquiet mirrored in his own frown.

"They found the body of one of my men in the harbor," Brand announced grimly.

"Was he hurt? Murdered?" wondered the princess, deeply

disturbed by the news.

"I don't know. Something's not right, though."

"Who was it?" inquired Keane.

"A fellow named Roloff. He's a notorious drinker, but he holds it better than anyone I know. It's not likely he'd fall in on his own."

"Was he attacked or injured?" Alicia pressed.

"Not as far as we can tell. At least, his body had no wounds. He appears to have drowned."

" 'Appears?' " Robyn heard the suspicion in the northman's voice. "You're not convinced?"

"No. Roloff was too sensible a sailor—and too good a swimmer—to suffer that fate. And then there's the expression on his face."

"What was it?" Alicia felt a dull sense of menace. This seemed like a bad omen for the start of a dangerous voyage.

"His eyes were wide open and staring, fixed that way when he died—as if something scared the stuffing out of him, and he never recovered even after he fell in the water."

"When was he last seen beforehand?" inquired Keane.

"His best friend, Luge, drank with him last night—apparently quite a bit, since he doesn't remember much past midnight. From the look of him this morning, I'd say Luge's memory won't be of much use to us."

"Does he remember where they were?" pressed the mage. "Perhaps someone else saw something there."

"No good," said Brandon with a shrug. "Luge doesn't even remember where they went."

"Ill luck for the start of a voyage," observed Tavish, with a shake of her head. "Let's hope that means this is the worst of it!"

The others found it hard to shake a sense of unease, but Brandon reminded them that the tide turned even as they talked. They carried their small bundles of personal baggage aboard, then returned to the docks. There the Earl of Corwell and Princess Deirdre stood to see them off.

"With luck, we'll return with your father," Robyn said to her younger daughter. "If the worst happens, you will be the next queen of the Ffolk."

Deirdre looked at her mother closely, her expression unreadable. Abruptly she reached out and embraced the queen, a hug that Robyn returned with full strength and held for long moments. When the two women stood apart again, their eyes were red with unshed tears.

"I still protest!" grumbled Randolph as the queen gave him a farewell embrace. "You'll need me!"

"I know," replied Robyn truthfully. "But Corwell needs a lord, and until our return, that's a job that's too important to entrust to anyone else."

Lord Randolph, as Earl of Corwell, would resume his normal duties. Deirdre would return to Callidyrr to oversee that large and populous realm.

The others filed across the boarding plank while the queen waved to the Ffolk who had lined the dock to cheer and wish them success. Alicia carried her changestaff and wore her sword. Her armor, like Brigit's and Hanrald's, was wrapped in oilskin and carefully stowed.

"Until our return!" pledged Robyn boldly, waving as she, too, crossed the gangplank. At the same moment, ropes were tossed free from fore and aft, and a light wind filled the *Princess of Moonshae*'s quickly bulging sail.

Brandon's crew of sixty handpicked northmen included his old mentor, Knaff the Elder, at the helm, and the gigantic Wultha. The group was the minimum needed to man the large longship, but that was all they had room for, since they had brought so many additional passengers on board as well.

Besides Alicia and Robyn, Hanrald, Keane, Tavish, Brigit, and twelve Corwellian longbowmen formed the ship's complement. The latter wielded bows that could shoot twice as far as any northman's bow, and their presence greatly enhanced the ship's defensive punch.

Yet even with nearly eighty voyagers aboard, the *Princess of Moonshae* seemed uncrowded. The vessel's smooth hull rested in the water, completely at home, rocking only slightly as men took their stations at rowing benches, mast, and helm. Ready hands pushed the bow away from the dock, and a few strokes of the oars brought the elegant prow with its graceful female figurehead around to the gap in the harbor breakwater. The wind remained light, yet it propelled the sleek vessel at an easy glide onto the placid waters of Corwell Firth, where they headed west under full sail, trailing a sharp, clean wake.

For all that afternoon and the first night, the coastlines of the firth slowly separated to the port and starboard. At dawn, the bracketing shores remained visible, but only as faint lines of green and brown along the distant horizon. By midmorning, the firth had widened such that they couldn't see land to either side, though it would be another day before they actually left the protection of Gwynneth's enclosing penninsulas and truly set a course upon the Trackless Sea.

"What heading will you sail, once we pass Moray?" inquired Brigit, as she, Robyn, and Alicia were joined by the captain in the vessel's prow.

"West by north," he said without hesitation. "We'll pass to the north of the Gullrocks and then swing to the west. That's where *I've* always pictured the elvenhome, anyway. If you know better, tell me now!"

The sister knight shook her head. "Actually, none of us Llewyrr—even Erashanoor!—are terribly clear on exactly where the island lies on an actual map of the Realms. We've always used the Fey-Alamtine rather than mundane transportation to reach the island."

"As to where it is," Robyn announced, "I think I can help us there. The goddess will certainly help me identify the presence of a large land mass before us if we can get anywhere in the vicinity."

"Well, all I can do is sail toward water that every sensible sailor avoids—avoids because that's where Evermeet is supposed to lie!" Brandon announced with forced heartiness.

A feeling of menace remained with Alicia, a dark sense of foreboding that had lingered since before the start of the voyage. It seemed incongruous now as she looked at the smooth water, sparkling in the light of a beaming sun.

Yet the feeling wouldn't go away.

* * * * *

Luge lay awake, trembling, disturbed by some terrifying knowledge within him, knowledge that he didn't grasp or understand, yet somehow *knew*. The stocky crewman, who had spent the last night of his shore leave in the company of the man called Malawar, had no memory of that encounter.

Now Luge continued to suffer his hangover, thirty-six hours after that portentous evening. He didn't recall the specifics of his own stark terror, but he knew that dark hole in his memory was the cause of his current unease.

In the morning, he had recalled nothing of the experience save for a lingering sense that his sleep had not been pleasant. The discovery of his friend's body had pounded his brain with shock, and since then he had passed through his duties in a haze. Roloff had been a lifelong companion, and his death—which Luge could't even remember!—tore at the sailor's conscience like a festering wound.

Nevertheless, it was that experience, a potent spell cast by the mysterious stranger, that now compelled him to stir.

His shadowy figure moved from the rowing bench, toward the gunwale of the *Princess of Moonshae*. All around, northmen and Ffolk slumbered, while the keen-eyed helmsman—currently Knaff the Elder—studied the starlit horizon and the smooth surface of the sea with cautious diligence.

Crouching, Luge moved low between the benches until he reached the rail behind the shelter of several water barrels. Here he raised his head, peering cautiously over the gunwale of the speeding longship.

Huddled in the shadows of the casks, blacker even than the dim starlight above, Luge reached into a concealed pouch—a flap that had been sewn into the lining of his sea cloak. His eyes widened in surprise—until that moment he had not recalled the pouch's existence, though he had been present when Malawar attached it.

Within, he felt several tiny metallic pebbles. He selected one with his blunt thumb and forefinger and withdrew his hand. A tiny tinkle sounded in the night, too faint to carry even to the ears of the nearby northmen but enough to identify the object as a small bell.

Still wondering why he was doing it, Luge dropped the bell over the side. It splashed into the waters squarely at the mouth of Corwell Firth.

In the water, the bell continued to ring . . . but now its sound was magnified a thousand-, a millionfold. The tinkle became a pounding dirge, and its weight carried it through the sea for dozens and scores and ultimately hundreds of miles.

* * * * *

Along the vast, kelp-lined ridges and plains of the Coral Kingdom, the tiny bell ringing four hundred miles to the north sounded a call to war. Huge sahuagin armies, camped for weeks along coral reefs, mustered forth, swarming up from the sea bottom, driving themselves northward. The fishmen swam with strong kicks, their companies spreading through the depths, some swimming high, breaking the surface occasionally to observe the surrounding sea, while others swam at different levels, with the deepest swimming more an a thousand feet below.

The huge scrags, long teeth gleaming even in the dingy waters of the kingdom's Deepvale, formed columns, twelve scrags per column, each column more than a match for any merchant crew of humankind. Hulking beasts nearly twice as large as the fishmen, the sea trolls propelled their sleek bodies through the sea with powerful legs and thick, webbed feet. Hair, like loose strands of seaweed, trailed back from round, scale-coated skulls. The columns of the scrags swam in the center of the army, leaving the lesser creatures to scout.

Some of the aquatic warriors bore weapons—silver-tipped

spears or curved, shell-studded scimitars—but most relied on their multitudinous teeth and sharp, curving claws. Others trailed nets, hopeful of seizing captives, and a few were armed with bows and arrows, though these weapons would only be useful in the air or at extremely short range when submerged.

A hundred such columns and companies gathered around the palaces of the Coral Kingdom, swarming upward, through waters that passed from purple to blue to aqua and then to the pale green of the surface. The sahuagin veered to the sides when the scrag columns swam, the fishmen cowering away from the mighty and infinitely evil sea trolls.

Other creatures, too, emerged from the depths to swell the ranks of the undersea army. Schools of sharks and sinuous formations of eels took position on the flanks of the force. The sharks were particularly useful, for they ravaged with sudden and bloody attacks any unfortunate dolphins or whales that stumbled into the path of the great army. In this way, the movement could be kept secret from the merfolk and titans, the two implacable enemies of the scrags and their allies.

To the north they swam, faster by far than any human army could march overland, riding a graceful northerly current to increase their pace still more. The army's master was Coss-Axell-Sinioth, swimming among them in the body of the monstrous squid, propelling himself faster even than the sleekest scrag could swim. The minion of Talos relished his new command and knew that the bell signaled a forthcoming opportunity to blood his troops.

As they moved, the leaders—Sythissal of the sahuagin and Krell-Bane, king of the sea trolls—knew that their speed would not in itself be sufficient to catch the human ship if it continued its course away from them. But that fact did not worry them. It was for this very reason, they reminded themselves, that Sythissal had built and placed the Mantas.

For several days the army swam northward, and in that time it reached the first bell dropped by the agent of Sinioth. By then, three more bells had been dropped, one during each night of the longship's steady journey to the northwest.

Yet the fact that the humans had three days' lead on the army still didn't concern the aquatic generals, for here, at the mouth of Corwell Firth, the strongest swimmers among them would mount the Mantas.

After that, the seizing of the vessel was a matter of near certainty.

* * * * *

After seven days at sea, Alicia began to wonder if she would ever see land again. They had passed to the south of Moray near dawn on their third day out, and later that day the surf breaking against the Gullrocks had been visible to port. Since then there had been no sign of anything except water and sky.

Alicia found herself enjoying the sights and the sounds of the longship. Watching the way Brandon thrilled to the wind in his face and to the pitching of the deck beneath his feet, she began to appreciate the fundamental differences between his people and hers. All the northmen thrived thus, while many of the Ffolk spent as much time at the gunwale as in their seats, especially during the first few days of travel on the open sea.

"Imagine if we'd met foul weather," the princess said to her mother as the longship glided easily forward, propelled by the same southerly breeze that had escorted them placidly for the entire voyage. "I think half the bowmen would have jumped overboard!"

"They were a sick-looking lot a few days ago," Robyn agreed. "But we seem to be getting our sea legs now."

"True," replied the princess with a nod. "If only the sea were the greatest challenge we have to face!"

"Have faith, Daughter," said the queen, placing a gentle hand on Alicia's shoulder. The princess stared at the blue-green water swirling past the hull and nodded.

She thought of her father and of all the obstacles that still lay in their path. A now-familiar wave of despair threatened to sweep her hopes away at the sight of the implacable sea. How could they hope to enter that alien realm? And if they did, what dangers would they face? How would they find the king?

"Faith," Robyn repeated, squeezing her hand with firm pressure.

"I'll try," Alicia pledged.

Robyn moved on to talk to Tavish, and Alicia remained at the rail, her mind drifting as she watched the limitless expanse of waves. She was soon joined by Brigit, who had spent a good deal of time with the princess on the voyage. Though the two were centuries apart in age, Alicia had found herself developing a bond with the elfwoman that transcended such trivial concerns.

"And how are you ladies passing this lovely afternoon?" inquired Hanrald. The earl, who had grown increasingly restless during the voyage, ambled over to the rail.

"Fox hunting," the princess deadpanned. She smiled at Hanrald, but she was surprised to see his eyes pass over hers and come to light on Brigit. Nonplussed, Alicia turned away from the earl, wondering at his odd reaction.

She stood on the port side of the *Princess of Moonshae*, near the stern. Feeling a vague sense of worry, she cast her eyes across the water, looking for something—anything—out of the ordinary.

Because of this musing, she was the first one to see the disturbance.

"Look!" the princess cried, observing a mass of bubbles erupt from the water's surface less than a mile away. "What's that?"

White froth broke from the water, tossing a large, oval patch of sea into a foam-streaked torrent. Pressure bulged upward, forming a maelstrom larger than the *Princess of Moonshae* was long, completely obscured by the turbulence across its surface. The water rose into the air and then began to flow away, pouring off a massive shape that still lay concealed by the foaming brine.

"It came from beneath the water!" shouted the princess, as others witnessed the sudden appearance. Men cursed, shouting to their gods for aid. Bowmen nocked missiles into their strings, while Brandon's northmen stood to their oars and their weapons, waiting for the prince's command.

"What's that?" Alicia asked as numerous small objects came into view atop the huge platform. They wiggled and moved like living things.

"Barnacles?" inquired Keane, without much hope.

"Sahuagin—fishmen!" Tavish announced, squinting. Obviously the bard's eyes didn't suffer any from her age. Soon the others could make out the scaly humanoids swarming all over the thing that now began to look like an oval platform of some kind.

"You are only partly right," added Brandon, his tone grim. "Look more closely. You'll see that the *little* ones are sahuagin, but . . ."

"By the goddess!" gasped Alicia. "What are the others, then?"

"Scrags—sea trolls, by the look of them." Several dozen hulking shapes, nearly twice as large as the human-sized sahuagin scattered across the broad deck, moved among the smaller beasts with an unmistakable air of command.

"Have you seen them—these sea trolls—before?" Unconsciously Alicia gripped the hilt of her sword, drawing it several inches from her scabbard before tensely slamming it home again.

"Never. Few have, who've lived to tell the tale," announced the Prince of Gnarhelm, not very reassuringly. "Full sail!" he shouted next, turning to the sailors nearest the mast. "Starboard rudder!"

The *Princess* lurched as the surface of the sail was turned to catch the maximum force of the wind. The longship reeled around to the north, but none of them questioned the involuntary course change in light of the circumstances.

"They can't move that thing through the water, can they?" inquired Alicia as the changing course of the longship carried the strange apparatus around to the stern.

As if to challenge her statement, the princess soon saw numerous long-handled paddles appear in the hands of the sahuagin who were clustered on top of the great, raftlike craft. She saw several long poles running the length of the hull, each straddled by dozens of the scaly humanoids. Below each pole, a narrow gap lay open to the sea, allowing the creatures to paddle not only from the edges but also right through the raft's hull. All along the vessel's stern edge and sides, the waters churned as scrags kicked with their powerful legs and webbed feet.

"It not only moves," observed Brandon. "It goes damned fast!"

Indeed, the ungainly-appearing object raced toward them with surprising swiftness, trailing a foaming wake. A white wave split before the thing's bow, but the flat shape seemed to ride higher and higher out of the water as it continued to pick up speed.

"Can they catch us?" asked the princess, staring at the huge craft, trying to analyze whether it closed the gap between the two ships. It didn't, as far as she could tell—but neither did it get any farther away.

"If the wind holds," the prince announced between clenched teeth, "then we might be able to make it. If not . . ."

"What is that thing?" demanded Alicia, determined to find some means of dealing with this challenge.

"It seems to be nothing more than a flat platform, probably with a neutral buoyancy—it neither sinks nor floats on its own." Keane had obviously been thinking about the object, for he answered without hesitation.

"Why would they use it? Why not just swim?" persisted the princess.

"Look." The mage pointed. The broad raft skimmed across the surface of the water, bouncing through the swells in clouds of spray, breaking a broad, foaming wave to either side of the blunt prow. "I think it lets them travel faster on the surface than they could otherwise swim. See? A number of them can rest, while the craft still makes good time."

"*Excellent* time," noted the northman captain grimly. More than two hundred sahuagin manned the great paddles, while an unseen number of scrags propelled the craft by musclepower. More than a hundred additional scaly monsters of the deep sat patiently in the midst of the wide platform, bearing weapons and ready—and rested—for battle.

"Dead ahead—another raft of the critters!" The cry from the bow, by the barrel-chested Wultha, paralyzed Alicia for one terrorized moment, but in that space of time, the Prince of Gnarhelm had leaped down the center of the longship's hull and was scrambling up the neck of the proud figurehead, the princess racing to join him.

"By the hundred curses of Tempus!" snarled Brand, and in another moment, Alicia saw the cause of his distress.

She recognized the pattern of bubbles, saw the swells of the Trackless Sea mound upward as they had when the other raft had broken the surface. But this time, the obstacle lay directly in the *Princess of Moonshae*'s path!

"Hard port—emergency helm!" shouted the prince. Even before the order was completed, the vessel heeled violently as Knaff the Elder pulled the rudder to port. Alicia lost her footing and tumbled to the deck, falling heavily as the longship crunched into the broad raft of the sea creatures with a timber-straining collision.

*   *   *   *   *

"Death to the humans! Attack!" hissed Krell-Bane, fang-toothed king of the scrags. The Mantaship beneath his feet staggered from the impact with the speeding longship, but the sleek vessel's keel rode up onto the raft, and now the ship was stuck there.

Two columns of huge scrags lurched forward, while the smaller sahuagin threw themselves with abandon at the gunwale of the longship. Human defenders quickly scrambled to their positions, but even as Krell-Bane exhorted his troops, he saw northmen fall, slain by trident and scimitar, tooth and claw.

In another moment, the first of the fishmen had scrambled

onto the enemy craft.

In the darkness of the depths below, the body of a giant squid lurked, hearing the sounds of battle, waiting for the report of victory. Sinioth would not involve himself in this battle. Instead, he would let his children bring the bodies of his enemies to him.

☙ 10 ☙

Dance of the Mantas

Brandon cursed, and veteran northmen sailors tumbled from their rowing benches, dislodged by the force of the collision. The *Princess of Moonshae* shuddered violently as a cascade of seawater surged over the gunwale. Alicia scrambled to regain her balance, certain that the hull of the longship had been fatally punctured.

But as she stood again, the princess realized that the deck felt solid under her feet, and she could see no sign of a crack in the solid planks of the hull. She tried to tell herself that, just maybe, the *Princess of Moonshae* was not finished yet.

If water was not pouring in, however, the same could not be said of the sahuagin. Dozens of fishmen leaped toward the longship's hull as soon as the two vessels collided. In a few seconds, many of them sprang to the gunwales and scrambled into the shallow hull.

Following the impact, the prow of the longship rested on the broad, timbered deck of the enemy raft. Stout, waterlogged beams formed parallel keels separated by the long strips of water. Under the weight of Brandon's ship, the bow of the raft wallowed beneath the waves. With the fishmen scrambling all around, it seemed as though the two vessels were firmly locked together.

Brandon shouted an inarticulate cry and split a sahuagin skull with his great axe. Wultha picked up one of the creatures in his huge hands, snapping the creature's spine before casting it into the faces of two of the corpse's charging compatriots.

Keane, meanwhile, snapped the words to a quick spell and crushed something like dried threads in his left hand. He pointed at the fishmen with his right. Immediately strands of gooey string shot from his extended fingers, wrapping themselves about several of the approaching monsters, binding them securely to the hull. The creatures snapped and snarled, but their most diligent struggles couldn't break them free. Even more were ensnared as they attempted to crawl over the original targets of the web.

Hanrald, holding his great longsword in both hands, cleaved his way through a pack of the sea monsters, slicing a huge scrag into pieces small enough that he could kick them over the side. The lack of armor, which he would have worn for any battle on land, didn't slow his aggressive tactics in the least. He shouted and roared, leaping this way and that, muscles tensing for each bone-crushing blow.

But not all of the attacks went the way of the humans. Three northmen in the bow fell, fatally wounded in the first rush before they even had time to draw their weapons. Others felt the kiss of sahuagin steel—hooks and spears, scimitars and tridents—as more and more of the creatures spilled into the longship's hull.

Alicia's keen longsword drove through the shelled breastplate of a scale-faced fishman, and then she gasped as the creature fell, for beyond it loomed a much more formidable foe.

Nobody had to tell her that this was one of the scrags. A wide mouth, like a shark's, gaped open to reveal many rows of short, barbed teeth. Stringy hair, like strands of pale kelp, straggled across the monster's smooth scalp, while pale, dead eyes stared with all the emotion of a fish.

But there was plenty of threat in the creature's actions as it raised a double-pronged spear and aimed it at the unarmored princess. Powerfully clawed feet gripped the gunwale as the creature loomed, monstrously huge.

"*Incendrius!*" Keane barked the single word that cast one of his most powerful spells, a magical command that caused a tiny pebble of flame to burst from his finger and drift, with a deceptively gentle and wavering flight, like a seed borne by a gentle breeze, toward the gunwale of the *Princess*.

"Down!" shouted the mage, then watched as Alicia scrambled back from the looming horror of the scrag.

The fireball exploded with a white flash that, for a split second, seemed to outshine the sun. The mage had pushed the center of the spell well past the longship's hull, but tongues of flame sizzled outward in a seething hellfire that licked along the gunwale and singed a corner of the sail. Several scrags perched on the rail vanished, incinerated to ashes in less than a second, and the following wave of sahuagin perished, shrieking, in another moment.

The respite gave the princess enough time to climb to her feet. She thought of her staff and immediately seized the shaft of wood, stamped it on the deck, and shouted the command: "*Phyrosyne!*"

The shaft began to grow, extending upward in shoots of green branches, planting feet to either side. The tree creature reached out with its tough, branchlike hands—and promptly fell over as the longship rocked on a gentle swell. The flailing branches knocked sahuagin and northmen down together as the magical being struggled to gain its balance on the unstable platform.

Exasperated, Alicia raised her sword against another scaly, fang-bristling face that appeared at the gunwale. She could hear the crunching and creaking of timbers as the two wooden hulls scraped together, a sound broken by the screams of sahuagin and scrags crushed between the vessels.

She sliced the head from one of the fishmen, ignoring the gore that spewed from its neck. The corpse toppled backward, and then once more she faced a huge sea troll. The creature sprang to the gunwale, balancing on its clawed, webbed feet while it brandished a trident over its head and thumped a fist against its solid, heavily muscled chest.

The princess darted forward to attack, deflecting the monster's forked weapon and gashing its thigh with her silver longsword. The creature bellowed and thrust, driving the prongs of its trident into the deck beside Alicia's foot. It struggled momentarily to pull the three-pronged spear free, and this was all the opening the princess needed.

Alicia aimed a wicked slash at the thing's scaly belly, watching as her keen steel sliced halfway through the vulnerable area. The sea troll gagged and choked, slipping backward as green blood spurted into the longship, across Alicia's legs. She paused, gasping for breath, waiting for the creature to fall dead.

Instead, she saw the gashes in the scrag's body slowly mend themselves, as if an invisible pair of healing hands pulled the sides of the wound together and bound them. For several moments, the monster wobbled, as if it would still perish, but then its eyes snapped open, boring into Alicia, and once again the creature raised its trident.

Forcing her dread to the back of her mind, Alicia lifted her sword to parry the coming blow, feeling as if she moved through a dream. The blade clashed against the gleaming steel tines, but one of the barbed tips scored a gouge across the woman's shoulder, tearing through her light tunic to puncture her skin. The princess ignored the pain, driving her own blade inside the creature's defenses, plunging the tip through the monster's belly and then pushing forward with all her strength.

Green blood splashed over her hand, and she felt the bile that rose in her throat. With a final shove, she forced the monster backward, off the rail, then clung to her sword with all her might as the beast fell away, almost dragging her weapon with it.

Finally she pulled the gore-streaked blade free and slumped against the gunwale, looking for her next opponent. A few sahuagin fought for their lives against the men of Brandon's crew, but they quickly met a gory fate. A pair of huge scrags, their bodies punctured by dozens of arrows from the Corwellian bowmen, stood back to back in the center of the hull. Brandon and Wultha led a charge that dragged the two creatures down to the deck. Numerous weapons hacked the sea trolls into immobility, and retching sailors tossed the grim remains into the sea, where they would doubtlessly regenerate.

Alicia could see that the *Princess of Moonshae* had at last passed the huge raft, breaking free to carve her course through the sea. Worriedly she looked ahead, remembering how the second raft had risen from the sea directly in their path. Now both craft of the aquatic attackers frothed through the water to the stern.

That knowledge was minimal consolation, however, for the flailing paddles on the flat rafts propelled both of them along the longship's wake with shocking quickness. The second vessel took a little while to get up to speed, but soon it was planing across the waves, driving forward even a little faster than the first one.

Still, the battle had ended for the moment. The oarsmen labored in the longship's hull, and the *Princess* moved with stately grace away from the attackers. Alicia's tree creature, still unable to gain its balance in the ship, settled in the hull, and she commanded it back into its staff form, irritated against her better judgement with her enchanted but clumsy ally.

Robyn stood at the stern, watching the two vessels and their complements of screaming, scaled monstrosities. Then she turned back toward the bow, looking upward at the wide sail that caught the gentle breeze—but not enough to pull them away from their enemies.

The High Queen closed her eyes and reached for the power of her goddess. The Earthmother heard and answered the call of her Great Druid.

And the sail bulged outward with a freshening wind.

* * * * *

The man awakened after a very long time . . . years, or perhaps a lifetime.

Perhaps even longer.

He sat up and looked around, reaching toward his side, driven by instinct to grasp for something. But what? Whatever it had been, it wasn't there now. *Nothing* was there now, beyond his skin and a pale white tunic that barely covered his nakedness.

A sword—that's what he reached for. He recalled an image now, indistinct but coming into focus. He saw a silvery blade, sensed its sharpness along both edges, *felt* the strength inherent in the gleaming steel.

Where am I?

The man looked around. His surroundings were dark, but not black. Long panels lined the ceiling, huge surfaces of opaque glass. From beyond, there issued a dull glow, like a distant lantern diffused through a mound of emeralds.

He saw a surface . . . for sleeping, the hard slab where he had awakened. A *bed*—he recalled the term from somewhere. This one was made of a hard substance, like rock, but a little softer to the touch. He ground granules of the stuff away with the palm of his hand. Not rock—what was it?

An image came to him of surf, of long white breakers pouring onto a beach, and blocky objects in the water—like this thing that made his bed.

Coral. The word came to him, and he felt a small measure of pleasure.

A noise sounded somewhere in the distance, and once again he reached reflexively for the sword. But something was strange in that motion, something beyond the fact that he had no weapon.

He looked down, and his eyes widened in shock. The movement felt unnatural, he realized, because he had only one hand! His left arm ended at the wrist, in a clean, well-healed wound that was nevertheless none too old.

Again the man looked around, at the strange canopy overhead and the walls of solid coral. He noticed a pool of still, dark water. There seemed to be no other way in or out of the chamber.

And then a deeper question came, beyond the wheres and the whys. The man slumped to the coral bed with a groan, but he resisted the urge to lower his head. Instead, he raised his face to the ceiling and spoke.

"Who am I?" he asked.

But no one and nothing answered.

* * * * *

Mastery of Caer Callidyrr was an idle pastime to Deirdre. The offices of her mother and father in truth required little attention during these summer days. Royal court was not in session, nor were there any pressing matters of diplomacy or war to concern her.

Instead, she found time for the tasks that were dear to her— the study of her magic, and the contemplation of the world she saw in her mirror.

It was to the latter that she found herself drawn more and more, as if she sensed that she could learn more from the glass than from any dense tome or musty volume.

Shortly after she had teleported from Corwell to Callidyrr, she located the *Princess of Moonshae* in the mirror. The image, she learned, displayed an easy affinity for locating Deirdre's mother or her sister. As soon as she imagined the wide expanse of Corwell Firth—and, on later days, the Trackless Sea—the image of the sleek longship came into focus. As always, she could move closer, like a gull diving toward the wavetops, and steady her vision with as much detail as she desired.

But that proved rather a mundane activity. There was little variance, as the days passed, in the activities of the crew or passengers on the long voyage. Even the weather remained fixed in its clear sky and light, favorable wind.

Deirdre had quickly thought of using the mirror to seek her father, but she found no such link as with her female kin. Instead, she probed the depths of the ocean, but saw only vast seas, giant fish, and a dark, featureless floor.

There was one more whom Deirdre desired to seek through the glass, yet thus far she had lacked the courage. Still, she remembered the tingle of recognition when she had spied him at the Corwell festival. This was the one she had called Malawar. There had been a powerful affinity in that sensation, as well as very real fear.

Deirdre felt nothing romantic nor even vaguely affectionate

in that attraction. Rather, she thought of Malawar as a mighty source of power, a source that she had barely mastered once, and then only to send it away. But now her mind had begun to think more ambitious thoughts: If she could but *capture* that power, channel it to her own ends . . .

The possibilities seemed unlimited.

* * * * *

The being that so occupied Deirdre's thoughts remained in the seas below the *Princess of Moonshae*. Sinioth lurked in the depths, awaiting the progress of the Mantaships with growing impatience. The gap narrowed, but too slowly for the avatar's desires. Sythissal, king of the sahuagin, remained below the sea with his master, while Krell-Bane commanded the attacking force on the surface.

It was the power of the accursed goddess, he knew, that sustained the unnatural wind. Normally the sleek rafts of the scrags should have overtaken the longship by now. But instead, he was forced to endure this crawling chase.

But the longship had sailed far from the Moonshaes now, and the great druid drew her strength from the very localized presence of the Earthmother. Surely she could not maintain this magic forever!

Seething with the impatience of his hatred, Coss-Axell-Sinioth tried to settle down and wait.

❧ 11 ❧

Goddesswind

"A week out from Corwell and they find us!" stormed Brandon, pacing back and forth in the *Princess of Moonshae*'s forehull.

In the stern, Robyn still stood like a statue, facing the sail, the canvas sheet billowed taut as ever, propelling the longship through the waters at a churning pace. Far behind now but still clinging to the long white trail of the vessel's wake came the two broad rafts and their clamoring passengers.

"Terrible luck, I know, but at least—" Alicia started to speak.

"Luck? There's no luck about it!" Brandon snapped, whirling toward her and interrupting. "They *found* us, somehow—here, eight hundred miles from the Moonshaes, in the middle of the Trackless Sea!"

Alicia glowered at him, but her anger was rooted in embarrassment. He was right, of course.

"There are ways a skilled sorcerer could locate us wherever we were," pointed out Keane.

"Did you see any sign of magic in that attack?" shot back the Prince of Gnarhelm.

"No."

"It's not like the sea creatures to use magic." Brandon's tone modulated somewhat, as if he suddenly remembered that he was surrounded by friends, not enemies. "And if they don't use it to attack, I can't imagine they've got wizards sitting around spying on us."

"What *do* you suspect, then?" demanded Alicia.

"I don't know," the captain admitted with a shrug. He looked around, at the casks and crates and seabags that lined the center of the longship's hull. "It's possible they might have placed something on board, some object that draws them like a beacon. I don't know how big it would be or even what it would look like, but it's all that I can think of at the moment."

They spent the next six hours tearing the *Princess of Moonshae*'s contents apart while the rafts drifted farther to the rear, never quite disappearing over the horizon. Every crate, every container of any kind was opened and examined. Crew members sifted flour from barrel to barrel and drained each water cask into another through a fine screen mesh. As to the search of individual crewmen, of course, every man was left to his own possessions—all the northmen and the Ffolk accompanying the expedition had been selected with loyalty as the top consideration.

All this time Robyn stood in rapt concentration, and the wind summoned by the goddess propelled the longship forward. The druid queen resisted any attempts to support her, shrugging off the few hands that came close. Her eyes were open, staring at the sail but focused on something much farther away.

"Nothing," Alicia concluded disgustedly after the search of the longship's bow was completed. She and Brigit had coordinated that scrutiny, and now the pair leaned on the rail, watching the gray-green water slip past a few feet below.

"I heard the captain talking," the elfwoman noted. "He said that if we can make it to nightfall, we should be able to slip away from them—and your mother can rest, as long as there's any breeze at all."

"I hope so," replied the princess, with a look at the sun. It was early evening, but the yellow orb was at least a couple of hours away from the horizon. And here, on the flat northern sea, she remembered that the daylight lasted for an hour or more after sunset. For a while, they stood in silence, unconsciously looking to the west—toward Evermeet, or least to where they imagined the elvenhome to be.

"Brigit . . ." Alicia looked down, wondering about the future, wanting to plan a known course to her father's rescue, though of course this was impossible. "I've been wondering about Evermeet. What's it like? Who rules there?"

"It is a wondrously beautiful place, dotted with clear lakes, covered with broad stretches of forest. It is also the largest, most populous nation of elves in all the Realms." Brigit turned to Alicia to make her point. "In fact, while elven realms in the outer lands are usually ruled by matriarchs or lords, Evermeet is ruled by a queen, the only true monarch in elvendom."

"Does she rule alone?"

"For the most part. She has many councilors, it is said, and a council of matrons acts as her advisers. I have heard that she is not afraid, however, to ignore their advice and make a decision on her own."

"When we get there, what will you say? Do you think the elves of Evermeet will help us?" Alicia wondered. "Or are there too many who feel as Erashanoor, that we humans are the enemy?"

"There are others more . . . open-minded," Brigit allowed, and then she laughed. "And there's no telling what your mother will accomplish, if she has the chance to talk to the queen."

"How can we be sure she'll get that chance?"

Brigit smiled, her face sympathetic. "With the determination of humans like you and Hanrald to back her up, I wouldn't be surprised to see it," the elfwoman said.

"I wonder if we can persuade them to help us—for the elves' own interests," Alicia questioned.

"I've been thinking about what your mother said—in the Argen-Tellirynd," replied the sister knight, almost as if she were musing to herself. "Doesn't it seem possible—even likely—that the same forces are at work against both of our peoples? That the dark powers commanding the scrags are the same that unleashed the Elf-Eater and closed the Synnorian Gate?"

"It *does!* I've wondered about that myself—but we have no proof. Can you be sure?"

"Can we be sure that *isn't* the case?" wondered Brigit. "And based on that premise, perhaps the only way to open the Fey-Alamtine is to defeat the forces that hold your father prisoner."

Alicia was forced to smile at the elfwoman's determination. "I wish you luck!"

"I believe that I can make the case," Brigit replied. "But I'm not sure that I'll find anyone impartial enough to listen—if we get there at all!"

"We'll get there!" declared the princess, more vehemently than she had intended. Trying to conceal her concern from Brigit, she looked aft.

She saw her mother standing as if carved from stone, with the proud sail billowing overhead. Beyond, past the transom and far down the foam-flecked line of the longship's wake, two black smudges lay against the horizon. These were the flat-ships of the sea creatures, and they remained well back.

Then her eyes were drawn back to the ship with a shock as Robyn groaned and staggered on the afterdeck. Immediately Tavish reached her side, holding Robyn's elbows and gently lowering her to the deck. Keane knelt beside the queen in another instant as Alicia raced down the center of the hull.

"I'm all right!" Robyn insisted as her daughter got there. Robyn sat up and brushed away the hands supporting her. "You'd think I was an old woman!"

"Are you really okay?" inquired Alicia, kneeling before her mother. For a moment, Robyn's eyes softened, and the younger woman saw a terrible exhaustion there.

"I . . . I just need to rest," the queen assured her.

For the first time since her mother's collapse, Alicia looked overhead. The once proud sail hung slack, undisturbed by any breath of wind, as if the real breeze had abandoned them at the same time as did the enchanted one.

"Swing out the oars! Clear those benches!" barked Brandon, and his crewmen scrambled to obey. He turned to Alicia, her own concern mirrored in his eyes. "We'll try to keep ahead of them until nightfall. Then we'll lose them in the dark and turn back to the west."

"Will that work?" asked Alicia, hating the sound of the question. Her faith was wavering, but she didn't want that fact to show.

"It's all we've got," replied Brandon with a shrug and a quizzical look at her.

Alicia rose from her knees and looked over the transom. Already, it seemed, the black dots had begun to grow.

* * * * *

In the darkest hours of the night, the longship *Princess of Moonshae* advanced across the black sea to the muffled strokes of oars, but no other sounds. For hours, the vessel slipped across the placid sea. The men labored at the oars. Even the Ffolk took turns wielding the heavy oaken poles, but they had no way of knowing whether or not the sea beasts on their great rafts were closing the distance.

Past midnight, the crew shuffled places once more. Those who had been resting took places on the rowing benches, while the exhausted sailors from the earlier shift tried to catch a little rest.

It was after this adjustment that the sailor, Luge, found himself at an oar, seated beside the gunwale of the longship. On each night of the voyage, he had performed his task faithfully, dropping one of the tiny bells over the side, plainly marking the longship's course for the pursuing hordes of the Underdeep.

Yet tonight he found himself with a problem. For the first time, the crew remained active through the hours of darkness, and Luge had yet to perform his duty. Not understanding why, he grew more and more agitated as time passed. Now he tried to maintain the pace of his oar while slipping a hand into his tunic, fumbling at the concealed pocket.

"Careful, by Tempus!" snarled a fellow sailor as Luge's oar collided with his neighbor's.

"Sorry," he grunted, turning to nod at the grumbling northman. At the same time, he placed his hand on the gunwale and allowed the tiny bell to drop into the water.

Immediately it began to ring.

*　*　*　*　*

The wind had abandoned them completely, Alicia told herself when she awakened to the pale blue light of predawn. An utterly still expanse of water surrounded them. It was too dark to see very far, but she had to wonder about the presence of the twin rafts.

Diffused light gave way to a banner of sunrise on the horizon, and details became apparent up to a mile away, and then two, except that there were no details, save for the eternal calm of the sea.

Then they could see three miles, and at the same time, they discovered the rafts. No one had to announce the observation; it was silently shared by every person on the ship. The two flat slabs came at them like huge, implacable sharks. They were close enough for the crew to hear the snapping of wide, fishlike jaws, and the slicing noise of the two massive rafts' passage over the water.

Not a breath of wind stirred the flat, seemingly endless sea. The only waves were the twin plumes cast by the *Princess of Moonshae*. The vessel, despite the efforts of the straining oarsmen, seemed to labor only with great reluctance through the water. In the hush, the rhythmic cadence of the sea beasts' paddling came to them, a dull pulsing that moved through the sea, sounding a beat of approaching doom.

"Stroke, you miserable lubbers!" shouted Brandon, but men could not increase their effort when it was already strained to the maximum. A martial chord suddenly rang through the air as Tavish again raised her harp, the need for stealth past. The playing of that enchanted weapon filled the weary sailors with strength, and once again the longship moved with a feeling approaching speed.

Yet it was not enough. After a few minutes of watching, it became apparent that the monsters still closed the gap between them.

"How did those devils find us?" spat the Prince of Gnarhelm, glaring to the rear as if his anger alone could incinerate the bizarre rafts.

"Through the dark of the night, no less," Alicia agreed. Subconsciously she looked for Keane. It seemed that now, with disaster so near at hand, the wizard was the only one who could offer them a chance of escape.

But he wasn't even paying attention. The princess saw him in the prow, peering before them, studying the flat water in their path. The mage's posture, his whole attitude, depicted raw tension. Abruptly he pulled a small vial of dust from a pouch of his robe and pinched a small portion of it between a finger and thumb. Then he let the dust fly, at the same time chanting the command words for a spell.

Alicia noticed that many of the crewmen were also watching the mage—as if they expect him to pull some kind of miraculous rabbit from his hat, she thought with annoyance. Then she realized with a flash of shame that she had been doing the same thing.

Abruptly all thoughts of salvation from that quarter were dashed when the mage stiffened, then whirled back to face Brandon and Knaff the Elder, who still manned the helm.

"Turn!" shrieked Keane, more agitated than Alicia had ever seen him. "That way—turn left!" He pointed, the tension in his body transferred in full to his voice. "Now, if you value your lives!"

Knaff hesitated a moment, looking to Brandon, but the captain didn't question the mage's warning. "Do it!" he bellowed, and the helmsman threw the rudder hard to port.

At her leisurely speed, the *Princess of Moonshae* didn't heel or rock from the force of the turn. Instead, the longship meandered through a sweeping, gradual change of direction. To Alicia, it seemed as though they were mired in mud. She stared at Keane, at the calm sea beyond him, and wondered if he had lost his mind.

A danger of the turn became apparent when she looked backward. The two broad rafts seemed much closer, and now, with the longship sailing across their path instead of away from them, they seemed to advance with shocking speed.

Then she became aware of a sound or vibration—an ominous rumble so deep that Alicia *felt* rather than heard it. The others, too, sensed the disturbance. All talk ceased, and even the oarsmen cocked their ears at the water as they strained with redoubled efforts toward their task. Alicia saw, with a sickening sense of shock, that the faces of many of the veteran seamen had blanched with terror.

The *Princess of Moonshae* began to tremble with a vibration that could no longer be doubted. It seized the vessel as if in a giant fist, and the longship quivered helplessly in its grasp. Still Alicia couldn't hear any audible noise, but the rumbling sensation reached into the pit of her stomach.

Then, finally, beginning like the roll of distant thunder, carried like an echo across a series of ridges, the sound came. Swiftly the rumbling gained force, and the hull of the ship shook so that it seemed as if the planks must soon be torn from the hull.

Tavish pounded her harp, tearing across the strings with her fingers, and the music rose up as if to challenge this unnatural disturbance. But it was no contest.

The only consolation came with a look to the rear. The two rafts of sea creatures were drifting as the monsters looked this way and that, obviously seeking the source of the same rumbling that afflicted the longship.

"At least we know *they're* not causing it," the princess remarked to Brigit, who once again stood beside her.

"They seem to be as worried as we are," the elfwoman agreed. "Though I'm not sure that's good news."

The momentum of the rafts had carried them well forward, into the same area where Keane had first sounded the alarm. Now they came about, veering to port so as to continue to close with the *Princess of Moonshae*. Like the humans, however, the aquatic monsters remained preoccupied with the mysterious vibrations that seemed to disturb this whole area of the sea.

"Look! On the surface, there!" shouted Keane, pointing toward the waters at the rear.

"*Under* the water!" Brand corrected. "Something's moving—fast!"

At first, they wondered if it might not be another of the flat rafts, for the appearance of bubbles and movement beneath the water was reminiscent of their arrival. In the stress of the moment, no one remembered that there had been no vibration preceding their surfacing. The current phenomenon also seemed to affect a larger area of water.

The rafts drove closer, propelled by the paddles once again, as the sahuagin and scrags who weren't rowing stood up on their platforms and brandished weapons and fists toward the humans. A trap was about to close. One raft approached the *Princess* from dead astern, while the other closed from port quarter.

And then the *Princess of Moonshae* pitched violently forward, her stern rising into the air, lifted by a powerful force from below. The longship shot ahead, sliding down a frothing wall of white water as if the ocean had been turned on edge. Spray flew upward, propelled by some massive undersea explosion, and a shower of water spilled into the rear of the suddenly careening longship.

The sea behind them continued to rise, swirling into the air, spewing a shower of brine to all sides but continuing to spin upward in a huge, towering column of seawater. A dark shape appeared in the liquid pillar. The raft directly behind the longship had been seized in the whirlpool and dragged upward with the force of the rising water.

"The Cyclones of Evermeet!" shouted Alicia.

Abruptly another of the great columns spewed upward from before them, and then a third and a fourth spouted from the surface. More and more of the vast, churning pillars of seawater spumed skyward, each more than a hundred paces across and apparently cylindrical all the way up the frothing surface. Water sprayed out from each, creating a drenching shower wherever the companions turned. Obviously the water thus lost was replaced, for the columns seemed to grow still larger as the awestruck witnesses watched.

Five hundred feet above them, the column of water spewed out the great raft. The flat vessel had swirled around and around the column, carried steadily upward until this point. For a few brief moments, the huge object seemed to float in the air, but then it plummeted seaward with steadily increasing speed. Hundreds of tiny forms spilled free, writhing in the air and clutching for some kind of support.

The raft struck the water flat on its hull, shooting spray for hundreds of feet to all sides and splintering into pieces from the force of the impact. Many of the raft's passengers landed atop the suddenly immobile object, perishing instantly from the long, screaming fall.

The *Princess of Moonshae* careened to the side, once again driven by the wind, which had freshened dramatically at the same time as the cyclones had appeared. Now Knaff the Elder guided them away from the nearest waterspout, steering as far from it as possible while still bearing west.

Within moments, white water surrounded them. Needles of spray lashed skin and stung eyes, while the roaring of angry water rose to a thunderous crescendo. Knaff, high on the helmsman's stand, tried to see what lay in their path, but he, too, was blinded by the torrent.

They might have reached the end of the world then, for with sudden abruptness the *Princess of Moonshae* plunged over the lip of an unseen drop, plummeting downward at breakneck speed.

* * * * *

"A Manta—destroyed!" Fury drove Coss-Axell-Sinioth to new heights of violence. His squid form lashed about in the depths of the Trackless Sea, the great tentacles crushing any scrags and sahuagin unfortunate enough to be caught by the stunning blows.

"But so are the humans!" hissed Krell-Bane, trembling before the avatar's rage. "They must certainly be dead!" The giant sea troll, master of his race and ruling monarch of the

Coral Kingdom, unwisely spat his own anger back at the giant squid. "They sailed full into the Cyclones of Evermeet, and it's common knowledge that no air-breather can survive that tempest!"

"Can you bring me their bodies?" demanded the giant squid.

Now the sea monarch trembled before the wrath of his master. Still, the scrag king was forced to shake his head in negative response.

"Where is the other Manta?" inquired the avatar, his tone dropping to a deep rumble of menace—like an undersea earthquake, thought Krell-Bane, distant but promising the imminent arrival of a crushing wave of pressure.

"It patrols outside the Cyclone belt, awaiting the humans," explained the scrag, hoping the news would be well received. "If the ship should somehow escape—and I assure your Excellency that that is virtually impossible—then—"

"I thought you told me that it *was* impossible," the great squid shape reminded the scrag.

"Yes. It is—for all practical purposes, of course. There's no way—"

"Enough!" snapped Coss-Axell-Sinioth, finally growing tired of his minion's groveling. "Send all the troops we can muster to form a line at the outer edge of the cyclone belt. If they emerge, they are to be tracked and observed—not attacked until *I* give the word. Is that understood?"

The sea beast bowed and nodded cravenly.

"Then begone!" commanded the great squid. "Return to me when you have news!"

The sea king darted away, quickly vanishing into the emerald depths. Coss-Axell-Sinioth watched him go, growling deep in his black heart. He itched for vengeance, but had no ready target for his hatred—nothing nearby, at any rate.

His thoughts drifted to the south, to the bright coral castles in the ocean shallows of Kyrasti and the air-filled prisons formed therein. Sinioth summoned the king of the sahuagin, who had waited safely out of the avatar's range. The fishman was considerably relieved that it was the scrag who bore the onus of the attack's failure.

"Come, my faithful one," ordered the giant squid, and the hulking sahuagin, the largest living member of his race, obeyed. "It is time for you to return to the grotto. There you must tend to the prisoner."

♣ 12 ♣

The Warder
of Evermeet

White water surged across the gunwales and showered from the sky in a seemingly endless stream. The dizzying plunge proved brief, but the sleek ship still raced blindly down a crashing wave. The *Princess of Moonshae* sagged in the water, loaded with the increasing weight of her own liquid ballast. All around, like a forest of massive columns, the pillars of water spewed upward, throwing seawater into the air with volcanic force.

"Bail! Bail for your lives!" cried Brandon, though nearly everyone aboard the ship was already doing just that.

The only exceptions were the Prince of Gnarhelm himself, who scanned the heaving water between the cyclones, looking for the safest passage, and Knaff the Elder, who clung to the rudder with a strength that belied his age. He may as well have been a part of the longship, feet nailed in place and wooden arms locked around the shaft with bands of steel sinew.

The High Queen lay still on a makeshift litter near the transom, her arms calmly crossed on her chest, as if she took no notice of the maelstrom around them. Her cheeks were pale and hollow, her breathing slow and deep.

"Starboard!" snarled the captain, and Knaff leaned on the rudder. The *Princess of Moonshae* scored a clean arc around the base of one of the monstrous spouts, racing like a diving bird, the force of the turn rocking the vessel far to the side.

"Now port—*hard*, man!" Brandon leaned to the left, as if his own weight would help the longship obey his command. Again Knaff anticipated the order, pressing hard in the opposite direction and hauling the vessel through the reverse of her previous turn.

They advanced with reckless speed, surrounded by vast

whirlpools, water that spumed and swirled with the unleashed energy of the mighty sea. The waterspouts in the distance seemed as inanimate as stone-faced mountains or landscapes. Nearby, however, the cyclones seethed and sprayed like living, flowing things.

Frantic sailors seized every bucket and cup, everything that could conceivably be used to scoop water. Arms churning, the crew bailed like madmen and madwomen. The water level in the ship remained just barely constant, as the *Princess of Moonshae* glided around the cyclones with lumbering grace.

Abruptly the longship hit a great wave, a swell that rose as a monstrous barrier in their path. Wind filled the sail, pressing forward and up, but the sleek vessel's momentum inevitably slowed. Brand clenched his teeth, looking at the crest that foamed and frothed above the figurehead. Then the *Princess of Moonshae* heeled away from the height, and for a sickening, drawn-out moment, the ship slid sideways on her keel, slipping down the wave and teetering, on the verge of capsizing. Only Knaff's skilled use of the rudder—Brandon didn't even try to command him at this perilous juncture—and the longship's superb construction and wide beam saved them from total disaster.

The helmsman guided the ship through a mad plunge down the flowing slope, through a dip between four pillars, and up a lower slope that blocked their path to the north. The vessel's speed carried them over this ridge, and for a moment, she perched on the brink of two swells.

Gasping from the strain of bailing, Alicia paused for a moment and looked ahead, awestruck.

The foaming pillars extended as far as she could see in all directions, intermixed by perilous whirlpools, all of it angry seawater, eager to chew up the longship and spit forth pieces of driftwood.

The only benefit—and it could not be overlooked—was that all sign of the pursuing rafts had been lost. Indeed, the crew took some heart from the fact that they had witnessed one of them destroyed. But now rows of pillars extended to the north and south for a dozen miles. The view to east and west was more restricted—columns of water stood directly before them in many places, and a second row of pillars blocked the view through the gaps.

Still, there seemed to be a rhythm to the churning mess between the spouts. The water rose into a whitewater crest, almost like a ridge of land, where each pair of pillars came relatively close together—as a rule, the narrower the gap, the higher the swell.

Conversely, the areas centered between three or four pillars tended to dip, with water flowing down into these shallow bowls from all sides. Knaff displayed breathtaking skill in guiding the *Princess of Moonshae* down these slopes, while Brandon studied the two or three gaps leading out of the bowl. Selecting the one offering the easiest passage, he commanded the steersman to turn, and the sleek longship shot upward like an arrow, propelled by the momentum of her downward run.

Spray filled the air, and often they sailed through blinding mist, but the two northmen looked upward, locating the columns that reached to the sky. Somehow, even with such scant navigational aid, Brandon and Knaff kept the longship afloat. A dozen times, a hundred times they avoided disaster only by the instantaneous press of Knaff's steady hand on the tiller, or by Brandon's keen eye spotting the one course allowing them a minimal chance of survival.

"Look!" cried Brigit from the bow, her voice thrilling with hope.

Alicia scrambled to her side, moving unsteadily from handhold to handhold through the lurching hull. "What?" she gasped, wiping the spray from her eyes.

"There! I see blue sky!"

"Yes!" It was true! A pair of wide, trunklike waterspouts stood before them, and beyond yawned an expanse of azure. They couldn't see the water below the pillars, for between the waterspouts loomed the largest ridge of heaving sea they had yet encountered. It looked like a precipitous mountain pass perched between two lofty, unassailable summits. Yet there was no choice—to the right and left, virtually converging columns of water formed sheer waterfalls, impossible to traverse.

"Dead ahead!" shouted Brandon as the *Princess* raced down the chute leading to the rise. Bobbing and twisting like a canoe in a torrential rapids, the craft plunged dizzily, seemingly out of control. Careening wildly, the longship keeled over, burying the port gunwale in spray. A tiny adjustment by Knaff and she heeled back, dipping the starboard rail toward the surface before bobbing upright.

Then the heaving slope lay before them, and the *Princess of Moonshae* raced into the water, climbing steadily but quickly losing the speed she had picked up on the descent. The sail spread wide, bulging with a following wind, but it wouldn't be enough.

For a sickening, paralyzing moment, the ship teetered on the brink of disaster, a downward slip that would inevitably turn her beam to the slope and capsize the sturdy craft. Alicia's heart pounded. Oddly, she felt fear only that they would end the mission before it had had a chance to begin.

"Father . . ." she whispered, staring into the churning froth, terrified it would be the last thing she said to him.

"By the goddess, give me *breath!*" shouted Robyn. Unnoticed, the queen had pushed herself up from her litter until she stood at the stern, leaning weakly against the transom. The *Princess of Moonshae* sank backward, and water surged into the hull, nearly sweeping Robyn off her feet. "*Blow, wind!*" she cried, raising both her hands.

The longship tipped sickeningly, and then a surge of wind exploded, billowing out the sail, creaking the mast as if it would tear the proud pole from the keel. Groaning from the strain, the vessel reeled at the edge of doom, the weight of the ship and all the water in her hull dragging her downward, but the miraculous wind, the power of the goddess herself, filling the sail steadily.

Slowly the longship broke from equilibrium, inching through the spray, plowing ever so slowly to the crest of the watery ridge. Then the bow passed the summit, plowing upward into open air. The *Princess of Moonshae* stood poised, bow pointed toward the sky, stern buried in white water. The Great Druid of the isles stood by the sheer force of will, commanding the power of nature to push the vessel the last few inches to safety. But still the longship teetered. . . .

And then Robyn groaned. Her face drained of blood and she dropped like a felled tree, slamming roughly into the deck. Disaster loomed as the ship slipped back toward the slope, but one more gust of wind kicked up, whether from nature or goddess did not matter. It filled the sail and pushed, and the sleek vessel at long last tipped forward, bow dropping and stern climbing.

They started down the slope, and Alicia's eyes were filled with dizzying impressions, all of them fantastic. She saw blue water stretched placidly before them, after this one final slope of spilling spray. They had passed the barrier to Evermeet! And then even more glad tidings, at the limit of the horizon—a long strip of solidity: land! It beckoned them with verdant and pastoral beauty, promising a safe harbor after the nightmare passage of the last day.

"Evermeet!" cried Brigit, spotting the land at the horizon. "We've made it!"

Cheers broke from everyone—northman, Ffolk, and elf— aboard the *Princess of Moonshae*. The proud vessel slid with dizzying speed down the last sloping wave, and this time the ride was exhilarating. Gracefully gliding away from the torrent of the waterspouts onto a surface of gently rolling swells, the longship leaned jauntily, once again heeling to the soft press of the wind in her sail.

As the companions watched, the seething barrier of the cyclones slowly settled as one by one the columns collapsed back to the sea. A swell of water rolled outward from the fading torrent, but the *Princess of Moonshae* easily cut through that minor disturbance. Finally she slid across a smooth and unmarked sea, with the growing line of the horizon beckoning them forward.

"They stopped after we passed," Brandon observed in quiet awe. "As if our presence triggered their appearance, and they lasted as long as we stayed within their domain."

Alicia patted the gunwale beneath her hands and smiled softly. "You said you'd sail her to the ends of the earth if you could. Was that close enough?"

"As close as I'd care to come," allowed the prince. "I would dare say that no other ship on the Trackless Sea could have made it."

"Nor any other captain," Alicia added, taking the northman's arm and kissing him quickly.

Then Alicia made her way back to her mother. Robyn lay senseless, her face as white as a corpse while Tavish cradled the queen's head in her lap. "She lives," said the bard softly, "but she's terribly weak. We must make landfall quickly. She needs a warm bed!"

"Evermeet!" said the princess softly. "We see it at the horizon. We'll make landfall before dark!"

Then something pounded into the *Princess of Moonshae* from below, crunching the heavy keel and lifting the ship dozens of feet into the air. Men fell to the deck, cursing or stunned, and the sleek vessel tumbled precariously to the side, nearly capsizing.

But this was no force of water or cyclone. The thing that had struck the ship was solid and powerful, moving very quickly. Alicia rolled across the deck at the stern, trying to draw her sword and get to her feet at the same moment. Even as she did so, her blood chilled to the announcement of Wultha, who stood at the rail and raised his huge battle-axe.

"Dragon turtle!" he bellowed, driving the blade forward with all the strength in his broad shoulders.

Alicia twisted to look, gasping in horror as a huge head, blunt-snouted and leathery-skinned, reared into view. Wultha's axe crunched into the broad nose, but then the creature's monstrous jaws spread wide. They closed about the bellowing northman, abruptly silencing his cries. When the dragon turtle's head vanished over the side, only the stumps of the huge warrior's legs remained standing grotesquely in place, bitten off cleanly at the knees.

The longship reeled to another crushing attack, and this time timbers splintered and cracked, and water burst through the hull.

* * * * *

The man sat in his emerald prison and wondered about the passage of time. He knew—or sensed, in any event—that he hadn't been here all his life. He remembered things of the outside—a sun, trees, highlands looming overhead, the feel of wind on his face.

Where were those things now? That was a question he couldn't answer. There were so *many* important questions— fundamental mysteries of his own life, his own past—and yet the answers to all of them seemed impossibly distant and unattainable.

Another important thought came to him then—not so much a piece of knowledge as a bit of a feeling. With a shiver, he looked over his shoulder, recognizing the feeling.

Menace. There was danger here.

"But *where?*" he groaned out loud. "Where am I?"

Food and water had come, he saw without surprise—the usual tortoiseshell bowls of clear water and raw fish. That had been his sustenance for a long time, he remembered, but not forever.

Menace. He reminded himself of the danger. But who was his enemy? How was he threatened?

Suddenly he remembered a huge shape, dark and indistinct of feature, wielding a horrible knife. By the gods, that *knife!* With a scream, the man seized the stump of his wrist with his other hand, staggering backward and slumping to his stone bed as the memories flooded back. . . .

He was screaming in those memories, and his arms and legs were restrained by terrible creatures with brutal claws. The man's face was bleeding and bruised, but more than one of the monsters had retreated, nursing a broken limb, before he had been fully subdued.

But then had come that *knife!*

And afterward, a drink. Now he was beginning to remember—a steaming goblet of sweet juice, delightful in taste and invigorating in sensation. He had drunk it greedily, and it had brought him some measure of relief.

But after he drank it, he had begun to forget. Now it had taken him great mental effort exerted over many hours just to remember that much. It was the drink that had made him forget!

Other memories trickled back, each slowly and reluctantly, like a timid hare lured from its burrow by a patient snaresman. He had been given the drink several times, he remembered vaguely, though only that first time did he recall with clarity.

Now he resolved, deep within a heart that had known long years of firm resolution, that he would not take the drink again. He didn't know how he had risen above its stuporific effects, but he knew that he would not willingly suffer those effects again.

He vowed to himself in the name of . . . he couldn't remember. Suddenly movement in the pool of water disturbed his meditations. He barely had time to throw himself backward upon the bed, feigning comatose slumber, before a large creature splashed to the surface and climbed from the pool.

He looked through narrowed lids and saw a huge sahuagin, the leering face a cross between a lizard and a fish. Bands of gold chain wrapped the creature's chest and loins. Webbed feet, studded with curving claws, flapped across the smooth floor as the creature advanced.

The sahuagin's back, he saw, bristled with long spines connected by thin webbing. The spines stood erect and alert now, and a pointed tongue slipped in and out of the distended, tooth-studded jaws. The man looked lower, to the monster's hands, which were webbed and clawed like its feet. One of these cautiously clasped the jeweled hilt of a scimitar borne at his waist, and the other held a tall bottle. The creature removed a cork stopper with its teeth.

From the top of the drinking vessel trailed a thin column of steam.

* * * * *

The dragon turtle came at the *Princess of Moonshae* from below, smashing the bony shell of its back into the hull with another timber-crushing blow, heaving the vessel far out of the water and sending her crashing to the side. Again the tumble very nearly capsized the battered longship.

Alicia caught a momentary glimpse of a monstrous snout thrashing in the water. A cavernous mouth gaped, and she saw bony ridges instead of teeth. With one bite, those ridges clamped onto the longship's starboard rail, ripping pieces from several stout planks. Blunt claws, each as big as a tall man's leg, appeared at the gunwale on either side of the snout, and the *Princess of Moonshae* rocked violently as the monster pushed against the hull.

The bowmen fired volleys of arrows at the beast when it showed itself above the gunwale. Most of the missiles bounced harmlessly from the heavy shell, but a few shafts punctured one of the monster's staring eyes. The turtle closed a leathery lid over the injured organ, effectively blinded on one side, though that did nothing to deter its aggressive attacks.

Next the raging beast ducked under the water to come up against the port side of the longship. Keane dove out of the way in apparent fright as the blunt head reared into the air, but then he spun and pointed. From his finger burst a lightning bolt that scored a gory wound in the dragon turtle's good eye.

The monster bellowed in rage, opening its jaw and belching forth a great cloud of steam. The blast struck the ship with explosive force, hissing through the air, searing flesh in a white fog. Several crewmen, caught in the killing heat, collapsed to the deck, writhing in agony.

Keane dodged beneath the killing cloud and then quickly

scrambled to his feet. Next he cast a blast of cold that ricocheted harmlessly from the monster's great shell after freezing the water there to a gleaming coat of ice. Again he chanted the words of magic, and a fireball drifted outward, exploding in a hellish blossom of flame. The blistering inferno sizzled the surface of the sea but didn't affect the monster. The dragon turtle simply dove to avoid the blast.

For a time, then, nothing disturbed the surface of the gently rolling sea. Endless seconds passed into an eternal minute, then another . . . and still there was no sign of the turtle's presence.

"Is it gone?" asked Alicia.

"Not likely," replied the Prince of Gnarhelm tersely. His intense manner prevented the woman from asking any further questions.

Abruptly the captain stiffened. "To the oars!" he bellowed, his voice booming through the boat and out across the sea. "Stop her in the water! Backward, men—hard!"

With his first word, the men of his crew sprang into action, seizing the long oars that were drawn into the vessel. The blades struck the water and churned backward with enough force to send Alicia stumbling forward from the sudden shift in the ship's momentum.

"Stroke, you weaklings! Full astern!" shouted Brandon, stalking down the center of the hull.

A great crack sounded at the same time as the longship's bow flew upward into the air. The blinded turtle hadn't struck the ship squarely, but several more planks splintered, and the craft rocked dangerously as it slid backward off the dragon's rising shell. Water spilled into the hull through several narrow, long gaps.

"By the Abyss, *still* it finds us!" hissed Brigit, her hand tightening around her sword.

"By sound!" Keane's eyes suddenly flashed, and he looked for Brandon. The turtle, meanwhile, vanished into the depths. In a few seconds, the magic-user explained his plan—and Brandon nodded grimly.

"Be silent!" ordered the Prince of Gnarhelm in a low voice that nevertheless carried throughout the hull. "Everyone remain perfectly quiet!"

As always, the crew obeyed even as the order was issued. Quickly the *Princess of Moonshae* grew still, drifting like a ghost ship with upraised oars and silent, staring crewmen.

Keane stalked to the starboard rail and murmured the words to a spell. Something splashed beside the longship and Alicia flinched unconsciously, expecting the return of the dragon turtle. Instead, she saw the effect of Keane's spell.

The mage had created an invisible wall of force, shaped like a square about twelve feet on a side and pressed flat against the surface of the water. Concentrating diligently, Keane shifted it first to the left and then to the right, so that water splashed around and over it. Then, still staring intently at the evidence of magic, the mage directed the force away from the *Princess of Moonshae.*

Splashing and swirling steadily, the effect of the spell moved farther from the longship, at right angles to her gentle course. After a few moments, they saw it: The water heaved beneath the wall of force, rising to reveal the great dome of the dragon turtle's shell. The blind creature thrashed about, seeking the thing it had heard, but Keane had already slid the invisible craft off to the side. It continued to churn its way through the water, and once again the monster heard it. The dragon turtle dove again, and they could imagine it following the noisy effect of the spell.

"Look!" Brigit's voice, a taut whisper, came to Alicia's ears alone. She turned and gasped silently. The shore of Evermeet loomed so close now that they could see individual trees and the gracefully sculpted outlines of tall, brightly painted buildings. Hues of blue, green, and amber mingled together on the small structures, creating a village that looked rather like a giant flower blossom.

Once more the dragon turtle broke the surface, more than two miles distant now and moving away fast. Safe from that threat, at least for the time being, Brandon directed their attention to a safe approach to shore.

"Soundings—constant," he ordered several crewmen, who took a weighted line to the bow and began to measure the depth of the water.

"Plenty deep!" came the reassuring reply.

"Lookouts—all along the hull," cried the captain next. "Be alert for *anything!* Sounding?"

"Still deep!"

Leaking from a dozen holes, listing to her battered starboard side, sail puffing from a few listless gusts of wind, the *Princess of Moonshae* crept toward Evermeet. Alicia stood beside the elven woman and shared her sense of awe. It seemed impossible that they were here, barely a mile away from the verdant shore.

"Still deep," came the announcement from the bow, followed by a strangled gasp. "Wait . . . I see something. What the—*stop!* Shallows—coral!"

Brandon whirled, ready to order his men to the oars. Before he could open his mouth, they all felt a wood-splintering crunch. At the same time, the longship stopped moving completely.

"Coral reef came from nowhere, Captain!" stammered the shocked sailor who had been performing the soundings. "The water was hundreds of feet deep, and then there it was, like a giant spike stuck as a barrier!"

"It may very well be just that," Brigit noted grimly. "How badly are we stuck?"

"With luck, the tide'll float us off," replied Brandon, with a worried look at the water that had started to trickle in through several new cracks.

"That's the least of our problems," announced Keane, with a meaningful gesture over the side. A quick look showed Alicia what he meant.

The water around the longship teemed with swimming figures—greenish and mottled blue creatures with elven features but webbed hands and feet. Each of the figures held a bow, with an arrow nocked and pointed at the longship.

With a sinking sensation in her heart, the princess looked around. The coastal guards had them completely surrounded. A quick count showed her there were many hundreds of them.

* * * * *

Deirdre returned to the mirror but again met with frustration. When she sought her sister or mother, she saw instead only a gray fog. It had been this way since they had passed the Cyclones of Evermeet. Whatever the nature of the arcane barriers protecting the island, Deirdre deduced that they extended into the realm of the arcane.

Nor did her continuing efforts to discover the location of her father yield any results other than a fruitless search of the limitless depths of the Trackless Sea.

More and more she had found her thoughts moving away from her family, away from any and all the people of her realm. Instead, her mind chased relentlessly after the one she could not find, the one she knew again walked the surface of the Realms.

Sooner or later, she vowed, her mirror would again locate the being she had known as Malawar, and when it did, her vengeance against him would be complete.

* * * * *

For a long, pregnant moment, the creatures in the water made no sound. Sunlight glinted from hundreds of arrowheads, a warlike and ironic contrast to the beautiful coral shallows, the mottled blue and green water reflecting the sunlight in dazzling hues.

The aquatic archers held their weapons horizontally so that both ends of their bows remained out of the water. The archers could shower the longship's hull with their lethal rain at a moment's notice.

"Be careful!" Brigit hissed. "They've been taught all their lives that humans are their mortal enemies. Don't let anyone do anything to give them cause to shoot!"

The princess studied the creatures in the water, realizing that they tended to be very fair-looking beings, with the pointed ears and narrow, shapely skulls of elves. The skin on their faces and arms, the only parts she could see above the water, varied in color from soft green to deep blue, even shifting through many hues on a single individual. The webbed hands and feet, however, couldn't help reminding the princess of a sahuagin.

"What are they?" she asked softly, realizing that Brigit stood beside her.

"The Aquis-Dulcio . . . sea elves," said the sister knight, her voice heavy with awe. "I've heard about them. All of us know of our cousins of the deep, but never have I seen one!"

Just then one of the sea elves rose, treading water with his feet. He opened his mouth, and a series of lyrical sounds came forth. To Alicia, it sounded like a pleasant song in which the singer made up nonsense sounds instead of words.

Brigit, however, stiffened and then listened with rapt attention. She responded once in the same language, and then the aquatic elf continued speaking. Despite the musical nature of the speech, the speaker's gestures and expressions convinced the princess he was delivering a harangue. His webbed hands clenched into fists, and he planted them firmly on his hips. Brandon, Robyn, and Keane observed the communication, gathering around the sister knight by the time the sea elf ceased speaking.

"What does he say?" asked the captain impatiently.

"They demand that we leave. They promise to kill us if we don't depart immediately."

Alicia's heart sank. "But don't they understand?" she objected.

"They understand that this is a human ship, and they insist that humans are not allowed here."

"Did you tell them why we're here?" asked Robyn.

"I told them who I am. The Sisters of Synnoria are known throughout elvendom, and being their captain gives me some status. I started to explain about the Synnorian Gate, but he cut me off and told me that it didn't matter—we had to leave." She didn't repeat the names he had called her, the filthy epithets—traitor and worse—for bringing the eternal enemies of elvendom to this sacred place.

"Does he see that we're stuck on an Abyss-cursed lump of coral?" snarled Brandon, stepping to the rail to glower at the male, who still held himself half out of the water. The northman started to raise his fist, but then apparently thought better of the gesture. With an inarticulate mutter, he turned back to the discussion.

Brigit leaned over the rail again and sang something back to the elf in the water. The sea elf scowled and came back in a minor, threatening key. The sister knight shrugged and turned back to the humans.

"I told him that we're stranded, that we *can't* get off of here. He . . . was insulting, but at least he didn't insist that we leave."

Hanrald listened intently, standing at the gunwale and flushing as he stared at the elf. He sensed that Brigit had been treated very rudely. "He's a pompous little wart, that one. I'd like to have the chance to teach him a few manners!"

Abruptly Alicia grew impatient and stepped to the gunwale. "We come in peace, and we seek an audience with your queen and her council of sages." She spoke in Common, trying to keep her voice light, her face friendly. "We offer no threat!"

She found herself the target of more arrows than she could count, all poised on the brink of launching. If any one of them slips, she thought, I'm dead.

Then Brigit stepped to her side. Again she spoke in that lyrical tongue, and the male replied. Now, however, several other males and a female joined him. All of them were covered by multicolored skin, fading through every shade of blue, green, and aqua in an effect that was really quite beautiful.

The female sea elf, who also rose from the water to sing, addressed Brigit and then the male. She was marvelously beautiful, with silvery hair that hung to the waterline in tight curls, concealing her breasts—but not the fact that she, like the male, seemed to be naked. Then she dove, her webbed feet popping out of the water just briefly. Alicia quickly lost sight of the perfectly camouflaged form as the sea elf disappeared into the dappled waters of the coral shallows.

"That's a little better," Brigit told them, still wary. "This one gave me her name—Trillhalla. She called the other one Palentor. She says that we're fortunate in where we've made landfall. The queen is in the Summer Palace, and that's not far from here. Also the names of Tristan and Robyn Kendrick are not unknown to her. Nor," she added quietly, "is Brigit Cu-'Lyrran. Anyway, she'll send word of our arrival. She warns that we have to stay here until she returns."

"That'll be easy enough," Brandon growled, with a belligerent look at the male who had been the first to speak.

Alicia, meanwhile, looked at the sky. The sun had passed into the region of late afternoon, and the magnificent forests of Evermeet, gleaming in a rainbow of colors, glowed beneath it. The water was placid, except for the graceful disturbance caused by the array of elven archers. As she looked, it seemed to her that their numbers continued to swell.

Natural enough, she thought, if humans are unknown here. They've probably never seen a longship before either.

With that not exactly comforting thought, she settled down on the deck with the rest of the crew to await the return of Trillhalla.

* * * * *

"Have you failed me, worm?"

The question posed by Talos was an awkward one for the avatar Sinioth. He answered as deftly as he could.

"We have trailed the humans to their destination. They are far removed from the prisoner, and we have two thousand warriors screening the seas against their escape. Should they try to sail, we shall annihilate them!"

"Very well," rumbled the Destructor. "Even the mirror

brings no image of them. I shall be patient—for now."

"Thank you, most merciful master!" pledged the avatar, thrashing his squid body through the depths in an ecstasy of groveling.

"But should you fail me in the end," continued Talos, "it will be more than the pathetic humans who face annihilation!"

♣ 13 ♣

A Queen of Evermeet

A snarl prowled across Brandon's face as he climbed aboard the stricken *Princess of Moonshae*. He and Knaff had completed their inspection of the hull, scrambling about on the coral outcrop that now, at low tide, held the longship completely out of the water. The Corwellian bowmen and Keane had stood an alert guard, though they all knew that their presence was for show only. The sea around them was a vast expanse of bobbing heads and torsos. Tavish, in a quick count, concluded that more than a thousand sea elves had congregated by now.

"As I thought, she's splintered in a lot of places where she's not holed clean through." The captain's tone was sad, almost brokenhearted, but also fiercely proud. "No other ship would have survived!"

"Can you patch the hull?" asked Robyn.

"Maybe. Give me two weeks, plenty of tar and timber, a forge, and a bigger drydock than you could find in the Moonshaes, and I might be able to make her seaworthy again. But she'll never be the same *Princess*."

The northman captain didn't try to keep the bitterness out of his voice. He looked at Alicia, his expression despairing, and the princess wanted to take him in her arms and soothe his pain. She remembered, with a tinge of resentment, that the northman would find such a reaction humiliating in the extreme.

"Look! Isn't that Trillhalla?" asked Alicia. "I hope she's bearing good news!"

They recognized the female sea elf, the only one thus far who had offered them the slightest willingness to listen, not to mention help. She was identifiable not from her features, but by the formed escort of warriors screening her approach. No less than a full score of large males swam before her, breaking the water like dolphins so that they could continually observe the humans.

Finally the formation broke apart in the shallow water before the reef where the *Princess of Moonshae* sat in her coral-bound trap. The dappled face of Trillhalla broke the surface, framed by her silver curls and growing rings of water as she raised her torso into the air. Palentor rose beside her, his face fixed in its familiar scowl.

"You, Brigit Cu'Lyrran," began the female sea elf in heavily accented Common, "are commanded to bring two of the humans and appear before Queen Amlaruil in the Summer Palace." Palentor turned to object, his face blanching with shock, but his reaction was halted by a sharp gesture from Trillhalla.

The female sea elf remained still, half out of the water, and it was several moments before the visitors realized that she had concluded her speech.

"I thank the queen—and yourself—for this gracious command," replied Brigit. The sister knight turned and, without hesitation, named Robyn and Alicia as her companions.

Meanwhile, a long, graceful canoe appeared, emerging unobserved from a concealed gap in the verdant shoreline. It was already halfway to the stricken longship before any of the companions noticed it. Then it was Knaff the Elder who, in obvious chagrin at its undiscovered approach, pointed out the craft.

The canoe was half the size of a small longship, propelled swiftly by a dozen paddlers on each side. A single long outrigger extended to the craft's starboard side. It had neither mast nor sail but was decorated in multicolored, flowered patterns along the hull, with garlands of real blossoms gathered in many places along the gunwale. The thing moved very quickly. Alicia thought it the equal in speed of a longship under full sail.

The craft slid easily into a tiny inlet of the coral reef—no more than six or eight inches of water—and came to a rest just a few feet from the longship. The three visitors climbed easily over the side, took two steps across the exposed coral, and were helped into the canoe by silent, muscular elves. These were not sea elves, but Alicia saw that their skin had a bluer cast than did the Llewyrr. Also, many of these elves of Evermeet had dark hair, a virtually unknown phenomenon among the elves of the Moonshaes.

They took seats in the bow of the slender boat on plush, cushioned benches surrounded by bouquets of brilliant flowers. The canoe moved smoothly but with surprising speed as it drew away from the longship and glided toward the tree-lined shore. Trillhalla swam beside them.

"The queen was surprisingly calm about your arrival," the sea elf announced, speaking in particular to Robyn. "Though the rest of the palace has been thrown into quite a stir. She, too, has heard of the High King and Queen of Moonshae. Synnoria is an important place to us in Evermeet, and the reign of you and your former husband has made that valley more secure than it has been in many years."

"Let's hope she wants it to go on for a few more," Alicia observed wryly. By then, however, the wonders of Evermeet drove the desire for further conversation away.

The trees, they saw as they neared the shore, sprouted a leafy mixture of blue, green, and silver foliage, all three colors combining when the breeze ruffled the branches into a glittering array of beauty. Colors seemed to shift and flow along the forest, which consisted of far greater trees than Alicia had ever seen or imagined. Even the saplings were the size of Corwellian oaks! The great mature specimens rested on trunks as large around as a good-sized cottage, towering hundreds of feet into the air.

Before Alicia noticed, Trillhalla, with a flick of her webbed feet, propelled herself from the water into the canoe beside the visitors. The sea elf seemed to have no regard for her nudity as she lay on the seat and let the sun dry the seawater from her skin.

Alicia didn't see the entrance into the forest before them, but suddenly the canoe slipped into a narrow channel. Despite the overhanging canopy of verdure, sunlight reflected from the silvery leaves and the clear water, making the hidden passage a bright, airy place. Here Trillhalla sat up and removed a plain white tunic from beneath her bench. Throwing the garment over her shoulders and pushing her arms through the sleeves, she tossed her silver-curled locks free. She looked, Alicia thought with amazement, as glamorous as any lady of an elegant court.

They glided along the watery passage for perhaps half an hour, and each twist and turn of the channel brought new wonders to their eyes, Synnorian and human alike. Birds of brilliant colors—bright red, emerald green, or deep, flashing blue—fluttered from tree to tree. At one place, a great hawk, pure white except for streaks of black on its folded wings, watched them from a lofty branch, its eyes glittering with intelligence.

In some places, the channel broadened to a wide pool, and occasionally they saw young elves splashing along the shores of these, swimming with carefree glee, pausing to stare in openmouthed wonder at the flowered canoe—or more likely, realized Alicia, at the strange and alien occupants of that graceful craft.

Finally, after a sudden twist in the channel, the forest fell away on either side, and the waterway flowed into a broad, placid lake. Across its mirrored surface, glittering with a beauty and majesty that took their breath away, the Summer Palace of Evermeet rose into the skies, in an obvious attempt to rival the glories of the heavens themselves.

The palace seemed to fly at first, like a gorgeous silver cloud. Turrets and towers of diamond, silver, and glass gleamed with millions of facets, expanding the light of the sun until the palace rivaled even that fiery orb in brightness.

Four massive pyramids, each hundreds of feet high, stood at the corners of the lofty palace, supporting the flat floor of clear crystal that formed the bottom of the structure itself. The whole thing remained poised in the air far above the lake. Wide stairways led up the pyramids, which seemed to sit on the water's surface, the summit of each forming one corner of the square base of the palace.

From these four corners, the palace rose dramatically. The platform was unwalled. Apparently its placement two hundred feet above the middle of a lake was enough to deter armed assault. Who knew, Alicia reminded herself, if war even existed upon Evermeet?

The keep soared upward for hundreds more feet and was surrounded by gleaming towers that climbed even higher. Narrow spires emerged from the center of the huge structure, and bridges of glass or silver—sometimes supported by weblike strands of golden cables, other times apparently freestanding arches—connected the highest towers and descended in graceful sweeps to the keep.

Alicia could not express her astonishment and wonder. Any words occurring to her seemed hopelessly mundane, even insulting, when used to describe a work of such consummate grace and beauty.

The first dose of reality came as they approached the base of the nearest pyramid, where finally the princess could see a wooden landing encircling the base of the stone edifice. Here stood a rank of crimson-coated guards, each armed with a sword and a shield. Above them, arrayed on the steps of the pyramid and seeming to extend into the sky itself, stood rank upon rank of elven archers, each holding a wooden longbow with a silver-tipped arrow nocked and ready for attack.

"Peace," Robyn murmured to the hard-faced guard who stood at the landing barring her path. He blinked in momentary confusion, then stepped back to study her with wary eyes.

"This way," the guard announced curtly, gesturing to the steps leading upward. As if there were any other way to go, Alicia thought. His eyes swept past the princess and came to rest on Brigit, flaring again with unrestrained hostility.

They really *are* upset that she brought us here, realized Alicia, wondering again at the generosity that had compelled Brigit to lead them.

Slowly, with a sense of awe and dignity, they made their way up the broad, steep stairway. The ranks of archers parted to let them pass, but some always remained ahead of them, backing smoothly up the stairs, all too ready to bring their weapons in line with the hearts of their "guests."

Alicia risked a look over her shoulder, where space yawned below her, yielding a vista of treetops and, far beyond, a line of blue sea, but immediately she felt a wave of vertigo sweep over her. Swinging her eyes back to the steps in front of her, she steadied her nerves and resumed the steady pace of the climb. The elves and her mother, she noted with annoyance, seemed to accept the climb with equanimity, even though Robyn had still not fully recovered from her ordeal sustaining the wind spell.

Finally they reached the crystal platform at the top of the pyramidical stairway. Now they could see that all four sides of the foundation provided access to the structure, as well as landings below for boats. Alicia's eyes were inexorably drawn upward, toward the crystal walls and glittering towers that filled her vision.

Twin phalanxes of elven warriors, standing on the glasslike floor, greeted them, bearing gleaming halberds held upright to form two rows of weapons. The formation also created an obvious aisle connecting the stairway to the entrance to the palace.

Their escorting guards stepped off the solid stone of the pyramid onto the transparent floor, and Alicia had to force herself to follow. She looked at her feet and beyond as she walked across a surface as clear as the air. The sensation grew increasingly unnerving the farther they moved from the pyramid, until soon only a surface of blue water was visible two hundred feet below. The princess noted that even the water below the multi-tiered palace was sun-dappled and gleaming. This immense structure apparently cast no shadow.

They crossed what might have been called a courtyard in a typical castle if it had been surrounded by a wall, with good, solid earth underfoot. Now it seemed like a test of nerves. Gradually they grew nearer their goal.

Once again Alicia found that her sense of perspective deceived her. The doors were much larger and farther away than she had first thought. They seemed to be made of solid gold, placed in the palace wall that was itself as clear as crystal. The princess noted to her surprise that even though she looked through the wall, it didn't seem as if she saw inside the palace. It was more as if she looked right out the other side of the massive structure onto a vista of lake and forest and sky.

Then she forgot everything else as, with a whispering sound as soft as a breeze, the golden doors began to swing open.

* * * * *

The man burned with hatred, a hot fire fanned by the bellows of a slowly returning memory. The scaly figure walked across the floor toward him, and the man's fury became a grim and deadly determination. Strange, he thought. There must have been some good things in my life. Why is it that the anger, the need for vengeance, comes back so strong?

He shook off the question, knowing that it was trivial. His vengeance *was* important, and not just for the slaking of his rage. It was important for his very survival.

He viewed the leering sahuagin through narrowed lids, saw the approaching bottle extended for the presumably dazed man to swill. Though he determined to thwart the creature's intentions, the man bore no illusions as to his ability to overcome the monster. Another memory returned. Though he had experienced many battles with the fishmen, the man had never seen a sahugain as large as this.

Instead, the prisoner played along, groaning sleepily, slurping at the vessel, spilling a great deal of the drink from the corners of his mouth, letting it trickle through his beard while his throat went through the bobbing action of swallowing. Finally, the flask empty, the hulking fish creature turned and flapped away, diving into the pool and disappearing.

Immediately the man rolled from his hard bunk and vomited, retching continuously, miserably, until he had nothing left inside of him.

After he had drunk some water and rinsed himself off, he felt the reawakening of anger. I will make it suffer; I will *destroy* it.

The intent was a blanket future for the man, a life's goal condensed into the image of a hateful creature who had drugged and maimed him. The man's purpose seemed clear, but even as he considered it, another shred of thought came to him.

A fit purpose for a man it may be . . . and I am a man. But somewhere in the back of his mind a voice whispered to him, speaking softly but convincingly: you are *more* than a man.

How? The question followed, and he puzzled it through. How can I be more than a man? And then he knew the answer, and another piece of his being fell into place.

Because I am a king.

* * * * *

Hanrald stood at the rail of the stranded *Princess of Moonshae*. He looked to the west, where the sun continued its descent over the elvenhome. If anything, he thought angrily, Evermeet looks even more beautiful in the light of sunset.

But not half so beautiful as the one his mind drifted toward with inexorable longing. Indeed, as her female features etched themselves in his mind, as her golden hair swirled around the face that smiled just for him, the earl's brain focused with unrelenting diligence on the impossible love that had seized and transformed his heart.

He thought, with surprise, how quickly he had earlier felt himself to be in love—and now at how fleeting that emotion had seemed.

For it was no longer Alicia Kendrick who occupied the thoughts of the proud knight. His feelings for her, in the light of memory, seemed no more than youthful infatuation.

Instead, Hanrald thought bitterly, his heart's longing had turned from one who was distant, perhaps unattainable, to one whose affections must inevitably remain aloof. For the Earl of Fairheight understood beyond doubt that he loved Brigit Cu-'Lyrran, Mistress Captain of the Sisters of Synnoria.

* * * * *

"Let Her Majesty ask the questions," Trillhalla coached as they passed down a long corridor of crystal walls, each of which seemed to provide a different vista of the placid lake and its pastoral valley, or of the seacoast beyond.

Alicia didn't need to be reminded. She was so overawed by these surroundings that she wondered if she'd have the composure to answer a question, much less to do any interrogating of her own.

Then abruptly they passed around a corner that Alicia hadn't even seen before them, coming to a stop before another pair of grandiose doors. Like the palace entrance, these seemed to be made of purest gold and swung inward with the same whisper of sound.

The princess had to restrain an audible gasp as they stepped into the throne room of Queen Amlaruil of Evermeet. There was no mistaking the monarch, for her throne of diamond-and-ruby-encrusted platinum hovered a full thirty feet above the floor, in the center of a chamber brighter and far more dazzling than anything the humans had ever seen.

It makes even the Argen-Tellirynd of Chrysalis seem like a farmer's shed by comparison! The thought, shocking in its truth, further awed the Princess of Callidyrr.

The great floor of the chamber was empty, but unlike the corridor and courtyard of the palace, this surface was visible as interlocking tiles of black, white, and red. The room itself was unbelievably vast. To Alicia's eyes, it seemed far larger than the keep itself, of which this was but a part. Gradually she realized that a very subtle mirrored effect of the crystal panels in the walls seemed to expand the space to almost limitless dimensions without mirroring the images of the occupants of the room.

Galleries lined the walls facing the queen's throne, each occupied by a small party of elven nobles or warriors, all of whom watched the visitors with keen interest and obvious suspicion. Beyond the queen there were fewer galleries, each of these occupied by a single, elegantly dressed elf, most of them elderly females. They're the Council of Matrons, Alicia remembered from Brigit's description.

The four women approached the center of the room, the walk taking a very long time, during which the throne of the elven queen slowly descended until it was perhaps ten feet over the floor of the chamber.

Trillhalla, quickly followed by Brigit, knelt and bowed deeply to the monarch. Alicia bowed formally, though she did not kneel. The High Queen of the Ffolk regarded this elfwoman as an equal, nodding her head politely in response to a similar gesture on the part of Queen Amlaruil.

The regal monarch was the most beautiful creature Alicia had ever seen. Even displayed as she was amidst a dozen fortunes' worth of gems and precious metal, she shone as a jewel that paled all the others to insignificance. Her eyes were very large, in the teardrop shape of the elves, a deep, warm green in color. Her face was slender, but her high cheekbones and firm chin gave her a look of authority that lay like steel beneath the velvet of her beauty. Hair of coppery red fell to her bare shoulders but was then swept into a clasp at the side of her head, where the strands gathered into the image of a soft-petaled rose.

The queen's eyes flicked past the humans after making a brief but thorough appraisal, coming to rest on the captain of the Synnorian horsewomen. Brigit had risen to her feet beside Trillhalla.

"Sister knight, you are known to us as an elf of courage and supposedly good judgement." The queen's tone was cold, her words clipped. "Tell me immediately why you bring these humans to Evermeet!"

"The tale is a long one, Your Majesty, and extraordinary, as you must know by our presence here. It begins with the closing of the Fey-Alamtine. That circumstance, as you doubtless realize, had as great an impact upon Synnoria as upon Evermeet."

Brigit spoke bluntly, and the elven monarch nodded as if she saw the point of the knight's last remark.

"Yes—the destruction of the gate is a most grievous affair."

"It was followed by an attack against Synnoria by a beast from the earliest nightmares of our people. We suffered the onslaught of Ityak-Ortheel, the Elf-Eater!"

The princess was satisfied by the sound of gasps and murmured comments suddenly echoing around the huge chamber. The report of the Elf-Eater's attack was obviously news to Evermeet, and anything that shook them out of their complacency was, to Alicia's mind, a benefit.

Brigit went on to describe the horror of the attack. Though she spoke without passion, in a clearly factual tone, there was none present who remained unaffected by the visual images: the trout farm's destruction, the Elf-Eater's march to Chrysalis across the watery causeway, the doomed charges by the sister knights, and the ultimate blasphemy, the destruction of the Argen-Tellirynd.

"Only the humans, with their sorcery—and their courage—could match the monster and, in the end, drive it away," continued the sister knight, warming to her topic. She described the intervention of the Ffolk as the decisive factor that it was. Finally, though it slightly altered the chronology of her recounting, she told them of Lord Pawldo's heroic sacrifice.

Next she recounted the reason the humans had come to Synnoria and that she had sailed with them to Evermeet. "Without the means to carry the fight beneath the seas, they must forever yield to the enemies who hold their king. But we elves once had ships, I know, that could sail under the water. All the humans ask—our *friends*, these humans!—all they ask, Excellency, is for the tool that will allow them to fight their battle."

Brigit sighed softly. A long time had passed, though no noise had disturbed her speech.

"Your Majesty, there is another compelling reason for us to aid these humans. The Moonshae Isles, of which Synnoria is a part, are beset by a menace that, I am certain, is tied in to the same force that has closed the gate and released Ityak-Ortheel from its nether hell. If we provide them with a vessel that they can take beneath the sea and strike at the heart of these evils, I believe that we shall find in that undoing the key to restoring our own valley to normalcy!

"They came to us in need, and yet their help has saved Synnoria so that the Fey-Alamtine can be restored! The very least we can do is answer their need with the power that we have at our disposal."

"You make a very compelling case," said Queen Amlaruil, nodding in apparently pleased response to Brigit. "It is as I expected—even anticipated."

Alicia couldn't keep her astonishment silent, forgetting for the moment Trillhalla's instructions about questions. "You *expected* us to come?" she asked.

"The Summer Palace is not always here at Dalloch-Krystas. I brought it here this year for the first time in more than twenty-five summers to place it near the Silluth, the Beaching Bay," replied the queen, as if that explained everything. If she had minded Alicia's question, she gave no indication, but the princess saw many of the courtiers on the balconies behind the queen glowering at her with unfriendly expressions.

"It is my command that the sea elves shall install a Helm of Zulae to the figurehead of your ship. This is the artifact you seek. It will take your ship beneath the surface of the sea. I entrust you, Brigit Cu'Lyrran, to ensure that it is returned to Synnoria at the conclusion of your quest." She paused, her expression wistful. "I wish you luck in your efforts to rescue King Tristan. He deserves a better fate."

For a moment, the three visitors gaped, stunned that they had succeeded. Trillhalla, meanwhile, gestured them to the door. The interview was obviously over.

"Thank you, Your Majesty," said Robyn, with a deep bow to the throne before she turned to follow the sea elf.

"The ship repairs!" Alicia whispered to Trillhalla. "We need to ask her about those!"

"No—not yet!" replied the sea elf, hoarsely. "You must settle for this."

But Alicia had already turned and, taking several steps toward the throne, addressed the regal elfwoman.

"Your Majesty, your generosity has given us a chance of success. I beg you, please, to increase those chances. Grant us the means to see our ship repaired. The hull was heavily damaged as we passed the cyclones and escaped your Warder."

"I'm not surprised," replied the queen, with a trace of a sniff to her tone. "No other human craft has ever survived those perils before now!"

"Can you not, in your generosity, grant us a sheltered harbor and some tools—a forge, and saws, and tar?"

"I see that you humans listen to instructions as well as I have always been taught to expect," noted Queen Amlaruil. This time there was no ignoring the sarcasm in her tone, but Alicia held her ground. After a moment, the monarch continued. "You may bring your crew ashore, but they must remain within two hundred feet of your ship. You can ask for supplies and we shall bring them to you. Under no circumstances are you to forage into the country of Evermeet, else I shall not be responsible for the consequences."

"Your conditions are most generous, Your Majesty," said Robyn, approaching Alicia with a tight smile. The human queen took her daughter's arm. Trillhalla stared at the princess with surprise, then shook her head in genuine admiration as they passed from the throne room.

"This way," she said with a smile. "Let's see if we can't get your people ashore by dark."

* * * * *

"The prisoner has been sedated," reported Sythissal as the giant squid slowly drifted through the spires and domes of Kyrasti. With the watch established over the boundaries of Evermeet, Coss-Axell-Sinioth had decided to return to the comfort of his own palace, there to await the word of Krell-Bane's army.

"Had he regained his senses?"

"No, Excellency. He remained as dull and clumsy as ever."

"Splendid," gurgled the avatar. "Though if it becomes necessary to take his other hand, we shall have to allow the potion of forgetfulness to wear off, that he may fully grasp the horror of his fate."

PART III: THE UNDERDEEP

❧ 14 ❧

The Helm of Zulae

Working the *Princess of Moonshae* free from her coral trap proved remarkably easy with the aid of a rising water level and a large contingent of sea elves. High tide occurred at sunset, and by the time the sun touched the horizon, the aquatic folk had lashed a dozen long, supple lines to the stricken longship's transom.

Hundreds of sea elves hauled on the ropes, and gradually the longship slipped gently off the reef, though seawater gushed into the hull from several holes that again dropped below the waterline.

Guided by Trillhalla, the men of Gnarhelm rowed the bruised and waterlogged ship through a wide channel in the coral barrier, a channel so cleverly aligned, Brandon realized, that no sailor in the world would find it.

This was the final layer of Evermeet's defenses, the captain reflected with chagrin—the barrier that had finally stopped them. It had all worked out as well as they could have hoped, of course, but there was something grating to the prince about having his vessel towed from the reef by people who had him at their mercy.

They approached the shore of looming forest, recognizing splendid maples and towering firs among other, more exotic trees. Even the familiar types grew taller than the humans had ever seen, with straight trunks and lush foliage. At first, it seemed as though the *Princess* steered toward a surf-swept beach, but as they neared the coastline, a channel appeared, slanting sharply to the left, all but invisible from the reef or beyond.

In the growing darkness, they entered the passage. Rugged cliffs of limestone rose as high as the masthead to the left and right, and elves with torches lined the top of the heights, illuminating the watery path as full night soon encloaked them. The crew rowed the weary longship along this channel, watching the firelight reflect from the water in a hypnotically beautiful display. The bright flames illuminated multicolored schools of fish meandering through water as clear as air.

Finally, with the last traces of sunset lost below the horizon, they passed beyond the torches and emerged into a cliff-walled basin. Splashing sounds indicated a waterfall somewhere nearby, invisible in the darkness, though the humans could see the encircling horizon of their deep grotto etched against the starlight above. Once they anchored, it didn't take more than a few minutes before the entire ship's complement found comfortable sleeping places—aboard ship, for most of the northmen; on land for Brigit and all of the Ffolk. Alicia found herself a soft and mossy niche between several rocks, comfortable and spacious enough for her to stretch and move around. Her mother and Tavish found similar alcoves nearby, and they collapsed with a sense of exhaustion mingled with accomplishment.

Alicia awakened to daylight, pleased to find that several thick ferns screened her bed with as much privacy as she could desire. Rising quickly, she pushed through the verdant growth to emerge onto smooth sand, a stretch of beach just coming under the light of dawn.

Sunrise revealed the true splendor of the voyagers' new surroundings, beauty that took Alicia's breath away as she beheld a small valley, lined all around with limestone cliffs—cliffs that enclosed a tiny enclave of paradise. Her eyes went irresistibly to the three waterfalls trilling into the rock-walled shelter, one sparkling like diamonds in the sun, the other two still cool in the morning shadow. Twin groves of great trees grew on the floor of the grotto, one on each side of the natural harbor where the crystalline water collected.

Much of the pool was surrounded by the same beach she now stood upon. She saw the gap in the rock walls of the grotto where the narrow channel drifted toward the sea and the

Princess of Moonshae had made her surreal torchlit passage.

Alicia couldn't imagine a more perfect haven than this secluded grotto. Seeing Brandon, already engaged in discussion with gray-haired Knaff, Alicia walked toward them. The listing *Princess of Moonshae* sat beyond, in a shallow bay of the main pool, as if she welcomed the chance to rest. A small channel diverted the waterflow from the area around the ship. With a closer look, Alicia saw that it had been dammed off by a cleverly designed gate.

"They must be draining it underground. Within a day that hull will be high and dry," observed Brandon, unable to hide his admiration.

"And they can open this lock here," added Knaff, pointing to a stout wooden gate that held back the waters of the pool. "When she's ready to float again, that'll add the water nice and gently."

Brand looked toward the channel to the sea, but instead saw Alicia coming. " 'Morning," he offered with a grin. "These elves did all that was promised as far as the drydock. Look at this thing!"

The princess could see that the water level under the longship had already dropped several inches below that of the pool. "Can you fix the hull?" she asked. Even to her landlubber's eye, the cracks and splinters in the formerly smooth planking gaped like grievous wounds.

"If they bring us the tools!" grumbled Knaff, again looking toward the seaward channel.

Alicia smiled at his impatience. "It's just dawn, you know. I'm sure they'll be here. I'm going to have a look around. Isn't it beautiful?"

She gestured to the waterfalls and groves, but the two sailors had already turned back to the ship, arguing over the repairs. Irritated in spite of herself, Alicia wandered away from the northmen, exploring.

She realized immediately that there was no easy way out of here except by water, a fact that suited both humans and elves, she felt certain. The high rock walls, carved by years of erosion into images of craggy faces and glowering visages, surrounded them, but allowed plenty of room for the crew to camp comfortably. Lush blossoms grew along the rocky face, and in places, pillows of moss had grown into perfectly formed chairs, couches, and beds. She had stumbled into a typically comfortable niche on the previous night.

Narrow trails twisted through the two groves, and though neither stand contained a huge number of trees, a person could take five steps down one of these paths and find herself surrounded by foliage as thick as the heart of any jungle.

A small portion of the space had been cleared for practical purposes. Northmen already erected tents, and Knaff supervised the construction of a small smithy and carpentry shed.

Alicia saw a silvery form break the surface of the water, and in another moment, Trillhalla reached the shallows. The sea elf splashed toward shore, lolling in the water as she greeted the human princess.

"I bring word—the Queen of Evermeet has ordered that supplies of seasoned lumber, tar, coal, and iron be provided. They are to be sent this morning . . . soon."

"That's great," the princess replied with a twinge of guilt. She realized that she didn't want to think about the repairs. She told herself that her father would understand, but the feeling unsettled her. She gestured to the splendor around them. "This place is so beautiful—so perfect. You're very generous to share it with us."

"It was Palentor's suggestion," she said.

"Really?" Alicia was astounded to think that the truculent elven warrior had displayed such kindness.

Trillhalla laughed, sensing her thoughts. "Actually, I'm sure he thought it would keep you confined and allow his scouts to keep an eye on you. But I'm glad if you find the surroundings pleasant."

The princess looked upward at the circle of rocky precipice that surrounded them a hundred feet above. Somehow even the thought of armed and watchful elves up there didn't detract from her pastoral sense of peace.

Brigit emerged from the forest behind them, and Trillhalla urged the pair to join her for a swim. The three females splashed through the water for some time, diving after schools of fish, exploring the coral formations under the pool. Finally they rested, Brigit and Alicia emerging from the water to flop onto the sand, already growing warm in the sun.

"I hope that you will all be comfortable here," said the silver-haired sea elf wistfully, relaxing in the water near the grotto's sandy beach.

Alicia and Brigit laughed. "I can't imagine anyplace *more* comfortable," replied the princess. Again she remembered her father, and a storm of guilt assailed her. She tried to force it aside, reminding herself that there was nothing they could do until the longship had been made seaworthy.

"Even Synnoria pales by comparison," Brigit added seriously.

For a time, in the warmth of the sun, they found it possible to forget about their quest, about the dangers that lay ahead. They had worked so hard to get this far that a few hours of leisure seemed no more than a just reward.

Trillhalla remained in the water but allowed her shoulders and arms to emerge as she looked at her visitors curiously. "It took great courage and great skill to reach our shores. It's quite a remarkable achievement, you know."

"There was no other way," replied the princess with a shrug. It was hard now for her to remember the tension and fear of their harrowing voyage.

"Your father is a great man. You must love him very much," noted the sea elf.

Alicia looked at her in surprise. Trillhalla spoke with a frankness that disconcerted the human woman. "That's true, I suppose. I—I just had to do something as long as there was any hope of success. I guess we all did."

"I wish you fortune for the remainder of your voyage."

The talk of their mission made Alicia restless again, and she sat up. "When do you think the supplies will get here?" asked the princess.

"Soon now, I should think," Trillhalla explained. "Palentor was placed in charge of their acquisition, and he's a fast and forthright worker."

"Even to aid those he despises?" asked Brigit wryly.

"He is a loyal servant of his queen," Trillhalla replied. "And besides, do not judge him too harshly. He commands the sea elves who patrol this portion of the shoreline. He was quite mortified that your craft made it so close to land."

As if to punctuate the sea elf's explanation, a long canoe came into view down the water channel that connected the grotto to the sea. A scowling Palentor sat in the bow, supervising the dark-haired elves who paddled the craft. The hull of the vessel, Alicia could see, was piled high with stacks of lumber and materials.

The male sea elf, they soon saw, rode the first of four great boats, each wider and heavier than the canoe that had carried the visitors to the Summer Palace. And each contained supplies necessary to repair the bruised longship—barrels of tar, iron for nails, even a bellows to fan Knaff's makeshift forge.

The females went to join Brandon and the others at the grotto's small dock, where the first canoe drew alongside. The boats were so big that they could only be unloaded one at a time, but eager northmen quickly formed a chain of workers, passing the crates and barrels from the elven craft to the work area, where Knaff supervised their organization and placement.

"You must be finished within five days!" barked the sea elf, standing straight before the prince of Gnarhelm and meeting him with his almond-shaped eyes.

"The queen said we could take as long as we needed!" objected Alicia, drawing the sea elf's angry eyes to herself.

He didn't withdraw from her gaze, but Palentor seemed surprised when the human woman stood up to his aggressive stare. Finally he blinked and cleared his throat. "I shall request independent confirmation of that fact. Your presence here is a disruption to our defenses. You place this entire coast in jeopardy!"

"I thought you said we were the first ship to make it this far. What do you guard against, then?" demanded Alicia, heating up to the confrontation.

"The surface of the sea may be blocked," replied the sea elf, his tone sincere, "and the cyclones may raise a barrier into the sky. But we have no control as to what passes *beneath* the surface of the sea, and it is the sahuagin and their foul kin, the scrags, who are our most persistent enemies."

"It's a relief to hear that humans don't fill that role *all* the time!" Alicia retorted. "Think—you've just named *our* enemies as well as your own!"

Palentor flushed, his mottled skin growing dark green. His lips stretched taut across his mouth, and for a second, Alicia wondered if he would strike at her. Her own fists clenched, reacting to the fury of his gaze. But then his expression softened—albeit minimally.

"It's true. Though we have prepared all our lives for the human menace, the only battles we have fought have been against the creatures of the deep."

"Then can't you see that we're not the enemy?" the princess demanded.

Suddenly Palentor's gaze narrowed, and Alicia felt uncomfortable as she saw his eyes boring into her. When he next spoke, it was with passion, not anger. "But for the elves . . . don't you see? Evermeet is *everything!* You humans will claim all the great continents eventually—Toril, Maztica, Kara-Tur . . . The elven populations in those places are shrinking, have been for thousands of years."

His voice dropped, but the princess sensed that he really did want her to see. "We *must* keep Evermeet secure, else our race will die out."

"I understand," she replied sincerely, and for the first time, she started to grasp the millennia-long conflict that had driven the elves to this island. "Please, Palentor—realize that we are not a threat to your island. We're grateful for the help of your queen . . . and yourself, but when we leave we won't be coming back."

"But others—"

"We won't tell people how we got here! And no other ship or captain could make it through your cyclones!" the princess argued, with a touch of exasperation.

Palentor looked at Brandon with a hint of respect mingling with the constant suspicion in his eyes. The sea elf turned back to Alicia, his expression hardening to its familiar lines. "I must see to the debarking of cargo," he said stiffly, turning back to the great canoes.

But the princess was gratified when she looked into those green, almond-shaped eyes, because for the first time, besides the anger and suspicion, she saw a hint of doubt.

* * * * *

The prisoner's mind continued to grow as his body purged itself of the memory-suppressing drug. He recalled things— images and sensations—but still had difficulty attaching names to those memories. He knew that he had been a king and sensed that this was a great thing, but he couldn't name his kingdom or remember his subjects.

The loss of his hand had grown in his mind, becoming more than a wound. It was an affront, an attack against his pride that he could not let stand. He had no clear memory of who had cut it off, but when that memory returned, someone—or some*thing*—would die. The man knew that he had killed before, and he remembered that killing was not a pleasant task, but sometimes a necessary one.

Most tantalizing of his recent memories was the image of a woman—a person of exquisite beauty and great tenderness. Her hair, long and black and silky, he recalled particularly. His mind drifted to images of that hair, of his hand stroking it, of his woman lying in a sun-speckled field of heather, with birds soaring above and towers of white piercing the sky near them.

It was an idyllic sensation, and for a moment, the recollection swept him along, warming his heart and even bringing an unconscious smile to his face. Then the memory dissipated and he looked around at his dank cell, and once again the rage began to swell.

This fury of his became a constant companion. It drove him to restless periods of pacing when he stalked the confines of his surprisingly large cage. He stared at the pool of water that served as the entrance. Where did it lead? How far did it go? The other features of his chamber provided even less promise. The dark green windows, slanting toward the top of the domed ceiling, swept overhead well beyond his reach. The lump of coral that served as bed, bench, and table was the only other object in the circular room.

Gradually he had noticed a pattern of darkness alternated by dim illumination through the panels in the ceiling, a cycle that seemed to approximate day and night. Once each cycle, shortly after the panels grew light—morning?—a monstrous creature brought him bare sustenance. The creature had the scaly skin of a fish, with thick strands of hair hanging across its scalp, and sharp teeth and claws.

The monster always emerged from the water quickly, surprising the man. The beast rose onto two legs, looming high over his head, glaring down at him with pale, emotionless eyes as it filled a shell cup with fresh water and placed a bowl of fishy gruel beside the pool. Then, with a shake of its bristling head, it dove back into the pool. And every time this jailer departed, the human king found himself staring at the rippled surface of the water. Where did it go?

Of course, his memory couldn't help him there, and to this end, he decided to explore. Water held no inherent fear for him. He knew that he was a proficient, if not a great, swimmer. He broke the surface in a dive, swimming through darkness for several seconds. Immediately, however, he realized that the loss of his hand created a severe handicap, rendering his swimming awkward and clumsy. Desperately he turned around, kicking hard to return to his cell, gasping in near panic.

For a full day, he avoided returning to the water, but after his jailer again brought him his miserable food, the man knew he had no choice but to try again. On this attempt, however, he relied mostly on his feet to propel him, while he felt along the dark passage before him with his hand and wrist.

Several times he repeated the dive, swimming carefully along the tunnel away from the pool. Each time his confidence grew, and he compensated more and more efficiently for his wound, mostly by kicking. He soon found that the tunnel branched, no more than forty feet from his cell, into three other passages. All of the corridors were water-filled from floor to ceiling—at least, at the place where they met the other submerged corridors.

At first, the man swam no farther than this intersection, returning to his cell and gasping for air as he emerged. But he found, as he practiced, that he swam a greater distance each time. His lungs expanded with the rigorous discipline of increasingly prolonged dives, until he explored some length of all three tunnels.

Finally, sensing that his guard would soon return with his food and drink, he paused to rest and consider what he had learned.

One tunnel, the straight route, continued to descend as far as he could follow, and he had nearly drowned the time he followed that passage a hundred feet past the intersection. The tunnels to the right and left, however, began a gentle upward slope after the junction, similar to the approach to the prisoner's cell.

It seemed a reasonable assumption, then, that similar cells might lie to the right and left. Would they be filled with air, like his? He had no way of knowing.

He fully understood the risks. He had already gone as far as he could down each tunnel while still making it back to his cell. If he went farther, he would have no choice but to go forward and either find air at the end of the tunnel or perish.

The decision was easy.

The prisoner spent some time in quiet contemplation. Somewhere he had learned to do this, to empty his mind and allow his body to fuel itself for maximum efficiency. In a flash, he remembered: The black-haired woman had taught him. His

skill had never approached hers, for she was . . . she had been
. . . a druid.

Robyn!

In the instant of recognition, his mind filled with joy, followed
by nearly intolerable pain. He groaned aloud as memories
came flooding back—delightful memories, each one of which
only increased his anguish. He was here, she was . . .

Callidyrr! The Moonshaes!

"I am Tristan Kendrick!" he shouted at his unseen jailers.
"I am the High King of the Ffolk, and you shall not have me!"
Pictures of two small girls—no, they were young women—
came into his mind. One was fair, the other dark like her mother. They were his daughters!

Roughly he pushed the tidal wave of memory aside. He focused on the task before him, studying the water, forcibly
quelling his emotions. His heartbeat fell, pulsing slower and
slower. Tristan breathed deeply, without thinking, filling his
lungs with air, forcing extra oxygen into his blood, grimly determined to press forward to the last gasp of his life.

He dove into the pool, cutting the surface like an arrow and
allowing his momentum to propel him halfway down the tunnel
leading from his cell. When he kicked, he moved his legs slowly, moving through the dark water with a minimum of exertion.
Feeling the wall beside him, he traced the path to the four-way
intersection. Here he veered to the right.

The tunnel rose slowly, and he allowed his buoyancy to account for some of his speed, though he still kicked gently. On-
ward through Stygian darkness he swam, feeling a rough wall
with his right hand. Occasionally his back would scrape the
abrasive ceiling of the tunnel. The pain he didn't mind so
much, but the sensation that he *couldn't* swim upward he
found starkly terrifying.

Tristan swam without thinking, slowly draining the air that
filled his lungs to bursting. Pain wrapped steel bands around
his chest, slowly constricting until a red haze swam before his
eyes. His throat tightened, and the urge to gasp for air swiftly
approached irresistible proportions.

How long had he been swimming? At least an hour, it seemed to his oxygen-starved brain. More than that, screamed his lungs, his tortured chest that could no longer supply the needs of his body.

Then abruptly the wall to his right ended. Tristan flailed mindlessly as the depleted air exploded from his lungs, but as he thrashed, he realized that rock no longer pressed against his back. Desperately driving himself upward with the last reserves of his strength, he felt his hand, and then his face and torso, break from the water and burst into an enclosed cavern that was filled with air.

He coughed and choked as he dragged himself onto a dry stone slab beside the surface of water. Dimly his awareness returned, and the king realized that he was in another cell, one very much like his own. The same dim green illumination trickled through the ceiling.

It was only when he stopped gasping that he looked up and saw that the room was occupied. He saw a man's face staring at him—a thin, emaciated visage with great dark circles under his eyes. The fellow was seated, chained to a wall, Tristan saw, with shackles around each of his wrists and his arms held spread-eagled to the sides.

The chained prisoner regarded him impassively. When the fellow shifted slightly, Tristan noticed something odd about his legs, and then his jaw dropped in shock.

The man had no legs—but not because he had lost them in an accident. In fact, his body below the waist had never borne a resemblance to humanity. It was a single, powerful limb, covered with green scales and ending in a broad-finned tail.

The creature, Tristan realized, was a merman.

* * * * *

For six days, the men of Gnarhelm labored on the hull of the longship, and gradually her bruises disappeared, her scuffs and scrapes vanished beneath fresh timber and tar. The *Princess of Moonshae* seemed to sit taller, prouder on the sandy base of the drydock.

Though the rudimentary forge belched out clouds of black smoke while Brandon supervised his men's making of nails and brackets, a constantly fresh breeze whisked through the grotto, clearing the air of fumes and soot. For the most part, the voyagers had taken little note of their splendorous surroundings once the equipment for repairs had been delivered. Good news had come as soon as the drydock was fully drained; Brandon's inspection showed that the longship's stout keel remained undamaged.

Alicia and Robyn both worked with unspoken urgency, knowing that their quest had a greater chance of success than they had previously dared to hope. Now they hauled firewood, stirred tar in large vats, and helped with other tasks wherever they could. Of course, the actual work on the ship was left to Brandon, Knaff, and a few experienced shipwrights among the crew. The prince would settle for nothing less than perfection.

The two women worked to the point of exhaustion, but even then they found it difficult to sleep. Memories of Tristan, imagined pictures of his current peril, drove them to restlessness. While they were sailing, there had been nothing that either of them could do to speed up their progress. Now, however, it seemed that each extra hour of work might bring them that much closer to departure.

Eventually, however, they realized that no matter how fast they piled up fuel or stoked the forge, the work on the vessel would proceed at a careful and methodical pace. Thus it was that one afternoon late in the week, with plenty of firewood stacked beside the fires and a surplus of heated tar available for the hull, Trillhalla prevailed upon the females—Alicia, Robyn, Brigit, and Tavish—to accompany her for a swim. They splashed through the narrow grotto to a secluded, sandy cove where they could enjoy a few hours of relaxation.

Alicia found that her concerns and fears seemed to fade as she lay in the soothing sun or splashed about in the coral shallows of the grotto, chasing schools of multicolored fish.

"Your captain tells us that the repairs are nearly completed,"

Trillhalla announced. "Soon Palentor will bring you the Helm of Zulae, the artifact that will enable your vessel to survive underwater. Then I suppose you will be on your way."

The notion of departing sounded the familiar note of guilt to Alicia, and her mother nodded seriously. "Yes. It becomes urgent that we sail. Tristan, I sense, is in terrible danger."

"Even worse than before?" asked Alicia.

"I don't know . . ." the queen replied, shaking her head as if to disparage the remark. Alicia, however, saw an expression of grave concern, even fear, hidden in the depths of her mother's eyes.

"I am glad for Evermeet that you have come," said Trillhalla bluntly after a few seconds pause. "There are too many of us who group the humans in with scrags and sahuagin. It is good that they see you are different."

"Too many like Palentor, you mean?" Alicia couldn't resist asking.

Trillhalla allowed herself a slight smile. "My poor compatriot has been thrown into a bit of a quandary by your arrival. You see, you've forced him to rethink a few notions about humans that he's held for more centuries than I've been alive."

"I'm glad!" Alicia declared.

"Such learning can flow in two directions." It was Queen Robyn who spoke, and her words were directed to her daughter. "It would be well for us to remember the acts that have driven elves like Palentor to believe as he does. Humanity is not blameless in this strife."

"No—I didn't mean . . ." the princess stammered, embarrassed. Of course her mother was right, but in the Moonshaes, the elves were safe in the sanctity of Synnoria. What did her mother's statement have to do with Alicia?

They heard shouts of greeting from the dockside, hidden from their shallow beach by a small outcrop of forest. Curious, they dressed quickly and started over to see what was happening.

"The helm!" Brandon cried as he saw the women. "Palentor's bringing it to the dock!"

They hurried forward and saw the by now familiar cargo canoe easing to wharfside. The taciturn sea elf was in the water, swimming toward the dock to emerge with a smooth, fluid motion. In the center of the craft was a surprisingly small object, covered beneath a well-padded blanket. Several elves of Evermeet lifted the thing from the vessel and placed it on the dock where Palentor waited.

"I hope you appreciate the value of this gift," began Palentor, speaking to Brandon and Robyn.

"Aye, that we do," replied the northman, with a frank look at the elf. "Even as we're surprised that you give it to us."

Palentor regarded Brandon quizzically. Then he bent down and swiftly unwrapped the blanket that had cloaked the Helm of Zulae.

The humans saw a larger than normal silver battle helmet with a full-face visor—so full, in fact, that it was even devoid of eyeholes! A sleek, ribbed fin jutted from the center of the object, sweeping from front to back like the dorsal fin of a fish. The sea elf nodded toward the *Princess of Moonshae*, with the proud female figurehead rising from the bow.

"Place this over the head of that carved figure," he explained, "and your ship will descend through the surface of the water. A pocket of air will remain over your crew, in the inverted shape of your hull."

"How does she move?" inquired the captain.

"The helm will propel her, although at much slower speeds than on the surface. You'll have to rig a second rudder to guide the ship up and down. Also, you must furl your sail before you submerge, or water pressure will tear it away quickly."

"Slower speeds, you say. How much slower?" asked the Prince of Gnarhelm.

"You'll make perhaps five knots."

"Does it have a time limit?" inquired Keane, staring in obvious fascination at the silver object.

"Indeed. It varies based upon the number of elves—I should say, people—in your crew. For a complement such as yours, I estimate that you will be comfortable for perhaps twelve underwater hours and capable of surviving for another twelve. Beyond that, though the mask will maintain the bubble around your ship, the air becomes stale and useless. Suffocation inevitably results."

Palentor looked them over, ready to challenge anyone to argue with him. None did. The picture he painted created a graphic image in the minds of all his listeners.

"When we're down there, then, we'd best pay attention to the time," Hanrald murmured dryly.

"I think we'll notice when the air starts to go bad!" Brigit affirmed.

The sister knight stood beside the earl, and it occurred to Alicia that they had been together a lot during the stay in Evermeet—at least, when Hanrald wasn't working with the men on the ship repairs.

Alicia's attention drifted to Keane, and she saw that the mage looked peaked, with dark circles under his eyes. He clutched several large tomes to his chest, as if he had been reading, and parted only reluctantly from his texts. Five days ago Trillhalla had brought him some books, and these he had perused ever since with obvious eagerness. Indeed, of all the men, he had been the only one who hadn't worked on the repairs. Instead, he spent his time reading in a secluded part of the grotto. Now, however, he listened carefully to the words of the sea elf.

"I—I feel I should warn you of something," Palentor said, as if he forced himself to speak despite great reluctance. "My scouts have reported a massing of the fishmen armies. Sahuagin and scrags, plus huge schools of sharks, which they use as their scouts, have collected just beyond the cyclone barrier."

The sea elf paused, and for a moment, Alicia wondered if he was preparing to launch a harangue against them for gathering the enemy to his shores. Instead, he spoke with real sincerity.

"We suspect that they await your departure. As I explained before, the cyclone belt is no barrier to undersea intrusion. They are not holding back an attack against us, for their numbers have been stable for several days and they have made no overt move toward the elvenhome. Instead, they screen the entire eastern coast of Evermeet."

"I suspected that might be the case," Keane noted. "Their pursuit was too diligent to break off on the suspicion of our destruction."

Trillhalla offered the next advice. "There may be a way to get you around that barrier," she said tentatively. "I'll have to talk to the queen."

"If not, we're helpless against them under the water, aren't we?" Alicia questioned. "After all, we can barely outrun them on the surface. They could easily catch us when we submerge."

"They can catch us, yes, but we're not exactly helpless," Keane continued. He raised the heavy books in his arms, as if the others might not have noticed them, then smiled at Trillhalla. "Thanks to our friends here, I have been able to learn a few new spells that might aid us. Water breathing, for one, and free action—and several others. If it comes to battle, they may prove very useful."

"Druids are not without useful abilities in this situation as well," Robyn pointed out.

Palentor looked at them all, his eyes wide and an expression of guarded respect on his features. "One thing that has not been exaggerated is the courage of humanity. I . . . begin to believe that you may accomplish your objective."

"*That's* a relief," muttered Alicia. She flushed when the sea elf turned his almond eyes toward her, then stared in astonishment as he concluded.

"Even more," Palentor added, with the first smile—albeit a small one—that the visitors had seen on his face. "I hope that you succeed."

With a quiet nod at all of them, the sea elf turned away and sliced through the waters of the grotto in a clean dive.

* * * * *

"Who are you?" croaked the chained figure, his tone weakened almost to the point of death.

"I am—" He wanted to say that he was Tristan Kendrick, High King of the Ffolk. Somehow that fact didn't seem important now. "I'm a prisoner here, like you. Only they didn't chain me."

"They assumed the water would stop you. I need more secure restraint." With a tight smile, the merman gestured with his fishy tail in case Tristan missed the point. "I am Marqillor, of Deepvale," added the prisoner.

"Tristan Kendrick, of the Moonshaes."

"I know those islands."

The words were like a flame of hope to the king. "You do? Where are they? Where are *we*?"

Marqillor shifted uncomfortably. "We are in the dungeon of Krell-Bane, in the heart of Kyrasti, his great fortress in the Coral Kingdom," the merman explained. "The cells of air, where Krell-Bane's most hated prisoners are kept."

The chained captive leaned his head against the wall, and his mouth worked weakly, as if he struggled for enough air to breathe.

"Can I help you?" Tristan asked, examining the brackets, both of which seemed secure.

"Water . . ." The merman gasped weakly and nodded toward the pool where Tristan had emerged. "It almost killed you, I know, but without it, I will die."

The king saw a large bucket near the wall of the cell and went to fill it. "To drink?" he asked as he returned.

Marqillor smiled and shook his head. "Throw it over me," he said. Tristan did so, and immediately he saw the merman's expression grow softer. He leaned back in apparent bliss. "Again . . . please?"

The human willingly soaked down his fellow prisoner, amazed at the abrupt transformation. Within moments, Marqillor seemed vibrant and healthy. He strained, albeit fruitlessly, at his bonds.

"Are they trying to kill you?" asked Tristan. "Is that why

they keep you out of the water?"

"No. They enjoy the torment, that's all. When I reach the point of complete collapse, they come and revive me. Sometimes I've awakened to find Krell-Bane himself observing me."

"Krell-Bane . . . tell me about him. Who or what is he?"

The merman described the scrag king and his race. "The sea trolls are the inherent masters of the sahuagin."

"Much the way trolls control orcs and goblins on the surface," Tristan realized. "And this is their palace?"

"Aye," grunted Marqillor. He looked at Tristan quizzically. "Do you know that you're five hundred feet below the surface of the sea?"

Now it was the human's turn to sag wearily backward. "I guess I'm not completely surprised, though how I got here alive I couldn't tell you."

"The scrags have ways," Marqillor stated. "Though normally they don't bother with the effort. They keep only prisoners who they feel will make valuable hostages."

The two captives looked at each other with the same idea.

"I'm High King of the Moonshaes," Tristan stated bluntly.

Marqillor smiled wryly. "And I am the Crown Prince of Deepvale," he concluded.

* * * * *

Sinioth lurked in the depths, seething with impatience. Were the humans dead, slain by the cyclones of Evermeet? Or did they still live, plotting and planning against his master?

The more he agonized, the more he convinced himself that the latter circumstance was the case. These intrepid voyagers would emerge again, he felt, bringing their longship against the aquatic army in their desperate attempt to carve a path to their king.

Yet even as he contemplated his great plan, with thousands of scrags and sahuagin effectively barring the sea east of Evermeet and the fast Manta floating just below the surface in the center of that great deployment, Sinioth's unease grew. They were resourceful, these humans . . . they had surprised him before.

More and more, he realized, the avatar of Talos should consider returning to his undersea monarchy. If the humans somehow passed his barrier of predatory sea warriors, he knew that he would finally meet them in the Coral Kingdom.

❧ 15 ❧

Embark to the Underdeep

"We'll be ready to sail as soon as the drydock fills with water," Brandon announced late in the afternoon of the day following the Helm of Zulae's arrival. "Knaff's rigged up the horizontal rudder, so the *Princess* is as good as new—maybe better."

Despite the fact that this was the culmination of all their endeavors, and Alicia had been eager to proceed all week, she found that the northman's announcement caused a melancholy reaction. Indeed, she was not alone. The longship's entire complement seemed to take the news like a dousing of ice water.

"We'll wait for first light, I presume," ventured Hanrald, standing beside Brigit. The sister knight looked around their grotto, and Alicia saw a trace of panic in her eyes, as if the elfwoman would suffer deeply upon their departure.

"Aye—and the tide, a few hours beyond. But we'll be well away from shore before noon," replied the captain. Even Brandon seemed to bite back a trace of wistfulness at the notion of leaving the idyllic elvenhome.

But of course there was no choice, nor really did Alicia welcome the thought of any further delay in her father's rescue. It was more that the sensations of the past eight days had been so pleasant, so relaxing, that the reality of a return to their quest seemed to loom like a many-headed hydra, threatening them with a dozen different fates, all of them bleak.

"Ready to get back to sea?" asked Keane, looking surprisingly undismayed by the prospect of sailing. "It should be—"

"No, I'm *not* ready!" Alicia snapped, annoyed that for once Keane should be prepared to embark on an adventure while she felt a deep reluctance. She looked at his pallid skin, at the circles under his eyes. "Where have you been all week, any-way?" she demanded, knowing full well that he had engrossed himself in tomes loaned to him by the command of the queen. Alicia's frustrations welled up and, as had so often happened during her childhood and adolescence, all of that anger focused on the convenient scapegoat of her familiar tutor. "We've been sailing the seas, living outside, and you're *still* pale!"

The magic-user turned away, hurt, and Alicia wondered why she had spoken to him so harshly. She felt little better after her outburst; her temper still smoldered with a low flame. Why does he let me do it? she wondered, wishing that for once the man would respond to her with anger of his own.

She threw herself into the frenzy of preparation and found release for her tension there. They had water barrels to fill, food to pack and load, and a final inventory, repair, sharpening, and polishing of weapons and armor to make.

"I'm not sure I relish a return to hardtack and stale bread," observed Brigit as they looked over their provisions, which had been unloaded when they beached the longship. Now they started to pass the heavy crates back into the hull.

Before dusk of that last night in the elvenhome, one of the great cargo canoes sailed into the grotto, propelled by its usual complement of elves. Trillhalla and Palentor stood in the bow, and as it neared the dock, the humans saw a wide variety of foodstuffs—melons of all sizes, large wheels of cheese, kegs of butter and honey—piled high in the center of the boat.

"A gift from Queen Amlaruil," announced Trillhalla, stepping lightly onto the dock. "Delicacies for the palate that may make your journey a little more pleasant."

Palentor stepped out of the canoe, bowing to the humans. The male sea elf looked remarkably unhostile, which is not to say he appeared friendly.

"The provisions of Evermeet are famed throughout elven-dom," he said stiffly but with a real effort to control his arro-gance. "The queen—that is, *we*—hoped that you would enjoy them as you embark upon this final leg of your quest."

"Your generosity—and your queen's—is overwhelming,"

Robyn said sincerely. She took a few steps forward, standing directly before the sea elf and staring into his eyes. "Thank you, Palentor."

The mottled green of the elven warrior's face darkened, and Alicia wondered if he blushed. He bowed with great formality before speaking.

"Perhaps . . . perhaps I should thank you," he said. "We live in great isolation here on Evermeet. Indeed, isolation is the key to our survival. But you have shown me that not all humans are rapacious destroyers as we have been taught.

"Your courage is obvious, and your skill—setting out for Evermeet and actually reaching our shores—is something that no ordinary creature would dare to do." His gaze shifted from Robyn to Alicia, who was staring at Palentor in surprise. "I hope that you find your father," he said.

"Thank you," was all the princess could reply, but suddenly the resumption of their quest became the most important thing in the world.

"The armies of the deep?" inquired Brandon. "Do they still await us beyond the cylcone belt?"

"Aye," replied Palentor. "They have gathered in greater numbers than I have seen. . . ."

It seemed that the sea elf had not completed his statement, though his voice trailed away. He regarded them carefully, and they sensed that he was trying to decide what to say next.

"There . . . there is a way around them," he finally announced. "A concealed passage through the reefs along the eastern shore that you could follow to the south, passing west of Belintholme, the Guardian Isle. That course should carry you around the cordon."

"How well concealed?" wondered the captain grimly.

"Perfectly. No charts have ever been made. It is mapped only in the minds of a few elves who have spent much of their lives in those waters. Anyone who tried to sail it without such an elf as a pilot would find himself—well, much as we found you—high and dry, a mile off the shore of Evermeet and going nowhere."

"The pilot, then . . . ?" Brandon prompted.

"These passages are keys to the final defense of the elvenhome!" Palentor snapped brusquely, as if he desperately wanted them to undertand. "Nevertheless, the queen has placed it in my discretion. If I choose to provide you with a pilot, she has granted you permission to sail the secret ways."

They waited, curious and tense. Alicia wondered why he had told them this much. She was sure Palentor's rabid belief in the sanctity of Evermeet's defenses would prevent him from allowing the humans to sail those concealed channels.

"You, Sister Knight, have shown me much by your example," continued Palentor, stealing a look at Brigit. "As you know, your staunch defense of Synnoria through the past centuries has not escaped our notice. Yet if one who has devoted her life to preserving the sanctity of an elven land sees fit to welcome humans there, perhaps there is good cause. I see now that there is.

"I will lead you along these paths," concluded the sea elf in a sudden rush of words. He glared at them for a moment, as if challenging someone to dispute him, but even so Brandon's reaction took him by surprise.

"I knew it!" boomed the northman, stepping forward to clap the much smaller elf on the shoulder. "You're all right, you know that, Palentor?"

The sea elf was too astonished to reply, but he smiled hesitantly as the crew raised a cheer. The elves produced great baskets of fruits and kegs of sweet wine, and the grotto rang with celebration, music, and dancing late into the night.

Alicia joined Robyn, Trillhalla, and Tavish on a blanket near the roaring bonfire. Keane and Brandon, and later even Palentor, came over to join them. The wine flowed sweetly, and as darkness settled across the grotto, the voyagers rose to a spirit of celebration.

"To our hosts! Their generosity stands as a shining example to all the Realms!" proclaimed Robyn, raising a crystal goblet of red wine. All the crew joined in the solemn toast.

"And to our guests," replied Trillhalla. "May their endeavor be blessed with success."

Thoughts of that endeavor again propelled Alicia. She felt certain now that, if her father lived, they would find him. Yet in the fellowship of the fireside, the camaraderie of their last night on Evermeet, she felt a growing wistfulness. The thought of her companions gave her strength, and she resolved to throw herself into the resumed voyage with every ounce of her energy.

"Where's Hanrald?" the princess wondered at one point when the company was well into their second cask of wine.

Brandon looked at her, his expression sly. "He's gone for a walk with Brigit, I think—at least, I saw them amble off together a few hours ago."

The princess looked around, trying to suppress her sudden shock. In truth, she had noticed the bond that had seemed to slowly develop between the couple, and every time she thought of it, it puzzled her. She felt a flash of jealousy toward the elven woman, a feeling she recognized as irrational, but it remained with her nonetheless.

After tuning her harp, Tavish sent songs of joy and celebration wafting through the camp. She played short, lively songs, ribald ballads, and sang gentle verses of love and valor—all of it music that floated through the night, a perfect counterpoint in sound to the idyllic grotto surrounding them.

Alicia listened to the songs dreamily. Idly she looked around again, wondering if Hanrald had returned, but neither he nor Brigit were anywhere to be seen.

Her gaze drifted over to Brandon, who looked back at her and grinned. She saw a light in his eyes. Was it the reflection of the fire, or something else? When she looked at Keane, the magic-user seemed morose, sitting quietly by himself and staring into the flames.

Abruptly the princess rose to her feet, surprised that her legs seemed slightly unsteady beneath her. Nevertheless, she started into the darkness beyond the pale of their fire. Soon the thickness of the grotto's grove surrounded her with foliage, blocking out the glow of the fire behind her and the glimmer of starlight overhead.

Alicia wondered for a moment why she had walked off like this. She couldn't find anything out here, and that, she admitted, was probably a blessing. Or had she come out here to find anything? Perhaps she wanted instead to get away. Everything seemed terribly confusing to her.

"It's the wine," she mumbled, turning back to the fire.

"The wine . . . and the firelight on your hair."

The voice was Brandon's, and it came to her as a shock. He had followed her into the darkness!

"Wh-what do you mean?" she demanded, startled.

"I didn't mean to frighten you," explained the northman hastily, placing his hands on her arms. For a moment, she froze, barely seeing his tall form in the darkness. But when he leaned closer, she raised her lips to his and they met in a long kiss.

It *is* the wine, she told herself as a torrent of emotions, thrilling and frightening, poured through her. His strong arms clasped her firmly, and she found that grasp comforting . . . and welcome.

"I love you, Alicia, and I would sail to the stars and back if that would win your love in return!"

The suppressed tension in his voice surprised Alicia, and it excited her to realize that she had such an effect on this proud and independent man.

And then they had no more time for words as their lips met in another kiss. Slowly, gently, Brandon lowered Alicia to the ground.

* * * * *

Keane watched and waited, staring at the place in the darkness where the northman and the princess had disappeared. A thicker blackness than mere night threatened to sweep over him, and his mind worked its way through a variety of imagined pictures—the two of them alone, in the woods, on this night of celebration and leave-taking.

For a moment, anger—unfamiliar, taut, and powerful—coursed through Keane. He thought of a thousand things he could do, ranging from a shower of light through the woods to violent, explosive magic directed at Brandon.

Even in a despairing rage, he could never hurt Alicia, and in point of fact, he knew that he would take no action against Brandon either. Yet it mollified him a little to imagine it.

Realizing that the celebration had lost its allure for him, Keane made his farewells and wandered off to his bed.

* * * * *

"How often do they come to you?" inquired Tristan, after Marqillor had regained his strength from the dousing of water. The merman's skin glowed, his eyes shone, and his voice came forth with a vigor that had not been there minutes earlier.

"Not often." The merman shrugged. "Perhaps every three days, though of course it's hard to tell down here."

"Recently?"

"No. That's why you found me in such bad shape. I'd suspect it won't be long now."

"How many at a time?"

"Just one." Marqillor's eyes flashed as he began to understand Tristan's point. "A big scrag. He comes out of the water and taunts me for a bit, kicks me and the like. Then he throws the water over me so I'll stay alive until the next time."

Tristan looked around, seeking something—anything—that he could use as a weapon. He had heard of the sea trolls, of course, and now he felt reasonably certain that the beast that had brought him his food was one as well. He had battled enough trolls in his life to identify the scrag as an aquatic cousin of that obscene race.

The only thing he found was the large bucket of hammered copper he had used to throw the water over the merman. "I'd rather have a sword," he observed, ruefully examining the distressingly flimsy container. He was weighing the fact that he would have to bear it in his single hand.

Tristan turned his attention to the metal brackets holding Marqillor's hands. Despite the corrosive rinsings, the manacles remained gleaming and clean, displaying a high level of craftmanship.

"It's no use," said the merman with another awkward shrug. "I've spent weeks tugging on them myself. The only way to get them off is with the key."

"Does that scrag carry the keys with him?"

"Yes—and a big knife, too." The merman's face creased into a slight smile. "He keeps the knife in the back of his belt, probably so that a prisoner doesn't try to grab it from him. Maybe that can work to your advantage."

At Marqillor's affirmation, the basics of their plan were set. Tristan took the bucket and crossed the cell, making himself as comfortable as possible in a shadowy niche beside the pool. He settled down for a long wait, yet strived to remain ready to scramble out at a moment's notice, trying not to let his mind dwell on the coming fight.

Still, images of horror and shock raced through his mind. Previously he had vanquished trolls while wearing metal armor, bearing a mighty sword, and more often than not, mounted on a stalwart charger, aided by resolute companions. The prospect of attacking one of the creatures unarmored and virtually bare-handed—*one*-handed, in point of fact!—struck him as rash to the point of insanity. Not insanity, he corrected himself—just brutal necessity.

Marqillor leaned back against the wall, trying to relax. Time passed with imperceptible speed. Tristan struggled to remain alert, holding the bucket, watching the water, silent but ready to spring forward.

The scrag came out of the water so quickly that it had fully emerged and stood dripping at the rim of the pool before Tristan even noticed beast's arrival.

Then his mind blanked momentarily in sheer panic at the size of the monster. It stood at least nine feet high. The creature possessed considerably more muscle than did the land-bound trolls he had encountered. Strapping bands of sinew rippled under its dark, fishlike skin as it stepped toward the imprisoned merman. Its feet and hands were webbed and tipped with long, wicked talons, and a burst of weedy hair covered the nape of the neck and extended halfway down the broad green back.

A wide belt was the scrag's only garment, and true to Marqillor's prediction, a silver-bladed, bone-handled knife was stuck through the waistband at the small of the creature's back. On the right side, looped through the belt, gleamed a keyring.

Tristan had no time to waste. The beast was certain to look around for the bucket and discover him, costing Tristan his only advantage.

At the same instant he came to the conclusion, Tristan acted. Holding the pail inverted in his hand, balancing it with the stump of his left wrist, Tristan sprinted from the niche, leaping toward the monster's shoulders. He brought the bucket down full over the monster's large, shaggy head. Bashing it with his wrist, ignoring the pain that shot like fire up his arm, he forced the metal container tightly onto the creature's great skull, where it stuck like a bizarre helm.

Immediately the scrag whirled, reaching for Tristan with two talon-studded hands, but the High King wrapped his arms around the beast's waist, following it through its spin and staying beyond the reach of those deadly claws. The scrag snarled as it turned, making a sound like water sucked down a drainhole.

Then the man grabbed the handle of the creature's knife and sprang away, bringing the wickedly curved weapon with him. The hilt felt rough to the touch, but the weight of a blade seemed natural in Tristan's hand. The monster, still snarling, reached for him with one talon-studded paw, and the human swung with all his strength. Keen steel sliced scale-covered flesh, a savage blow that lopped the limb off at the forearm. He heard Marqillor's shout of encouragement, but then his vision filled with the tooth-studded horror springing toward him, the creature's sharklike mouth gaping wide. Though the bucket still covered the monster's eyes, it did nothing to block the grotesque mouth.

As savagely as any beserk northman, the sea troll attacked the insolent human. If the creature felt any surprise at Tristan's presence, the fact didn't delay a furious reaction. The High King fell back, whipping the blade this way and that to block the monster's flailing attacks. Each time the sharp steel bit into the scrag's flesh, but the wounds did nothing to diminish the fury of the attack.

In fact, Tristan felt a shudder of piercing horror when he looked at the stump of the thing's wrist, where moments before the human had severed the hand. Tiny claws already sprouted there, growing longer as he watched. Soon they wiggled grotesquely as the bleeding wound gradually regenerated the hand.

For a moment, the monster paused, raising its hand to the bucket and tugging at the obstruction. Tristan took advantage of the moment to strike, driving the blade into the scrag's good arm, chopping deep into flesh and bone—though not with enough force this time to slice off the limb. With an angry howl, the beast kicked outward, and the man barely evaded the blow.

Both wounds were temporary, but for the moment, the creature's hands were useless. It could neither attack nor lift the bucket from its head. It paused, gasping for breath, its mouth gaping to reveal rows of triangular teeth, fangs gleaming faintly even in the pale emerald light. For a moment, the sea troll turned its face to the water, obviously considering the merits of a tactical withdrawal. The latter possibility meant disaster, Tristan realized, for if the creature escaped and returned with assistance, they were lost.

But in the monster's temporary halt, he saw his chance and dove forward, thrusting the stump of his arm through the large keyring. He used his momentum to carry him past the beast, spinning it in a circle as he charged.

The scrag dropped its blunt nose to bite this pesky attacker, but the monster's own steel dagger darted in to stab the creature's soft tongue. With a strangled gasp, the sea troll lurched backward, and the keys broke free from the belt as the wounded creature thudded heavily to the floor.

"Don't let it get to the water!" hissed Marqillor desperately, watching the monster wriggle toward the pool.

Tristan leaped on the thing's back and drove the dagger through the scaly skin, into the base of its wicked brain. Instantly the scrag stiffened, jerking reflexively for a moment and then growing still.

"*Hurry!*" urged the merman, straining in his iron brackets. "It'll be up again in a few minutes!"

Although Tristan had seen the horror of regeneration in trolls, it seemed even more sickening in this monstrous creature from the sea. Desperately he searched through several keys—fortunately there were only half a dozen on the ring—and found the one that clicked the manacle free.

"Kill it again!" barked Marqillor as the scrag started to kick and groan before the second bracket was released. Tristan left the keys with the merman and returned to dispatch the monster with another thrust to its brain. By the time he finished, Marqillor had succeeded in working himself free of the final bracket.

"Thank you, friend," said the merman, using his long tail and his hands to propel himself over to Tristan and the troll. He looked up at the human for a moment. "You wait here," he said, and then he slipped silently into the water and disappeared.

For a moment, Tristan was too shocked by the merman's disappearance to react, and by then it was too late. All he saw were the spreading rings on the surface of the pool.

And then once again, beside him, the sea troll began to stir.

* * * * *

The secret passages through the coral reefs would have been impossible to find, according to Brandon, without the guidance of the sea elf Palentor.

"The thing is, they look like shallows," the Prince of Gnarhelm explained in amazement. "And what looks like the passage as often as not is studded with those great spires of rock or coral. That's what caught us on the way in."

The Prince of Gnarhelm had been garrulous and friendly since they had departed from Evermeet, as if on their last night together he and Alicia had settled all of their doubts. To the princess, however, the situation was exactly the reverse. The unease she had felt before was magnified tenfold now, into a raging chorus of tension and anxiety.

Her disquiet increased as she began to suspect how much her dalliance with Brandon had hurt Keane. The magic-user had spoken barely two sentences to her since they had boarded the ship, but she noticed him looking at her frequently, though he dropped his eyes quickly whenever she tried to meet his gaze. His unhappiness brought guilt into Alicia's emotional maelstrom, and finally she devoted herself to the voyage, spending a great deal of her time in the bow, watching the sea elves guide them through the narrow channels and gaps.

For two days, the *Princess of Moonshae* continued to slip southward, hugging the shoreline and working through the mazelike pattern of reefs, shallows, and channels. The tall trees of the Elvenhome rose off to their right, never more than a mile away. By keeping this close to shore, Palentor informed them, they should avoid observation by any scouts that the seaborne army might have sent to search for them. Palentor told them that he had dispatched squads of sea elves to patrol the seas beside their route in a further attempt to avoid observation.

So far they seemed to have been successful. There had been sign of neither scrag nor sahuagin. Frequently a blanket of thin mist obscured the reaches of the sea, further securing their progress from detection.

Now Alicia couldn't wait to get on with their task, across the open sea and then . . . down. None of them had talked about it very much, but they all felt some apprehension about the efficacy of the Helm of Zulae. Of course they believed it would work—otherwise the entire mission would have gone for nothing—but nevertheless, the unnatural method of travel couldn't help but disturb sailors used only to the sunswept expanse of the surface.

The horizontal rudder installed by Knaff trailed behind them, just above the water level so it wouldn't impede their progress on the surface. Yet a disturbing fact was forcibly reminded to each voyager when they saw the silver helmet gleaming in the middle of the hull. They would be voluntarily *sinking* their ship!

Still, progress remained steady, and always the heavy bank of land lay to the west. Then on the second day out from the grotto, they began to notice that the land swept away, no longer running north to south but instead commencing a great curve away from them—the southern terminus of Evermeet. A low, rocky horizon loomed to the south—the Guardian Isle of Belintholme, according to the sea elf.

"Sail due south for two or three hours from here," Palentor instructed the Prince of Gnarhelm. Brandon. "That'll take you beyond the reefs. Then you can swing your course around to the east and a little south."

"Aye—and thanks," grunted the northman. Brandon had come to respect the sea elf mightily. Also, he fully understood the value of his guidance on this embarkation, for it had saved them from the pitched battle that would have inevitably ensued if they had sailed straight east.

"It—it has been my pleasure," replied Palentor, with apparent sincerity. He and Trillhalla took a few moments to say good-bye to the others in the crew, and then the sea elves disappeared over the side into the mottled waters.

For a few moments, they watched the pair until they vanished. Then, favored by a strong westerly wind, with the sea before them calm and inviting, the *Princess of Moonshae* started on the final leg of her quest.

* * * * *

Darkness shrouded the longship, though a dim phosphorescence gleamed in the white water pushed aside by her racing bow. The sail stretched taut, pressed by a steady wind, and Brandon himself had the rudder as they charged through the night. It was a few hours after sunset on the first day of their return to the open sea. Belintholme had vanished astern sometime during the afternoon.

The Prince of Gnarhelm fixed his eyes upon the waters ahead, and the sleepy lookouts, too, kept their attention on the ocean surface surrounding the boat. None looked for trouble in the shadowed confines of the hull.

But that was where Luge stirred, once again kindled to the task that he did not understand—or even acknowledge, once the morning sun crested the horizon. Now the little northman crept to the gunwale, undetected by his comrades. His hand reached into the secret pouch, removing one of the tiny bells, as it had done every night of their outbound voyage from Gwynneth. In a quick motion, he cast the object over the side and crept back to his bench.

Below and behind the speeding longship, sinking steadily into the depths of the ocean, the tiny bell began to ring.

*   *   *   *   *

The vast undersea army hovered in its screen, stretching more than two hundred miles along Evermeet's coast. Creatures of the deep, the sahuagin and scrags kept their distance from the coastal shallows around that great island. The deadly defenses of the sea elves were well known to these aquatic raiders. Nevertheless, they formed a solid cordon along the drop-off, where the coastal shallows plummeted into ocean depth.

Coss-Axell-Sinioth slipped along the length of the great formation, unable to dispel a sense of unease, although he was pleased with the alertness, the barely contained killing frenzy, he saw among his minions. His huge squid body loomed great among the teeming scrags and sahuagin, and an escort of giant barracuda cleared the waters before the avatar wherever he went.

The remaining Manta Sinioth held in the center of the line, crewed by his most powerful sahuagin and several elite corps of sea trolls. Krell-Bane himself, the monstrous sea troll, captained the great raft. The army was poised and ready, prepared to strike any place along that vast front.

Of course, there was a possibility that the longship had been sunk, but it was a likelihood Coss-Axell-Sinioth did not believe. This belief had nothing to do with sensing the life-force of his enemies or anything like that. Instead, the feeling owed its persistence to Sinioth's sense of destiny: He couldn't believe the issue would be settled without a direct battle between the human foe and his own undersea minions.

The sound of the bell thrumming its basso resonance far to the south came as a rude shock to the avatar of evil. The humans were afloat—and more significantly, they had somehow slipped past his great army!

Immediately Sinioth mustered his minions, sending them in a great swarm following in the wake of the elusive and speeding longship. The avatar pictured the rage of Talos should his quarry escape them, and he drove his creatures with brutal lashes of his tentacles.

Then, a day later, another bell followed, and a third on the night after that. The three bells formed a perfectly straight line, and Sinioth had no difficulty drawing that line to its inevitable destination: the underwater city of Kyrasti, the heart of the Coral Kingdom.

Grimly Coss-Axell-Sinioth left the army of the deep under the command of Krell-Bane. The sea troll king pursued the *Princess of Moonshae* aboard the speeding Manta, leaving the vast majority of the scrags and fishmen to swim in the raft's wake. The aquatic monarch slowly narrowed the gap, but it would be a close thing.

The giant squid, meanwhile, sped southeastward at speeds that far exceeded those that even the Manta could travel. Sinioth would go to Kyrasti, there to prepare for the approaching threat.

Perhaps, to be on the safe side, it would also be necessary to kill the prisoner.

☙ 16 ❧

The Final Manta

Deirdre spent her days in Caer Callidyrr idly, when she did not immerse herself in the studying that seemed to expand the horizons of her knowledge on a daily basis. The affairs of the kingdom required little of her attention, and her irritable reaction to any interruption ensured that the servants and advisers sought to solve any problems themselves rather than risk the wrath of the young princess.

Many times during these days she sat before her mirror, scanning the wastes of the Trackless Sea without success. She did not believe that her mother or sister were dead. Deirdre was certain that, if this were the case, she would know beyond doubt. Still, their disappearance frustrated and concerned her. She wondered if they had established some means to screen the *Princess of Moonshae* from arcane observation.

Then, in the sudden revelation of a summer's dawn, she saw them again, coursing south by east now. The meaning of the course was clear to Deirdre: They had reached Evermeet and now proceeded with the next step of their mission.

Her first reaction to the discovery of her mother's party was an upswelling of relief. She knew now that the longship had no defenses against her scrying, although Evermeet did. Nevertheless, now she would be able to follow the continuation of the mission in her glass. She felt a growing measure of excitement as the *Princess of Moonshae* plunged steadily through the swells.

Casting forward, using the mirror once again to press below the surface, she looked for some sign, some clue of the Coral Kingdom's existence. She could find nothing, but she didn't believe this was because of any such arcane barrier as screened Evermeet. Instead, she suspected that it was simply because she didn't know where her target lay, nor was she linked there by a bond such as drew her to her sister and mother.

Yet if her search for the undersea realm failed, her reconnaissance provided her with another bit of information that hit the young princess with a bolt of anger and excitement. There in the ocean depths, she encountered a presence . . . a thing that was full of menace, and also familiarity. She searched carefully, sensing its nearness.

She found that essence in the body of a giant squid, but she knew that the flesh was merely a disguise. Immediately she felt the soul of the one she had known as Malawar.

She had found him again! Deirdre met the news with dark determination, resolving that this time the avatar of her enemy would not escape.

* * * * *

Tristan killed the sea troll for the tenth time, though leaden weights seemed to tug at his arm. The dagger lost more of its edge with each blow, and finally fatigue began to drag him toward the floor. How long could he endure, holding off sleep in order to maintain his grim vigil?

He reflected on the bitter confines of the submarine lair. Not only did it entrap him, but it limited his air. The only way to permanently kill a troll, as far as Tristan knew, was to burn it. Yet here, even if he had been able somehow to start the creature ablaze, the smoke would probably choke him. A grim joke for the troll, he thought without humor, if the creature reached from beyond death to claim the life of the one who had slain it.

Where was Marqillor? Would he return? Tristan had no idea how much time had passed since the merman had disappeared so abruptly. If the human had been abandoned, he knew his life would last only until he fell asleep, for then the troll would regenerate uninterrupted, rendering the fate of his sleeping captor inevitable.

Splashing water, the first clue that he had dozed, startled Tristan awake, and he sprang to his feet clutching the dagger.

"Hold, friend!" declared Marqillor, curling his tail beneath him at the edge of the pool. The merman raised himself to the height of a kneeling human as he spoke.

"Where were you?" demanded the king, embarrassed at his lack of alertness.

Abruptly more water splashed upward, and again, and each time the pool disgorged another merman until more than a dozen had gathered around Marqillor, sitting at the edge of the pool with their long tails trailing into the brine. The aquatic creatures examined the sea troll—which Tristan hastily dispatched again—and regarded the human with expressions of clear respect.

"I went to pay a call on some friends," Marqillor announced. "They wanted to meet you."

"Can we get out of here?" inquired Tristan, knowing it would take a stunning bit of sorcery to transport him to the surface in any state approaching alive.

"I don't know. The surface is far away, and if you swam the distance quickly, the rapid change in pressure would surely prove fatal."

"What can we—I—do, then?"

"We can go to the palace of Kyrasti," explained Marqillor. "That's the great dome where Krell-Bane and Sythissal hold court. It's the very heart of the Coral Kingdom. More significantly, a portion of the throne room is filled with air. You will be able to survive there."

"Sythissal." The name was familiar to Tristan. The sahuagin king had been his enemy for more than twenty years. "But who's Krell-Bane?"

"The king of the sea trolls, and a very evil monarch he is. Krell-Bane is the most hated enemy of the merfolk, and we have been given a marvelous chance to strike him!"

"Why is it so marvelous?" Tristan wondered.

"Because you freed me," explained the merman prince. "The perimeter of the scrag king's palace is well patrolled by sharks as well as by his troops. The interior of the castle, secure as he imagines it to be, is not nearly so well protected."

"How far is it?"

"Several miles," admitted Marqillor, placing a hand on Tristan's arm as the human's face fell.

"I can never swim that far," Tristan acknowledged with a shrug. To come so close to escaping, and now to be thwarted by such a trivial distance!

"There might be a way," offered Marqillor, studying Tristan's face. "It is not without risk, and it requires great courage on your part, but it may be possible for you to make it."

"I'm ready to try anything," said Tristan—and he meant it.

* * * * *

"Dead ahead, Brandon," Robyn quietly announced to the Prince of Gnarhelm. The northman nodded. For five days, he had followed no compass but the intuition of the Great Druid, yet he didn't begin to doubt the acuity of her direction.

The wind had favored them for the first two days but then faded to a lackluster breeze. They made headway, but their listless wake sliced placid waters, a far cry from the white slash trailing the *Princess of Moonshae* when she was under full sail.

"Look—in the water!" announced Brigit, her voice terse and commanding.

The others saw them, too—sharks, in a great school gathered around the longship. Schools of the ugly fish, triangular fins slicing the surface of the water in menacing patterns, approached from fore and aft until dozens of the predators surrounded them, spread in a wide escort around the longship. The marine predators had no difficulty matching the *Princess of Moonshae*'s speed.

One of the longbowmen took aim at a huge gray shark as it approached the hull. His arrow pierced the sleek body, immediately coloring the surrounding water pale red. Moments later, the ugly fish closed on their stricken fellow, tearing the body apart in a thrashing orgy of killing.

"Look! Here come more of them!" announced Keane as more fins appeared, slicing through the water from the north. Additional bowmen raised arrows and took aim.

"Don't shoot," the queen suggested. "The blood will only draw replacements—faster, I'm sure, than we can kill them off."

"Makes sense. Save the arrows for the sahuagin and scrags," Brandon agreed.

"Look!" For an hour or more, Knaff the elder had been observing a strange blot on the northern horizon, until finally he made his terse announcement, calling the discovery to the attention of the others.

"It's one of those damned flat ships!" cursed the captain as soon as he saw the object. He looked critically at the sun, the sail, and then back to the pursuing Manta.

"They'll be on us with hours of daylight to spare," he announced cryptically.

Robyn came to the stern and looked. "I could try to raise the wind . . ." she said tentatively, turning to look at the Prince of Gnarhelm.

Brandon met her gaze, then shook his head firmly from side to side.

"There's only one of 'em now. I think we should take our chances in a fair fight. We're sailing into the heart of their territory, and it doesn't make sense to let that ship hug our tail while we do it!"

"I agree," Alicia said firmly, turning to her mother. "And we serve no purpose exhausting you before we get there!" The princess's readiness for battle surprised even herself, but Alicia found herself looking forward to crossing blades with the aquatic horrors on the Manta. After the long days of travel and repair and further travel, her emotions distressed her. Brandon continued to make her nervous, and she couldn't look at Keane without a stab of guilt.

It seemed proper now that they would begin to settle this matter, writing the solution in blood.

True to Brandon's prediction, the Manta had closed to within a few hundred feet by midafternoon. Alicia studied its approach, clearly able to distinguish the long platforms separated by strips of churning sea. Hundreds of fishmen paddled furiously, and the blunt prow of the raft rode up on the swells, the flatship surging forward like a great flying fish.

The humans readied themselves for battle, and it seemed to the princess that her mood was shared by the rest of the crew. She saw no reluctance to face the sea beasts. Indeed, many of the men displayed smiles of grim satisfaction at the prospect of battle.

As the splashing raft drew steadily nearer, the crew of the longship studied their foes and prepared to mount a defense. First to strike were the Corwellian longbowmen.

"Aim for the sahuagin, men!" Hanrald urged. "Your arrows'll be wasted on the sea trolls!"

The ten Ffolk archers fired volley after volley of steel-headed death from their powerful weapons. Most of the missiles angled with precision onto the unprotected decks and rowing benches of the Manta, and dozens of the scaly fishmen squirmed from the impact of the deadly rain. Their comrades simply pitched the slain over the sides to lighten the load for those remaining. Sharks swarmed among the corpses, relishing the gruesome feast.

The High Queen faced the approaching craft and held her staff in both hands. Alicia, beside her, carried the changestaff for the time being, but her sword rested in its scabbard at her belt. More arrows poured onto the Manta, but they seemed to put little dent in the teeming sea beasts.

Then, to the horror of the humans, the raft surged forward, veering toward the longship's rear quarter. The prow of the Manta, Alicia saw, was not so blunt as she had imagined. In fact, it narrowed to a sharklike snout, and through the froth of the wake, they could see the gray reflection of a metal-tipped ram!

Robyn recognized the impending disaster clearly, and she raised a prayer to the goddess Earthmother. Even through the deck of the longship, past the thousands of feet of brine into the ocean depth, the power of the great druid touched that of her deity and the words of the spell came forth.

"*Cadeus, devor-ast!*" cried the High Queen, and the command words touched the power of wood. Trees were the most stately children of the goddess, and thus ever susceptible to her will, even after they had been torn from the earth, their timber turned to the uses of creatures such as humans . . . or sea trolls.

Timber such as the heavy shaft of the ram.

Robyn's spell warped the great beam, twisting it downward and forming a great curl back toward the Manta. The creaking force of the twisting wood shrieked against their ears, but the shaft did not splinter. Instead, it held its new shape, the great timber curling downward into the water, pointed harmlessly toward the ocean floor. The sudden increase in drag slowed the great raft like an anchor, and disaster was averted for the moment. As the Manta lurched to the side, waves of water rolled over the long rowing benches, dragging the craft still slower and carrying many of the sahuagin right off their vessel.

A huge scrag, wild strands of weedy hair blowing around its head, snapped and shouted at the crew members, many of whom scrambled back aboard and returned to their places on the long benches. Slowly the flat ship picked up speed, until it again approached the pace of its quarry.

But though no longer threatened by the ram, the *Princess of Moonshae* couldn't pull away from the deceptively swift vessel. Keane cast a fireball against the bow of the Manta, incinerating a dozen sahuagin and a trio of scrags—but even that lethal explosion made little dent in the numbers on the wide raft.

The thing was surprisingly huge, Alicia saw—far bigger than she had previously imagined. Not only was it longer than the *Princess of Moonshae*, but the Manta's tremendous beam also increased its carrying capacity by dozens of times. She counted six of the great rowing benches, each little more than a long pole running fore to aft, straddled by dozens of sahuagin. From the pole the creatures dipped their paddles into the water that slid below them. The Manta had five long slots in its deck for just this purpose.

The sharks swarmed in closer, as if they, too, sensed imminent bloodshed. Several more sahuagin, slain by arrows, toppled into the water, and the ravenous shark pack immediately swarmed around them. The blood in the water drove the fish into a frenzy, and the surface of the sea roiled from the savage orgy of feeding.

"We can't keep this up forever!" Brandon declared, drawing Robyn and Keane aside.

"What do you suggest?" inquired the queen.

"We attack," the Prince of Gnarhelm stated bluntly. "We grapple with the bastards. We kill them or kick them off of that accursed raft, and then we burn the thing!"

"They outnumber us ten to one," objected Robyn. "That's too rash!"

"More like five to one," suggested Keane, who was studying the Manta intently. He frowned in concentration. "Of course, we'll need to leave a guard behind on the *Princess*. It wouldn't do to have them swim under her and come up on the far side."

"You're not seriously thinking of this, are you?" pressed Robyn, turning to the magic-user. Then her brows tightened. She knew the time for debate and decision was short, and finally she sighed. "I don't have any other solution. Let's do it."

"The sharks . . . they might keep the fishmen out of the water," suggested Alicia, who had joined them.

"Too risky. They kill the wounded, sure, but they're under the control of the same forces. Better to leave the bowmen on the longship. They'll have to use swords if it comes to that. Bring up the casks of oil. We'll need help if we're going to burn the raft."

Within a few minutes, the plans for the attack had been made. The Manta plunged along to the rear, within long bowshot range, but the archers had ceased shooting some time ago in order to conserve their arrows.

"Now!"

On Brandon's command, Knaff brought the longship into a tight turn to port, cutting across the Manta's path. The monsters howled as they surged forward, once again closing the gap while the *Princess of Moonshae* veered across the raft's bow. Gradually the ungainly Manta began to swerve after them, but now the longship cut back, carving a broad S on the sea before the plunging raft.

Both vessels had slowed considerably during the maneuver, and when Brandon gave the command, his northmen plunged a dozen oars into the water, bringing the *Princess of Moonshae* to a sudden stop. As the Manta surged alongside, humans cast hooks and harpoons, each attached to a long line anchored to the longship's hull. Some twenty of these grapples stuck, and in the blink of an eye the two huge vessels lunged together, hulls grinding, lashed in a battle to the death.

Bowmen poured volley after volley into the monsters at the edge of the raft. Keane called upon lightning and fire, raking one bench with a lightning bolt that blasted two dozen sahuagin to pieces. He sent a great fireball to blossom in the middle of the enemy troops, sending many more of them hissing and shrieking into the sea. Next Keane pounded the Manta with meteors, huge stones that splintered pieces of timber from the hull, crushing the scaly warriors struck by the magical bombardment.

"*Phyrosyne!*" cried Alicia, stamping the base of her staff against the hull, hoping the tree creature could maintain its balance better than it had the first time she had summoned it in the longship. Immediately the shaft began to grow, and as the twin feet appeared, the being braced them to either side of the hull, growing taller and taller until the leafy, branching form rivaled the height of the mast itself.

No earth elemental could serve the Great Druid here, but Robyn's powers drew from a broad arsenal. She barked a command, again calling on the power of her goddess, and this time her servant arose from the sea itself. A foaming, manlike shape grew from the waves beside the Manta, scrambling onto the raft and bashing several sahuagin overboard with watery—but very solid—limbs. Humanoid in shape, it grasped the Manta with two arms, pulling itself aboard the pitching craft where it stood up on two broad, sloshing feet.

The lurching figure of frothing brine possessed real crushing power in its whitewater fists. The elemental scrambled across the raft and crushed any of the scaled monsters foolish enough to come within reach. Even the scrags tumbled away, battered and broken, from the summoned creature's powerful blows. Under the onslaught, the first rank of monsters fell back, leaving fifty or more of their number dead on the deck.

"Let's go! The path's as clear as it'll get!" cried Brandon, whooping and raising his battle-axe as he scrambled over the gunwale, followed by his crewmen and their Ffolk allies.

Brandon led his shouting northmen, with Hanrald, Alicia, and Brigit in their midst, against a mass of fishmen who had evaded the elemental and surged back to battle human foes. The two forces met in violent melees of hacking and stabbing, chopping, snarling, and hissing bodies. The cursing of wounded northmen mingled with the reptilian gasps of battered sea creatures.

The lurching figure of Alicia's changestaff lifted itself methodically over the rail of the longship, and though it staggered on the planks of the pitching raft, it picked up a squirming sahuagin and snapped the creature's spine with a twist of the tree's great limbs.

From the afterdeck of the longship, Tavish took up her lute and sent forth a martial song. Her fingers struck the strings of the enchanted instrument, a treasure from the tomb of Cymrych Hugh himself, bestowed upon the bard by the will of the goddess. Now she called upon those strings for all the power at their command.

Chords resonated in the wooden box, rolling across the combatants with different effects. The music attacked the creatures of the sea with raw violence, an excruciating assault against their senses. The jarring force of the notes forced some of the sahuagin back, driving many of them to press their hands over their heads in an attempt to block out the horrendous noise. Even the scrags barked and growled, discomfited and annoyed by the sounds.

To the humans, charging onto the pitching deck of the Manta, the music sounded a trumpet cry of courage, urging them forward in a cause they knew must be just. Hoarse northmen bellowed cries of battle, mingling with the bard's vibrant notes, and Hanrald and Alicia shouted the name of Callidyrr as they raised their swords and charged across the heaving planks of the Manta's deck.

A lightning bolt crackled over Alicia's head, blasting a gap in the rank of sahuagin standing ready to meet her. Hanrald's two-handed sword chopped a pair of the creatures in half, while Alicia stabbed one and quickly parried another's return blow. The second one lunged a fatal step too far, and her dripping blade drove through its neck to make her second clean kill.

Alicia saw her changestaff slip and fall, splashing through one of the slots in the hull, but then the limbs extended across the rowing bench, and slowly the stiff wooden shape scrambled back to the Manta. A huge scrag leaped at it, splintering one armlike limb with a crushing axe blow, but the tree being's other arm wrapped swiftly around the scrag's ankles, pulling the beast to the deck. The monster howled in pain as the wooden form twisted its body into a crippled mass of scaly flesh, finally tossing the grotesque thing to the sharks.

"Attack! Take the fight right to 'em!" bellowed Brandon, gathering his crew for a charge.

The water elemental and the prince led the lumbering assault. The humans formed a V-shaped wave with Brandon at the point as they battled their way across the rocking deck of the Manta. Several men fell through the rowing slots in the chaos of the battle, plunging into water churning with hungry sharks, but there was no stopping to save them as the battle rose to a furious pitch.

Alicia's vision focused on an array of fang-studded mouths

and ripping, wickedly curved talons. Her blade claimed victim after victim, and she drew comfort from Hanrald's steady presence at her side. On the other side of the earl, Brigit Cu-'Lyrran held her own, her silvery longsword streaked with the green, red, and black blood of their fishlike enemies.

Robyn advanced in the rear of the attacking wave, going to each of the sea trolls wounded or temporarily slain in the battle. To these wretched predators she touched the tip of her staff, and the body crackled into flame, sputtering an oily cloud of black smoke into the air. The legs and arms of the horrid beasts shriveled into the flames as the magical fires devoured their grotesque fuel.

Arrows showered overhead as the longbowmen, standing at the rail of the *Princess of Moonshae*, continued to support the attack. When the assault carried halfway across the Manta, a huge scrag organized a counterattack, a rush of monsters that took the humans by surprise. Several crewmen fell, and Alicia lost her footing on the blood-and-water-slicked deck.

She teetered at the brink of a foaming slot in the deck, sensing the sharks thrashing below, eager for her blood. Desperately she reached out, but her hand slipped across the slick timbers. Then she felt a firm grip under her arm, and Keane pulled her backward, just beyond the thrust of a monstrous scrag. Her feet splashed into the water, and she felt a sharp cut in her calf as a snapping shark narrowly missed a meal.

The mage barked a command word as a sea troll—the hugest Alicia had ever seen—raised a monstrous trident. Keane pointed over Alicia's head, and she saw bolts of magic explode from the mage's outstretched finger, each of the missiles spattering into the chest of the monster, driving it steadily backward until, after nearly a dozen blasts, a mass of sahuagin rushed forward, blocking the magic-user's line of fire. The fishmen swarmed around the water elemental, and though many of them fell from the creature's crushing blows, finally the enchanted being collapsed into water, flowing back into the sea from which he had come.

Brandon personally led a charge toward the huge scrag. The

other monsters deferred to the great creature, who wielded a monstrous double-bladed sword. The Prince of Gnarhelm struck at the thing with his axe, and the sea troll slowly, steadily gave ground.

Hanrald and Knaff the Elder stepped in to guard the captain's flanks, while Alicia turned to look back to her mother, intent on protecting her against any monsters who might break through the rank of northmen. She saw a monstrous sea troll fell a crewman and charge forward with an upraised spear aimed straight at the High Queen's heart!

But Alicia leaped across a slot of churning seawater, getting there first, chopping savagely to hamstring the charging monster before it could cast its weapon. The beast fell and she cut its throat, stabbing hard to penetrate the scrag's scaly armor. Quickly her mother stepped to her side, stamping her staff against the sea troll and starting its incineration.

Brandon and the monstrous scrag chopped and slashed back and forth, the northman swinging his great battle-axe with bone-crushing force, the scrag wielding the massive sword as if he were a lumberjack striving to fell a tree with a single blow. Again and again the two metal blades clashed together, neither fighter able to gain an advantage as they leaped and dodged across the blood-slicked planks of the Manta's deck.

Cries of alarm drew their attention back to the *Princess of Moonshae*, where they saw a dozen sea trolls scrambling over the sides—the type of attack Brandon had suspected. But the longbowmen were ready, throwing down their missile weapons and meeting the attack with cold steel. The ten Ffolk archers battled desperately to hold the longship, and though three had fallen by the time Hanrald reached them with reinforcements, the scrags were all slain or sent bleeding back to the depths.

The huge scrag battling Brandon lunged for the captain, sweeping his great sword through a great arc with enough force to slice a human body in two if it connected. The northman ducked as the blade whistled toward him, barely evading the strike. As Brandon sprang back to his feet, the double-bitted axe whipped upward, the edge biting deep into the scrag's belly. The monster howled and dropped the sword, which bounced off the deck and vanished into the sea. The scrag spun, ready to dive after the weapon, but Brandon's blade struck again, squarely between the monster's shoulders. It fell to the deck with a thud as the Prince of Gnarhelm chopped it again, this time fatally. In another moment Robyn reached them, touching her staff to incinerate the beast before it could regenerate.

Next Keane and Robyn combined to sweep a surging wall of flame across the last corner of the Manta where they still met resistance, finally clearing the enemy vessel of foes. Fires smoldered in many places where Robyn had torched the bodies of the sea trolls, and the frame of the raft itself burned in several spots.

"Oil!" cried Brandon. "Bring those casks over here!"

Crewmen made ready to cast the longship free as the flammable liquid was poured liberally over the deck of the Manta. Pools of oil caught fire as soon as they touched the smoldering sea trolls, and quickly the surface of the raft was engulfed by flame.

The humans beat a hasty retreat to the *Princess of Moonshae* and quickly drew in the lines that lashed the two vessels together. Sunset began to shroud the sea as they hoisted sail and caught the freshening breeze, the same breeze that fanned the fires aboard the burning Manta into an inferno of destruction.

The great raft blazed into the night, a shrinking ember on the horizon, as the speeding longship once again followed her course to the southeast.

* * * * *

Talos and Malar watched the unfolding drama through the window of his enchanted mirror, beholding each scene as Deirdre observed it—peering over her shoulder, in effect, at the longship and its desperately battling crew.

The Destructor felt the woman's interest in the avatar even as he saw the failure of Sinioth's plan to trap the longship. Would the servant of evil fail him again? If he did, Talos vowed that it would be Sinioth's last failure.

Then once again his thoughts turned to the dark-haired princess as Deirdre focused her attention on the enchanted—and very dangerous—glass.

❧ 17 ❧

Kyrasti

"We're close now," Robyn announced, full of certainty. She didn't try to explain her assurance, nor did any question it. Faith had guided them across hundreds of miles of the Trackless Sea. Now that same faith told the queen that her husband was near.

Sunrise cloaked the *Princess of Moonshae* in a fine mist, but pale blue already domed overhead with the promise of a clear day. A good breeze had carried them through the night, and now it ruffled the sea into cheery whitecaps.

The longship left a swath of wake through the swells, cresting each and pouncing forward to the next as if the vessel herself sensed the nearness of their goal. Alicia stood in the bow, wanting only to finish the voyage soon—for better or worse.

The Helm of Zulae, still sitting on a rowing bench before the mast, gleamed in the first rays of sun to break the mist. Alicia looked at the powerful artifact and at the vast expanse of featureless sea. How could they possibly know when to dive, where Tristan was held below the unchanging waters?

Her mother, however, had no such doubts. Robyn, too, remained in the bow of the longship, her eyes closed in concentration. Tristan's presence grew in her heart and her mind, filling her with hope and determination. Finally, less than an hour after the pale dawn, she turned back to Brandon. From his position beside the helm, the sea captain looked at her expectantly, and she raised her head in affirmation.

"It's time," Robyn said softly, the words carrying clearly to every member of the crew.

Brandon nodded. News of the impending descent washed swiftly through the ship, and the men alternately looked upward at the sun, knowing that they might be beholding it for the last time, and down at the suddenly menacing sea. Would those waters soon swallow them?

"Ready with the helm," cried Brandon. Hanrald and Brigit picked up the artifact and carried the gleaming object to the bow, where they stood behind the figurehead and awaited Brandon's next command.

"Steady on the rudder," the captain instructed Knaff, who stood at his usual post. "Furl the sail, lash down anything loose, and ship the oars!"

His crew leaped to obey, every man determined to do his best. The familiarity of the tasks lent necessary stability to the strange prospects before them. Knaff himself tested the horizontal rudder they had affixed, insuring that the wide, short stabilizer could move freely up and down.

"Can it work?" asked Alicia, only half-joking as she stood beside Keane and watched the enchanted figurehead.

"Don't you think it's a little late to wonder about that?" replied the magic-user. Alicia laughed, though Keane hadn't intended the remark to be humorous. She took his arm and he sighed—sadly, she thought. The two of them turned their attention to the captain, and the princess felt Keane's arm tighten beneath her clasp. Unconsciously she clasped him more firmly.

"All stand by!" Brandon cried, looking once more at the sky. If the Prince of Gnarhelm was nervous, however, he didn't betray it in his posture or his voice.

"Now!" he called sharply, chopping downward once with his hand.

Hanrald and Brigit smoothly raised the Helm of Zulae over the wooden figurehead. Carefully they lowered it, pleased as the smooth silver headpiece came to rest firmly on the female features of the proud carving. The helm seemed to shrink slightly, so that it rested firmly on its wooden perch.

Immediately the longship settled lower into the water, with an unsettling lurch that was obvious to every member of the crew. Before anyone had time for second thoughts, Brandon looked at his helmsman with a grim smile. "Let's go," he said.

Knaff instantly pushed down on the horizontal rudder, driving the wedged platform into the water at the vessel's stern. The manuever raised the longship's after quarter, angling the bow downward into the waves.

Alicia felt a slight tilting of the deck below her feet, and suddenly the horizon canted to the side. She grasped the gunwale with her left hand, still clutching Keane's arm with her right, as the *Princess of Moonshae*'s prow sliced through the surface of the sea.

Waves rolled to either side, and the sensation that the ship was sinking underneath her was impossible to avoid. Frothing, angry turbulence to port and starboard surged higher and higher, until it rolled *above* them, but none of the water spilled into the hull.

More and more of the ship plunged beneath the surface, until the roiling maelstrom formed a tube enclosing the forward half of the vessel. Alicia, standing amidships, took a last look at the sun, and then white water surrounded her. She turned aft and saw Knaff the Elder's teeth clenched in determination as the stern of the longship followed the rest of the vessel under the surface of the sea.

She looked along the length of the hull, upward through a column of air, like seeing the blue sky through a window or from a hole deep in the ground. Then foaming brine closed over the rudder, and the ship slipped below the surface of the green, rolling water.

Suddenly, and pleasantly, the turbulence around them settled. No longer was the water white and frothing. Instead, it flowed past them above and below in a smooth green wall. Only where the mast broke the dome overhead did a line of wake appear. To the rear of the ship, a foaming trail bubbled as water closed behind the *Princess of Moonshae* while she moved through the sea.

The helm masking the longship's proud figurehead propelled them forward, and if they moved slower than on the surface, no one thought of complaining. The dome of air remained over the crew, the air pocket shaped very much like a second hull, the same shape and size of the longship's.

"She's girded for war now," Keane observed softly, with a long look at the silver-helmed figurehead. He might have spoken of the whole ship, Alicia thought. They were *all* ready for war.

Grim-faced crewmen sat at their benches, staring at the green water flowing past a few feet from their faces. Awed by the powerful magic, none of the sailors broke the silence. Instead, they clutched weapons close at hand and maintained a wary watch on the sea.

We can do it! Alicia felt the strongest thrill of hope she had known since their quest began. They sailed *under* the sea! With a moment's guilt, she admitted to herself that she had never fully convinced herself that the helm would work. Of course, there remained the matter of finding her father and vanquishing any of his captors who stood in their way, but these seemed minor concerns to the princess. Anticipation consumed her. Her emotions surged closer to joy than they had in several bleak months.

A gray shape flashed through the green water, catching her eye with a start. She thought she saw another, and then a third. Alicia strained to look. Illumination in the boat was weak, filtered as it was through a steadily increasing blanket of brine, and she wondered if the shapes had been products of her imagination. Then she saw rows of teeth inside a gaping mouth lunging from the water toward her face!

"Shark!" cried the princess, drawing her sword as she quickly stepped backward. The complacency of her earlier mood vanished in the instant of attack. Inches from her skin, grotesque jaws snapped shut with a loud slap, but before she could stab with her weapon, the hateful snout disappeared into the water.

"Help!" shrieked a crewman, and Alicia whirled to lay horrified eyes upon the northman writhing in pain, the jaws of a huge shark clamped on his shoulder. He twisted and screamed, trying to lunge toward the center of the hull. The rear half of the great fish remained in the water as it struggled to pull the fellow from the hull.

Several of his comrades leaped to his aid, driving the shark back with blows of sword and axe, and finally the fish released its victim. The man collapsed to the deck, groaning piteously, as blood spurted from torn skin and flesh.

"Over here—look out!" Shouts of alarm rang through the hull. The *Princess of Moonshae* shuddered repeatedly to the bumps of dozens of blunt heads bashing into the timbers of the hull.

Water exploded into the boat across from Alicia. She turned just in time to see several huge sharks almost thrash free from the green sea. Their jaws closed over the arm and head of a stunned northman, and before the wretch could even scream, they dragged him back into the protection of the briny liquid. The princess whirled just in time to stab a shark that had lunged at her unprotected back. A scream from the bow told her another crewman had not been so quick or so fortunate.

"Stand them off!" shouted Brandon, chopping wildly at the churning water with his axe and driving one of the piscine carnivores back, but only for a moment. Another fellow, one of the Corwellian bowmen, screamed as a huge shark dragged him into the water.

Robyn stood in the stern and made a snap decision. Turning to the transom, she dove into the water. At the same time, she called upon the power of the goddess, a power she had used often before, but never in this way.

She shifted her body into the form of an animal with the ease of long practice, but this time—as her limbs turned to fins and her head formed a long, bullet-headed snout—she forced herself to grow. Her size expanded far beyond the limitations of human mass. The power drained her resources but infused the druid with might *now*, when she needed it most. There would be time later to recover, or so she hoped.

Quickly Robyn grew, her shape stretching, narrowing to a driving muscular tail. Patches of white and black appeared across her skin, and the powerful flukes of her tail drove the great mammal forward. Air exploded from the hole at the back of her neck, and she opened a cavernous mouth, knowing that teeth had multiplied and grown there, longer and sharper than any shark's.

The ravenous killers still swarmed around the *Princess of Moonshae*, intent upon their quarry—so much so that the swift onslaught of a killer whale into their midst came as a complete surprise. Robyn attacked with savage fury, her love for her husband and daughter magnified, it seemed, into a consuming maternal rage by the great body encasing her.

In seconds, a dozen sharks floated, ripped and lifeless, in the wake of the onrushing mammal. More suffered·the crushing bite as the whale surged on, and many not killed were left crippled in the water, irresistible prey for their cruel and ravenous fellows. Great jaws slashed and crushed, and though many of the fish turned to snap at the whale, they couldn't slow her driving attack. The druid felt the tearing pain of sharp teeth raking her flanks, slashing her fins and tail, yet she drove forward in relentless onslaught.

Sensing the need for air in her great lungs, Robyn propelled herself upward, drawing the enraged sharks into slashing pursuit. She rose quickly, beating them to the surface and exploding into dazzling sunlight. Exhaling with a burst of steam, the great mammal then drew in a large lungful of air. Then, twisting gracefully in the air, she dove into the midst of the shark pack.

Crushing with her powerful tail, biting and slashing with her massive jaws, the killer whale again tore through the savage fish, again ignored frenzied jaws that ripped at her own skin. More and more of the sharks turned toward easy feeding on the carcasses of their mates, slain by the deadly whale. Those who still dove after the longship Robyn pursued, attacking without mercy, biting to at least cripple each shark that came within range of her jaws.

Finally the harrying carnivores fell away, discouraged and defeated by the druid in the body of a whale. They circled in the distance, menacing and patient until Robyn rushed at them. Then the fish scattered in the face of her ominous approach, and by the time the whale turned back to the longship, the sharks had lost interest in their mission. The survivors returned to partake of the feast that their heavy casualties had provided them.

The *Princess of Moonshae* continued to descend away from her, but the druid circled warily for several minutes, ensuring that the vicious fish did not return. Finally, convinced that they would remain content with their current spoils of battle, she rose once more to the surface, breaking into the sun and spouting steam from her nostrils. Drawing a deep lungful of air, she lifted her tail to the sky and dove.

Like a sleek harpoon she plummeted into the depths, soon making out the incongruous shape of the proud longship coursing forward through its alien environment. The killer whale swam to the ship, and as she reached the pocket of air, Robyn allowed her body to return to its human form.

Wearily the queen tumbled into the longship, where she barely felt welcoming hands lift her to the deck, laying her down gently and spreading a warm blanket across her. As if from a great distance, she saw that her legs and arms were covered with bites, many of them bleeding. The whale hadn't escaped the battle unscathed.

Then, as Alicia and Tavish knelt to tend her wounds, darkness rose around her and the High Queen slipped away.

*　*　*　*　*

Again Tristan's lungs felt as if they would burst. All around him pressed dark water, dragging against his body from the force of his movement. He clung to the strap of leather, feeling the sea rush past his body, sensing the impenetrable depths yawning for great distances around him. Yet still he held on and held his breath . . . until at last his lungs could stand it no longer.

Then, as he had been instructed, he exhaled.

He felt the cloud of bubbles ripple along his chest and knew a momentary panic at his lack of air. Then he felt a body beside him, hands seizing his head and other lips pressing to his own. Eagerly Tristan opened his mouth and inhaled, feeling a welcome rush of oxygen enter his lungs.

That's one, he told himself as he again determined to hold his breath as long as he could. One of the mermen had given him air—another precious minute or two of survival here in the alien deep.

Marqillor had explained it to him: Each merman could breathe underwater, through the use of gills located at the nape of the creature's neck. Though the creatures also had lungs, these organs were not used when a merman swam underwater. Thus the aquatic humanoid could take a lungful of air and hold it, just like any human swimmer, except that the air would not be depleted by use, since the merman didn't need it.

But Tristan did. Again he reached the limit of his endurance and gasped out a cloud of bubbles, and another merman swam before him and gave him the gift of air.

Two, the human silently tallied.

Marqillor had also explained the limitations. While all the mermen had taken a breath of air before they left the dungeon, they could not generate additional oxygen in their lungs while they swam. The use of the gills bypassed the air-breathing organs entirely. Thus Tristan could count on but one breath from each of his companions, and he knew they had to swim for several miles.

There were thirteen mermen in the party. Marqillor hadn't been specific about their destination, except to promise him that there would be air in Kyrasti, the domed palace of the Coral Kingdom.

All Tristan had to do was make his thirteen precious lungfuls last that far.

The king of the Ffolk held on to a leather belt around Marqillor's waist, so that none of Tristan's energy was expended in swimming. Even if he had two good hands, he could never have hoped to approach the speed the merman attained with no difficulty while hauling his ungainly human cargo.

Vaguely he sensed that it grew darker around them, and he knew they swam down some kind of tunnel. He saw turbulence ahead and heard strange cries ringing through the water, followed by the sharp clicking sounds of underwater combat. The mermen had stumbled upon several sea troll guards and swam into the midst of the guardpost, furiously attacking their hated foes. Marqillor's warriors slammed into the larger creatures, bashing them with their muscular tails.

One of the scrags whirled, thrusting a sharp trident through the body of a speeding merman. Air and blood escaped the body in a foaming cloud as the unfortunate creature sank, motionless, toward the bottom. Other mermen slashed in, quickly disarming the scrag and then beating the sea trolls into senselessness.

The crucial count continued, amid darkness and pressure and the eternal chill of the ocean depth. Five, eight, finally ten of the mermen sustained Tristan with the breath of their lungs. They swam above a deep chasm, with cliff walls plummeting to inky black depths below him, and then they crested a low wall. Once again a huge pair of scrags floated before them, but the mermen attacked mercilessly, and by the time Tristan reached the scene of the fight, little more than bubbles floated in the water to indicate where the two sea trolls had stood their guard. Most of the mermen were armed by now, bearing weapons they had acquired from slain guards.

Then the eleventh merman gave Tristan the breath of life, and he tried not to think of the few minutes of air that remained. He knew that one of his escorts had been slain, so he suspected he had one more breath available to him. If they didn't reach some sort of cave before then . . .

Abruptly he noticed growing illumination in the water around them, and then they plunged through an undersea doorway, bursting into a huge circular chamber. Several monstrous sea trolls, the largest specimens Tristan had yet seen, surged toward them as Marqillor darted upward, dragging Tristan behind him. The human king growled in silent frustration. With his lone hand holding on to the merman's belt, he didn't even have a fist with which to defend himself.

In another moment, however, the merman and the human broke through the surface. Tristan exhaled and gasped for breath, thrashing his arms to tread water. Only after his straining lungs had recovered did he take notice of the fight that raged around him.

A huge ceiling curved overhead, creating a great domed chamber. Only the top portion of the room contained air, but Tristan saw several niches in the walls just above the water level. The human splashed over to one of these while he tried to make out the murky figures below him.

Pale emerald light spilled into the room through crystal panels in the ceiling of the chamber, much like the windows that had illuminated his cell except that these were much larger. In that light, Tristan saw figures darting through the water below, mermen fighting with their tails and captured weapons as they rushed the palace guards.

A monstrous sahuagin, dark green, with a spiny ridge along its back, sprang upward from the dais in the center of the chamber where it had previously floated. Tristan saw golden chains trailing from the creature's neck and suspected that the creature must be one of the masters of Kyrasti—perhaps even Sythissal himself! The human clutched his steel dagger as he saw the beast swimming toward him.

The monstrous beast broke the surface of the water in a cloud of spray, reaching a taloned hand toward Tristan's leg but recoiling as the blade slashed toward the green-scaled limb. The fishman settled back into the water, its spiny dorsal ridge cutting a streak through the brine as it dove out of reach. Whirling, the monster fixed the human with a hate-filled stare.

Tristan felt a hot flush of combative joy. Battle had been joined, and the outcome now depended on speed and strength and skill. The sensation brought back a flood of emotions—not so much memories as impressions. He remembered the fierce delight of hard-won victories, the bleak despair of defeat. Fear and fury, triumph and grief—he was certain he had known them all.

And he knew that most of his battles had been victories.

"Fight me, lizard!" Tristan challenged, ready to battle the creature then and there. His missing hand was insignificant. His righteous rage, he believed, made him the match of the larger sahuagin.

But the monster apparently lacked courage to equal its physical size. It turned and dove toward the bottom of the chamber, seeking the great dais or one of the exit corridors Tristan could see in the wall at the base of the dome.

Now, however, all the other sahuagin had perished. Only mermen swarmed around the monstrous fishman. Several of Marqillor's warriors seized the big sahuagin by its flailing limbs, dragging it to the surface and casting the beast unceremoniously into the niche where Tristan lay.

"This is Sythissal, King of Kressilacc—a prize captive indeed," Marqillor explained. He cast a scornful look at the enemy lord as the sahuagin backed into the corner, prodded by several tridents in the hands of mermen.

"An old enemy of mine," added Tristan Kendrick, studying the scaly face. Sythissal bared his teeth in a snarl.

"And of Deepvale," spat Marqillor, driving himself out of the water with a single flick of his powerful tail. He sat next to Tristan, facing the sahuagin lord.

"Are we trapped here?" asked the human king.

"Sanamarl has barred the doors," explained Marqillor, gesturing to one of his comrades in the water below their niche. Tristan saw one merman—Sanamarl, obviously—swim a quick circle around the periphery of the dome.

"Even now," continued the merman prince, "a few of my best men have made a break for freedom, striking out for home before we reached the palace. If they're successful, they may be able to bring help. Deepvale is not terribly distant, though admittedly it would be a costly venture to send our army against Kyrasti."

Tristan looked around the great dome. He saw scrags swim past the crystal windows, but he could see no way they could readily enter the chamber short of bashing down the stout stone doors.

"Fools—you're both insignificant fools!" The words, spoken in a hissing version of the common tongue, came from the great sahuagin. Several tridents, borne by swimming mermen, pressed menacingly against Sythissal's belly. The creature crouched as far back into the niche as he could, sneering in hatred.

"Perhaps so," Marqillor replied. "But the fools are holding steel to your skin."

"I don't matter," spat the sahuagin king. "It is my *master*. When he comes, you will all be destroyed!"

Tristan stared at the savage creature. On many occasions in the king's own lifetime, this monster had hurled predatory armies against the coasts of the Moonshae Islands. Indeed, it had been the sahuagin whose onslaught had first provided the necessity that linked the northmen and Ffolk in peace. Always those incursions had been thrown back, but at grievous cost in villages burned, helpless people slain.

Yet now that he had the enemy of all those years before him, Tristan felt the rage and fury slowly drain from his body, replaced by a great weariness. What was the point of a lifetime of war? Would it merely bring the adversaries to their shared doom here at the bottom of the sea?

A thunderous force rocked the dome of Kyrasti then, rumbling through the water below, shaking the very foundations of the great structure, seeming to make the very reef itself tremble. Tristan saw long cracks ripple along the walls as something smashed against one of the doors, causing the water to churn with turbulence. When the human looked down, he could barely make out the floor of the chamber. The seawater in the dome grew murky, as if a dark cloud slowly spread through it.

Abruptly the merman called Sanamarl vanished into that murk as the area of opacity continued to expand, obscuring more and more of the floor. Within a few moments, the inside of the chamber was as impenetrable to sight as the silty water of a placid river.

In the next instant, a tentacle lashed out from the murky water, thrashing around the niche and grasping the sahuagin king around the neck. Sythissal screamed, a high-pitched, keening cry of pure terror. Quickly the tendril tightened its grip, dragging the monarch into the water. Tristan gasped and slashed, but his blade struck only hard coral when he missed the whipping, snakelike limb.

The great sahuagin screamed and writhed in the grasp of the heavy tentacle. Then, as Tristan and the mermen watched helplessly, a great form rolled across the surface, ripping and tearing at Sythissal with tentacles and a sharp, chopping beak. They heard the crunch of bone, saw the rending of scaly skin. The sahuagin's screams slowly gurgled to a halt, but the sharp beak continued to rend the reptilian body.

In moments, the fishman had been torn to shreds, leaving only gory remnants to float through the turbulent water of the throne room.

"What *did* that?" gasped Tristan, trying to comprehend the massive size of the tentacled intruder.

"It's a giant squid," Marqillor noted, trying to peer through the still murky water. "The biggest one I've ever seen."

Then, as the creature rose to the surface once more, more tentacles—several as big around as a man's waist—snaked toward the mermen and their human comrade.

* * * * *

The *Princess of Moonshae* moved with stately grace through depths layered with blue, aqua, and then a deep, cloaking green. The ship had been underwater for many hours, though Brandon could only guess at their course, since Robyn had lain still and unaware since their submergence. Finally the longship entered a realm of dark purple, where the water seemed to press against the wooden hull and its magical dome with ominous and inexorable pressure.

Alicia still knelt beside her mother, relieved to see that the queen's wounds had healed for the most part with almost miraculous speed.

"It's the goddess," Tavish whispered reverently. "Her healing comes to a druid when she changes her form for another's."

For hours, the queen lay motionless, while the princess and Tavish washed and bandaged her wounds and tried to soothe her as best they could.

Finally Robyn fell into a restful sleep. Now, as she slumbered, Tavish came back to watch over the High Queen while Alicia climbed stiffly to her feet and began to check the blade of her sword. She would need the weapon very soon, she suspected.

"Look!" came the cry from the bow, where Keane and Hanrald maintained a steady watch. "We're coming to something."

It seemed as if the submerged longship had sailed into a forest of widely spaced tree trunks. Tall spires rose around them, and as they passed between two of the columns, they saw undulating terrain below them, dotted with numerous circular objects that almost certainly had to be buildings.

"Those are spires—towers," announced Keane, studying the shafts rising from the ocean floor all around them. They towered far higher than any surface structures, the sleek proportions of giant needles extending very nearly to the surface. "The sea floor is shallow here, as if this is a high ridge . . . a mountaintop on the ocean's bed."

"Guards!" shouted a northman, pointing into the darkness around the nearest of the pillars. Numerous fishlike forms swarmed toward them, like a great school of humanoid swimmers.

"Stand ready!" called Brandon. The bowmen took up their arrows while the northmen raised their weapons and stood in a protective circle around the hull.

"The spells—now is the time!"

Keane turned, seeing Hanrald and Brigit speaking to him together. The two knights had donned their armor. Silver plate encased them both from the waist up, with chain mail to guard their legs and arms.

"The spells from Evermeet," Brigit added quickly. "The queen gave you scrolls, with spells for underwater movement and combat. We need them—*now!* We'll create a diversion and draw some of the defenders away from the ship!"

The magic-user blinked, trying to think as the aquatic attackers swarmed closer. "I agree," he concluded after a split second. After all, the two knights were some of the best fighters among them.

Keane quickly unfurled the leather parchment, hurriedly reading over the words to the spells, each of which would provide its target with the ability not only to breathe underwater, but also to move through the sea as if the liquid was no more obstructive than air. In moments, he chanted the brief commands and passed his hand through the careful symbology of the spell.

"We'll go out and meet them. We'll try to draw as many of them off as we can," explained Hanrald. The earl looked up at Alicia, who had joined them in the bow.

"Farewell, princess!" boomed Hanrald, with a bright smile at Alicia. "We battle yon foe; it is the way of the knight, after all!"

Alicia felt a great fear for her friends. "Take care," she said quietly, stretching upward to kiss the suddenly blushing Hanrald. She turned to Brigit with a wan smile. "Don't let him get into too much trouble!"

The elfwoman smiled sadly and touched Alicia on the arm. "It is too late for that, I fear," she said.

Then, as the swarming fishmen were almost upon them, Brigit and Hanrald dove over the side, racing through the water as swiftly as if they sprinted over a grassy field. The two dropped to the surface of the submarine ridge, landing lightly on their feet after a hundred-foot descent. Immediately they began running over the rough terrain, dodging around large outcrops of coral that loomed like giant boulders before them, and within a few seconds, they had disappeared from the view of their companions in the longship.

The voyagers saw scores of the attacking monsters swerve downward, pursuing the two knights. Scrags spread into a wide screen, swimming dozens of feet above the ocean floor, while many sahuagin darted into the ravines and gullies where the two intruders had vanished.

At the same time, the rest of the swarming predators continued to press toward the *Princess of Moonshae*. The complex of towers and domes was well defended, and more and more of the guards appeared in the distance, swimming toward the fight.

"Phyrosyne!" cried the princess, stamping her changestaff against the longship's hull. Immediately the shaft grew upward, though the tree creature twisted low to prevent its upper branches from breaking into the water over their heads. Thus propped in the hull, the wooden fighter reached out with knotty branches, ready to defend the ship against the wave of attackers that surged against them from all sides.

For an hour, Alicia's life became a maze of battle as she joined the crew of Brandon's ship in a desperate defense of their beleaguered vessel. Only the shock of their appearance and the success of Brigit and Hanrald's diversion, it seemed, gave them any chance in this battle, for no sooner had they vanquished a company of scrags or sahuagin than a fresh formation arrived to take its place. If the sea creatures had all attacked together, she knew, the battle could have had but one grim outcome.

Robyn recovered her awareness as the battle began and rose to her feet to aid in the fight, remaining in the body of a human this time and wielding spells instead of her own flesh. Tavish frantically played her harp, and as always the enchanted instrument caused the human warriors to forget their fatigue and their fear, striving their utmost to win this all-important battle.

The changestaff fought as steadily as any courageous human warrior. It broke the backs of fishmen and scrags alike, seizing their bodies in its firm branches and twisting with inexorable force, tossing the crippled remains back into the sea as it searched for another foe.

As it was, they battled desperately with spells and steel, arrows and axes, and they just barely managed to hold the swarm at bay. The water in their wake was littered by the torn bodies of the sea creatures, while many brave northmen and Ffolk gasped out their last breaths in the blood-spattered hull of the longship. The air grew thick with the stench of sweat and blood and saltwater, until each breath clogged in the throat, burning lungs and providing precious little oxygen for the breather.

Desperately battling men and monsters crashed over the benches, around the casks of stores, and even up and down the mast, but in the end, every attack was driven off, at a dear cost in blood.

"There—some kind of castle!" announced Brandon, peering through the murk toward a mountainous structure rising before them.

"All around us—a huge compound!" exclaimed Keane, his tone full of wonder that almost succeeded in vanquishing his fatigue.

Spires arose from a sea bottom that undulated through a series of steep-sided ridges, the huge protruberances of the massive coral reef that formed the foundation of this undersea realm. Twisting towers of shells, gleaming with mosaics of pearl, silver, and gold, studded the coral hills. Domed buildings, many with panels of emerald-colored crystal set in their roofs, clustered among the towers. There were no walls in this city. They would be no more useful here than they would on the surface against attackers who could fly.

The central feature of the submarine vale was a huge rounded structure that occupied the center of a shallow depression. All around it circled ridges of coral, occupied by towers and other lesser buildings. The huge structure was built as a series of great domes, piled one atop another until they reached their highest point in the center, which consisted of a great rounded chamber with panels of clear crystal set all around the curving wall.

"It's got to be the palace!" cried Robyn. "Go there—to the top!"

The ship sailed into the great bowl, surrounded by coral towers. The huge dome before them looked like some kind of undersea mountain, except that its surface was marked with turrets and balconies and was broken by many great panels of green crystal, providing glimpses into the shadowed chamber below.

The *Princess of Moonshae*, free of pestering attackers for the moment, came to rest beside one of the portals. Eagerly Alicia stared through the murk, not sure what she would see but full of more hope than she had felt in months.

Nevertheless, the sight that met her eyes was too shocking for any reaction, at least until a second had passed, enough time for her to confirm her identification and find her voice.

"It's Father!"

Alicia stared in astonishment as the shapes below the glasslike panel came into view. She saw Tristan in a shallow alcove at the side of the domed chamber. "We've found him!" she cried in pure elation.

Then Alicia saw the monstrous creature rolling in the waters before her father and she screamed in horror, for the whirling shape reached toward the king with a pair of grasping tentacles, slithering through the water like eels. She saw Tristan squirm desperately in their clutches, dragged slowly but inevitably toward the water.

* * * * *

Sinioth surged and thrashed in his fury. First had come the news that the prisoner had escaped his cell, and now the humans dared to come against him here, in Kyrasti! He had tried to prepare himself for this possibility, but the reality stunned him beyond disbelief.

Sythissal, of course, had paid for his failure to secure the prisoner. The captor had been put to death—justice, to Coss-Axell-Sinioth. As he well knew, should he himself fail, Talos would show him no greater mercy.

But Coss-Axell-Sinioth was not one to dwell upon his defeats, except as they fueled his rage and propelled him to vengeance. Now the prisoner, and then his rescuers, would pay for their arrogance and pride.

☙ 18 ☙

Floodwater

Tristan looked up in amazement. Moments earlier, he had noticed a shadow across the emerald pane over his head, but when he saw the outline of a northman longship there, he thought he was losing his mind. The ship heeled over, presenting her beam to the window, showing a hull filled with humans!

Then Tristan saw his wife and his daughter, faces he had forgotten in the haze of his drugging, but that now poured back with the full force of memory—and he was certain that he had gone mad.

"Robyn! Alicia!" His voice came out in a strangled gasp. Tristan stood up, ignoring the chaos in the room behind him, and reached toward the high window with his one good hand, imploring.

The tentacle grasped his ankle before he saw the giant squid's attack. A powerful force jerked the king backward, toward the floor of the throne room. Never had water terrified him as much as it did now, when the full wealth of his life came flooding back.

Desperately Tristan kicked at the tentacle around his leg, chopping with his dagger, realizing the blade was too dull to have much effect. He cast the useless weapon aside and struck with his bare hand and even the blunt end of his wrist, yet his resistance made no difference. Irresistible strength jerked him from the niche and into the water. Tristan barely captured a breath before the monster dragged him below the surface.

The king ignored the pain flaming through his arm and focused his hatred and rage against the massive beast that sucked him under the water. The creature seemed full worthy of that hatred. Something unnatural lurked in those murderous

DOUGLAS NILES

red eyes, flaming like coals to either side of a beaklike mouth. Smaller tentacles flailed around the beast's horrid maw, but the two massive tendrils securing Tristan had no need of help.

A figure swam before him, and Tristan saw Marqillor approaching the squid. The merman wielded a large trident, acquired from a vanquished scrag, and now he shoved the weapon with full force into the giant head, flexing his powerful tail in a surge that pressed the tines deep into the creature's monstrous body. The squid twisted away, thrashing at Marqillor with a tentacle, movement enough to allow Tristan to fling his head and torso out of the water, gasping a breath of air before the monster once again pulled him down.

Other mermen swarmed around the monstrous beast, striking at the squid with whatever they held, sometimes with merely their hands and tails. Tristan kicked with all his might, struggling to break free. He cursed the mutilation of his left arm, feeling that if only he had two good hands, he would be able to defeat the beast. Even in his oxygen-starved delirium, however, he recognized the thought as madness. The monster was too huge, too mighty to be vanquished by a man and certainly not here, in its natural environment. Finally the air exploded from Tristan's lungs and the fight abandoned his body. It required too great an effort to hold onto his breath.

But then he felt strong arms around him. As his mouth opened reflexively to gasp in water that would choke him, he felt a merman's face before him, and instead of water, he inhaled a lifesaving lungful of air.

The merman who saved him paid with his own life, Tristan saw, as the writhing squid wrapped the fellow in looping tentacles, whipping him toward that crushing beak. Other fishfolk tried to save their comrade, but it was too late. The mouth crunched over the victim's midriff, and the sound of breaking bones snapped horribly through the water. The dying merman's mouth gaped, emitting a cloud of thick blood into the water.

Once again Tristan managed to work free, pulling himself to the surface and splashing into the niche, finally, as he watched for tentacles. Alone and unarmed, of course, there was little he could do to defend himself if the squid determined to have him.

But at least, he vowed, the monster wouldn't get him without a fight.

* * * * *

"This way!" Hanrald cried, driving his huge sword through the body of a scrag that swam in his path. The human dove into the narrow passage, closely followed by Brigit, the sister knight stabbing another pursuing sea troll as she guarded their rear.

They darted around a corner in the passageway, and Brigit stopped to pull a metal lever protruding from the wall. Immediately a large rock settled from the ceiling to the floor behind them, pushing bubbling water out of the way and solidly blocking pursuit—but also barring their return along the same route.

The knights paused to catch their breath.

"That worked even better than I thought it would—our diversion," Brigit gasped, flashing a wan smile. Though dark water pressed around them, thanks to Keane's spells they were able to talk and breath as easily as they did on the surface.

"How many were chasing us?" Hanrald wondered aloud, remembering the frantic minutes of pursuit, the fleeing fighters just barely able to outdistance a whole swarm of swimming monsters. All of them, he thought with satisfaction, had been distracted from their original target, the *Princess of Moonshae*.

The pair had battled their way through a savage cordon of sea troll guards, finding that the enchantment of the spell gave them great freedom of movement. They could slash and parry as if only air blocked their blades. Thus their superior skill outclassed the scrags, who, though they fought in their natural environment, employed little in the way of tactical finesse. Some of the monsters didn't even carry weapons, and those who did used them primarily for thrusting—easy attacks to parry for a skilled swordsman or swordswoman.

Also, the two knights found that they could run at very nearly full speed, thanks to the effects of the spell of free action—their feet found solid purchase on the sea floor, and the water did not obstruct their forward progress.

"I think we diverted a hundred, at least—maybe more," Brigit guessed. "Enough, I hope, to let the others get into the palace." How they would get away again, with the full wrath of the Coral Kingdom aroused against them, remained an unaddressed problem.

"They're still out there," said Hanrald, leaning his ear to the stone. Sounds of prying and scraping came clearly through the water, though as yet the barrier showed no willingness to budge.

"Let's hope they don't break it down for a few minutes," groaned Hanrald, exhausted from the long minutes of battle and flight. They had raced along the circular wall around the undersea palace until they reached this labyrinth of towers and tunnels. Now, in one of those tunnels, they saw the rock that separated them from their enemies start to wobble.

"How long before we should get back to the ship?" Hanrald mused.

Brigit looked at him and shrugged. "Maybe we ought to move on," she suggested. Keane had told them that the spells had a very finite time limit, and neither of them had to stretch his imagination to come up with a picture of what would happen when the magical protection wore off.

Hanrald started down the corridor at an easy lope. Brigit easily kept pace as the passageway curved through a long descent. Abruptly it ended, opening onto a balcony carved into the side of a deep undersea chasm. The far side of the chasm stretched as a sheer cliff no more than a hundred feet away.

"They're coming after us," reported Brigit, spotting the swimming forms of several scrags following them down the winding tunnel.

"Let's go!" shouted Hanrald, raising his sword in one fist

and taking Brigit's hand in the other. The pair leaped from the balcony, kicking their feet and swimming with their hands. The force of their jump carried them far from their start, floating through the water like birds soaring through the air. Far below, the base of the chasm darkened to a midnight black—and then they were past, landing on a balcony across the canyon much like the one they had jumped from. Without hesitating, they darted through a doorway into another submarine passage, still racing forward.

Abruptly they came into a large room, domed like many others they had seen. A dozen tunnels opened in the walls of the chamber, and an equal number of diamond-shaped crystal panels spiraled around the ceiling.

"Which way?" wondered Hanrald, at a loss.

"We can't go back," Brigit informed him after a quick look behind. "We'd better move on, *quick!*"

Hanrald turned to the right and charged down one of the passageways. Immediately a large scrag loomed before him. The creature jabbed with a trident from a darkened niche in the side of the corridor. Surprised, the knight grunted as the weapon pierced his rib cage. Hanrald staggered back in mute astonishment, watching the water around him begin to redden.

Brigit whirled past him, disemboweling the scrag in one vicious slash. The creature floated to the side, but a quick look back showed her that their swimming pursuers were closing in rapidly.

Beside her, Hanrald's eyelids drooped, and his motionless body drifted toward the floor. As gently as possible, the elfwoman nudged the knight into the alcove that had concealed the scrag. Then she turned to face the pursuing sea trolls, deflecting the lead scrag's harpoon and splitting his face down the middle.

More of the monsters swam forward, but the sister knight sliced and slashed so skillfully that each of the beasts felt the edge or the tip of her blade. Warily they backed away from the elfwoman's silver sword, content to hover in the passageway beyond, blocking escape to the right and left but making no immediate move to attack.

Hanrald's eyes fluttered open. The knight's consciousness returned slowly, belaboredly, mainly because of an awareness of crippling pain. Each breath he drew slashed like a hot iron through his chest. He tried to focus his vision on something, anything.

He noticed a brightening of the shadows in the back of their niche. He forced himself to a sitting position, looking closer, increasingly hopeful with what he saw.

"Brigit!" he said, intending to bark commandingly and surprised that his voice came forth as a mere feeble gasp. Nevertheless, the elf woman turned around after checking to see that the scrags remained well back from her blade. "Look—stairs. They must lead to one of those towers above the palace."

The sister knight saw that a tightly spiraling stairway led steeply upward from their alcove. "Let's go!" she exclaimed. "We can try to get the attention of the ship from there!"

Hanrald smiled warmly, grasping one of her hands in his. "A good plan," whispered the earl, "for you. You'll have to leave me here to distract them. You make your escape—get back to the ship!"

Brigit smiled and said nothing. Instead, she leaned over and kissed the human knight on the lips.

"Up! Climb, dammit. I can hold them, but not forever!" groaned the man, struggling to sit up and look around.

"Shhhh," whispered Brigit, holding his head in her hands. Hanrald had lost a lot of blood, but she reduced its flow by pressing a cloth against the wound. "In a little while we'll go together."

Hanrald shook his head, wincing in pain at the movement.

"Don't argue," urged the elf. "Just rest for a moment."

Hanrald looked around wildly, as if he *had* to change her mind. Then he slumped backward, relaxing with a wan smile. "We took on a good lot of the buggers, didn't we?" said the earl with a low chuckle. "And we led 'em on quite a chase as well."

Brigit looked back into the corridor. She counted at least a dozen scrags, but all of them floated well back from the alcove, having learned the painful lesson taught by the elfwoman's sword.

"We make a good team," she said, turning back to Hanrald. She was horrified by the pallor of his skin, the distant expression in his eyes. Don't die! she urged him silently.

Suddenly, with surprising strength, Hanrald sat up and looked into the sister knight's eyes. "I love you, Brigit Cu-'Lyrran!" he pledged, and his own eyes were serious and sane. "And never did I think to be saying that to one who was as good with a sword as myself!"

She smiled and kissed him, wanting to say the same thing to him, but somehow she was unable to speak. The thought, after all these centuries, that she would come to love a human seemed to her like some grand joke of the gods if she thought about it too much.

"Come on," she whispered, after several more minutes. "Let's climb those stairs."

* * * * *

In her mirror, Deirdre watched the desperate approach of the longship. She saw the splendors of the Coral Kingdom, of the Kyrasti, and the savage defenders swarming out to battle for their home. Her inspections drifted downward, and she noticed with interest the presence of her father, the king. The sight of his peril brought a strange thrill to her heart.

Yet her attention focused most intently on the body of the giant squid—or, more accurately, on the corrupt soul encased within that grotesque body. She wanted to strike out at Malawar, to punish him further for the hurts, real and imaginary, he had inflicted upon her. Desperately, grievously, she wanted to return those injuries a thousandfold. And at the same time, she wanted to use him, to exploit his destruction for her own gain.

Deirdre grew more and more fascinated by the avatar of evil, watching the huge body flex through the submarine chamber, thrashing in battle with lesser creatures. Partly her desire was for vengeance, but in greater part it was a lust, a craving for the power that the great beast contained within its unnatural form. Power that could belong to Deirdre, once she prepared the means of mastering it.

Yet, still, she lacked a weapon.

* * * * *

"Down!" commanded Brandon. He pointed, in case Knaff misunderstood his intent, but the bow of the longship already dipped in response to the helmsman's touch. Below, the huge dome of the palace rose through the emerald depths. For the time being, the *Princess of Moonshae* was free of immediate enemies. Except for the scrags who had charged away in pursuit of Hanrald and Brigit, the monsters who had resisted their initial approach were all dead. Even so, the air in the boat remained dense and fetid. Sweat rolled from each crew member in steaming rivulets.

"Hold on!" the captain shouted in warning. "We're going to ram!"

Alicia clung to the mast, her sword in her hand and her eyes on the huge crystal pane before the *Princess of Moonshae*'s bow. The longship rocked downward as Knaff pressed on the tiller, and then she lunged ahead, the proud figurehead with the gleaming silver helm driving toward the smooth, transparent surface.

The crash nearly tore Alicia loose from her perch, but she held tightly to the stout timber, staring in shock as the emerald plane shattered. A great bubble of air erupted around them as seawater plunged into the space of the huge undersea dome. The longship followed the flood, the narrow bow plummeting through the aperture into the dome. Ten feet of the hull followed, and then the widening gunwales wedged firmly against the sides of the shattered window.

A gangly figure tumbled past Alicia, and she saw the flailing form of her changestaff spilling like a felled tree toward the bow. Branches thrashed out as the thing tumbled past the figurehead, and then the trailing limbs wrapped around the wooden prow. The tree being arrested its fall at the last possible minute, an instant before it tumbled into the maelstrom below.

White water flooded past them, thundering in a cascading torrent into the vast, circular chamber, but still the enchanted blanket of air over the longship maintained its protective presence.

Alicia searched desperately below, seeking her father through a chaos of white water and flailing bodies. Then she saw Tristan in the grip of a writhing snake. She watched in horror, screaming unconsciously, as the king disappeared beneath the surface, and at the same time, she made out the huge creature thrashing there. Appalled, she understood that the thing grasping her father was not a snake but a mere appendage of a much larger monstrosity.

Tristan flailed back to the surface, grasping about with his hand, pounding his arm against the tendrils around him. He reached for something, anything, but nothing met his grip, and once more he vanished.

Robyn dove forward, and once again Alicia saw the sleek form of white and black, the whale's teeth and the powerful, driving flukes. The killer whale dove at the squid, and her wide jaws clamped around the widest tentacle, near the base of the writhing limb. Both sea creatures flailed through the great room, and Alicia saw her father flung free from the squid's grasp.

A huge scrag swam out of the shadows, a long trident extended before him. The beast drove the tines of the weapon into Robyn's flank, and the killer whale twisted reflexively, releasing the squid with an involuntary flexing of her powerful jaws.

The tentacled horror dove away at high speed, coming to rest in a murky cloud at the bottom of the huge chamber. Alicia realized that it had released the cloud, providing its own cover as it retreated from the fight.

But now another wave of sahuagin and scrags attacked the trapped *Princess of Moonshae*, swarming from the surrounding towers and walls as if they had gathered their strength for this massive rush. In the chamber, Alicia saw things that looked like humans, until she realized that they had huge fishlike tails. Mermen! Several of the aquatic beings swam across the room to circle protectively before Tristan.

Water continued to pour into the cavernous dome through the shattered window, and consquently the air pocket shrank steadily, raising the level of the choppy surface. The High King splashed to one of the niches in the wall, but soon the rising sea forced him out. Swimming, he started through the turbulence toward the *Princess of Moonshae*'s prow, the proud figurehead jutting through the ceiling, now no more than a dozen feet above him.

"Father!" cried Alicia, scrambling down to the bow, holding on to benches and sailing lines to keep her balance on the steeply inclined surface. She barely caught herself at the figurehead, holding tightly to the stout timber as she leaned over the rail. Beside her, she saw the lanky form of her changestaff, also clinging precariously to the prow.

Desperately the princess looked around, gathering a coil of rope and then searching for Tristan's head, but the king once more vanished into the frothing turbulence.

Then she saw two of the mermen and her father's bearded face between theirs. Slowly they made their way toward the longship, circled protectively by the great killer whale.

"Here!" Alicia shouted, throwing the line and securing the end around the trunk of her changestaff.

Then the water bubbled around the trio, and Alicia screamed as one of the mermen rose from the brine, the tines of a scrag trident emerging from his chest. Blood turned the water pink as the brave creature perished.

The lashing limb of a monstrous tentacle suddenly whipped through the water again, and Alicia saw the squid shoot up from the floor. Tristan shouted something, then vanished with shocking suddenness. The princess saw a flash of black and white skin, a tall dorsal fin, and then the powerful killer whale disappeared after the monster.

"No!" cried Alicia, shaking her head in anguish. Then, before she stopped to think, she drew her sword and dove headlong into the water, aiming the blade like a harpoon at the place she had last seen the great squid.

She felt slick, leathery skin before her and drove the blade into the monster's body, feeling it lurch away from the force of the blow. Opening her eyes, Alicia saw nothing but bubbles, but then a hand came into view—a *human* hand! She reached out and grabbed it, kicking upward and raising her head above the surface in time to gulp one precious gasp of air.

Something wrapped around her leg, and she chopped with her sword, still holding on to the hand. For a moment, she glimpsed Tristan's face as the king broke from the water and drank in a breath, then father and daughter plunged below, caught in the nest of snakelike tendrils.

Alicia saw the darting forms of mermen around them, the black and white skin of the great druid nearby, and she drove her keen blade again and again into the tough body that seemed to drag her and her father ever deeper into the flooded chamber.

And then abruptly they broke free. She swam upward in a frenzy, feeling her father kicking beside her. Just when she thought they must certainly drown, their faces broke from the water only a few feet from the longship's bow.

"Here!" The frantic voice belonged to Keane, who threw a rope toward them. Alicia and Tristan seized the line and hung on for dear life. "Pull!" cried the mage as a dozen crewmen scrambled to help him.

They strained against the weight of the pair in the water, but the footing in the steeply canted hull proved treacherous. The king and princess started to rise from the water, but then several crewmen slipped and they plunged back into the maelstrom.

"Help!" cried Alicia, choking on spray and turbulence,

knowing that her friends already were doing everything in their power to aid them.

Yet one heard that call and answered. The gangly form of the changestaff had slowly pulled itself back into the hull, though several of its limbs still firmly grasped the figurehead. Now the tree extended a long knotty limb down toward the two Ffolk in the water. Alicia and Tristan grabbed at the branch, clinging tightly as the tree being slowly lifted them free of the water, toward the tenuous safety of the longship's hull.

Aided by the frantically straining Keane, in another moment the pair tumbled over the rail of the ship, collapsing in the bow as water continued to thunder downward around them.

"Break her free, men!" shouted Brandon, chopping at one of the frames where the ship was braced into the broken window. Pry bars, axes, and hammers all crunched against the coral surface of the dome, chipping and bashing in a desperate effort to enlarge the entrance.

"The pressure's too great!" Keane shouted over the thunderous cascade. Brandon saw that the water pouring into the dome held them firmly in the gap.

Spray splashed over Alicia and she whirled in surprise, seeing the sleek killer whale leaping from the water that now surged nearly onto the longship's figurehead. The great mammal teetered on the gunwale for a moment, and then the High Queen of the Ffolk tumbled into the hull beside them. Once again in human form, Robyn knelt beside her husband, tears of relief glowing in her eyes.

The pounding cascade slowed as finally the chamber beneath them was fully flooded. They saw no sign of the squid as the crew again pried against the frame jammed around the vessel's bow. Abruptly the *Princess of Moonshae* lurched. A chunk of the dome wall fell away, releasing the longship but twisting her hull with brutal, unforgiving force. Planks splintered along the keel, and water exploded through the gap, quickly swirling around Alicia and Tristan as they tried to scramble to their feet.

Slowly the longship began to float upward, toward the surface and the sun. Marquillor and his surviving comrades swam out the broken window, diving for the shelter of the coral ridge below. Water continued to flood the hull in a roaring cascade through a gap at least twelve feet long and more than a hand-span wide.

Grimly Knaff took his position at the helm, and the *Princess* began to move forward, trailing a bubbling wake at the stern. Her bow rose slightly, but so much water sloshed in a large wave toward the stern that the helmsman had to quickly bring the ship back to level. Dank air stung their eyes and caused their lungs to strain for breath as the ship wallowed through the depths.

"We've got to get Brigit and Hanrald!" Alicia shouted to Brandon, who stood near Knaff in the stern.

"Where are they?" demanded the captain, peering through the turbulent seas. They could see no sign of the knightly pair.

"Look!" Tavish called in alarm as a giant shadow moved through the broken window, emerging from the dome to follow them into the sea. The blunt body, the long tentacles—all were dolefully familiar.

Yet even that fact paled against the significance of the ruptured bow. Water gushed around their knees, rising higher every second.

It seemed clear to them all that the *Princess of Moonshae* was fatally breached.

* * * * *

Through Deirdre's mirror, Talos observed the escape of the human prisoner, and vengeance against his servant's failure crystalized into determination in his evil, immortal mind. His presence, always a shadow when the princess used the crystal, now formed into a conscious thought—knowledge that he projected into the young woman's mind.

"His name . . ." came the voice of Talos. Deirdre stiffened, frightened yet at the same time intensely thrilled. She felt the touch from beyond her world, beyond her existence, and she knew that a source of great power reached her.

"His name is Coss-Axell-Sinioth."

The voice faded, but Deirdre's attention had already fixed on a plan—a plan that she could at last put into action.

Finally, now, she had her weapon.

❧ 19 ❧

To Sun and Sky

Painfully Hanrald grasped at another step, and then one more, pulling himself up as he had for the last half hour—one stone stair at a time. The deep wound in his side wracked his body with waves of agony. He had no idea how much blood he had lost, but from the amount of the crimson liquid that continued to drift around him, he knew that he must be pretty thoroughly drained.

But Brigit still wouldn't leave him. He had tried again to persuade her, halfway up the agonizing climb, when he had been convinced that he couldn't make it. Again she had insisted that she would wait until he was ready. Ultimately the only course left to the earl—the only way to save the elfwoman—was to make this climb.

Meanwhile the sister knight defended them both, fighting below him on the stairway, backing up the steps, holding the scrags at bay if they tried to pursue too closely. Fortunately the great beasts usually hung well back, having learned several painful lessons about the Synnorian warrior's skill with her keen elven steel.

During the duration of his climb, Hanrald noticed steadily growing illumination above him, the promise of escape that had kept him moving, had brought him back from the edge of utter despair. The steps were very steep, and he knew that he had climbed more than a hundred, though he had forgotten to keep an exact count, a fact that he chided himself about as he neared the top.

Finally Hanrald came around a spiral in the staircase that ended in an aperture above him—a rectangular gap that was the source of the pale green light, the illumination that had drawn him this far. Cautiously he raised his head through the hole, discovering that they had indeed reached the top of a tower. Aqua-colored seawater surrounded him, stretching to the far limits of the horizon. Above—and so terribly, impossibly far away—he could see the sun-dappled reflections of the surface.

Without hesitation, the knight crawled onto the floor of the flat stone platform that capped the tower, finding a circle no more than twelve feet across, lofted more than a hundred feet above the floor of the sea. He saw that the tower stood proudly at the rim of the great undersea bowl. Below him, some distance away, he made out the multidomed structure of the huge palace.

Among the towers and domes of that edifice, he observed many companies of scrags and sahuagin, mere dots in the water at this distance. Hanrald crouched flat on the exposed surface, thankful that, for the moment at least, none of the monsters seemed to notice the human's presence. Instead, they swarmed about the palace, clearly focused on an enemy closer to hand.

Brigit scrambled out of the opening beside him and looked back down the stairway. "The scrags are just down the stairs," she warned. "They have no intention of letting us get away."

"Look!" cried Hanrald, spotting a heavy metal trapdoor lying open beside the entrance. With great effort, the two of them lifted the portal and dropped it over the opening, where they swiftly bolted the barrier shut.

"Rest for a moment," the sister knight said quietly, and for once, the man needed no coaxing. He slumped, all but unconscious, onto the flat coral surface.

The elf stood up and studied their surroundings. Sunlight brightened the surface of the sea, reflecting from the waves like multiple facets of diamonds, still at least three hundred feet above her. Many spires like the one they now occupied rose around them, and she noticed numerous shell-covered, domed structures dotting the rolling surface of the great reef below.

A swarm of creatures near the largest of these domes caught her attention, and she saw bubbles and turbulence in the water there. Then a familiar shape—the longship!—moving slowly, emerged from the turbulence. Even from this distance, a mile or more away, it seemed to Brigit that the *Princess of Moonshae* wallowed heavily in the water.

Still, the elfwoman's heart filled with renewed hope. She leaped to her feet, her silver breastplate gleaming in the bright water, and frantically began to wave.

* * * * *

"We're sinking!" Brandon snarled from the stern, angrily watching seawater flood into the longship's hull. It seemed to him a cruel irony: A powerful magical barrier protected the ship from tons of water weighing heavily above them, yet a simple gash in the planking seemed likely to doom them all to a watery grave. Already the vessel wallowed sluggishly, and in a few more minutes, she would inevitably become too heavy to rise through the sea.

Alicia noticed, for the first time since they had broken free of the dome, that the lanky figure of her changestaff had crawled back into the bow of the longship. It perched, like a gigantic mantis, near the figurehead, as if it tried to crouch out of the way of the frantic voyagers in the hull.

Her mind seized upon a desperate idea, and it was obvious no one else had another plan to suggest. "There!" the princess commanded, speaking to the creature of wood, the powerful servant of the goddess . . . and herself. Would it comprehend? The princess pointed to the gash in the ship's hull, addressing the animated tree. "Can you seal that hole—stop the leak?"

Slowly, deliberately, the creature extended a limb into the water gushing through the gap, and then another. Finally it reached into the hole with its remaining branches, gaining solid purchase on the outside of the hull. Then those sturdy limbs contracted, pulling the trunk of the tree into the long, narrow crack, compressing the flow of water until the spurting leak had slowed to no more than a thin trickle. The changestaff pressed itself even more tightly into the gap, blending into the planks of the hull, and in another moment, the leak stopped entirely.

"By the gods!" Knaff grunted in gruff appreciation. "We might make it yet!"

They had no time for congratulations, however. A quick look in any direction showed huge schools of swimming scrags and sahuagin, rapidly closing in to attack. Columns of sea trolls formed the vanguard of the onrushing force, while vast waves of sahuagin followed quickly in the wake of their larger cousins. The creatures might have been schools of minnows when viewed from a distance, but they rapidly closed the gap, quickly expanding to more menacing dimensions.

It seemed the creatures of the sea had the *Princess of Moonshae* dead to rights. The longship wallowed in the depths of the sea, short of air and slowed by the unnatural environment. Everywhere the crew of Brandon's vessel faced a teeming collection of hungry monsters of the sea, while the humans had difficulty even drawing enough breath to stop panting and gasping.

The air in the magically enclosed longship continued to grow increasingly foul. The crew had been underwater for nearly a full day, and the strain showed on faces streaked with sweat, mouths hanging open, reflexively gasping for oxygen that was not to be had.

And yet, under these conditions, the northmen and Ffolk prepared to fight their most desperate battle yet. Never before had they encountered nearly the number of beasts that now swarmed toward them. Above and below them, to port and starboard and astern—indeed, everywhere but directly in front of the ship—the gathering schools of warriors approached. The crew could clearly see that they faced far more attackers now than had gathered to block their initial approach to Kyrasti.

Yet no one would even acknowledge the possibility of defeat.

The voyagers universally rejected the thought that now, after their miraculous rescue of the High King, they might fail to reach the surface or see the shores of Moonshae again. Every man and woman aboard vowed quietly that he or she would see that sky, breathe the fresh air that hovered so close above them.

Besides the warriors thronging through the water, the humans faced the reality of yet another grim threat. Brandon and Knaff, in the stern, saw clear evidence of the ominous form that slowly followed in their wake.

The image of the giant squid grew ever larger, emerging from the darkness of Kyrasti to advance toward the still-sluggish longship. The Prince of Gnarhelm saw that the creature delayed beginning its attack, obviously waiting until the troops surrounding the vessel had a chance to initiate the assault.

"Look there, to the west!" shouted Knaff the Elder, his voice booming through the hull of the longship. They followed his pointing figure past the bow to the one region where they had previously seen no threat, gradually discerning another mass of warriors advancing rapidly toward the *Princess of Moonshae*. These submarine troops swam through the water in long ranks, ranging across the full depth of the reef waters from surface to floor. Hundreds of fresh warriors surged toward them, still far away but closing the distance quickly, approaching from the only path of escape that had lain before them.

"*More of them?*" groaned Alicia, following the loyal helmsman's indication. The additional figures emerged from the haze of distance, swarming toward them as quickly as the palace guards.

Alicia's eye, however, was drawn to a flickering point of brightness in the direction of this new advancing force, yet not so far away. She looked more closely, positive she had seen the flash of silver or some other bright metal. Then she was certain.

"It's Brigit!" the princess cried, gasping for enough breath to shout in the foul atmosphere of the hull. She pointed to the spot of radiance, barely making out the desperately waving arm. "There! We've got to get to her!"

Slowly, with noticeable reluctance, the *Princess of Moonshae* pushed through the water, cutting a course toward the knight, but unable to avoid hundreds of savage enemies on all sides.

* * * * *

Luge huddled behind his shield, a wet and bloody sword in his hand. The terrors of this undersea journey continued to assail him, yet like any true man of Gnarhelm, he stood ready to follow his captain wherever Brandon led. He had slain sahuagin, sliced deep wounds into scrags, battled sharks and worse, all for the love of his prince.

But now he felt something even more horrifying, darker and far more sinister than any of the mortal foes he had battled to this point. The evil centered in the giant squid that pursued them. The beast had terrified Luge when he had first witnessed it in the flooding dome, and even then somehow it had reminded him of a black-bearded man who had come to him in The Black Salmon Inn.

In the terror of that recognition, he remembered things about the crew's last night in Corwell, memories his mind had tried very hard to shut out. He saw the death of his friend Roloff, the terrified sailor strangled by the dark man, then cast casually into the harbor. Finally he knew a sense of obscene violation, and he recalled the magic the stranger had worked on him, twisting Luge's mind to the evil fellow's own dark will.

Then, not knowing the cause of his compulsion, though it grew to irresistible proportions as the squid neared the *Princess of Moonshae*, Luge felt a different urge. He wanted to serve, to *help* this monster.

He waited only for the creature to tell him what to do.

* * * * *

Brigit and Hanrald clung to the narrow platform, hearing a steady battering against the metal door from below. However, the iron bolts holding the portal shut were thick and uncorroded. It didn't seem that their most dangerous threat would come from that direction.

That, reflected Brigit grimly, left only every other direction as a potential source of sudden, violent death.

"Do they see us?" asked Hanrald weakly, unable to focus his eyes on the distant longship.

"Yes—they're coming," the sister knight told him, trying to make her voice sound more cheerful than her thoughts. "They'll be here soon. Just try to rest for a few more minutes."

In truth, the *Princess of Moonshae* remained near the distant palace, lumbering through the water with barely perceptible motion. Clearly she had again suffered grievous damage, and Brigit doubted it would reach the pair of knights before Keane's spells ceased to protect them.

"Yes . . . rest," Hanrald agreed dreamily, closing his eyes and again slumping to the platform.

Frantically Brigit looked around for some source of hope—and it was then that she saw the new force of swimmers approaching the battle. They came from beyond her tower, swarming straight toward Brigit and Hanrald and, beyond them, the embattled longship. Brigit saw hundreds of the piscine forms, and she knew that these fresh assailants would reach her long before the *Princess of Moonshae* could get close.

The female knight noticed something different about these warriors. They swam more naturally, and faster, than did the scaly creatures of the Coral Kingdom. Even in the depths, light glinted from sharp spearheads and tridents, growing steadily more visible as the hundreds of swimming figures rushed closer.

She could tell for certain that the newcomers would reach them before the longship did, and she knew that she and Hanrald, exposed on this high platform, would make easy prey for the numerous attackers.

Nevertheless, she raised her sword and prepared to exact a stiff price for her life.

* * * * *

On the ship, the voyagers also watched the newly arriving force spread out, thinning their ranks to drive forward in a final burst of speed. In moments, they swarmed around the tower top where Brigit stood, but the newcomers pressed on, inflicting no harm to the elfwoman.

"Mermen!" cried Tristan Kendrick in sudden recognition. "They're here to *help* us!" He indicated the swimming figures, now sweeping past Brigit and Hanrald, surging toward the undersea warriors of Kyrasti that now advanced against the longship.

The mermen warriors of Marqillor's realm swept into the ranks of Sythissal's army with brutal savagery. In a matter of a few seconds, a vast, seething melee swirled through the water as mermen, sahuagin, and scrags darted high and low, both companies quickly entangling in a desperate underwater clash.

Dozens of mermen surrounded the scrag columns. The fish-tailed humanoids darted in, stabbing with their long, sharp weapons and then diving away before the larger, less nimble scrags could return the assault. Schools of sahuagin and mermen mingled in slashing attacks, many clouds of pink froth and motionless bodies marking the wounded and slain on both sides.

The warriors of Deepvale were outnumbered by the defenders of Kyrasti, but they used the speed and surprise of their attack to disrupt each monstrous formation. As it had when the *Princess of Moonshae* made her bold approach to the submarine palace, the monsters' inability to concentrate seemed to cost them their chance for an easy victory. Still, however, the melee raged through the sea, at great cost in lives to both sides.

"The squid—it's closing in!" shouted Alicia, looking to the

rear with growing alarm as the beast rushed at the ship. A volley of arrows—a small barrage, for only four of the Corwellian bowmen still lived—plunked into the water, but the huge beast ignored the pinpricks.

Cursing, Knaff clutched the helm, holding the longship steady. There was nothing else he could do, no evasive action that could hope to elude the monstrous pursuer. The squid spurted forward, reaching out with long tendrils toward the *Princess of Moonshae*'s stern.

* * * * *

Brigit Cu'Lyrran, Mistress Captain of the Sisters of Synnoria, sat atop the tower, still hundreds of feet beneath the surface of the Trackless Sea, and watched an army of mermen make their slashing attack against the predatory humanoids of the Coral Kingdom. A sense of dull amazement possessed her. She still couldn't bring herself to believe that these hundreds of warriors had passed her without attacking. Where they came from, who or what had summoned them—these remained mysteries.

"We fought well, Sister Knight," Hanrald said weakly. The human sat up enough to look over the edge of the platform, watching the longship approach through the murk, seeing the battles raging through the sea. The vessel still bore the Helm of Zulae, gleaming brilliantly at her prow, and the ship approached them slowly. Nevertheless, their companions had nearly a half-mile to go before they reached the stranded knights.

"That we did," Brigit replied, kissing him gently on his pale forehead. "I'm proud to have fought beside a knight such as you."

But already her words sounded thick in their ears, and as Hanrald reached out a hand, it met increasing resistance—the pressure of the water, a clear indication that the protection of the spell had begun to wane.

The Earl of Fairheight felt a sudden penetrating chill, and

with a sidelong look at Brigit, he knew that she had experienced the same thing. The sea had surrounded them ever since they left the ship, but now it pressed against their skin, obstructing movement and blocking speech as the first of Keane's spells, the enchantment of free action, slowly dissipated. If it hadn't been for their heavy armor, the natural bouyancy of their bodies would have floated the knights right off the platform.

With the passing of this effect, they knew that it was only a matter of time—minutes, or perhaps merely seconds—before the protection of the second enchantment faded.

That, of course, was the spell of water breathing.

* * * * *

The time was *now*, Deirdre knew. Her teleportation spell, coupled with the knowledge gained from her mirror, gave her the ability to travel instantly to the point of decision. This time, however, before she cast the spell, she picked up her mirror. Wrapping the glass once more in its leather blanket, she clutched it beneath her arm and concentrated upon the precise enchantment.

Teleportation was always a tricky matter. Normally the spell depended upon the sorcerer traveling to a place that she knew very well; otherwise it was impossible to coordinate the point of arrival with the real world. Although an error of five feet to one side or the other might not make a lot of difference, a mistake that brought a magic-user through a teleportation five feet too *low* would almost certainly prove fatal.

But such was the unerring accuracy of the visions in Deirdre's mirror that, so long as she was certain to take reasonable care, the sorceress had no difficulty performing a teleportation to a coordinate she had pinpointed through her arcane scrying glass.

Now she carefully chanted the words to her spell, calling into her mind the picture she had witnessed scarce moments before. In a twinkling instant, she vanished from Caer Callidyrr.

As she expected, the mirror provided her with an uncanny sense of precision, for she arrived in the stern of the longship, appearing so suddenly that Knaff the Elder nearly stumbled over the stern in astonishment. Brandon gaped at her in shock as she brusquely stepped passed him, advancing to the transom and staring intently through the wake.

There, drawing quickly nearer, she made out the shape of the giant squid—the being she would no longer call Malawar.

* * * * *

Marqillor's warriors ripped through the line of Sinioth's followers, individual mermen diving amid the scrags and sahuagin, stabbing with long spears while they used small, tortoiseshell bucklers to deflect the weapons of the scaly carnivores.

At the same time, the squid closed on the stern of the longship, racing upward with lightning speed, reaching with those grasping tentacles to wrap the *Princess of Moonshae* in a crushing grip.

However, at this precise moment, the younger Princess of Callidyrr appeared on the longship's rear deck. Northmen cursed and growled at the woman's startling sorcerous arrival, some making holy signs in an attempt to ward off evil, but Deirdre ignored them all. She had attention for only one target, and that one swam in the dark waters of the *Princess of Moonshae*'s wake.

"*You!*" Deirdre cried, her gaze piercing the squid's body with almost physical force. "You escaped me once—but not again!" She yanked the leather wrapping off the object she held in her hands, revealing a gleaming surface of reflective glass.

Then Deirdre raised her hands, still holding the crystal pane, and the horrific monster recoiled from her gesture—or was it the mirror that caused the avatar to cower? Tentacles lashed through the sea as the creature dove, dropping out of sight beneath the longship's hull. The next moment, the squid shot upward, slamming into the keel, rocking the vessel violently. The sudden impact knocked Deirdre and a number of crew members to the deck.

The young woman screamed—out of fear for her mirror, not for herself. Landing flat on her back, she clutched the glass to her chest, and somehow it remained unbroken. All but spitting in her fury, Deirdre sat up, gingerly cradling her mirror, trying to scramble to her feet.

A sailor lurched forward from his bench, his shortsword raised, lunging toward Deirdre. He was a short man, but the gleaming steel in his hands driving toward her breast amplified his image in the horror-stricken eyes of the princess. She kicked out at him, tumbling backward as the man brutally stepped on her leg. Trapped, she squirmed helplessly, holding out the mirror like a fragile shield. Her attacker raised his sword and started the blade on a fatal plunge toward the young woman's heart.

"Luge!" shouted Brandon, furiously leaping after the crewman, but it was too late. The tip of the man's bloody weapon drove at the mirror, and the dark-haired princess cried out in anticipated pain.

Hot magic crackled through the air, exploding from Keane's finger as the mage stood in the bow. His spell arced down the length of the hull, seizing the sailor in a grip of paralyzing power. Luge's back arched and his lips stretched back from his clenched teeth as violent, killing magic wracked his body. In a second, his body, scorched as if it had been burned in a fire, dropped, rigid, to the deck.

A tentacle lashed over the gunwale, but Alicia chopped fiercely at it with her sword, sending the limb writhing back into the water. The shadowy form of the squid's body suddenly loomed into sight, its whipping tendrils flailing into the boat, seeking the black-haired princess. Deirdre scrambled back and raised the mirror, confronting the beast with its own monstrous image.

"I *name* you!" she shrieked. "You are Coss-Axell-Sinioth—

and you are *mine!*" Triumphantly she lifted the glass high, shoving the reflective surface forward, straight toward the looming avatar.

Then the vengeance of Talos ripped forth, and the form of the avatar writhed in the grip of something greater than itself. The mirror shattered of its own will, shards of glass exploding outward to puncture the monster in a thousand places, rending the huge body into a gory mass of bleeding wounds.

Sinioth's bellow of agony sliced through the water, a wailing screech of unspeakable torment. A shimmering wall of crystalline fragments circled the squid, driving through its flesh, tearing the huge form into pieces and then ripping those pieces into smaller and smaller parts.

Deirdre stood awestruck, overwhelmed by the stunning release of power. She stepped involuntarily backward, raising her hands before her face to ward off . . . what? The circling, silvery specks of glass continued to tear at the monster until there was nothing left to rend, but then the magical storm swirled back toward her.

Slivers of the broken mirror whirled around her, forming a glittering cocoon, obscuring her from view. Then, as if propelled by some invisible command, the spiraling cyclone of glass enclosed her even more tightly, until the shards flew straight toward the woman herself. They drove like needles into her skin, but left no marks, dripped no blood.

Deirdre screamed in overwhelming horror, collapsing to the deck and curling into a ball of terrified flesh. She slapped frantically at her skin as the darts of glass pierced her, yet still she showed no evidence of wounds. For several seconds, she continued to scream, and then her cries faded to a whimpering wail. Finally, shivering, she pressed her face against the planks of the hull and lay there. The only sound she made was a soft moaning.

Robyn knelt beside her daughter, and Tristan brought a woolen blanket to cover her. Gently he lifted her in his arms, noting with surprise how much smaller she seemed now. "Sleep, child . . . brave daughter," he said softly, cradling her head on his shoulder. Slowly her trembling lessened, though it did not cease altogether.

Knaff guided the longship beside a tall tower, where they had seen Brigit and Hanrald. The knights expended their last breaths as the vessel approached, but they crawled to the edge of the platform and, weighted by their armor, toppled over the side into the hull. Even the stale air in the *Princess of Moonshae* began to restore Brigit's strength, though Hanrald lay pallid and motionless on his back.

The sea around them continued to brighten, shifting in reverse through the spectrum of purple to pale green they had experienced on the way to the bottom. As all the crew felt the increasing strain of breathing the foul air in the ship, the undersides of individual waves came into view. Closer and closer to the surface the longship came as every voyager stared eagerly upward, unconsciously straining for the clean air.

Around them, the creatures of the Coral Kingdom remained disorganized, losing heart after the death of their immortal master and driven into flight by the savage attacks of the mermen of Deepvale. The mermen harried their enemies back toward the confines of the palace, and the monsters seemed content to withdraw to that massive lair, leaving the rescuers to their well-earned freedom.

And then finally the *Princess of Moonshae* crested the surface, sending a cascade of water showering off the hull. She wallowed low in the waves, though her gunwales remained safely above the waterline. Although bright sun washed around them, no breath of wind moved the stale air away. They could still barely draw a breath.

It was Keane who, after a moment, understood the nature of the problem. He scrambled into the bow and swiftly removed the Helm of Zulae from the longship's figurehead. In an instant, all of the stagnant air gusted away, replaced by a fresh sea breeze.

Hanrald's wound stopped bleeding finally, and as Brigit and Tavish affixed a bandage, the knight smiled wanly, too weak to talk. Yet when he took the sister knight's hand, the pressure of his grip spoke volumes of words.

Brandon came to kneel beside the Ffolkman who had proved such a stalwart companion. For a moment, the two proud warriors clasped hands.

"Your diversion," the prince told the two knights sincerely. "That's what cleared the path to the palace. Without it, we could never have made it."

Then the Prince of Gnarhelm rose to his feet, stepping to the charred body of the sailor, Luge. The pouch of the man's tunic lay open, a flap torn away from the inside lining of the crude garment. Several silvery objects had fallen out, scattering on the deck. Brandon picked one of them up, hearing it tinkle slightly, and Keane leaned over to examine another of the tiny balls.

"It's magical," said Keane, after casting a quick detection spell. "I'd wager these are how they kept locating us out in the middle of the ocean."

"Poor devil," observed the captain. "I don't think he ever knew what it was that had hold of him."

Closer to the stern, the High King of the Ffolk rested in the arms of his wife. Deirdre had fallen into an exhausted slumber. The princess seemed almost comatose, though they could see no sign of any wounds on her skin. Nevertheless, the sight of those sharp slivers of glass piercing her skin remained with them all, leaving a blanket of grave concern.

Alicia sat beside them, dazedly remembering the events of the past day. Too exhausted to move for the time being, she felt weak and dizzy—a delayed reaction, she knew, to the tension of the battle and rescue.

"My love," Tristan said, gently touching Robyn's cheek. His voice choked, blocking further words.

A shower of spray cascaded into the hull as Marqillor rose from the water, resting his elbows easily on the longship's gunwale, his tail splashing lazily in the water below.

"Glad you made it up here," said the merman with a grin. "If it hadn't been for you, Tristan, I'd still be drying out in that cell."

"I, for one, will welcome the chance to dry out!" sighed the king, reaching out to clasp the merman's hand. "But thank you, too, my friend."

"We did it together," replied the Prince of Deepvale. "It took rare courage for you to win my freedom. My people have tried to return the favor."

"How many did you lose?" asked the king, his tone dropping in concern. The carnage among the mermen, he feared, had been horrendous, yet without them, the longship's crew certainly would have been overwhelmed in the depths.

"Too many," came the sad reply. "But not without some gain. I think it will be many years before the scrags decide to make war against Deepvale again."

"And the Moonshaes, too—we can hope," replied the king.

"Farewell, Tristan Kendrick!" offered the merman then. He pushed himself from the hull, arcing his back and splitting the water in a clean backward dive.

Keane came to Alicia as she rose and leaned against the gunwale, looking across the sun-dappled expanse of sea. For once, he found his voice when he needed to.

"When you were in the water," he began seriously, "it seemed as though my own life was hanging by a mere shred. I understood something then, Princess. Without you, my life would have no meaning; I would have no reason to exist." The tall magic-user cleared his throat, the familiar awkwardness returning.

"I guess what I'm trying to say," he continued hesitantly, "is that if you want me, I'll be—"

"Ho! What a ride!" boomed Brandon, coming up between the pair and wrapping a brawny arm around each. Keane squirmed uncomfortably while Alicia laughingly disengaged herself.

"Yes . . . yes, it was that and more," she agreed softly. She looked at Brandon, and then back to Keane, offering each a warm smile. Then she slipped between them and walked by herself to the bow.

A fresh breeze rose from the south, bulging the longship's

sail and propelling her smoothly northward, across seas that lay smooth and inviting, a clear path beckoning them toward the Moonshaes.

Toward home.

Epilogue

Talos and Malar had no mirror now to observe the progress of their mortal servants. That artifact had been a necessary sacrifice in order to conclude the transformation they desired. But that fact bothered the Destructor little. Most of those servants, after all, had perished violently within the last day.

The loss of Sinioth seemed a minor thing to him now, and the deaths of Sythissal and Krell-Bane mattered even less, given the way things had been resolved. After all, the power of the avatar was not gone . . . it had merely been converted into a new form. That form would rest for a while, of course. Even the chaotic Talos knew the value of conserving his assets. Yet sometime not too far in the future, his new servant would be ready to serve.

All in all, Talos the Destructor and Malar the Beastlord were not displeased.

FANTASY ADVENTURE

THE LONG-AWAITED SEQUEL TO THE MOONSHAE TRILOGY
Druidhome Trilogy
Douglas Niles

Now Available - Book One
Prophet of Moonshae
Danger stalks the island of Moonshae, where the people have forsaken their goddess, the Earthmother. Only the faith and courage of the daughter of the High King brings hope to the endangered land.

Coming in March 1993 - Book Three
The Druid Queen
Threatened by an evil he cannot see, Tristan Kendrick rules the Four Kingdoms while a sinister presence lurks within his own familiy. At stake is the fate of the Moonshae Islands and the unity of the Ffolk.

FORGOTTEN REALMS
FANTASY ADVENTURE

Other books by Douglas Niles

The Moonshae Trilogy   **The Maztica Trilogy**

Darkwalker on Moonshae
Black Wizards
Darkwell

Ironhelm
Viperhand
Feathered Dragon

The ultimate struggle
of good and evil . . .
At stake, the survival of
the Moonshae Isles and
the peaceful Ffolk. High
King Tristan Kendrick
and the druid Robyn
confront an evil that
has invaded the land,
manifesting itself in the
form of an army of giant
firbolgs, dread
Bloodriders, and
the beast, Kazgaroth.

Tucked into a farflung
corner of the Forgotten
Realms lies the savagely
beautiful land, Maztica,
where vengeful gods battle
in an epic struggle for
supremacy, with human
pawns as gamepieces.
Pitted against these warring
titans are Erix, a former
slave girl, and Halloran, a
mercenary. Will they be
able to save the land–or
themselves?

VOLUME II IN SSI'S SPECTACULAR NEW *AD&D*® COMPUTER FRP EPIC!

The explosive sequel to *GATEWAY TO THE SAVAGE FRONTIER* is here at last! ***TREASURES OF THE SAVAGE FRONTIER*** is based on the award-winning game system used throughout SSI's famous gold-box series.

New features: Movement and combat are subject to the effects of weather. Players can now interact with NPCs – even have romances! Plus, in some situations, combat reinforcement can give you extra help when you need it most.

You'll find much more to explore – *and the freedom to explore it the way you want!*

Available for: IBM and AMIGA.
Visit your retailer or call 1-800-245-4525, in USA and Canada, for VISA /MC orders. To receive SSI's complete catalog, send $1.00 to:

STRATEGIC SIMULATIONS, INC.
675 Almanor Avenue, Suite 201
Sunnyvale, CA 94086

novels

Heart of Midnight
J. Robert King
Casimir, who inherited his father's lycanthropic curse, fled from both his home and his heritage. Now the young werewolf must embrace his dark powers to prevent his own death and to gain revenge on his monstrous father.

On Sale December 1992.

NOW AVAILABLE

Vampire of the Mists   Christie Golden
Jander Sunstar, an elven vampire, is pulled into the newly formed dark domain of Barovia and forms an alliance with the land's most powerful inhabitant, Count Strahd Von Zarovich, unaware that Strahd is the very enemy he seeks.

Knight of the Black Rose   James Lowder
The cruel death knight Soth finds a way into Ravenloft, then discovers that it is far easier to get in than to get out—even with the aid of the powerful vampire lord, Strahd.

Dance of the Dead   Christie Golden
Larissa Snowmane is a dancer on a magical riverboat that journeys to the zombie-plagued island of Souragne. The music is chilling, the captain is sinister, and Larissa must master the Dance of the Dead to save her own soul.